SHADOWS ON THE AEGEAN

Also by J. Suzanne Frank

Reflections in the Nile

SHADOWS ON THE AEGEAN

SUZANNE FRANK

WARNER BOOKS

A Time Warner Company

Warner Books, Inc., 1271 Avenue of the Americas, New York, NY 10020
Visit our Web site at http://warnerbooks.com
⬤. A Time Warner Company

Printed in the United States of America

ISBN 0-446-52090-X

Book design by Giorgetta Bell McRee

In memory of my grandmothers:
Katrina Hawthorn Roy, 1907–1996,
who taught me a love for beauty and kindness,
and Irene Mings Green, 1911–1998,
who taught me a love for God and a zest for life.

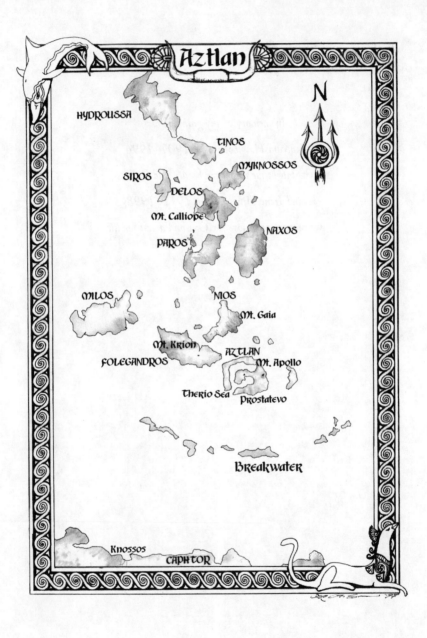

GLOSSARY

Suggested Ancient Pronunciations

adept—name for scholar-student

agape **(ah-gáh-pee)**—a Greek designation of divine, unconditional love

akra **(áhk-rah)**—Greek for tip

Alayshiya (ah-láy-shee-ya)—ancient Cyprus

al-khem **(áhl-kim)**—literally "from Egypt"; the precursor to alchemy, and ultimately chemistry

Apis (áy-pis)—the name of the region's bull god

ari-kat **(áh-ree-khat)**—Egyptian term for synthetic, used most often in reference to stone

artemisia (áhr-tee-mee-ja)—the Greek name for wormwood; the herb distilled into absinthe

Arus (áh-russ)—son of Zelos

Atenis (ah-tín-is)—daughter of Zelos and Ileana; chieftain of the Clan of the Muse

athanati **(ahth-áh-nah-tee)**—Greek for "immortal"

athanor **(áh-tha-nor)**—a beehive-shaped oven used by alchemists

atmu **(áht-moo)**—Egyptian for dusk

Aztlan (áhst-lan)—the fictional name of the empire inhabiting the Aegean in the mid-1800s B.C.E.; also the name for the central island

Cheftu—(chef-too)

cubit—measurement equaling eighteen to twenty-two inches

Daedaledion (dáy-duh-lée-dee-on)—the astrological/astronomical observatory in Knossos

Daedalus (dáy-duh-lus)—inventor of the Labyrinth, the air sail

decan—chronological measurement, roughly an hour

Dion (dée-on)—son of Zelos; chieftain of the Clan of the Vine

eee—Greek exclamation

ellenismos **(ell-ín-ees-mos)**—term for the enlightenment of Greek culture

eros **(áir-os)**—a Greek designation of carnal, erotic love

Etesian (i-tée-sjan)—Greek winds from May to October

Golden—term for the ruling Clan of Aztlan

hemu neter (**him-óo-nee-ter**)—Egyptian designation for first among the physicians

henti (**hín-tee**)—Egyptian measure of distance

hequetai (**héck-a-tay**)—Greek for political advisory board or cabinet

Hreesos (**hrée-sos**)—the Golden One; title for the ruler of Aztlan

Ileana (ill-ee-án-ah)—the Queen of Heaven; Zelos' wife; Kela-Ileana

Irmentis (er-mín-tis)—youngest daughter of Zelos and Ileana

ka (**kah**)—Egyptian word for the soul

Kalo taxidi (**kah-loh-tax-ée-dee**)—Greek blessing on the dead, wishing "good journey"

kefi—Greek for a time of revel

Kela (káy-lah)—derivative of *kalos*, Greek for beauty; the ancient mother-goddess

khaibit (**kháy-bit**)—Egyptian word for vampire

kheft (**keft**)—Egyptian word for demon

kollyva (**kóll-ee-vah**)—Greek dinner of the dead; favorite foods are prepared and shared

kreenos—lily-derivative drug

kur—Egyptian measurement of dry weight

Ma'at (may-aht)—Egyptian representation of justice and universal balance

maeemu—Greek for monkey

mafkat—Egyptian word for powdered turquoise

Manoula—Greek for Mommy

mastic—an adhesive from the lentisk tree

Megaloshana'a—the Great Year

Megaron (**még-ah-ron**)—an audience chamber

mnasons (**máy-son**)—Aztlan priests who specialize in building and architecture

natron—an Egyptian salt used in embalming and chemistry

Neotne—a female survivor of the Mt. Calliope eruption

Nestor—son of Zelos; Aztlantu ambassador/envoy

neter—physician

Niko (née-koh)—friend of Phoebus; of the Clan of the Spiral

nome—the districts of Egypt

okh (óhkh)—an exclamation

Pateeras—Greek for Father or Papa

Phoebus (fée-bus)—son of Zelos, the heir to the throne

pithoi (pl.)—Greek for large clay storage jars

pothos—a Greek designation of ambitious desire where the object is conquered

prion (pree-on)—a specific type of protein

psyche (sí-kee)—Greek for soul

Ptah—(tah)—Egyptian god of craftsmen

rekkit—Egyptian for the common people

rhyton (rí-ton)—a vase or flask used in offerings and at state functions

sa'a (sáy-ah)—son of the heart

sem-priest—the highest rung of the Egyptian priesthood

senet (sin-étt)—Egyptian board game

Sibylla (si-béll-ah)—Greek for prophetess or seer

skeela (skée-lah)—Greek word for bitch

skia (skee-áh)—Greek word for a shade or phantom

Sobek—Egyptian crocodile-headed god

Spiralmaster—title of the clan chieftain of the Scholomance

tenemos (tín-i-mos)—sacred enclosure

Theros (théer-os)—Greek word for summertime, name of the lagoon

Therio (théer-ee-o)—Greek word for beast

theea (thée-ah)—Greek word for aunt

tholos; tholoi (pl.) (thó-los)—an underground grave

tsunami (sóo-nam-ee)—Japanese term for tidal wave used in geology

udjet (ood-jét)—the Eye of Horus symbol

ukhedu (ook-hay-doo)—Egyptian concept for a physical/spiritual source of illness and discontent; transmissible to the body through the bowels

ushebti (oo-shéb-tee)—an Egyptian funeral statue that served as a proxy for the dead in the afterlife

w'eb-priest—the lowest rung of the Egyptian priesthood

w'rer-priest—the second rung of the Egyptian priesthood

Yazzo (yáh-zoh)—a Greek cry to move forward, to follow, to come

Zelos—the king, the Golden Bull of Aztlan

THE CLANS OF AZTLAN

Clan of the Horn—Hydroussa and Tinos; capital Kouvari; chieftain Sibylla

Clan of the Vine—Naxos; capital Demeter; chieftain Bacchi, Dion

Clan of the Wave—Siros and Myknossos; capital Ariadne; chieftain Posidios, Iason

Clan of the Stone—Paros; capital Pluto; chieftain Nekros

Clan of the Flame—Milos; capital Prometheus; chieftain Talos

Clan of the Spiral—Aztlan; Spiralmaster Imhotep, Cheftu

Cult of the Snake—Nios; capital Basilea; Kela-Ata Embla, Selena

Cult of the Bull—Folegandros; capital Atlas; Minos

Clan of the Muse—Delos; capital Arachne; chieftain Atenis

Clan Olimpi—Aztlan; chieftain Zelos, Phoebus

FOREWORD

The Elixir of Life. The Fountain of Youth. The Philosopher's Stone. Under different names and guises, we have searched for immortality throughout time. Using religion, science, and myth, we have sought eternity. But are these all the same: dawn, noon, and evening of one day? Are they different facets of the same truth? What determines myth, and what defines fact? Is truth hidden in the shadows of fable? Hidden, because ultimately we believe only what we see.

PROLOGUE

THE WORLD EXPLODED IN LIGHT and I felt myself freed—the constraints of skin, blood, and bone slipped away and I knew that the core of my person, my *ka*, had left its ancient Egyptian shell.

No longer was I wearing the flesh, the mind, the persona, of the priestess RaEmhetepet. For the first time in more than a year I was purely Chloe—a twentieth-century diplomatic brat; an artist; a retired air force lieutenant; a Levi's-wearing and coffee-drinking English-American. I was no longer ancient or Egyptian. None of RaEm's thoughts or perceptions clouded my mind.

I had no curiosity about RaEm's missing Egyptian lover, Phaemon. Instead I wondered about my Egyptologist sister, Camille. I thought in English, then Egyptian. The order had been reversed. I had vivid recollections of traveling at fifty-five miles per hour, of transatlantic flights, of chocolate, coffee, and cigarettes. Of diet Coke.

I was once more only myself.

Before this concept settled, a scream of unbearable agony followed me through a channel of fire. It ripped at me, shredding a heart that beat only in a metaphysical sense.

The fire burned me, consumed me, but did not destroy. My senses were jumbled so that I heard it and tasted it, instead of seeing it and smelling it. Through it all a cry, a plea torn from deepest soul, encircled, echoed around me.

"*Chloe!*"

I recognized the voice. My husband, Cheftu—my lover—taken from me by fate, or circumstance, or the divine. I felt his grief through the void. His pain was so intense, a cleaving ran down to my marrow. I wanted to join my voice to his, to reassure him . . . but what reassurance was there? Was this dying? Was this the end now, my battle service done and death really nothing more than not being?

Yet I *was!*

Suddenly, in the midst of the dreadful, pressing loneliness, I was comforted. A tangible sense of love, acceptance, and rightness flowed around me, billowed me up, carried me. It gave me ease. For a time—for time was meaningless—I rested.

The physical pain that time travel brought surrounded me in an instant. I was taken from cool refreshment to the fire. I understood in a flash how gold felt. Heated, cooled, beaten, and molded . . . perfected.

Tension coiled all around me, radiating from me and through me. I was being reduced, expanded, in an agony of displacement. My spirit self hunkered down, bracing, preparing to roll.

A face appeared before me suddenly, a woman with blank blue eyes, curling black hair, a woman of striking beauty. A body to let, I realized. No one was home. Before I'd made a decision, I was flowing through her wide, empty stare. I screamed, and as her flesh became mine, my fear was given voice. Her skin shaped over me, stretching to my height, adapting to my blood, my DNA. Like a wetsuit, this new body tugged over my spirit, clothing it. A hundred million pins pressed into me as the carnal casing grew tighter, closing over me, my atoms readjusting, my cells merging into the empty carcass.

The sensations were wrenching, too much to endure. As I gave myself into the drift of black peacefulness, I felt the rage, the hating frenzy, of another spirit, outside me.

It shrieked, furious, lethal . . . and hopeless. "That body is *mine!!*"

PART I

CHAPTER I

S IBYLLA?"

They were gathered around her, nymphs and matrons, their heads clustered so that Sibylla could barely see the stalactites that hung like drops from the top of the cave—or the red lintel that cast a faint shadow on her face. Feeling uncommonly chilled, she allowed two of the Kela-Tenata healing priestesses to help her to her feet. They solicitously walked her out of the cave and into the fresh air.

The beautiful land of Caphtor! It was the Season of the Snake, when the earth renewed itself as a serpent sheds its skin. Rains had fallen, misting the whole valley. In the distance, sunlight glinted off the distant dark waters of the Aegean. Faint winter shadows were cast in the dormant olive and grape groves surrounding this sacred mountain, the dwelling place of the oracle.

Residence of the Sibylla.

It's *my* winter home, she thought. Breathing deeply to purify her body after the ecstasies of prophecy, she felt something cut into her ribs and looked down. Attire that seemed both ordinary and foreign clothed her. She wore a brightly patterned belled skirt and a tightly fitted, short-sleeved, waist-length jacket with very little front. An embroidered waist cincher pressed her full breasts up and out, blatantly visible through the sheer blouse she wore in winter.

A curl of dark hair lay like a comma on her tawny breast . . . yet it looked odd. What was a *comma?* Sibylla shook her head, dispelling the strange impressions. She didn't feel completely herself. Was a vital element of her *psyche* still traveling for the goddess Kela?

Sibylla looked out then and shuddered. Instead of seeing the fields where olive and fruit still slept until spring, she saw destruction. A veil slipped over reality for a moment, and once again she became the oracle.

The tiny village at the foot of the mountain was nothing more than a smoldering pile of ruins. White and gray particles fell from the sky, covering the ground, suffocating the vegetation, standing as deep as a child was tall. She looked at the faces of the women around her and saw them disfigured; blistered, bleeding, with charcoal tongues protruding from lipless mouths. She looked at a nymph, a bride-to-be, and shrieked in fright. Swollen with child, the girl fell into the flames, her screams rising momentarily above the roar of fire.

"Mistress?" One of the charred bodies moved. Sibylla was rooted like a vine. "Mistress, the Kela is upon you?"

"Flee!" she cried in a voice stronger, deeper, than her own. "Your days of peace and joy are limited in this valley! Beware the Season of the Lion! In his days, all will die, the earth itself will feel his wrath!" She looked over to the sea and saw a wall of water crash onto the land, stripping away *henti* of earth as if they were grains of sand. "Days of darkness, nights of fire! The earth will vomit you up, the sea will swallow you! Protect yourselves and your loved ones. You must flee, you must flee!"

Shuddering and weeping, Sibylla collapsed to the ground. They clustered around her, no longer corpses but deeply frightened women. Respectfully they carried her inside to rest on her makeshift couch. Sibylla felt a malevolence stirring in the shadows. A *skia* dwelt here, an angry spirit with no body. She wept, her eyes closed. Sibylla wanted to beg them to stay, to not leave her alone with the *skia*, but exhaustion had sealed her mouth.

"The Kela is still upon her," she heard a woman whisper. "Her eyes are still green."

Green? Sibylla knew that she should be frightened by the news that her eyes were the wrong color, but she was heartened. Her eyes were green. My eyes are blue, she protested. *Not anymore,* said another voice inside her.

Fleet steps pounded away from the mountain toward Knossos. She knew that other Kela-Tenata would arrive and take her away into the quiet of the Daedaledion. Nay! She must say more, tell about the mountains coughing blood and mortar, of skies where no stars were visible, of sunrises filled with gore, but she was too tired, too weary. Your days are few, Sibylla wanted to say to the villagers. Please, please, you must go. The Lion comes, he will ravage. You can return, but you must go. Flee before the Lion.

Flee!

She awoke in darkness, her heart pounding as though she had run to Knossos. Sibylla stumbled to the mouth of the cave. Exhausted as usual after a period of prophesying, she accepted wine and preserved fruit from some of the village women. They worshiped her as an aspect of the Great Goddess. She spent the Season of the Snake, when she had fewer clan chieftain responsibilities, dwelling in this lonely cave fed by the local women. Here she administered wisdom and acted as the voice of the Kela.

The Great Goddess was the giver *and* taker of all life. With one hand she created, with the other she destroyed. She was a pentad deity, represented as maiden, bride, matron, midwife, and hag. She was the progenitor of the bull god Apis, she was his seducer, his bride, his wife, and, eventually, his slayer. She was the moon, he was the sun; she was the odd numbers, he the even; she was serpent, swallow, and ax, he was lion, bull, and boot. The lives of the gods paralleled the life of the land; soon the land would reawaken and Sibylla would join the other priestesses in welcoming Kela.

Sibylla would return soon to Kallistae and the palace. The seasons of growing and reaping would be upon the Aztlan empire and she would step once again into her position and authority. The chaos of Aztlan Island would all but erase the memory of these cool, quiet fields, the snow-capped mountains in the distance. This was the nineteenth summer, the summer of great change in the empire.

Aztlan Empire? the voice inside her said. *Where am I? Is this a Mexican resort? Please don't tell me I'm an Aztec.*

Sibylla shuddered at the voice and forced her thoughts to this summer. Her cousin Phoebus would become *Hreesos*, the Golden Bull, while his father, Zelos, would be made *athanati*, immortal. Phoebus was nineteen; this summer the sun and moon would stand as one. This summer the new heir to the throne would be conceived. This summer would mark the end of the reign of Zelos and the beginning of Phoebus' nineteen summers on the throne. The annual midsummer festival would be fourteen, not the usual seven days.

What are you talking about? Where am I? Where did you get those names? the voice pleaded, its fear tangible.

Sibylla ignored it. Kela-Ileana had ruled as Zelos' wife and personification of the Great Goddess for the same nineteen summers. This summer the nymphs of Aztlan would challenge her position as Queen of Heaven. Through a series of footraces and mazes, the queen and the chosen racers would match strength and resilience. If Kela-Ileana won the competitions, she would marry Phoebus. Becoming pregnant in thirty days would confirm her position as the Great Goddess and Phoebus' wife, ensuring another nineteen summers' reign. If she proved to be infertile with Phoebus, then her position would be yielded to the runner-up.

Yielded to the runner-up? Does that mean she gets a lovely parting gift? The voice alternated between fear and scoffing. *What is a runner-up wife? God! Where am I?*

Silence yourself! Sibylla hissed. As a member of Clan Olimpi, she would compete for the role of Great Goddess and Phoebus' wife. While tradition decreed *Hreesos* must be golden haired, his wife need only be Clan Olimpi, religiously trained, and fertile. The prosperity of the land related directly to the Great Goddess's fecundity. The queen must conceive within thirty nights of the sacred marriage.

Sibylla sighed; it was too early in the seasons to concern herself. The race was moons away.

Race? Moons? I have a bad feeling about this.

Arching her back, feeling unused muscles stretch and pull, Sibylla tried to enjoy the restfulness of Caphtor, to ignore the strange voice that spoke to her in a language she didn't fully comprehend. On Kallistae, the wind would be whipping around the palace, the sun not even touching Ileana's chamber, the *Megaron*, until well after its zenith. Cold, rainy, and noisy, the island shrieked with the winter wind.

Sibylla pitied the Mariners, Aztlan's navy. Winter, the Season of the Snake, was forbidding on land. How much more terrifying on a ship? The Mariners sailed from port to port, checking on the various outposts of the empire, trading food for stones—seeking for certain stones. Sibylla shrugged. Her pity was wasted: each clan had its responsibilities.

Instinctively she touched the clan seal around her neck.

Nice necklace, the voice said.

The gold seal showed a snake swallowing its tail, signifying her name day, and was inscribed with horns for her clan. It had hung around her neck since she'd come into adulthood. Each chieftain wore a similar golden seal. The only time they were removed was during the Council meeting, when the chieftains were stripped and unadorned, representing every man and woman. The meeting convened every nine years and in the nineteenth year, during the Season of the Bull.

The Season of the Bull? Is that summer? Please, someone tell me where I am. . . . The voice trailed off despairingly.

"Help me, Kela," Sibylla prayed under her breath. Surely she was hearing *skia* talking to each other.

As Kela was the goddess of women, the Apis bull Earthshaker was worshiped only by men. The priests had pyramids on Aztlan Island and the other four "Nostrils of the Bull" throughout the empire. The peaked Nostrils cast Apis' hot, sometimes putrid breath into the air. The priesthood worshiped diligently, for if the Bull's ire was raised, he was a destroyer. He breathed fire, melted gold, boiled the springs and rivers, and made the mountains bleed molten rock.

The freshness of the rain-soaked fields recalled Sibylla, and she smiled in anticipation of the year: the nineteenth, the *Megolashana'a.*

Her earlier visions of horror had faded. Sibylla could not believe Kela and Apis would seek to destroy their own people! Surely the Great Goddess was not truly bidding them to leave their homes? Was there another meaning, perhaps? Symbolized by these dreams?

Her mind felt clearer now, her skin once again familiar. When she was an oracle, the spirit of Kela inhabited her body, speaking truths, answering questions. Only a small part of her intellect would stay behind, as an anchor for her wandering *psyche*. Extensive training had taught her never to let the silver noose, which linked her traveling spirit and her Kela-inhabited body together, to stray too far. She could be lost forever then, doomed to wandering as a *skia*.

Sibylla acknowledged, however, that some part of her was missing. The silver noose had come undone, and she feared that part of her *psyche* was wandering. Something else had come back in place of herself. *Someone* else.

Me! the voice said.

"My mistress?" someone called, and Sibylla looked up gratefully. The young bride-to-be approached. Sibylla accepted the offering of corn from the nymph's outstretched hands.

"You spoke of destruction yesterday," the girl said.

Sibylla looked away.

"Will my husband be safe?"

The humility of the young woman's question brought tears to Sibylla's eyes. The nymph asked not for herself, but for the boy she loved. *Your vision looks like footage from a* National Geographic *special,* a voice inside her said. Sibylla stiffened, chilled by the voice. The interloper was speaking. Nay, it must be Kela.

"I did not see him in the vision," Sibylla answered. The girl's night-dark gaze searched hers, then dropped away. Sibylla knew her words were false, but what hope to tell a bride she would not live to see her firstborn?

So tell her to go to the other side of the island, the voice said. *Surely she has relatives there. It won't hurt them to get away for a while. It might even save their lives.*

Please let this be the Kela speaking to her in a way never before experienced, Sibylla prayed.

Not hardly, the voice scoffed. *C'mon, this kid deserves a break.*

If I instruct her, demand she move, Sibylla countered, would that not be changing what is decreed to happen? If she loses her home and fields, what matter is it for her to live?

Within her Sibylla felt a heavy, lost sigh. *We can only try. Those things that cannot be changed are not. . . .* Sibylla felt the voice retreat, wounded and hurting.

"You have family in Phaistos, nymph?"

"Aye, my mistress."

"After you are wed, go there."

The nymph's eyes grew round. "Phaistos?"

"It is the wish of the Kela."

Sibylla rested her head on the rock, listening to the sounds of the nymph scampering down the stony path, returning to the village. The creature inside her smiled.

Way to go, Sibylla.

No one saw.

They began in the dark depths of the ocean, peaks built by the fury of the earth. An arc of islands swept through the wine-dark sea, heights of death intermixed with cradles of savage and gentle beauty: Milos, Hydroussa, Tinos, Siros, Myknossos, Delos, Naxos, Paros, Nios, Folegandros, and the connected islands of Kallistae and Aztlan. Some had spewed their fury before humanity inhabited their slopes; others would remain silent for centuries more.

As the African and Eurasian tectonic plates slowly nudged each other, ripples and ridges shuddered through the earth, compressing rock, fueling fire, building tension, creating this volcanic sweep of islands on the plot of earth to someday be called the Aegean microplate. Massive earthquakes on the ocean floor were felt only as bare tremors in the clear air, thousands of meters above.

Stealthily the molten core had risen. What had once lain a day's sail beneath the crust of the earth had crept into four channels that ran like veins inside the beautiful mountains of the Aztlan empire: Mount Apollo, Mount Krion, Mount Gaia, and Mount Calliope.

The weakest channel was on Delos, an island of artists. Mount Calliope loomed above them, an inspiration for paintings, for poetry, for the soul. The artists did not feel the increasing heat beneath their sandals. No animals had yet become victims of gas poisoning. Thousands lived in Calliope's shadow, celebrating feasts in its groves, making love in its crevices, giving strangers directions by its location. They did not know liquid death lurked inside the mountain. Hot, boiling with rage and rock, creeping through the narrow passageway that led to the throat of the cone.

Thousands of years had passed since the last eruption. A mass of land now resided on the bottom of the purple ocean, testimony to the earlier wrath of the earth. The mountain had spewed rocks the size of ships for days, raining scalding ash on the round island. Fire had reached the heavens, and the tales of destruction became part of myth and legend.

Then the mountain had slept. Minutely the cone had risen from the depths of the ocean. Green grass had covered it and birds had flocked to it, and each year it was bigger and higher, its soil more fertile. A tribe had reclaimed it, growing purple grapes and flavorful herbs and fig trees, raising their crops and rearing their children, unaware.

No one settled on the peak, for the high places were forbidden by the deity the tribe worshiped. Iavan, the ancient patriarch of the tribe, told of how the deity had saved his family because of the goodness of his grandfather, Noach. This family, and the animals they had gathered up, had been spared from the waters that had drowned the earth. Because of this nameless deity's rescue, the tribe that sprang from Noach's loins was ever faithful.

As the cone grew and time passed, the god passed from practice, then memory. Rising from the same stock were others who worshiped the earth, the sky, and the sea. They identified the island cones as Nostrils of the Bull, whose roars sometimes shook the earth. In great piety and vanity they tipped the cones with pyramids, their sides emblazoned with precious stones, their interiors vast caverns where their priesthood lived.

Beneath the floors tiled in gold circles, black stripes, red swirls and squares, the volcano grew. Like the bull god who controlled it, the mountain's rage was consuming and unfocused. It waited, the heat that could vaporize a man, building, growing more intense than any metal worker's forge, its capacity pulled from below the ocean, where cataclysms were born, in the molten womb of the earth.

It waited.

THE AZTLAN EMPIRE

ILEANA LINED HER LIPS CAREFULLY with the sharp edge of the ocher, then moved the color stick to her nipples, adding a drop of water and painting them, too. A few good pinches brought them erect. She smiled, pleased.

Her many summers had been good to her. She still had the figure of a nymph, and the legends of her beauty brought sailors and gifts from around the empire and beyond. Zelos was hers, for a little while longer. Ileana swallowed, a tremor of fear playing with her brow. At midsummer festival her husband's son would become the ruler and she would become a widow. Phoebus had hated her as a boy. Now, at age nineteen, he hated her even more. Ileana had not lived so long and so well that she didn't recognize danger. Phoebus would as soon kill her as see her, but Ileana had no intention of stepping down as Queen of Heaven.

There was no doubt she would win the footrace. However, Phoebus would have his satisfaction if she were unable to become pregnant in the time allotted. She refused to think of the penalty for losing: the Labyrinth.

A piercing shriek came from the corridor, and Ileana patiently finished her makeup. A peacock strode in, screaming, his tail closed. Ileana turned on her stool, snapping her fingers for a serf to hand her seeds. "Come along, my beauty," she said, throwing its food on the painted floor. "Show me how lovely you are." The peacock ate the seeds and screamed for more. "Not until you show your colors," Ileana admonished her pet.

Obligingly the male strutted forward and preened, opening the multicolored wonder of his tail. "Those two and that one," Ileana said to the serf. The peacock screamed again, closing the fan of his tail, but the serf was fast and already held three long, eyed feathers in his hand. Three, a number to honor the Great Goddess. Laughing triumphantly, Ileana turned back to her water mirror. Deftly the boy tucked the feathers into her crown of corn gold hair.

"The feathers make your eyes as fathomless as Theros Sea," the boy said.

Admiring her reflection, Ileana leaned back against him, her head against his chest. She feasted on his expression of admiration reflected in the mirror, then waved him away.

Immediately he bowed, stepping back. She snapped her fingers and two handsome men, long limbed and narrow waisted, opened her chamber's doors. With a final tug of her seven-tiered skirt, befitting her role as mother-goddess, Ileana stepped to her carrying chair. Before she asked, a rhyton was handed to her. It was a slender pointed cup fashioned from mother-of-pearl and gold, pointed at the end to stay fixed upright in a graceful metal stand or the ground. She snapped her fingers and the men proceeded slowly so they would not step on the wandering peacocks.

The walls of the palace, with their life-size paintings of priestesses and princes in worship and parade, sailed by in a haze of gold, scarlet, black, and white. Sounds of the festivities—music, the clatter of earthenware and alabaster, and the low trill of laughter—caressed Ileana's ears as she was carried down the wide staircase to the queen's *Megaron*.

The guards set her chair down gently and assisted her out. Shooing the peacocks into the spacious chamber, Ileana smiled as silence fell. One solitary flute played as she sauntered in. The guests, her subjects, stood with bowed heads and arms raised in supplication.

"Kela-Ileana, Queen of Heaven, Mother-Goddess of the Harvest, Mistress of Aztlan," a high voice sang.

She took her seat at the elevated edge of the company: with a snap of her fingers the feast returned to life. Her rhyton was refilled, and before she could sink it in the ground a male voice spoke. "Fairest Heaven, may I?"

Slowly she raised her gaze. By the strength of Apis, this man was a beauty! His smile indicated he knew this well. Irritated by his arrogance, Ileana plunged the rhyton's end into the ground. His shock was visible. Was she the first to refuse him?

Looking beyond him, she called out to her stepson, "Arus! Tell me, who is this man to think he can approach Heaven on the strength of his smile?" From the corner of her eye she saw the youth's cheeks redden.

Arus, his hair unfashionably short, but bearing a *most* impressive nose, leaned forward. "He's the youngest Troizen prince. Not enough man for an Aztlantu woman." He smiled and turned his attention back to his companion.

Ileana snapped for food and waited in silence, watching the courtiers of Aztlan. It was a gay group since *Hreesos'* grayheads had gone to an annual symbolic sea skirmish.

Her gaze flickered quickly over the women present. Summer approached, when she would have to defend herself and her goddess-given throne against the nymphs who chose to challenge her. The Coil Dancers were priestesses, but not Olimpi. She dismissed them. Long ago she'd learned their sexual tricks and had gone on to perfect them.

She saw the occasional fresh-faced nymph; however, they were not priestesses and therefore no threat to the Queen of Heaven. A clanswoman or two roamed the room, their years proclaimed by the backs of their hands. Age alone would prevent them from catching her in the footrace.

Three women were her true rivals: Vena, Selena, and Sibylla. Ileana smiled at a courtier attempting to woo her through gifts. Even if one of her clanswomen managed to win the race, she would still have to wait a moon to see if Ileana had become pregnant. Then Ileana had several moons when she could pretend pregnancy before she was discovered. Those moons would be fatal for any potential successor, giving Ileana time to get with child.

Ileana knew she was fertile, she was the goddess on earth. However, she might have to work to find the right partner. It was the timing of the thing. Racing always disrupted her moon-cycles, and to become pregnant immediately afterward . . . she needed Kela's help. The courtier blushed as Ileana directed her most charming smile of gratitude at him. The gift was worthless, but he was blond—he could be useful.

The young Troizen prince had not spoken, not even glanced her way. Intriguing, Ileana mused. He refuses to cower before my beauty or to flee my legendary wrath.

Deliberately she turned to him. He stared straight ahead. Ileana narrowed her eyes. He was not as tall as an Aztlantu man, but he was broader shouldered and more sinewy. His body was sleek skinned and oiled, firm young flesh that rippled as he moved.

He was a blond.

Per Aztlantu custom he wore a belled, patterned skirt, but strangely he had no waist cincher. A flat link necklace was his only adornment. No makeup tinted his lips or ringed his eyes. He turned to her, challenge and carefully banked lust in his deep green eyes. "Are you pleased with what you see . . . my mistress?"

His arrogance was tinged with charm. He wasn't afraid of her, and Ileana found the difference thrilling. Playing with him could be entertaining. "Thus far," she said, husky voiced. She rolled a date on her lips before eating it, licking the sticky residue away slowly. "However, I cannot make a decision based *only* on what I behold."

His eyebrows were not plucked or painted but grew densely, leaving only a narrow gap over the bridge of his nose. Ileana felt a catch in her throat. His nose was exquisite, large and bold; his mouth was wide.

"Even your beauty cannot win you that honor," he said, rising to his feet. Ileana smiled coolly at his retreating form; he was a prince of Troi, *eee?* The man was a peacock; she admired his spirit. She had insulted him, so he had responded in kind. A worthy lover, to give as good as he got.

Ileana was not finished with him yet.

She saw him embrace a Coil Dancer; holding the girl's bare breasts in his hands, he kissed her mouth with the fervor of youth. Ileana felt desire's flood rise. Two blond men; who would know if Phoebus were not the true father?

"He's quite a stag, is he not?" hissed Vena.

Too entranced to recall that she hated Vena, Ileana agreed.

"He's fostering here. His name is Priamos, the youngest son of Troi."

"Why we foster an enemy's whelp, I do not know," Ileana mused.

"Well, if a mistress of your stature and summers knows not, then few of us have any chance at that wisdom," Vena said with a smirk.

Ileana remembered instantly that this above-herself Shell Seeker from Milos was among her rivals. She smiled sweetly. "My poor dear, don't lust after a younger son, it demeans the clan. I know you must doubt yourself now—your charms, your ability—it must be difficult to have a lover flee." Ileana spoke over Vena's sputtering protests. "But I overstep your feelings. I do not know. I've never been put aside."

Vena's rose complexion was mottled with fury. "I could have Nestor back!"

"He fled to Kemt to get away from you! *Okh!*" Ileana said, touching her lips in feigned chagrin. "I apologize. What is the tale you are bandying about? He volunteered on a diplomatic mission for dear Phoebus, is that the right myth?"

"I could have any man on any shore in the empire!"

Ileana lifted her rhyton to her lips. "Men being what they are, *having* is no challenge." She sipped her wine, feeling the peppery bite of oregano and thyme mixed in. "*Keeping* is."

"What a wonder you know the difference after nineteen summers wed to *Hreesos*. Tell me, Kela-Ileana, has he slept on your couch more than once?" Vena arched her back as she spoke, throwing her perfect body into a pose that halted conversation at two tables.

Ileana smiled coldly, careful not to let emotion tug at her face. "*Hreesos*, my Golden Bull husband, may have rutted and rammed a selection—"

"A wide selection—"

"—of cows . . . but he always returns to the fold."

Vena, her violet eyes black with anger, clenched her fists. She would be trouble, Ileana thought. She was beautiful, healthy, Olimpi, and her background as a Shell Seeker qualified her. How could Ileana stop her?

"Mistresses, the air fair crackles with your words." The speaker dropped down between them, as careless and graceful as a black cat.

"Already you stink of the grape," Vena said to him, throwing her chestnut curls over her shoulder.

He grinned. "But I am *of* the grape." He deepened his voice and bellowed, "Dion Bacchi, inheritor of the Clan of the Vine!" Leaning forward, he placed a love bite on Vena's breast. "Besides, last Season of the Lion, when you were beneath me, also crushing the grapes, your comment was, 'Aye, Dion!' " he trilled in a falsetto. After flashing a wicked smile at the laughter of the courtiers, he sipped from Ileana's rhyton and turned it so that she drank from the same spot. "However, if we are to discuss the scent that I recall from the experience, I would say it was fi—" Vena cuffed his head and marched back to Arus. The courtiers returned to their conversations as Dion lounged beside Ileana's feet.

"Where is Sibylla?" she asked. Best to know where one's rivals were.

Dion reached up and plucked shrimp speared with rosemary from the glazed dish before her. "You know full well that she loathes both of you."

"As do you?"

His smile was charming, melting the severe lines of his face. In a lover's purr he said, "I do, Ileana. With all my heart, I do."

In Aztlan, Dion was the ideal—tall, broad shouldered, wasp-waisted, with black hair that fell to his waist. His eyes were large and dark, deep as an oracular pool. Seeing him reportedly drove the clanswomen wild with lust—a screaming pack of hounds in heat who roamed the hills in the white of the moon. Despite his youth, he seemed aged, knowing that no one could refuse him. Ileana hated herself for not being above the physical call of a man she loathed.

"You have an odd way of showing it, feeding me wine—" Ileana stopped, staring at *Hreesos'* whelp. Carefully she wiped her mouth on the edge of her garment, then picked up the empty rhyton. She willed her fingers to cease trembling as she felt the bottom for residue. Holding up her fingers, she saw glittering grains in the dregs. "You poisoned me?" she rasped. Where had her taster been?

Dion smiled.

"Tell me!" Ileana hissed.

He smiled wider, speaking only to prevent her from shrieking for the guards. "Never poison, Ileana." He clicked with his tongue, a sound of dismay. "Nay, your death should be savored." He licked his fingers, his tongue caressing the pads. "Anticipated." His gaze grew darker, more intense, and Ileana felt her body tighten in response. He took her palm and licked it; fire rippled through her body. "Why, it should bring at least as much pleasure as your life has brought grief."

"You are dismissed," Ileana said tightly.

"Shared," Dion continued, his fingers stroking his chest in minute movements that made her hands itch to take over the responsibility. "Shared equally by those whom your life has cursed. How many lay their death at your door? Do you need counting strings to keep tally?"

"You go too far with your accusations and blasphemies," Ileana hissed.

He continued as though she had not spoken. "However, your days are numbered. You are too old to bear the next Golden."

She rose abruptly and the company fell silent. Dion lounged at her feet. Ileana snapped her fingers and her chair was brought immediately. As she sat, Dion rolled over, his face level with her feet. He kissed the arch of her foot tenderly, his lips finding the sensitive skin between her sandal straps.

"You test me, whelp."

"I will bid a scribe attend you; age has probably affected your mind, as it has your body," he said sadly. "How your beauty has faded, even more so than your intellect. Perhaps the scribe can assist you with the list. We can start with your own mother, my mother, Phoebus' mother, Nestor's mother—"

Ileana snapped her fingers and they left, but Dion's count remained in her head. How she had fought for her throne! From her earliest memory she'd known she would be Queen of Heaven. She wanted it, deserved it. In one bold action she had grabbed it. No one could prove anything, though suspicions were raised. Ever after, bodyguards, food tasters, and a rigorous physical regime worked to protect her. She'd spent a lifetime defending her position. If the reigning Queen of Heaven died while in office, *Hreesos* could choose anyone, any of the many whores he'd impregnated.

He would have no choices: she would have no assassins.

So she'd eliminated the many women who had presented her husband with sons.

They had given him perfect children—Phoebus, Dion, Nestor . . . The babes from Ileana's own exquisite, golden body were female. She would not be usurped by her own daughters, ugly though they were. Not by Atenis, her strangely silent, homely firstborn, nor by Irmentis, the child of the night. The goddess Kela had been in her Season of Blood, and Ileana's youngest daughter bore the marks of her wrath.

As the embodiment of Kela, Ileana was creator and destroyer. She had made certain neither girl would seek pleasure in Zelos' arms. She was Kela, with Kela's authority, power, and position. What she wanted was divinely approved, for she wanted it. Ileana had removed the desire to rule and to wed from her daughters; she would not be a victim of matricide.

Ileana was assisted from the chair and entered her rooms. Light glowed in alabaster basins, and Leia played softly on the lyre as Ileana's young serf stood naked, anxious, and prepared to serve.

He untied her waist cincher, released her skirt, and led her to the lustral bath. Too tired to resist, she shuddered as she stepped into the warm water. The memories never faded; indeed, they grew more potent. The serf offered her *kreenos,* and Ileana hesitated, then took some. The drug brought her no peace, however. The specters from her past rose up before her.

Once again she was thirteen, slipping into her mother Rhea's chambers. Zelos, Ileana's older brother and Rhea's son, had just left the apartment, and Rhea was sprawled on her couch, naked and defenseless.

Ileana, tall and gawky for her age, had hidden an obsidian blade in the folds of her tunic. She was only a Shell Seeker and thus did not wear the layered skirt honoring the Great Goddess. She stepped quietly toward the sleeping woman, the sound of Rhea's soft snoring beating in the girl's head. Blond hair, so like Ileana's, flowed over marble white shoulders. Kela-Rhea wasn't aging: she would never lose the footrace, she would never step down as Queen of Heaven.

She raised the blade in both hands, then Ileana plunged it into her mother's back. Like the animals Ileana had practiced on, Rhea struggled, screamed, and tried to flee the knife. The cone shell poison worked quickly, however—in an eyeblink Rhea could no longer move. "My bath," she gasped. "Ba—a—aa-ttt . . ." Her body jerked violently, the poison controlling her. Finally, she was still.

Ileana ran to the balcony and pulled in a fellow Shell Seeker. The nymph's first taste of wine had made her groggy, and the poppy Ileana had added made her malleable. They traded tunics, Ileana's blood-splattered one now clothing the dazed girl. "Hold on to this," Ileana whispered to her onetime friend, wrapping the nymph's fingers around the knife's haft.

Ileana heard footsteps in the corridor. "Don't let go for anything," she hissed.

Ileana watched from the shadows as the narrow double doors opened and two guards ran in. They saw the girl, her position condemnation enough, then realized Rhea had not even been killed in her bath. She would never dance on the Isles of the Blessed.

Without the purification of the lustral bath, she was eternally dead. Soldiers bathed before they went to war, the ill were bathed if the condition was feared fatal. Newborns were birthed in a shallow pool, in the event they died. Rhea was lost forever.

Following the guards, Zelos ran in and threw himself weeping on Rhea's body. With the same blade Ileana had used to take Rhea's life, Zelos took the girl's. Ileana's path to the Queen of Heaven's throne was now cleared.

Blinking herself back into the safety of her bath, the distance of those many summers, Ileana forced her mind to calm. No one had guessed, no one had even known she'd been there. Feigned sorrow over the death of her mother seduced Zelos' heart, and sexual skills beyond her years had won her a place in his bed. She'd stepped easily into the role as Queen of Heaven.

No one knew. She was safe.

But safe until when? And whom? Safety was an illusion; danger always lurked. Friends were enemies waiting for opportunity, children were the seedlings of one's destruction, and even the goddess was fickle in her affections. Kela-Ileana destroyed any realities of danger. Danger lived and breathed in Vena, Sibylla, Selena . . .

Not for much longer, however.

CAPHTOR

SHE WOKE UP IN THE DARKNESS OF THE CAVE, but instead of feeling familiar it felt foreign. Once again Sibylla was uneasy. She rubbed her eyes and reached for the alabaster lamp to her side.

A gust of icy wind blew through. "That body is mine!" she seemed to hear around her. "Give it back to me!" It sounded like her own voice, fear filled and furious. Why would her voice be outside her? It's the part of my *psyche* that didn't return, she thought. It hates me for that. The voice carried on the wind, and Sibylla, hands now shaking, lit the oil lamp.

She lived in a simple room with whitewashed walls; a mattress of dried leaves and herbs lay on a shelf. Her few belongings from Kallistae were grouped atop a small trunk. Two other skirts and jackets hung on pegs.

That's a really beautiful contrast, she heard the voice inside her say, *but what does it mean, and where am I?* Sibylla looked at the saffron-and-crimson skirt against the white-and-black-bordered wall and had to admit it was striking, though so commonplace she didn't know why she had suddenly noticed it. She ignored her own mind's question of where she was. She was in Caphtor, in the cave, where the spirit of Kela dwelt. Across the sea were the other islands of the Aztlan empire— her home. She knew where she was. Sibylla rose and began to straighten the already neat room.

Something unspeakable had happened, was happening, to her.

She felt . . . lonely. It was an odd feeling, one Sibylla couldn't recall having felt before. Images flashed in her mind, a man, not unlike the men she saw all around her, yet different. He glowed through her perception, and she saw things in him that were shielded from most eyes. Integrity, skill, honesty, wit, sensuality . . . they poured from him in tinted beams of light. She'd never seen him before, yet she knew him.

Some part of her mind wept for him. This memory, this vision, was not her own.

Was this a message from Kela?

The voice within screamed in frustration, and Sibylla fought the urge to run, run all the way to Knossos if need be. This chamber with the wailing *skia*, her mind with the weeping unknown *psyche*, were too strange for her.

She pulled a cloak around her shoulders and walked outside. The lamp flickered feebly behind her. White chalky dust clung to her skirts and feet. She breathed deeply of the night air, feeling its sting burn in her breast. Above, stars hung like grapes from the arbor of the sky, and Sibylla felt tears in her eyes.

Why in the name of Kela would she be weeping? Her sense of loneliness and despair was so great, so engulfing, that she could not keep the sobs from rising. Her crying was loud, harsh in the still night. Sibylla had no idea how long she wept, how many times she wiped her face and hugged herself, desperate to feel the concern of one other person. An unknown, unnamed person.

Finally exhausted, she stumbled back to the cave's entrance. Malevolence hit her in the face like a stench. Recoiling, Sibylla looked into the shadows. *Skia* awaited her. Breathing deeply, she forced herself deeper into the cave. The *skia* surrounded her, pummeling her mind with anger, betrayal, pain, fury, whipping her into a pulpy emotional mass.

Sibylla ran the last steps to her shelf bed and huddled beneath her cloak. The very night seemed to whisper to her: she had never desired to see the dawn more. The flickering lamp went out, and she screamed, quaking.

Skeletal fingers poked her, prodded her, and Sibylla retreated in fear to a corner of her mind. Another part of her, a stronger, more adaptable *psyche*, stepped forward.

Chloe pulled the cloak off her head and stared into the darkness.

Holy shit! Once again, she was sharing someone's body. Was she sure of that? Who am I? she asked herself quickly. Chloe Bennett Kingsley, second lieutenant, serial number 044-65-2089. Born December 23, 1970. Middle child of an American diplomat and an English archaeologist. Older sister Camille, an Egyptologist. Younger brother

Caius, a professional black sheep. Grandmother Mimi, deceased. Degree in communications art. She lived at 767 Amber Lane, Dallas, Texas 75007.

Chloe swallowed. Those were the facts of her life. So far, so good.

So where was she? She wasn't in her own skin—she didn't have black hair. So who was the host body? Her vision of this current world seemed to be viewed through rippling water. Nothing was clear. Nothing was recognizable. The other *psyche* in this body, Sibylla, treated her as if she weren't here most of the time. Definitely not welcome, Chloe realized. It was one of the few clear thoughts she'd managed to have over the past—how long had it been? *How can I figure anything out when I can't even see to "drive"! We need to negotiate a body lease agreement. Living in this body is like moving a puppet; I am a breathing Punch & Judy show. Oh God.*

Where was Cheftu? The pain of his loss was so crippling that she whimpered in the darkness. They'd had such a short time. If she hadn't returned to the modern world, and she was guessing that she hadn't—caves were rather outmoded accommodations—then where was she? Where was he? Had he stayed in ancient Egypt? Had he moved forward in time? Did he truly understand she'd not wanted to leave? Had he, oh God, was he alive? Chloe shut her eyes tightly, holding back more tears. Did he know she was alive? Did he know where she was? Did *she* know where she was? Where was here?

The vision, Sibylla's vision of destruction, rose behind Chloe's eyelids. Because it had not been "her" seeing it, the edges were torn and it was faded: a mental daguerreotype. Waves, fire, earthquakes . . . was she here because of her emergency management training? Not to mention her emergency management *experience*. When the going got tough, the tough ate locusts.

Oh Cheftu, oh dear God I miss you. . . .

Chloe shook her head, the intention taking a few moments to result in action. She didn't feel quite settled in this body. *I sound like the next guest on Jerry Springer, "Modern Women and the Ancient Bodies They Inhabit."*

"I'm really losing it." Even her voice was a little different—not to mention the language!

If I am here, sharing Sibylla's body, then where is the body of RaEm—my former hostess—where is my body, and where is RaEm? If RaEm and I changed places before, is RaEm still in modern Egypt in my body? Has Cammy realized I'm not me?

Where was Cheftu? I need you, she thought. I was stupid not to have admitted it before. God, Cheftu, I need you! He alone would see the humor in this, understand how she could feel like laughing at the farce of it while she cried at the reality of it.

Chloe wrapped her arms around her waist. Fires, monster waves, and earthquakes. Welcome to Sibylla's world. She wanted something so badly, almost as much as Cheftu's touch, as a glance from his golden eyes. She could have bounced quarters off her nerves. If she *had* quarters. . . .

She licked her lips. *Man, do I want a cigarette.*

DAWN CAME, and with it the women of the village. Startled awake and disoriented for a few moments, Sibylla didn't understand their language. She blinked, focusing on a woman's rapidly moving lips, and felt herself slide into the comfort of knowing. The voice inside groaned in frustration and turned away, leaving Sibylla in control of herself once more.

With smiles and gentle orders they dressed her in a five-tiered red-and-saffron skirt and jacket, lacing her corset and brushing her hair so that it fell in waves to her waist. Cool kohl ringed her eyes and colored her eyelids. No one commented that her irises were still green.

That other *psyche* is still inside me, Sibylla thought.

She took some bread, and together they walked through a gentle rain into the main cave. There was no prophesying today, just the companionship of young and old alike, listening to the tales of the village, the daily trials of smoky fires, cranky men, crying babies, and irascible donkeys. The Season of Rains was for rest. Just as the earth and the sun and the sea rested, so did the villagers.

The women had brought wool to card. Sitting around the fire, they passed out implements and fleece for carding. Sibylla accepted two of the pronged plates and put a puff of wool—*Looks like a bunch of cotton balls,* she heard in her mind—between the plates. With a synchronized motion she rubbed the plates together, stretching and straightening the wool. It was loud work, with all twenty women chattering, and the conversation grew louder to be heard over the slap and scrape.

At the sun's zenith they took a break and walked outside. The light was pale, the ledge before the cave slick from the storm. The younger women played with a small ball, kicking it into the air, laughing and giggling as their elders sliced cucumbers and spread goat cheese on flat bread.

A group of nymphs challenged one another to footraces, mimicking the games at the midsummer festival. After loosening their waist cinchers, they stripped off their skirts and ran barefooted back and forth, tagging each other, shouting encouragement, and causing such commotion that one mother banned them all to the next ledge. "Go run there, and we will all watch you," she said with a smile.

"Nera, you did that just to get them away!" an older woman whispered, her voice almost drowned out by the girls moving to the ledge below.

"All season Lillina has been racing! Up and down the muddy lanes, back and forth through the fields! By the skirts of Kela, if that girl doesn't calm down, I may make her eat wood!"

Sibylla laughed, knowing this woman would no sooner beat her child than she would beat the oracle. The women of the village laughed as they sliced onions and broke cheese onto coarse winter greens. As they sipped wine from the matriarch's vineyards they discussed how to follow Kela's wishes. Should they flee before the Season of the Lion? Leave in the middle of harvest?

However, if Kela said to move, they would pack up their looms, their donkeys, and their white-clothed infants and move. They believed the goddess loved them and protected them. They didn't understand why, but they believed. If only Aztlan had so much trust, Sibylla thought. Even if the very Nostrils of the Bull spewed blood, Sibylla doubted the Aztlantu would believe. Hundreds of years free of conflict with earth or mortal had made them arrogant. They had no fear or respect. Would they leave their lush garden villas, the cobbled streets and shops where any merchandise known to the Aegean could be purchased? Would they leave their vineyards overlooking the glittering wide expanse of Theros Sea?

If they did leave, where would they go?

After lunch the village women retired to the shade of the hill, *sitting like crows on a phone line,* Sibylla heard in her mind. She dozed, feeling the sunlight on her breasts, face, hands, and feet. Her mind seemed still, content to be part of this community of women. When they awoke, they drank more wine. Today was special because the sweet girl who had been in Sibylla's vision was marrying after the full moon. Would Mistress Sibylla bless the union by attending? The vision was faded, easy to forget. A marriage party would hearten them all. Sibylla agreed with a smile.

The bride was almost fourteen summers. Her body had developed a little ahead of her spirit. Surrounded by her aunts, cousins, sisters, and mother, she listened wide-eyed as her grandmother took her hands and described the mysteries of the wedding night. With giggles and suggestions from the matrons, the girl's questions were answered and her sparkling brown eyes were no longer fearful.

Sibylla sat back, contemplating the differences between Caphtor, a rural vassal, and the cosmopolitan islands of Aztlan. Was this what Aztlan was like before the clan structure, when families were linked by blood ties only? In Caphtor everyone did a little of everything; had their own garden, owned their own goat, carded their own wool, wove their own cloth. At home in Aztlan, each clan had a separate responsibility to the empire. The Mariners sailed the sea, the artisans on Delos beautified the empire, her own clan fed and cared for the cattle.

Together they entered the sacred cave and bathed the bride in the icy waters of the sacred spring. They rubbed her skin dry with fresh herbs and flowers, then led her outside. An elderly aunt mixed henna and with graceful strokes began to paint the bride's hands.

Sibylla's glance fell to her own hand, long fingered and elegant. She wore no symbol of marriage. No tattoo wound around her wrist and over her fingers, declaring she was wed. Would she ever love like that? *I already have,* she heard an impatient voice say. *I lost him, and what the hell am I doing here?*

Disoriented, Sibylla ignored the voice in her head and focused on the celebration. This was her youngest grandchild, the weathered woman leading them had announced proudly. May it be the wish of Kela that she have a great-granddaughter by next harvest. The bride blushed as the women laughed. Sibylla shrugged away her sense of unease—the vision was false, surely.

Kela wouldn't let them come to harm, would she?

The women of the village brushed the bride's hair, braiding sections and tying in an odd number of trinkets in honor of the goddess as bride. In Aztlan the bride would wear gold and silver and precious stones, but the Caphtori were poor and found their wealth in herbs, flowers, and ribbons. The situation worked to the benefit of Aztlan.

Finally the bride's hands were finished, vines and flowers winding over her palms and inner wrists, the butterfly of Kela in the center of her left palm.

Please don't let this be for naught, Sibylla begged Kela. She is so young, so full of life. Please spare these people.

Sibylla thought she smelled burned flesh in the air already.

CHAPTER 2

JANUARY 1996, EGYPT

THE SECRET HAD BEEN GUARDED FOR AGES. Hidden beneath and within tons of stone, waiting for those chosen.

A living sentinel, the last lion sat in a rare patch of shade in Egypt's eastern desert, his tawny gaze fixed in the distance where humans toiled, moving the earth, scrabbling beneath it like jackals. They were working in the den where his ancestors had died. There they had given their lives, watching, waiting, and defending.

It was his turn.

Only his instinctual need to return to this den motivated him. He licked his paws clean, watching the humans. They had now all descended into the den.

Rising to the call he felt, the old lion began to hobble his way across the sands, to end his life where it had begun. To end his ancestors' mission.

To reveal the secret.

SWEAT TRICKLED BETWEEN HER BREASTS, but Dr. Camille Kingsley ignored it, as she ignored everything that interfered with her excavation.

Bubbles of excitement boiled in her blood. Anticipation that she didn't dare voice. They were so close now. She could feel it in the air: all her senses were on full alert. So close, so very close! The swishing sound of brushes on stone was musical in its rhythm. Please let this be it, she petitioned blindly.

After a cartouche had been found inscribed on the rock above them, funding for this project had escalated. The excavation had stepped into the spotlight, and Cammy was lucky she was still a part of it. Though she was an expert on the early eighteenth dynasty, she still was a lowly postdoc. Fortunately her location (already being in Egypt) and her role in the early finds (as one of the diggers) had helped her case.

The cartouche they found was Hatshepsut's, the woman pharaoh of the eighteenth dynasty and arguably one of the most powerful female rulers in history. Finding anything from her reign was miraculous, not to mention suspicious. Why would she have carved her name way out here in the eastern desert? No one could answer that question, at least not in a way that made sense.

Please be the find of my life, Cammy thought again.

She heard one of the others coughing from the centuries of stirred-up dust. Cammy kept at her detail work, brushing away the wall dust in fragile layer after layer, searching for the slick plaster the ancients had painted here almost 3,500 years ago. If this room had been anything more than a storeroom, the Egyptians would have painted the walls. It was their way.

The cavern was eerie. The subterranean room had apparently also served as a lion graveyard. Piles of bones had been found and removed. Within the chamber her team of Egyptologists had found some of the most amazing papyri ever unearthed in Egypt.

The huge, elaborate drawings were in a style unlike that of the ancient Egyptians. The ink and papyri unmistakably placed them in the early eighteenth dynasty. An enigma wrapped in a mystery most assuredly, she thought. The drawings were so odd, so debatable, that the team leaders were relieved to have the discovery upstaged when Rameses the Great's sons' tombs were found. The drawings could still be an elaborate hoax.

But the cartouche was not.

Pharaoh Hatshepsut.

Her near twenty-year reign had brought peace, prosperity, and foreign trade. She had then been usurped, presumably murdered, though by whom was anyone's guess. Her nephew Thutmosis III had taken the throne. During his long, bloodstained reign he had become one of history's greatest conquerors: the Napoleon of ancient Egypt.

Cammy pushed her glasses back onto the bridge of her nose and blinked, then blinked again.

Ink!

With trembling hands she brushed lightly at the dust. There, beneath it, was the faintest tracing of a line. She frowned. The paint wasn't typical; it was far too thick and inconsistent. Swallowing carefully, she continued to brush away. A fine crossbar. Another line, parallel to the first. A few pieces of the ink flaked off, and Cammy bit her lip to keep from cursing. She rubbed her sweat-soaked face on her dusty shirt, then brushed away some more at the wall.

A ladder—the common symbol used to portray climbing to Osiris. The means to get to heaven, to the afterworld . . . which meant the chamber . . .

It was a tomb!

"Jon," she said calmly, calling the head archaeologist.

A tomb? Hatshepsut's cartouche above? Was it possible that this was Hatshepsut's tomb? The tomb prepared for her in the Valley of the Kings had never been inhabited. Would Pharaoh have built a tomb on the east bank of the Nile? In the middle of the desert? It was unheard of, but so was a female pharaoh.

"Jon," she said a little louder.

Above them she heard muffled screams, which she ignored. Hatshepsut's tomb? The idea was too fantastic!

"What the——!" said Brian, the Aussie.

Tearing her gaze away from the ladder drawing that stretched up the wall, Cammy looked over her shoulder.

A golden roaring blur soared in from the opening in the roof. Camille heard her screams mingled with the others. A giant cat! A lion? The rushing of blood in her ears was so loud that she couldn't hear. The lion advanced on her, his massive chest spattered with blood, tufts of fur missing from all over his body. Cammy's mind dashed from utter darkness to fears of rabies, attacks . . . He advanced and she stepped backward, crashing into the seven-foot wooden ladder that leaned against the wall.

Ironic that it leaned in parallel to her new discovery, Cammy thought fleetingly. She couldn't look away from the lion. Clumsily she backed her way up one step and then another and another, hoping the angle of the ladder would support her.

The lion growled low in his throat and swiped at her with a massive paw. Cammy shrieked and clambered up another step, her trembling arms reaching toward the ceiling for balance. He sat down, his shaggy head and huge mouth just inches from her sandaled feet.

With a whimper, Cammy scooted onto the highest step, her shoulder blades against the ceiling, her legs tucked close to her. The lion roared and Cammy cringed, backing against the ceiling. She felt her hands, already near the meeting point of wall and roof, go up . . .

And inside the rock.

"Camille! I've got him in my sights! Duck!" Jon's voice filled the chamber a moment before the lion leaped.

An explosion rocked the room and Cammy grabbed the rocky ledge above her, struggling to hang on and pull herself up to safety as the lion collapsed against the ladder, sending it crashing onto the dirt-packed floor.

Cammy glanced up and into a hallway, lit with the dull gleam of gold. This *was* it!

Then the ceiling gave way.

Gold. Dust. Darkness.

Camille opened her eyes. The shock of waking up in a hospital had diminished only slightly in the past two weeks. Impressions she still didn't fully understand clung to her. She rubbed her face with her shoulder. At least she felt fairly safe here. Gold, dust, darkness . . . what were these images from? Her gaze drifted over the baskets and bouquets of flowers assembled for Camille Kingsley, Ph.D. Egyptology. She felt more like a child than a professional woman.

She didn't remember anything about the dig, the fall . . . trained her entire life for archaeology and she couldn't recall anything. Gold, dust, and darkness. She wished she could reach into her mind and see what she had seen. If she had seen anything.

What a miserable way to spend the winter season.

It still hurt to breathe, but not as badly as before, so she knew her ribs were mending. Her nurse, Fatima, smiled as she uncovered Cammy's breakfast. Hospital food was hospital food, even in Egypt. She looked at the window toward the modern town of Hurghada on the Red Sea. If she had to stay in this nouveau tourist trap, then she'd much rather be on the beach!

Patiently she opened her mouth, hating that she had to be spoon-fed, but with her left arm broken and her right wrist tendon torn, she literally couldn't get her hand to her mouth. Fatima told her she had visitors waiting. Cammy let Fatima brush and twist her long brown hair away.

After an assisted trip to the bathroom and a rinse of her teeth, Cammy gratefully climbed back in between the sheets and fixed a smile on her face. She wished they wouldn't come. She felt horribly guilty: just seeing their false-bravado faces made her cringe inside. They were unemployed because of her.

After the lion collapse incident, the Egyptian Antiquities Authority had closed the dig as unsafe. If Camille hadn't held on to the roof, it might not have fallen and they could all still be working. Big ifs that had no effect on the situation now.

Negotiations were under way to reopen the dig, but it was the Middle East. Time was fluid. Today, tomorrow, next week, next year . . . who knew? A dozen people had to be bribed, then they bribed another dozen. The wheels of government weren't just slow, they were only recently hewn. Until that far-off day when they received permission again, the eastern desert dig was sealed, an iron grate was installed over the well, and three guards patrolled twenty-four hours a day. The university had pulled the grant, terrified of lawsuits.

Jon was the excavation leader, most recently the lion killer and her rescuer. She got chills when she realized what the lion could have done to her. Yet even when he had swiped at her, his claws had been sheathed. It was a strange detail she hadn't noticed until she thought about it afterward. If only she could remember other details.

Brian the Aussie still wore a white bandage around his head, giving his rakish good looks a piratical twist.

Clyde, a talented photographer and copyist whose skill rivaled that of Camille's sister, Chloe, was from one of the Carolinas. Blond and slender, with a gentle, slow accent, he had inspired a handful of crushes. All the young nurses wanted to be his wives, fatten him up, and give him golden-haired children.

Lisa was the only other woman on the team. Her specialty was in mid–eighteenth dynasty funerary objects, though she was well versed in many other eighteenth-dynasty artifacts. When it was apparent the cavern was eighteenth dynasty, she had come in from Cairo.

"We brought you this," Lisa said, laying a tabloid on Cammy's coverlet. "If laughter is indeed the best medicine, this article will cure you."

"It's amazing what the public will believe about archaeology," Brian said. "It's bunk. Just like the 'Curse of Tutankhamen' all over again."

Clyde opened the pages for her, and Cammy, mystified by the chortles and giggles of her usually reserved comrades, skimmed the headlines that reported Elvis sightings and the scoop on alien lovemaking techniques. "Should I even ask how you found this? Which one of you reads it?" she asked.

Jon turned beet red. "My sister mails me anything that even mentions Egypt. Go ahead, read it."

Clyde turned the next page, and Cammy stared, openmouthed.

ARCHAEOLOGIST TALKS TO GOD THROUGH MAGIC STONES! the headline proclaimed in huge letters. It was always a bad sign when the headline used exclamation marks. The story continued in the same overblown fashion. "Renfrock Holmes, the real-life 'Indiana Jones,' finds the telekinetic devices to tune *people* into God's frequency!" read the subtitle.

"Oh no, please not Renfrock," Cammy said. "How he even got a degree is beyond me."

"Keep reading," Lisa said. "It gets better."

"Beneath the waters of Israel's Lake Kinneret, Renfrock Holmes has unearthed the keys to talking to God.

"'God Himself told me where to dig,' the world-renowned archaeologist said, pointing to a sandy finger of land that leads into this deep lake, the site of much of Jesus' teaching and the base of operations for the rabbis who wrote the Talmud."

Cammy skimmed over the paragraphs extolling Renfrock's brilliance, his tête-à-tête with God, *"just like Moses, God made me take off my shoes!"* and found the actual details of the artifacts.

She read it twice and looked up. "No way. This is unbelievable."

Jon chortled. "You'd think that even Renfrock would realize no one would buy this story."

"An Egyptian leather pouch, containing two stones that Holmes believes are 'telecommunication devices with God—'"

Cammy resisted laughing—it hurt too much.

"'The pouch is circa 960 B.C.,' Renfrock said. 'This may be the same pouch the priests used to carry the stones when they fled the invading Egyptians.'"

"Did Egyptians invade Israel in 960 B.C.E.?" Cammy asked.

"Keep reading."

She slogged her way through a poorly written paragraph in which Renfrock claimed that *"through electromagnetic impulse"* the Egyptians had used the stones to build the Pyramids. Cammy couldn't help it; despite the pain she hooted with laughter.

The article concluded with Renfrock's challenge to establishment archaeologists to *"have faith"* and *"believe in the truth of legends."*

"Wasn't there a legend about some stones the Hebrews had?" she asked, flipping idly through the rest of the paper.

"Yes. They were called the Urim and Thummim," Clyde said. He had a general Near Eastern background, as opposed to the strictly Egyptian dynastic education the rest of the team shared.

"Strange names," Lisa said.

"In Hebrew, 'im' is plural. They mean Justice and Mercy. Or Lights and Perfections, depending on the translation," Clyde said. "According to legend, David's high priest used them to learn what battles he would win."

"David?" Brian asked.

"King David? The guy who slew Goliath? Did any of you go to Sunday school?" Clyde asked with a smile.

"You're saying he could talk to God?" Jon asked. "What a load of bullshit."

"How did the stones work?" Cammy asked.

"Well," Clyde said, his cadence slowing, "no one knows how exactly they were used, but the high priest carried them around in his ephod, that jeweled breastplate he wore, and they kept Israel out of a lot of trouble."

"What happened to them? I'm assuming, since I've not heard of them in any museum or collection, that they were lost," Lisa said.

"The Bible doesn't mention them after the dividing of the monarchy, i.e. after the death of Solomon in 930 B.C.E."

"So Renfrock got his dates wrong," Jon said, shaking his head in disgust.

"When did they come into being?" Brian asked.

"They're mentioned biblically with Moses and Aaron, though that could be anachronistic. It's rumored that Saul had a pair *and* David had a pair. Heck, there are legends that say Noah had 'em on the Ark and one of his sons took 'em," Clyde said.

"Noah? His sons?" Jon asked.

"Even I know this," Brian said. "Noah had three sons: Ham, Shem, and Japheth. All the peoples of the world—"

"The world as seen by the Hebrews," Lisa said. "I don't think Asia or Australia were included."

"Nah, I doubt they were," Brian said. "Shem became the father of the nations called Semites. Arabs and Jews, et cetera. Ham was father of Egypt, Canaan, Libya, and Ethiopia."

"Most of Africa, then," Cammy said.

"Japheth is credited with the northern peoples: his offspring populated the land from the Caspian Sea to the Greek Isles."

"Actually, Greece was fathered by Japheth's son, Noah's grandson Javan," Clyde said. "In Hebrew the word for 'Greece' actually is 'Javan.'"

"So one of Noah's sons stole the stones?"

Clyde shrugged. "It's just a legend. No verification anywhere."

"So Noah allegedly called God for a weather report using these stones?" Cammy asked with a chuckle.

"One would hope *that* weatherman would be more accurate," Jon said.

"'The forecast calls for rain,'" Brian said. "'A lot of rain.'"

Lisa chuckled. "'Rain to last for weeks. Don't plan on gardening, there won't be any ground.'"

Cammy wondered: Was it possible that Renfrock had really found this Urim and Thummim? "Is it—"

"No. They were mystical talismans, probably just some pretty rocks, and David had unbeatable luck, so the legend grew," Clyde said. "If Renfrock has found anything, it's just—"

"Poppycock," Brian suggested.

The conversation moved away from the news article, and the group discussed their options while the dig was closed. Since there was no end in sight and it was midseason, the team was scattering. Camille and her sister, Chloe, were due to fly out of Cairo at the end of the month, to meet their parents at the Kingsley villa on the Greek isle of Santorini. Cammy's mom would be there, fresh from her new excavation in the Aegean. Cammy's dad was still in negotiating mode, who really knew where. Brian was returning to Melbourne, Lisa to Chicago, and Jon was off to Turkey. Clyde had gotten a last minute job with a team in Israel.

If only she hadn't grabbed the ceiling, if only the dig hadn't collapsed—Camille fought down her feelings of guilt. She struggled to look happy and wished them all a great season. Everyone left except Clyde. Recently they'd begun to play cards together. Cammy could stuff the cards in her cast and with her mobile right fingers select and discard. Clyde was good company, and she helped him with his Arabic while they played. Fatima was everywhere, fluffing pillows, fetching them tea and pastries with shy smiles.

Cammy was losing by two hands when Chloe walked in.

Clyde was head over hiking boots in love with Cammy's sister. In normal circumstances, Cammy would have been thrilled. However, Cammy hadn't really liked her sister much in the past year. The intimacy they'd once shared was gone, just when Cammy really needed it, too.

"How are you feeling?" Chloe said, brushing a kiss over Cammy's cheek. She was wearing a short skirt, heels, and a clinging top. It was bare and daring for the United States, absolutely scandalous in the Middle East. Chloe's cultural sensitivity had flown out the window along with her artistic ability, sweet nature, and sardonic tongue. Her long red hair fell over her shoulders, and her lipstick and heavy eyeliner underlined a sensuality Cammy had only recently seen in her sister.

Clyde went mute. He never knew what to say around Chloe. His neck turned red, and sweat beaded his upper lip. A soft touch on his shoulder and another on his knee made him drop his cards. Cammy had witnessed this drama for the past weeks. Had Chloe always had this effect on men? It was odd, but Cammy sometimes felt as though someone else watched the world from behind Chloe's eyes.

Of the things that had changed in the past year, the changes in Chloe were the oddest. About a year ago, the Kingsley family had suffered a terrible scare. Chloe had gone missing on her birthday. Anton Zeeman, a Dutch doctor, was the last person who had seen her. When a chamber in Luxor Temple had been found splattered with blood, he had been held for her murder.

Tests had shown that of the two types of blood present, neither was Chloe's rare AB-negative. Cammy had been consumed with guilt. Chloe had been in Egypt at Cammy's request. Despite the fact that Chloe was an adult, a military officer, and an entrepreneur, she was still Cammy's kid sister. Cammy still felt responsible. Anton had gone free once the bloods were analyzed.

Cammy shivered as she remembered the night he'd shown up at her door, pleading with her to believe him, to let him help. He hadn't killed anyone. Not only had she forgiven him, but they had somehow wound up in bed, having the most cataclysmic sex Cammy had ever experienced.

Don't even go there, she admonished herself. Anton had realized it was a mistake; he'd never even called. Sick with guilt and worry, Cammy had returned to her dig and buried herself in work. Chloe had been found in early March. The feeling of relief was something Camille would never forget.

Nor would she forget the eerie sensation of Chloe's hysterical blindness or the fact that her sister's eyes, once green as palms, were now brown. Concussion, the doctors said. Severe trauma related to a concussion. Odd, but not completely unheard of.

Eye color was the least of the changes. Chloe, an artist to her very core, had not picked up a pen or paintbrush in almost a year. Moreover, she refused to leave Egypt, draining her accounts in Dallas. She had moved in with a young Egyptian named Phaemon, a man Cammy had never even met. She exhibited a stunning disregard for her parents' feelings and their father's reputation.

In the Middle Eastern mind, one's daughters were the honor of one's household. Chloe was performing a slow hatchet job on their father's role as a negotiator in the elaborate Middle East peace knot. Chloe knew that the Arabs, Palestinians, and even the Israelis were losing respect for her father, but she didn't seem to care. She treated him like a stranger when he came to see her. They'd never had the best of relationships, but this was extreme, even for them. Chloe had adamantly refused counseling, or talking to anyone, even family. She claimed she remembered nothing, she just wanted to be left alone.

Aside from her height and her red hair, Chloe was unrecognizable.

Camille *still* felt responsible. She also wasn't sure she even liked her sister anymore.

"Who is winning?" Chloe asked, resting her long-fingered hands on Clyde's shoulders. Cammy pitied him: he was obviously fighting for composure, and when Chloe began kneading his shoulders, telling him how tense he was, Cammy wanted to scream. Deliberately she lost her hand and yawned.

Clyde, with his Carolina manners, rose immediately. Holding his jean jacket in front of him, he wished them both a good day. Chloe brushed a kiss on his cheek, and he stumbled from the room, crashing into Fatima and making his confusion worse. The door slammed behind him, and Cammy listened to his footsteps retreating up the hall.

"What a geek!" Chloe said, throwing herself into the chair by the bed.

"If you don't like him, why do you lead him on?"

She shrugged. "It amuses me."

"He's a colleague of mine, but more important he's a nice, sweet, aboveboard guy. Leave him alone, Chloe."

"He's a big boy. If he doesn't want to play, he will tell me."

He doesn't stand a chance with you, Cammy thought. You've turned into a man-eating predator! "Do you and Phaemon have holiday plans?"

Chloe frowned for a moment, as though she didn't understand Camille.

"Is he joining us in Santorini?" Cammy said.

Her sister's fair skin flushed a little. "Phaemon is another religion, not sharing in these holidays, so I will be with him."

"What religion is he? Do you realize that you've been with him almost a year and I've never officially met him?" *Other than the time I walked in on you two having sex in my bedroom and you invited me to join you.* Cammy felt her own cheeks heat. What had happened to Chloe? It was enough to make one believe in alien abductions, she thought, glancing at the tabloid.

Chloe dug into a stack of fashion magazines she'd brought. "He is rather, uh, shy."

"What does he do? Where is he from? Phaemon is an interesting name, ancient almost. . . ."

"You are very inquisitive this morning, Cammy. You are feeling better, and this is how you repay my willingness to drive halfway across this barren land to be with you?" Chloe's voice was raised, her brown eyes unreadable.

The tension hovered while Chloe flipped through her magazines and Cammy replayed her words. She hadn't been that harsh, had she? Weary from unease, she closed her eyes and turned toward the window. What she wouldn't give to be back on her dig.

Gold, dust, darkness . . . What had she seen?

PART II

CHAPTER 3

ANCIENT EGYPT

U SER-AMUN SIGHED AND SCRATCHED HIS HEAD. His scalp itched. The solution that felt so refreshing when his head was just shaved made it itch horribly once it was dry. He rubbed his wiry fingers along the base of his neck and behind his ears. A loud meow made him open his eyes. His cat, Ner, sat before him. "You think I should pet you before scratching myself?" he asked, running his fingers over her pointed ears until the low resonance of her purr filled the room.

Someone knocked at his door; User bade him enter. The priest was young, not fifteen Inundations, his pale brown eyes wide. "Life, prosperity, and health to you, noble User-Amun, *neter* of the House of Life. I am to bid you come to the temple. There has been an accident."

User placed Ner on the floor and rose, tightening his sash around his sagging belly. "What kind of accident?" he asked, pulling vials and ointments from the shelves that lined the room.

"A man, trampled by an Apis bull," the boy said. "There was another, but she is dead."

The physician turned, pausing for a moment. "This man still lives?"

"He was pressed into manure and mud," the boy said. "He managed to shield his face and let the mud take his body. Still, he has traveled far in his journey to the Afterworld." The boy looked down. "Even now he may be at Anubis' gates."

User handed his heavy parcels to the boy and drew the door closed behind them. "Which priest is it, son?"

The boy shrugged. "I know not, my lord."

After the appropriate greetings, User was led to the victim. One look at the man's body and the physician knew any aid would be in vain. Burning with fever, he was near death. His pulse was jumpy, his body stinking of manure. Bruises mottled his chest, legs, and arms. He would not live; it would be a waste of time and energies to care for him. The living needed the little food available in this time of famine. Better to let him embrace Anubis. "How did you find him?" User asked.

"He was lying on his belly in the mud, his face turned into his shoulder, his hands protecting his sex," the priest said.

User picked up one of the victim's long-fingered hands and saw a heavy tiger's eye–and-gold scarab ring. Was this man a royal scribe to wear such fine jewelry? He had hair, so he was certainly no priest. Two of four fingers were broken; at least User-Amun could set them. When he pried open the man's fist, a string-tied papyrus package fell from his palm.

Using linen bandages, ointment, and heavy rush stems, User flattened the man's hand into something resembling human. It would not do to enter the underworld without use of one's left hand. He prayed in a sonorous tone from the Book of the Dead: "'Fix tightly the bones in my neck and back. Let the linens embrace me.'"

User ran sensitive hands over the body. Though the lung was not pierced, a rib or two were broken. The man's ankle was swollen, and User administered cooling waters and bandages for it. "Give him to the House of Eternity," he said. "He sleeps too deeply and his wounds are too extreme. He will die soon. 'Together my arm, wrist, and elbow are joined,'" he intoned.

The priests covered his body and prepared to carry him. "My

lord," the *sem*-priest said, "there is also a woman to take to the House of Eternity."

"A woman?" User frowned at the man. How did a woman come to be in the bowels of the sacred bull's running ground in an all-male temple? Beckoning, the man walked into another room. Again the stink of manure.

She was so mangled that even in the afterlife her body would be of no use to her. Hooves had pounded her body into a pulp, bruised beyond identification. "No rings, no indication of who she was?" User asked.

"Nay, my lord. All of the priests on duty have been questioned."

"Her linen is fine stuff," User-Amun said, touching the once bright sash wrapped around her waist. Good-quality leather sandals shod her feet, and her hair was real, not a wig. User looked more closely at her body.

Strangely enough, neither of the victims had the appearance of famine sufferers. Both were firmly built, with clear skin beneath the muck, hair that was lustrous and well rooted in the scalp. User picked an instrument out of his basket and opened the woman's mouth.

The priest hissed in shock. Never had either of them seen such healthy teeth! Strong, white, and not even one missing! Fear pricked User-Amun's spine, and he made a gesture against the Evil Eye. Her face was pummeled, her eyes blackened. On pure impulse he drew back an eyelid.

In his thirty Inundations of serving the House of Life, User had never been so frightened. "Isis! Protectress!" he pleaded.

The woman's eyes were blank. Not just sunken or rolled into her head. She had *no* irises . . . just white orbs.

The priest had stepped away, fingering his *udjet* eye amulet. User looked at the woman's body again. Something unearthly was being played here.

"When was she found?"

"The twenty-third of Phamenoth."

The most fearful day in the Egyptian calendar. *Khaibits*, fanged shades, and *khefts*, laughing demons, roamed the night. Unexplainable things happened. Wise men locked their doors and prayed for Ra's light. Why had the priests waited so long to summon him? Death was so common in the two lands now that even the priesthood was behind schedule. "Destroy her," he said in an undertone.

"My lord?"

"Her *ka* fled her body before death. Her eyes, the windows of her soul, are empty. She is a shell, abandoned. Her body is broken, of no use in the afterlife. Something beyond our knowing has happened." He looked at the scared priest. "We must protect ourselves and destroy her corpse!"

"We cannot do that here, my lord. We are a temple! Perhaps the House of Eternity . . ."

"Nay, fool! They will seek to preserve her. We cannot let that happen. Come. Now. We'll offer her to the Nile."

The priest slowly nodded agreement, his hand never leaving his amulet.

"Nay, wait," User-Amun said. "Tonight. We'll do it tonight."

"So where does she stay?" the priest asked, frantically backing away from the corpse.

"I have the responsibility of the man, the woman is yours until tonight."

"Why must we do this?" the priest whispered.

User-Amun paused in the doorway. "Her *ka* will not return to this body. Should a *khaibit* or *kheft* wish to, however, they could bring *ukhedu* life to her."

The priest blanched. *Ukhedu* was vile poison. It filled a body when someone was sick. Medicaments and prayers fought the *ukhedu* for possession of the body. It was the basis of evil in the human condition. It brought madness, destruction, uneasy death. A body under the control of the *ukhedu* would upset the balance of Ma'at, the equilibrium of the universe.

Once on the other side of the door, the *sem*-priest barred it. With trembling fingers he set his seal in the wax, forbidding entry. Two *w'rer*-priests were assigned to help User-Amun with the man's body. Together they began to make their way to the House of Eternity.

"My lord! My lord!"

User paused. They had just left the mud-brick *tenemos* walls of the temple, carrying the wrapped body of the victim between two shaven-headed priests. A *w'eb*-priest ran up. Cow dung and mud covered his feet and hands, and he quickly crossed his chest in respect.

"Aye?" User growled.

"I found this, my lord. It was lying underneath the man, between him and the woman." The boy held out his hand, and User reluctantly received the muddy thing. With a production of disdain he wiped it off and stared.

A ring. White and yellow gold were interwoven, and inside each loop was a chip of amber, or citrine. "It is too small for a man," User said. The priest shrugged, crossed his chest again, and ran back to the temple.

Thoughtfully User tucked the ring into his sash and bade the priests walk on.

Noph was a changed city with the famine. Though it was nearly the Season of Growing, none of the *rekkit* could get to their farms. The Nile had overflowed again and water stood in the fields, making it impossible to sow seed. Earlier in the year, rats had invaded the city. All the sleek cats working every decan Ra gave them could not eradicate the vermin. Dozens of people had died; dozens more lay ill.

Then there were the insects. They swarmed over the standing water, then attacked the people. No house, no person, was safe. Most of the population lived with weeping sores from the illnesses the mosquitoes brought. Again, dozens of people had died.

User was glad he was an old man. The biting bugs had no interest in his leathery skin and sour blood. Though his bones ached and his teeth were rotten, still he could move; so he worked, bringing aid where he could and mixing herbs for those in need of more potent relief.

They passed through the market section. In past Inundations this was such a pleasant experience: children and animals, fat and thin *rekkit*, mothers with babies, fathers with produce. User shook his head. Egypt was surviving, but her *ka* was weak from the lack of fresh fruits and vegetables. Life begat life.

Thank Osiris for Pharaoh, living forever's! insight and inspiration, which had made Pharaoh gather up excess in the Inundations of plenty to share with the *rekkit* in these Inundations of hunger.

The imposing structure of the House of Eternity took up the full block. The whitewashed walls and papyrus-topped columns in red, blue, and green were reassuring, as they should be. User gestured to the priests, and they followed him to the delivery entrance in back. Whitewashed slabs were placed uniformly in the courtyard for just such occasions. The priests laid the body down, and User dismissed them, then knocked on the door.

A scribe opened it, his bulk filling the width of the doorway. User had worked with him before; he was an idiot. How could it be that in a three-year famine this scribe still looked as though he dined at Pharaoh, living forever's! table nightly?

"I need to arrange for a body," User said, smiling pleasantly.

"Dead?"

"*Haii*, well, he is dying."

The scribe looked up. "Nay, my lord. We take only the already dead."

"He is dying. Quickly."

"Not dead yet? No entry."

"I am the first physician of the House of Life! I assure you, this man will be dead by tomorrow's *atmu!*"

"I am sorry, my lord, but only the already dead may enter."

User-Amun sighed. How inflexible the idiot was. "Look at him! In the sleep of death, broken limbs, probably shattered bones. He bleeds inside, see the bruises? There is nothing that can be done for him. I promise you, he will die tonight!"

"Only the already dead, my lord." He backed up as though to close the door, but User stuck his foot in the crack.

"Look, my brother of Amun, I am busy. I have neither the time, nor the desire, to take him to my practice, watch him die *there*, then haul his carcass back *here!* Do you understand me?"

"Just following my orders, my lord. I cannot help you. Already dead."

User-Amun ground his teeth. He was fully tempted to strike the comatose patient on the head and be done with it. Only the confession in the prayer of the dead, *"I have not deprived any man's life or ambition,"* prevented him. "By the feather of Ma'at," he shouted. "He's going to *die!* Let me leave him here!"

The victim chose this moment to mutter and thrash about.

"Who is going to die?" a pleasantly cultured voice asked from behind User. He watched the eyes of the idiot scribe widen, and the man dropped into a sloppy bow. As User turned his heart sank. He suddenly knew he should not have left his home today. The gods were not smiling upon him.

Imhotep. Pharaoh's physician and offspring of the brilliant designer of the Pyramids. Stones the size of bird's eggs glimmered at the man's throat, wrists, and fingers. He was tall and unspeakably ugly, with features that were so disproportionate they looked like a mask. His teeth were decayed, rattling in his head and giving him the breath of a crocodile, but his gray eyes smiled. His gaze moved beyond User's hasty bow to the half-wrapped body of the unknown victim. "The man you are so certain will die?" he asked with a gesture.

By Sobek's tail, User thought, my career is finished. "Aye, my lord. In such a time as this we must trust the gods' will that some be taken."

Imhotep raised the man's eyelid, then checked the voice of his heart. "Skilled work on his hands," Imhotep said. "It is well that a man not enter the afterlife without use of both hands."

"Aye, my lord," User said, exhaling silently in relief. He glared behind Imhotep's back to the incompetent scribe in the doorway. Perhaps this would make the man yield? "His injuries are mostly internal and far too serious." User shook his head in pity. "He looked a strong man, but perhaps Isis wanted him more."

Imhotep was looking at the man's ring. "Have you seen this before?" he asked. "Is this man a scribe?"

"I know not, my lord." User indicated the black hair matted to the soon-to-be-corpse's skull. "He was found in the Apis run, but he is not a priest with hair like that."

Imhotep's gaze touched the man's legs and chest, both liberally sprinkled with hair. "Very odd," he said. "Great pity that we cannot ask him."

User watched as the great physician's eyes narrowed.

"How long, say you, does this man have?"

Aware of the listening idiot, User said, "A day, two at most."

"Is it not in your vows as a *neter* in the House of Life to care for this man until he meets Osiris?"

User felt his face warm. "My lord, this man is doomed. I would wager a month's grain that he will not wake again." A gleam flickered in the great one's eyes. Had the whisperings been true, then? Imhotep was open to any wage making? Perhaps this unfortunate victim would not be buried, unmourned, by the state.

"If you choose to waste your grain that way, let me sweeten the wager. I will treat this man for three weeks. If he dies before then, I will pay for his burial and tomb."

"What if, by unlikely chance, he lives, my lord?"

"Then he is mine and you repay me for my costs: treatment, time, and skills."

Sweat ran down User's back. Truth of it, the man could linger for three days. To take his word back now would be admitting he'd exaggerated. But three weeks? Thirty days? Impossible. "As my lord suggests," he said, keeping his tone even.

With a curt nod, Imhotep's guard loaded the body in a cart and began walking away. "I am here on Pharaoh, living forever's! business," Imhotep said. "I will send a messenger if the man lives and will expect your compensation by return message."

User nodded, crossing his chest in relieved respect.

"Tell me again, where was he found?"

"The Apis chamber."

"Trampled only?"

"Aye, my lord, though he has some cuts. They are not gore marks, nor do they look like hoof marks. Perhaps he received them a short time before he was hurt?"

The great one paled and made a motion of protection against the Evil Eye. "Could they be teeth marks?"

User frowned, picturing the wounds. "Aye," he said slowly. "But from a large animal. Perhaps even the bull."

Imhotep rattled his loose teeth. "The gods' best to you," he said. "Life, health, and prosperity!"

User bent low until the footfalls of the jogging slaves were gone. The scribe saw the look on his face and hurriedly shut and bolted the door. Swearing, User walked home.

I was just on this road, User thought. Now, though, it was dark. Not as fearful as darkness on the 23rd of Phamenoth, but still he felt the breath of *khefts* on his neck. Hurriedly he passed through the temple gate. The priest waited, his kohl-ringed eyes glittering in the torchlight. From the darkened rear of the temple User could hear the sound of singing priests, taking the god Ptah to his couch.

Silently the two men walked into the chamber. The body of the woman was there, no longer stiff, the flesh warm from the heat of the day. Decay was setting in, and User felt his gorge rise. In protection against wandering *khefts* and *khaibits*, he had bound an amulet around his throat and one on each arm. Prayerfully he covered the corpse with cloth.

The *sem*-priest, chanting softly, bound a black cord around her waist, then knotted it. Had he wanted to destroy her *ka*, her spirit, he would have written her name on a papyrus scroll and bound it into the cord. Since they were destroying her body only, it was unnecessary to use her name. A boon, since her name and identity were unknown.

Instead they offered prayers of protection for her *ka*, already loose on the face of the earth. Once the corpse was wrapped and tied, the priest picked up a wax figure of the woman. This was the most sacred of ceremonies, the vilest of Egyptian ritual. But it was necessary protection. Egypt was already weak with the famine, with sand-crawling Asiatics invading from across the desert. The red and black lands did not need a *khaibit* wandering the marshes.

With a sharp bronze blade the priest cut off the feet of the wax figure. Was it User's imagination, or did the corpse jerk, as though she felt the knife? In an inversion of the prayers of the dead, the prayers recited by the deceased as they traveled through the afterworld, the priest chanted. *"When Ra's light shines on these fields, you cannot rise to walk through them."* He cut off the figure's hands. *"Creativity is taken from your hands. You cannot fashion yourself."* The priest's voice was trembling as he raised the hilt of the knife and bludgeoned the figure's face. *"You are blinded, you cannot find the river, the land. You cannot see to revenge or wreak de-*

struction or take what is not yours." He cut its head off. *"In the protection of Osiris, I cut off my sister's head. I beg the counsel of Osiris that this one's ka is admitted to the afterworld. You cannot seek revenge."*

He laid down the blade, picked up the pieces of the figure, then wrapped them in the edge of the linen. After letting themselves out a side door, User and the priest carried the body into the star-strung night, reciting prayers that were as rote as their names.

"Hail, long-legged beast, striding from the cornfield, creature from the House of Light. I've seen nothing in the world but beauty. May we live forever!

"Hail, priest of incense, smoke, and flame, fresh from the soul's daily battle, I've taken nothing from life but strength. May we live forever!

"Hail, wind in my face, blown from the mouths of the gods, I returned the goslings to their nest. The hawks soar freely above the cliffs. May we live forever!

"Hail, devourer of shadows, terror lurking in the entrails of mountains, I extinguished no man's life. I took neither his life nor his dreams. May we live forever!"

They stood at the pre-Inundation edge of the Nile, supporting the body between them, water at their waists. Clumsily they tucked rocks into the linen wrappings. The priest was weeping freely now as they recited the final prayer.

"May the light shine through us and on us and in us. May we die each night and be born each morning and that the wonder of life should not escape us. May we love and laugh and enter freely into each other's hearts. May we live forever!"

The splash seemed loud: then she was gone. Wherever her *ka* had gone, it was now trapped there. The two men gripped arms, looking out into the dark river. "May we live forever," User whispered.

IPIANKHU, LITERALLY "He Who Is Called 'Alive,'" jolted awake. Sitting up, he slowly focused on the room around him. He was not in the dark confines of his prison cell, where despair was an odor that clung in the night, where men's panicked cries to stone gods filled his ears.

He breathed deeply.

Instead, his wide, opulent chamber was washed in dawn's glow. The white linen sheets that draped his couch were tinted pink and orange. The covered body of his wife moved gently as she breathed. This was his home. He was safe. Free. The most powerful man in Egypt, next to Pharaoh, living forever!

So what had awakened him? He rose stiffly, went to the alcove, and washed his face and hands. He looked into the bronze reflection for a moment. At sunrise his foreignness was most apparent. The light seemed to catch fire on the red stubble of his chin and scalp. His skin was sprinkled with freckles, beaten into one copper mass by the sun. His eyes, the brownish green of the Nile, contrasted with his bronze brows and lashes. He looked away. A decan with his brush and paint-wielding manservant, and Ipiankhu was as Egyptian as any other man.

He pushed away from the mirror and he walked to the door over-looking his courtyard. The famine had killed any beauty that had once dwelt there. Vegetation rotted in stagnant pools of water. Yet the famine would last only four more Inundations. This he knew; he'd been assured of it.

Ipiankhu raised his gaze to the sun. *Go to Pharaoh!* a powerful com-mand whispered through his questing mind. Senwosret needed him. The knowledge seized him and he clapped, waking his manservant to prepare him for an audience. When slaves came to get him less than a decan later, they were stunned. Surely Ipiankhu was an awesome mage!

Pharaoh Senwosret was sitting up on his couch. His bare head was covered, lines formed by Inundations of worry drawing down his face, free of makeup. The film that covered his eyes and was ruining his vision seemed thicker today. His eyes were murky, filled with poi-son, like the Nile. Ipiankhu prostrated himself.

"Rise, my wise one," Pharaoh commanded. "I have dreamed!"

As happened every time he interpreted a dream, Ipiankhu saw im-ages flash in his head: His childhood and the arrogant dream of the sun, moon, and nine stars bowing to him. The beautiful mantle pro-claiming him heir to his father's herds, the same mantle ripped from his body by his half-brothers. The clammy, rodent-ridden chill of the well where he spent countless days and nights in sheer terror. His beautiful employer's face changing from lust to hatred as though a sculptor were reshaping her features before Ipiankhu's eyes. The haughty demeanor of the baker who had died. He felt a chill race through his blood, and in his heart he begged for assistance. "My Majesty, if it be the Unknown's will, I shall interpret."

"I was in a desert. It was cold, not hot, even though Ra blazed down." Senwosret licked his lips. "Before me the dunes and sands were losing their colors. An incense-thick gray fog surrounded me. Then all became darkness. Out of the darkness I heard an angry growl, the sound of a big cat in pain. Blazing fire engulfed me, and I saw the world in brilliance and a mountain cat with eyes like molten gold standing before me. He held a knife in his mouth." Senwosret looked away. "Then I awoke." The pharaoh chewed on his lip for a moment. "Could it be a sign to go to the temple of Bastet?"

Ipiankhu sighed. He doubted the Unknown would send Pharaoh to worship a stone image. When would the man under Egypt's double crown realize his gods were nothing? Ipiankhu wondered. Of course, Senwosret could not worship Ipiankhu's god, not being of Ipiankhu's tribe. His tribe . . . Ipiankhu pushed away his thoughts and focused on Pharaoh. "I must pray for the wisdom of the Unknown," he said. "Only by his—"

"Aye, I know," Pharaoh interrupted. "Only he can see and tell you. You are merely a vessel." He sighed. "What a pity your god will not allow you the honor of realizing your gift and accepting it as your own."

"It is not mine," Ipiankhu began their common argument.

Pharaoh waved him away. "I have no heart for your words today. Go, do what you must to interpret. I shall not see your face in court until you know why I have had this dream."

"But the Aztlan envoy, My Majesty—"

"What do you have assistants for? Surely you have trained at least one Egyptian to parry Aztlan's threats and smile through bared teeth?"

Ipiankhu bowed and backed from Pharaoh's sight—there was no need to respond. Once on the other side of the double doors he swore. Responsibility weighed on him; Aztlan was pressing dangerously, and he and Imhotep had to defend Egypt . . . somehow.

Ipiankhu's anger was washed away by something more potent. A call more visceral, more urgent, than desire or marital devotion, daily duties or fleeting power. *Forget not your first love.* The unmistakable whisper filled his head. With quick commands he delegated his day's duties, then Ipiankhu prepared to meet with his Unknown God.

AZTLAN

PHOEBUS FEINTED TO THE RIGHT, catching his opponent in the chest with a prong of his triton. The Mariner fell, and Phoebus pulled back. "That is enough," he said, handing a serf the tall metal staff with its covered tines. "A good match."

"My gratitude, Golden One," the Mariner said, bowing.

Phoebus, Rising Golden Bull of the Aztlan empire, looked up at the balcony, where Niko, his dearest friend, was engrossed in a scroll. Though practice had gone well, and Phoebus was certain to be ready for the ceremony, he was disappointed that Irmentis had not come in. Hadn't she been here, clinging to the shadows, the safety of the torch-lit chamber? He thought he had felt her gaze on him, almost as tangible as a touch.

Pushing his long blond hair away from his face, he accepted a damp linen from a serf and wiped away sweat from the fake battle. The Season of the Snake had been warm this year, a strange omen that no one knew how—or dared—to interpret. Phoebus swallowed hard at the thought of the upcoming rituals. He was nineteen; he had spent his whole life training for this, the *Megaloshana'a,* the Great Year.

"*Pateeras, Pateeras!*"

Phoebus turned when he heard his firstborn's call. "Eumelos!" The boy launched himself into Phoebus' arms, embracing him with the sticky heat of a child. For a few moments the pride Phoebus felt, knowing that this squirming bundle of intelligence and impulsiveness was his, threatened to send him to his knees in gratitude.

Eumelos belonged to Phoebus, the one thing his stepmother,

Ileana, could not claim. He was Phoebus' greatest joy. Though he would not inherit the throne because he was not born of the mother-goddess, he would sit on the Council someday. Smiling through sudden tears, Phoebus looked at his son. His hair was blond, like Phoebus', his eyes the same sky blue. At five summers his face was still gently rounded with childhood, but soon he would boast the sharp lines and prominent nose of his clan. He would be the living image of Phoebus.

Spiralmaster even thought the boy showed oracular potential, a trait gleaned from his aunt Sibylla, Phoebus guessed.

The boy pulled away. "That last move was really surprising, *Pateeras*," he said, imitating Phoebus' feint and slice. "I have watched for moons and I never saw that before! That should really take them." Eumelos danced around, his thin body fluid as he dodged and stabbed invisible opponents. "Are you ready to fight the bull?"

"I *dance* with the Apis bull, Eumelos. Fighting is only man to man."

"I wish I could dance with the bull someday," Eumelos said wistfully.

Phoebus dismissed the serfs with a snap of his fingers. "You are destined for great things. Dancing with the bull . . ." He trailed off. There was nothing he could say; the boy wouldn't rule. There was nothing he could do. Tearing his gaze from Eumelos' questioning blue eyes, Phoebus asked him how he had spent his day.

"Scholomance was boring! I would rather be with you! Learning to fight!"

"An Olimpi clansman must have a mind as sharp and agile as his body," Phoebus said, reciting the words he'd heard so often. "Conflict is rarely profitable. It is better to compromise and profit from tribute."

"Like Caphtor pays tribute?"

"Aye, very like Caphtor."

Together they mounted the sweeping staircase, bowing briefly at the inset altar of horns, honoring Kela. For luck they plucked the two-headed ax out of its resting place and turned it. The double-edged blade represented the two sides of Kela, a giver and taker, for the goddess cut both ways. If your fortune was bad, you turned the ax to improve it. Likewise, if your fortune was good, you turned the ax, surprising bad fortune and thus diminishing it. Better to turn the ax yourself than to have your enemy do it.

Geometric patterns of red, gold, and black crept across the ceiling, floors, and walls. The bright floor tiles were warmed by an enormous fireplace in the center of each room, the expansive roofs supported by red columns that tapered down to the floor. In this room, one of a thousand in the palace of Aztlantu, nobles mingled with commoners, all seeking out their clansmen in these last days before the Season of the Bull, this growing season, and the meeting of the Council.

For just a moment fear rode Phoebus. After that meeting he would dance with the Apis bull. How he acquitted himself there would decide whether he was worthy of entering the Pyramid of Days and undergoing the tests of the Rising Golden. He dismissed the fear as Eumelos' nonstop commentaries continued. "Niko!" Phoebus called.

The violet-eyed man looked up, yanked from his world of words and formulae into the chatter of the palace. Niko blinked twice, his gaze finally focusing on them. Despite his brilliance, he often had trouble remembering the commonplace—food, women, bathing.

"Practice is over already?" his friend asked, running his hand over his tangled, waist-length white blond hair.

"Aye. The sun has moved three times in the sky." Phoebus' voice dropped to a whisper. "Did Irmentis come?" he asked, despising himself for his weakness.

Niko shook his head. "Aye. I spoke to her, as you bade me." He fumbled, gathering his scrolls. "I think she loves you, Phoebus. However, her love is not *eros.*"

Phoebus' cheeks burned that his best friend would know the woman whom Phoebus desired did not want him. Even if her love was *pothos*, if she desired him as an ambition, a goal, an end to accomplish, that would be something. But pure *agape*, only with her heart . . . Phoebus lifted his gaze to his friend's. "Did she say more?"

"Only that she despised Ileana and would not challenge her. She seeks another kind of justice."

"The only justice is for that *skeela* to have a knife through her heart," Phoebus whispered.

"Treason, my friend," Niko said, rising from the wave-backed stone bench. "Irmentis also asked for more of her drink." His voice was tight with disapproval.

Phoebus ignored him. "When I am ki—"

Niko turned to the boy. "So, Eumelos, what wisdom did the Spiralmaster share today?"

"He said we were all silent and blind and wouldn't recognize the hands of the gods if they pinched us on our—"

"*Okh*, really?" Niko said, lifting Eumelos onto his shoulders. "You need to talk to Spiralmaster," Niko said, frowning at Phoebus. "He seems to grow more disrespectful and more erratic by the day."

Phoebus watched as Niko hoisted Eumelos' wiry body high in the air, pretending to fly the length of the decorated room. In every slash of turquoise paint Phoebus saw the feral gaze of his stepmother, Ileana.

How he would love to sink a knife in her belly.

"So have we heard about the sea skirmish's outcome?" Phoebus asked. Niko slid Eumelos off his shoulders, and the boy raced away.

"Everyone is watching from Myknossos," he said.

"What are the odds this time?"

"Aztlan will be victorious, as always."

Phoebus didn't ask how Niko knew. Despite his seeming removal from the commonplace world, Niko knew everything; he was a fountain of information. "I asked about the odds."

"As good as the chances of your becoming *Hreesos*," his friend said with a rare smile.

They walked through the press of people. Women in bright skirts, dark hair curling and kohled eyes flashing, stood in clusters like bunches of flowers. Men in short kilts or long belled skirts mingled with Mariners carrying shields and quivers. *Hreesos'* private guards with their cropped hair guarded the far doorway. A school of scribes sat in one corner. Damp clay plates lay before them, over which their fingers moved rapidly, embossing tiles tied to their fingertips and knuckles, pressing into the clay the language of Aztlan in pictographs of men, shells, weapons, and symbols.

Once outside, Niko looked at him. "Where are we going?"

Phoebus smiled, squinting at the sunlight shining off the Pyramid of Days. "Dion invited us to view his newest experiment."

Niko frowned. "I am supposed to be in the library doing research for Spiralmaster, Phoebus."

"I know, but this will take only an afternoon. You can spend all night in the library if you need." They walked toward the land bridge that attached Aztlan Island to the crescent-shaped Kallistae Island. Mount Apollo rose before them, harsh and forbidding in the winter light, its slopes bare and brown. Two other bridges, designed by the finest *mnasons* in the priesthood, attached Aztlan to the northern and southern tips of the crescent-shaped island of Kallistae.

"What are you researching for Spiralmaster?" Phoebus asked as they walked to the north bridge.

"You remember his elixir?"

"Aye, his eternal project." Phoebus smiled at the Scholomance pun for Spiralmaster's obsession.

"His eternity project," Niko corrected. "Aye, well, he is convinced there is a secret ingredient."

"That he will find in the library? What is it, dust?"

Niko's gaze was solemn. "Nay. Something our forefathers knew and we forgot. I'm looking for it."

"That means you are reading every scroll, every tablet?"

"Aye. Every one."

Phoebus slapped him on the back. "You are too dedicated, my friend." He stopped. The bridge, carefully wrought from woven metal, cording, and enormous *ari-kat* stone pylons, stood before them. Narrowing his eyes, Phoebus turned to the left, the edge of the cliff approximately eight hundred cubits above Theros Sea.

What mischief was Dion up to this time? Then they saw it, a square of white floating in the air between the tip of Kallistae and Aztlan. "By the stones of Apis," Niko breathed. The men ran, joining a few Scholomancers and one of the head instructors, Daedalus.

Suspended between heaven and earth in a cradle amidst wings of flax and bone, Dion floated. Niko and Phoebus watched as gusts of wind coming through the channel carried him higher and higher. "How will he get down?" Niko asked. Pretending not to hear or ignoring him, Daedalus laughed as the inheritor to the Clan of the Vine rose upward in his air sail.

"What do we tell Sibylla if he gets hurt?" Niko whispered.

Phoebus blanched. Though Sibylla was exquisite and blessed by Kela, her temper rivaled that of Ileana. Sibylla had rescued Dion from a cave of wolves, where *Hreesos* had hidden him after Ileana had killed his mother. The two were the same age and almost inseparable, though not linked by *eros*. Sibylla would make them all eat wood if Dion were hurt.

"Pray the winds are gentle," Niko said in response to his own question.

"We checked the omens of the wind priestess," Daedalus said, twisting his Labyrinth key pendant. "She does not fear for him."

Phoebus and Niko exchanged dubious glances.

A bigger group was gathering on the cliff's edge. Word had spread that Dion was in the air, and groups of women from all over the two islands clustered for a chance to see him.

"Phoebus, my master!"

The Rising Golden turned at the cry and saw a palace serf running to him. Panting with exertion, the serf handed Phoebus a tiny roll of paper. Niko met his glance questioningly. "Nestor. He's in Egypt," Phoebus reminded him. Carefully he unrolled the note.

"Egypt barters. We will win. N."

"How goes it?" Niko asked quietly.

"Egypt still seeks to negotiate, but Nestor is certain of victory."

"Is it necessary to rule Egypt, too?" Niko asked. His question was not meant personally or as a challenge, Phoebus knew. Niko was a Scholomancer: he viewed every situation from each known angle, then two more.

"Egypt rules the Nile. They have honored their agreement to stay off the seas, but we need Egyptian grain. The clans cannot continue to support us completely. The soil is losing its strength. We will deplete it if we are not careful."

"Caphtor doesn't provide enough?"

"Not once she's fed her own, nay."

"So how goes the plan?"

Phoebus sighed, squinting up to see Dion's tiny figure, still floating in slow circles. It was rather nauseating to watch. Phoebus was glad *he* wasn't floating up there merely on flax and the word of a priestess. "Nestor has threatened invasion if they don't send a fifty percent tribute on produce, grains, and cattle."

"Is not Egypt suffering a famine?"

Phoebus shrugged. "That is what rumor says, but it is Egypt! They have so much space—"

"Not much water, Phoebus."

"Actually, too much water, from reports I've heard. Anyway, those are Nestor's demands."

"What will he settle for?"

Phoebus looked at his friend. "Bulls."

"Aye, your rituals," Niko said, understanding.

The wind died suddenly and the craft dropped. The crowd gasped in unison, watching as Dion and his contraption fell below the level of the cliff. A moment before he hit the water, a gust of wind buffeted him upward. As the onlookers peeked over the edge of the cliff, Daedalus commanded the Scholomancers to prepare a launch to retrieve Dion should he land in Theros Sea. The wind pulled Dion back up, and Niko spoke as though nothing had happened.

"Have we always gotten the Apis bulls from Egypt?"

"Aye."

They watched in silence as Dion floated level with the edge of the cliff, only ten cubits away. "How is it?" Phoebus shouted. Dion's mouth moved, but his words were torn away by the wind. They were close enough to see each other's face, and Phoebus smiled as Dion shouted mutely, careening suddenly away from the safety of the islands, above the open sea.

"But we have always paid for them before?"

"What?" Phoebus asked. His clan brother's figure was getting smaller and smaller.

"The bulls, we've always paid before?"

"Aye. We've paid well: gold, animals, Coil Dancers, stones. We offer tokens this time." Phoebus ran a shaky hand through his blond hair. "Dion seems to be on an unfriendly wind."

"You don't think the wind priestess would be wrong, do you?" Niko focused in the distance where the speck of white floated above the blue sea. "If Sibylla really does have direct communication to Kela, let us hope she is interceding now." Two water craft, minuscule compared to the expanse of the sea, sailed swiftly after the runaway Dion. "Have you heard rumors of blessed stones?"

Phoebus watched, his forehead damp, wondering how to get Dion back. Niko's tendency to change the topic was sometimes bewildering. "Blessed how?"

"Direct communication with a mighty god."

He turned to his friend. "What?"

Niko shrugged. "I have found oblique references to such stones in some of the older writings."

"Is this the thing you are seeking in the library? What do they do?"

Niko shrugged. "You ask them questions and they speak."

"Speaking stones? Niko, you jest. A child's myth—"

"Nay. These stones let you talk directly to a powerful god. Just think, you could ask anything and learn the truth. You would know when was a safe time to engage battle, or if a storm were brewing, what fields to leave fallow, who is untruthful . . . There would be no more guesswork."

Phoebus frowned. "We would be as children, always asking the permission of a parent."

"Phoebus, Spiralmaster could ask this deity what else belongs in the elixir."

Back to the elixir. Spiralmaster was an old man; perhaps his mind was beginning the final journey without him, Phoebus thought.

"Look!" Niko shouted.

Dion had caught an updraft and soared above the cliff. The crowd scattered and the vessel twisted, as though in a giant grasp. With a ripping noise that echoed over the cliffs, Dion fell to earth, lost in his flax wings.

He landed with a thud, and the waiting dozens ran to him. Scholomancers pulled the cloth away and helped him stand. He listed to one side and was instantly supported by a young woman, her painted breasts heaving with excitement. "It worked!" he shouted, and the Scholomancers cheered.

Phoebus and Niko pushed through the crowd. Dion's face was alive, his dark eyes purged of ennui. "How did you bring it down?" Niko asked, looking at the mangled sail on the ground.

"I used a cord, designed to tear the sail enough that I could control descent." Dion winced as he stepped on his left foot. "Somewhat, anyway." The nymph was running her hands over his body, checking for damage in places that bore no chance of injury. A path cleared for Daedalus, and Dion pushed the nymph away, embracing his partner in design. Niko knelt on the ground, inspecting the understructure, a cleverly woven basket of bird bones, hewn to be lightweight and fixed with wax.

The group began to make its way to the palace, Dion in a riding chair carried by the Scholomancers, Daedalus speaking to a group of students that trailed his saffron-and-blue geometric-patterned robes, clinging to his every word.

Niko and Phoebus walked toward the rear, where the nymphs and young men flirted back and forth. The moment was near perfection, Phoebus thought, a synthesis of all that Aztlan could and should be.

If only Irmentis could be with him. In the sunlight—here—in flesh and spirit. He thought of her, asleep in her dark catacombs. Tonight he would not see her. It was a full moon, and she danced with the women on the hills, and with Dion. He was the only man who dared to learn the women's mysteries.

Phoebus made a mental note to send Irmentis more of the potion he had made her. He'd even given it her sacred throne name. Artemisia. At least the green milky fluid could ease the pains that often gripped her. Insensible, yet suffering, she would stare into the distance, frozen like a doe. Did her spirit journey? He thought not; it seemed more likely that she was trapped in the grips of some violent *skia*.

Phoebus clenched his teeth. If only he could be close to her, really close. She should be his consort, *she* should be the Queen of Heaven. Arousal flowed through his veins; deliberately he focused on something else. Lusting after Irmentis was as much an element of his existence as Eumelos was his son. She alone truly knew him. She saw beyond the "Golden" to the shadows that dwelt with him. She knew his fears for Aztlan, his worry that the empire was outgrowing itself.

She shared his sick sense that the Clan Olimpi had become less than glorious. Only with her could he share the omens he'd seen and heard. She would watch him, with dark, knowing eyes, eyes that made him want to flee into her body and soul, to share that part of herself she kept for the moon alone. He wanted her for his queen. She could easily win against Ileana, why did she not try?

His *eros* love was also *pothos*—Irmentis was for Phoebus the most valuable of prizes. He must win her; he wanted her more than anything, even more than his throne.

Niko wandered off to the library when they returned to the palace. He offered no farewell, and Phoebus knew his mind was already on the dusty leather-and-gold folded tablets, on scrolls. Greeting cousins and citizens on his way to the Scholomance, Phoebus decided to visit the Spiralmaster.

The Scholomance was built at right angles to the palace. The rooms for the six thousand students and instructors were constructed along narrow, dark corridors that ended at staircases that also served as light wells. Huge porticos supported with red columns, the walls painted in the fluid style of Aztlan, bordered every side. The largest covered balcony housed the instructors' suites, each side open to sunlight. The instructors taught from the comfort of their couches or chairs, the students attending them, reciting and repeating the wisdom of Aztlan until it was theirs.

The Scholomance was reserved for Aztlan's brightest clansmen and -women. Intent on exploring every aspect of life in the mind and body, the Scholomance had created the astronomical pavement of the Daedaledion in Knossos and collected an extensive menagerie on Aztlan Island. No clan distinctions existed within the Scholomance; all of its adepts became Clan of the Spiral.

Education, like most things in Aztlan, was a dance. This dance led through the labyrinth of the mind. One set of steps formed by rote and ritual complemented another set composed of imagination and experimentation. The same steps executed from differing angles produced two utterly different dances. Agility, suppleness, strength of body and mind were required with both. This versatility and elegance of thought characterized the mind of a Scholomancer.

Phoebus and Niko had met in the Scholomance when they were five summers old. From the first they had been close. Phoebus, aware of his destiny even then, had been suffering over the loss—the murder—of his mother and the separation from his clan sister, Irmentis. Niko had been painfully shy. His natural curiosity was winning out against the protective shield he'd worn for his earliest years against his instinctive realization that he was not like the other clan children.

The Rising Golden flattened himself against the wall as a group of children raced past, screaming and pushing. The walkways were narrow and open. A fall to the ground would be fatal, yet boys Eumelos' age ran on, oblivious of the danger. Older scholars sat along the wall, drank wine, and argued. A Scholomancer would debate any topic at any time; the purpose was to learn how to turn a problem around and find the solution hidden within.

Phoebus stepped into the darkened room of his mentor. The old man was nowhere about, so Phoebus went to the painting of a door, pressed the hidden catches behind a panel in the correct pattern, and waited as it opened slowly. Spiralmaster was in his lab.

The smells of *al-khem* wafted up the stairs, burning Phoebus' eyes and throat. He walked carefully in the near darkness. The steps were worn smooth and he had fallen before, his leather sandals sliding out from him. Landing in an undignified heap at Imhotep's door had been a humiliating way to start the day. Phoebus held on to the railing.

Unlike the wide, square staircases of the outer rooms, this one coiled around in on itself. True to his title, Spiralmaster was a master of every tool, technique, skill, and discipline ever pursued at the Scholomance. His skills were as intercoiled, complex, and mysterious as the inside of a shell.

Phoebus paused outside the door, straightening his attire. Spiralmaster was also fastidious.

"Enter, Rising One!" Spiralmaster called. "How I loathe when you are indecisive! There is work to do!"

Phoebus pushed open the door, and the Spiralmaster turned to him. Though he labored in the service of *Hreesos* and Aztlan, the Spiralmaster had been born Egyptian. Myth said that his ancestor, the first great Imhotep, had been birthed in a tumultuous time for Aztlan. He'd stolen Aztlan's secrets of *al-khem* and used them to wheedle his way into the court of Pharaoh Khufu.

Forever after, Imhotep I's pyramids were called Egyptian. Imhotep had stayed, reared a family full of more Imhoteps. The generations of magi had alternated between serving the courts of Egypt and the courts of Aztlan. The Spiralmaster stayed here, his oldest son in Egypt, and another in Hattai. Aztlan's Imhotep and his eldest son hated each other.

Spiralmaster was wizened, but still very, very tall. Despite the many years working in this laboratory in the bowels of the Scholomance, his skin was ruddy and dark. His head was shaved, elaborate tattoos carefully drawn on his scalp and down his back. His enormous ear-lobes were weighted with earrings that shot white and blue fire from unknown, unfaceted stones. Lengths of brilliantly patterned cloth wrapped over his narrowed shoulders and around his waist, their fringed edges brushing his sandals.

Recently, Phoebus thought, he looked even thinner.

The seal of the Clan of the Spiral, of which he was chieftain, hung against his wrinkled chest. Other seals, vials, and papyri scrolls dangled from a cord around his scrawny waist.

Phoebus greeted him respectfully. No one knew the age of the Spiralmaster, but the animation in his eyes made him seem the compatriot of every young dreamer who walked through the door. Imhotep lurched as he turned, and Phoebus watched as a vial fell to the ground and shattered. The Spiralmaster ignored it.

Fastidious Spiralmaster leaned against a broad table, his shoulder apparently twisted, his feet surrounded by shards of glass. Phoebus kept his features carefully blank.

"Are you practiced?"

"Aye, master."

"You know that I cannot teach you more. Either it is inherent knowledge at this point or you are truly not fit to rule."

Phoebus' felt his cheeks redden. "I am prepared."

"Do you know the formulas?"

Phoebus gaze dropped. One misstep and he would die. "I am prepared," he repeated.

Spiralmaster peered into Phoebus' eyes. The older man turned away. "Then let us discuss what happens after the ritual."

"Just so," Phoebus said, taking position next to one of the long tables in the room. "Tell me, what does happen?"

Spiralmaster turned away, catching himself abruptly before he fell on the shattered vial. His eyes glittered. "You have plans for a new city?"

It was a leading question, one the Council was certain to ask. Phoebus felt a tingle of anticipation. This city was his best chance to make a mark, a lasting mark, on Aztlan. "Aye. Between Mount Apollo and Echo. It is a perfect natural port. Easier for foreigners to sail there than to enter the lagoon."

Spiralmaster shook his head in agreement.

"Chieftain Atenis is dealing with the decoration of the city," Phoebus continued. "I've spoken to Talos and he assures me that the new metal he is working on will resist corrosion."

Spiralmaster motioned for him to continue.

"Well, other than receiving approval from the Council on moving clan families there, it is done."

Spiralmaster cracked his knuckles, a sure sign of pondering. "My old brain is tired, boy. Tell me again, why do you need this?"

Phoebus hid his smile. Spiralmaster's brain was sharper than any dozen young Scholomancers, but this was an easy way for Phoebus to practice what he was going to say to the Council. "In building Prostatevo, we put the best the empire has to offer in one place. No longer will chieftains have to travel to all ten clans; instead they can trade whatever they need in one centralized location."

Pacing, Phoebus elaborated. "Each section of the city will be dedicated to one clan. Within that section members of that clan will live and work, communicating with the clan's seat in order to arrange shipping routes."

"It is a radical idea. We haven't had people live apart from their whole clan in generations of summers," Spiralmaster said, his delivery obviously mocking Chieftain Nekros.

"Visitors to our empire will see the effectiveness of Aztlantu rule: the uniformly built city, the skill of the artisans and workers, a modern port, and a beautiful temple to Kela. All this will symbolize and epitomize the might of Aztlan."

"What about Apis?"

Phoebus turned. "There is no Nostril of the Bull on which to build. Those who seek to pay homage to Apis can travel easily by boat to the Pyramid of Days on Mount Stronghyle or they can go overland to Mount Apollo."

Spiralmaster sat in silence, and Phoebus waited. "You didn't answer the question about the radical—"

"Aye!" Phoebus sighed deeply. "It is a new reign, Council members. I am *Hreesos*. Prostatevo will bring greater prosperity to our empire. It shall be done."

Spiralmaster chuckled. "Nekros won't like you for that—he's losing a brother after all—but he will respect you."

Phoebus approached the table where Spiralmaster had been working. "What are you doing?"

"It's the elixir."

"Jus—"

"Before you say anything, boy, I want you to know how close we are."

Phoebus looked at the vials and bottles of dried animal and vegetable matter. "It cannot be done," he said.

Spiralmaster growled low in Egyptian and pulled Phoebus behind him. They walked to the darkest corner of the room, and Spiralmaster proudly turned back a curtain.

A pig lay on its side, breathing shallowly. Its eyes were glazed, but it was alive.

Phoebus felt a chill run through him. "You did it?"

"Aye. The broken child's blood beats inside the pig's body."

Sunset before yesterday, a child had fallen from the cliff. His neck had snapped, but a low ledge had prevented his body from being dashed on the rocks. While his blood still flowed, Spiralmaster had attempted to transfer it into the body of a pig. The two essences were the closest, he felt. The elixir would bond them through *al-khem*, a pig with the blood of a human.

It was obscene. It was fascinating.

"Has it moved? Can it?" Phoebus asked.

"Now that we know we can move the blood of a child into a pig, I want to know if the reverse is also true," Spiralmaster said.

"Is the pig going to live, actually be able to eat and rejoin his herd?"

Spiralmaster prodded the pig with a long, trembling finger. The pig grunted but did not move. "If blood can be shared from one creature to another, then life can indefinitely be sustained. Life is in the blood."

"My master," Phoebus said, "are you saying you could share blood from man to man?"

Spiralmaster fixed his dark gaze on Phoebus. "If we can give fresh, live blood to a dying, nay, even a dead creature, then we can revive it."

"You think to revive the dead with living blood?" Spiralmaster ignored him, and Phoebus shuddered, offering a prayer to Kela for protection.

"Spiralmaster! Spiralmaster!" The cry was fear filled and impatient. Phoebus helped the older man into the other room. A scribe, his eyes wide, sweat streaking down his cheeks, quickly greeted them both. "Master, you must come. A great illness has overtaken my bloodfather!"

Laboriously they climbed into traveling chairs; Phoebus dared not leave Spiralmaster's side—at times the mage could barely walk. They were carried through the maze of rooms in the palace, down the hill, and across the bridge into the city of Daphne. The scribe, a budding Scholomancer, was the son of an Aztlantu merchant. The villa was huge, surrounded by a vineyard flowing down the terraced hillside to the sea.

Women clustered around the central fireplace, watching the man lying in richly dyed linens. None of them would step close to the sickbed. "When did this happen?" Spiralmaster asked.

"He has not been himself these past days," said an older woman Phoebus guessed was the merchant's wife. "He's been unable to eat, unable to sleep. He insisted on going to the harbor, and he collapsed on the pier yesterday. He has been like this ever since."

Phoebus knelt, touching the man's forehead. No fever, no sweat. "Any sign of wounds or bites?" Spiralmaster asked.

"Nothing, my master," the woman said. "We have bathed him and oiled him."

They are ready for him to die, Phoebus thought.

The woman continued speaking. "He doesn't speak, just laughs and stares." The patient was motionless, his gaze unfocused as he stared up at the painted ceiling. As they watched, his throat moved convulsively, fighting for air.

"Check his esophagus," Spiralmaster commanded.

Phoebus knelt, and opened the man's mouth, turning his head away at the patient's putrid breath. In a frenzy of motion, the patient shuddered, kicking blindly, pushing Phoebus away and laughing . . . a maniacal, eerie sound. Spiralmaster pulled Phoebus back.

"What did the Kela-Tenata say?" Phoebus asked.

"She gave him an infusion of moonstone and asked us the same questions you ask. My masters, what is wrong?"

"Why isn't she here?" Phoebus asked Spiralmaster in an undertone. This man was obviously dying, he'd had his lustral bath to ensure his entry to the Isles of the Blessed, yet his healer had left before doing everything possible?

"She said there was much illness in the city today. Even while here, three messages came for her," the merchant's wife said.

Phoebus and the Spiralmaster requested privacy. "Have you seen this before, master?" Phoebus said, expecting the answer to be nay.

"Aye."

"What? When?"

Spiralmaster staggered to a carved stone chair, leaning against it as though he couldn't bend properly to sit. "Something is affecting *Hreesos'* cabinet members."

Phoebus' skin prickled.

"They are dying like flowers. One day full of health and drooping the next day. Dead on the third." Spiralmaster gestured to the prone figure. "Most of them succumb like this, drowning in their own lungs, or starving because they cannot swallow."

As if on cue, the man began to choke, his face purpling, his eyes pleading. Before they could call his family or medicate him, he was gone. *"Kalo taxidi,"* Spiralmaster said, closing the man's staring eyes. "Summon his women to prepare the *kollyva.*"

Phoebus, shaken by the suddenness of the man's demise, stepped into the next room. "Your master requires his meal, he has begun his journey," he said carefully.

The women began to cry. For the next nine nights they would prepare his favorite foods, so that as he journeyed through to the next world he would not hunger. It was the final honor his family gave him.

Phoebus turned to the window, the weak sunlight falling on the street outside, two children playing noisily on the ground. The Clan Olimpi had a far different, a far more explicit final honor.

The Rising Golden shuddered.

CHAPTER 4

CAPHTOR

THE MOON WAS WANING, the landscape misted with silver. Firelight flickered over the assembled women and the naked body of the young bride. Painted wedding designs now covered most of her body, transforming her firm young flesh into the mysterious and divine. Mystic symbols of crescents, horns, sacral knots, and birds were woven together with labyrinthine patterns.

Sibylla felt the night air on her bare breasts, her hair against her exposed back. With a prayer to Kela she threw the herbs into the fire, their sweetness and tang carried on sparks into the heavens. Tonight was the night of Kela's blood. The night of purification. Tomorrow was the start of everything new.

For the bride it would be entering into her husband's bed, for others it would be the last week before greeting Kela. The seasons were changing. Already the wind was warmer, the sun shone longer. A new beginning could be seen everywhere in the land.

She felt the fire's warmth on her skin, heating her front, making her back feel colder. Tonight, for some reason, she felt unfamiliar with herself. Her body seemed excruciatingly sensitive—she felt every frail hair on her body, every spot of skin. She burned for something, an indefinable lust. Sibylla rubbed her face. Tonight was about joy and ecstasy, not for thought and reason.

Carefully she chewed a laurel leaf, throwing her head back as she felt the night embrace her. She turned her back to the fire, knowing her body was limned with light. Raising her voice, she began to sing, moving her body slowly, praising Kela's wisdom for forming woman. The steps that had once come thoughtlessly seemed slow and awkward tonight, and her mind felt uneasy within itself. *I'm definitely going to take dance lessons next chance I get,* she heard her mind say.

Others joined in. Naked women: old, young, pregnant, withered. With wine in their veins and joy in their souls they sought a spiritual freedom in dance. More women came from the shadows, more voices joined, each singing her own song, the resulting dissonance a dimension of beauty unquestioned and accepted.

Slowly they moved around the fire, passing the wineskin, reveling in the sensations. The dance grew faster, moving in a tighter circle, their fluid movements becoming one. Sibylla felt an arm around her waist and gripped the shoulders of the woman next to her as they moved in a flurry of sweat and scent, celebrating the mystery of themselves.

Closest to the fire the young bride danced alone, learning her body, teaching herself to recognize the sensuality within her. Her elders watched as she practiced a seduction of her new husband. Amid laughter and suggestive comments, the matrons demonstrated alluring looks and sensuous gestures. Sibylla laughed, thriving on the feeling of community, the sense of belonging. Yet she was confused. She had danced like this almost every moon of her life. Why did it feel so sacred tonight? Why did it seem so rare?

The circle grew slower as the bride's dancing grew more frenzied. As she was approaching completion, her mother and grandmother stepped forward, soothing her, stopping her. Now she would have no fear of marriage, no terror of what the night would bring. Indeed, it would be a feat to keep her from rushing the young groom! She had learned how to conjure passion, a sacred gift.

The hills were darkly gray and the moon small when the group fell asleep on the ground. Sibylla huddled beside the dying fire, staring up at the mass of stars, aching. Something significant and internal was missing. She hugged herself in the night, wondering for what or whom she grieved.

"Mistress?"

An old woman stood above her. Age had not been kind or gracious to her body or face, but her eyes were soft in the predawn darkness. "You are lost," the woman said, awkwardly sitting down beside Sibylla. Her words touched the oracle, and Sibylla began to weep. Old arms wrapped a cloak around her and pulled her close, rocking her gently, speaking nonsensical words of comfort. Sibylla cried all the harder. She hadn't felt the nurturing love of another woman in so long. *It was almost like having Mimi again,* her mind said. Before Sibylla could ask who Mimi was, a flood of sorrow submerged her and she grieved in a grandmother's arms.

AZTLAN

Dion blinked, focusing on the ring of women. It had grown very dark; the sun would soon rise. Still they were dancing and laughing, wine and herbs in their veins. They were his cousins, his sisters, his lovers, the mothers of his children, and the mothers of whom he'd been robbed.

All cavorted naked in the darkness. All save Irmentis, who never removed her tunic, no matter the weather or the dance. Even in the midst of these hundreds of women she was alone. A young nymph had been by her side all night, and Dion had seen them share more than one chaste kiss. He smiled at the thought of telling Ileana her dark daughter enjoyed the lips of women, but he would spare Irmentis Ileana's wrath. Anyone could see her with Phoebus and know she enjoyed men also.

Dion leaned against a tree. The haze of drugs was clearing as the night grew cooler, and Dion knew it was up to him to make them all go home. Somewhere behind him a stick cracked. A subtle sound, a stealthy one.

He saw Irmentis raise her head. Her eyes were dark holes in her pale face, and she turned unerringly toward the sound. Slowly she got to her feet, smoothing the cheek of the nymph and stepping away. She uncorked the vial that hung at her waist, drained it, and tucked it back into the cording.

Dion watched her lean figure step toward the treeline, alone. Setting a trap for the interloper? A few cubits away, a young girl stepped too close to the fire. With a shout Dion raced to her, momentarily forgetting Irmentis as he pulled the intoxicated child to safety. Cradling her against his chest, he looked for Irmentis. She was gone.

He handed the child to a young nymph, who kissed him passionately in gratitude. Extricating himself from her embrace, he walked to where he'd last seen Irmentis. He froze at the sound of hounds baying in the distance. Irmentis' dogs combed these hills and forests. He cocked his head, listening intently.

A shout, a scuffle . . . a horrified shriek.

Dion looked back at the women. A few still clustered before the fire, but most were asleep on a rug of leaves and pine needles. Another shout . . . a man's cry of agony. Dion raced into the clump of trees, his night-adjusted eyes helping him to navigate the uneven terrain, the jumble of fallen branches and large stones.

He smelled blood before he arrived.

In a small copse of trees bodies littered the ground. Irmentis' rangy, long-nosed hounds sniffed at the remains: four deer and one man, his body bleeding black blood into the silver ground. Dion turned, looking for his clan sister. He recoiled when he saw her.

Hunched over a dead deer, her body poised like a feeding lion, Irmentis licked her fingers. They were dark with blood. The rumors were true, then: Irmentis feasted on fresh blood, yet only the man was bleeding.

Kneeling beside him, Dion realized the man had begun his final journey. "What is your name?" he asked. "What clan?"

He was a young man; what was left of his throat bubbled with

blood. "Acteon," the man whispered. "The deer . . . are dying all ov—"
Blood spilled from his lips, and Dion bade him farewell.

Dion approached his clan sister warily. She was more than a
huntress tonight; she was a predator. "What happened here?"

"My hounds smelled the deer, he interfered," she said. It took Dion
a moment to realize she was crying, her tears falling on the head of the
stag she cradled in her lap. "This whole group is dead. Why, Dion?"

He surveyed the four fallen stags. None had wounds that he could
see, and they all lay on their sides, as though they had died in their
sleep. Nor could they have been dead long, for rot hadn't set in.
Something internal had killed them.

"Have you seen this before?" he asked Irmentis, touching the face
of a stag. No marks, nothing.

"Recently. Deer are dying in the dozens. Look at this." Irmentis
walked to the other three, checking the same thing.

Dion saw patches of fur rubbed bare, as though the animal had repeatedly scratched or been scratched. "These aren't fatal," he said.
"Scratching isn't deadly."

"They all have it, the same marks."

"Did the others?" he asked, kneeling beside Acteon. The sky was
growing brighter. "Dawn comes," he said gently.

"I do not know," she said, rising gracefully. He avoided looking at
her bloodstained hands and mouth. "I will check the pelts." They
walked quickly back to the bonfire. Irmentis feared the sun; it burned
her pale skin horribly. Rousing those who would journey across the
water with them, Dion led a dazed, staggering crew toward the beach.
The sun was just peeking over the horizon when a wave of earth
moved beneath their feet.

A heaving, tearing sound filled Dion's ears, drowning out the
screams of the women. He dropped to his knees as the ground quiv-
ered like a terrified animal. Dion whirled, facing the direction of the
Cult of the Bull's Mount Krion. No fire; they were safe.

"The sea!" he shouted to the naked women. They stumbled down
the hillside, the ground still rumbling with aftershocks. The startled
cry of one woman gave way to a loud, dying shriek. Dion drew to a
halt, then ran back to the dark gash in the earth.

The woman was gone.

The crevice ran down to the shoreline. He followed the white figure of Irmentis, herding the dazed women along. He looked toward Kallistae and wondered if they too had felt the earthwaves. The vessel was filled with terrified, shivering women. Irmentis had already curled into herself, covering her body with a densely woven cloak.

After seeing his uncle Nekros suffer, Dion knew that the sun would still manage to burn her, even through the cloth. Casting off into the rough waters, he rowed hard, his body streaked with sweat and dust. The Aztlan pyramid's flat top shone with the rising sun.

His head throbbed as he pulled the boat across the roiling sea, thinking of the night, the deer, dying from scratches. What had precipitated the earthwave? Had Irmentis taken sustenance from the dying man? Finally the boat slid into the tunnel beneath Aztlan Island, beneath the Labyrinth—whose name was never said—which housed the few criminals the clans produced.

The women were taken by the waiting serfs, and Dion rowed to his small cove, tying his boat and climbing the treacherous stairwell to his apartments. Naked and filthy, he was once again grateful for this secret entrance, which allowed him to come and go unobserved. He leaned against the door, exhausted.

The dark-haired nymph who was his dresser, his serf, and privy to most all his secrets met him with outstretched arms. In her he buried his fears and doubts, the lingering sense of loss that permeated his world. He ran his fingers through her curls and slowly turned her around.

In this manner, he could forget.

EGYPT

IMHOTEP WATCHED HIS PATIENT. Fever gripped the man and he tossed and muttered in his sleep. The hemp rope that kept him from harming himself was cutting grooves into his wrists and ankles. Without the restraints, Imhotep feared the patient's thrashing about would loosen the wrappings and he could possibly damage himself more. Imhotep was determined the man would not die.

Imhotep had a wager to win.

The patient cried out incoherently, desperately, then subsided into a fitful rest. At least the coma, the feared sleep of death, had broken. The man was still burning with fever, and despite the patient's improvements, Imhotep felt a growing sense of failure as he watched the increasingly hot body. Only the victim's face, bandaged according to custom, and groin were unmarked.

If he survived, this man would owe Ptah, god of mud and spreader of manure, a huge offering of beer and bread. Manure had cushioned the weight of cattle running across him. Still, three cracked ribs, two broken fingers, a fractured ankle, and internal bleeding were grave injuries.

The man's *ka* caused Imhotep the greatest concern. The mage sensed the man wanted to die: his *ka* was embracing the *ukhedu*. His body had grown hot and still hotter, so hot that Imhotep had shaved him, ridding the nonpriest of his heavy black hair and the matting on his chest and legs. The fever continued to rise.

They had washed his body, flushed him through with emetics; still the fever rose.

Imhotep walked around the room, trying to see through the rising incense. He completely blocked out the priests' droning prayers for healing or death. For reasons he didn't fully understand, Imhotep wanted to know who this man was and how he had reached the bowels of the temple undetected.

He wanted answers. The man must reach consciousness. Imhotep turned to the slaves, priests, and women. "Begone!" They fled his ugly face and rattling teeth.

With deft gestures Imhotep drew out the packet he kept close to his body at all times. One of the mysteries of Aztlan. The power of his forebears. Quickly he scooped up ash from the brazier and spread it on the ground, forming a circle that was as wide as the *w'rer*-priest's couch on which the man lay.

With his index finger Imhotep inscribed the symbols for fire, water, earth, and wind. Then he wrote the figures, the letter numbers that gave Aztlan their power. Using the side of his hand as a straight-edge, he formed the angles, intersecting them as he had been taught to by the Spiralmaster of the Scholomance himself.

Another quick glance over his shoulder and Imhotep brought out his inheritance from his grandfather, also Imhotep. A golden pyramid filled the palm of his hand, topped by a tiny jewel, the Seed of Creation, which refracted the dim light to all corners of the room. Imhotep laid the pyramid onto the ash, its magical dimensions filling the circles, then took out a sliver of mirror.

Within a few moments the penetrating light of the stone was centered between the wounded man's eyes, the invisible third eye of understanding. With infinitesimal movements, Imhotep woke the man's mind. "Why are you here?"

"I am a tool," the unconscious one answered mentally.

"A tool of whom?"

"The highest God."

Imhotep faltered for a moment. "Fight this death around you," he commanded.

"Why?" the man asked.

"What is your greatest wish?" Imhotep asked.

"To love her forever."

"Who?"

No response.

"Who?" But the moment was gone; the purity of emotion and thought had been defiled. At least now he knew what to say, Imhotep thought. Carefully he gathered his tools and scattered the ash. This man would live. It was deceitful, but Imhotep would force him to live.

He put his mouth next to the man's ear. "She is in danger," he said. "Grave danger. I fear it may be too late. She has no one but you. Can you help her?"

Coldly he watched the man press his lips together in grief. The patient was very ill; even manipulation would take a while. Imhotep pulled a stool to the couch's edge. "She is in danger," he repeated. "Grave danger. . . ."

CAPHTOR

SHE WAS IN DANGER OF BREAKING AN ANKLE, Chloe realized. How did these women run on the rough ground around here? Unlike training grounds in her time, this track was just a well-worn goat path, complete with stones and potholes. What I wouldn't give for a pair of Adidas, Chloe thought.

I should be grateful I haven't had a cigarette in over a year, otherwise I wouldn't be running. Period. Though outwardly she was Sibylla—she'd stepped into her skin and zipped it on like Spandex—Chloe knew she was in her own body. Her own lungs, muscles, strengths, and weaknesses had to be harnessed to run this race.

Shielding her eyes with her hand, she watched her teammate round the curve. The young woman, a Shell Seeker, ran hard, arms and legs pumping, breasts bouncing, ribbon-tied braids streaming behind her. I really hate running, Chloe thought.

She tensed her body, her hand outstretched for the woman's palm. The force of the slap made Chloe's wrist ache, then she was off, running barefoot, dividing her energy between holding her bare breasts with one arm and dodging the holes and stones. The faint shouts of encouragement faded away as she turned into a small valley, a stream running beside her. Chloe's breath was loud in her ears and she could feel her lungs starting to burn.

A moment's hesitation, then she was across the stream, cutting through the small copse of trees. . . . *ouch, ouch, pine needles, ouch!* She hopped on one foot, then was back onto the goat path. Sweat was dripping down her back and she could once again see the waiting women. I hate running, Chloe thought, then took off.

She hated running, but she hated losing worse.

Wincing from the stony path, she focused on her waiting teammate, forcing her legs to move faster, struggling for breath. She slapped the girl's hand and jogged off to the side, bent over and breathing hard. Her muscles trembled and she felt dizzy.

"Sibylla, you will never qualify," a well-meaning voice chided. "On all other fronts you are the strongest contender, but if you can't catch Kela-Ileana, it doesn't matter."

Trying to catch her breath, Chloe asked, "Has my time improved?"

"From the last Season of the Bull, aye, it has." The woman chuckled and clicked her tongue. Chloe raised her head and looked at her. Despite her short hair, tunic, and kohl makeup, she was every inch a coach. Visions of field hockey danced in Chloe's head. Apparently Sibylla wasn't a good runner, either.

"What is Kela-Ileana's time?"

"About three times the speed of yours."

Chloe didn't ask how this woman kept track without a stopwatch or even a concept of seconds. Three times faster was unbeatable. So she didn't qualify. Big deal. She was here for disasters, not for track and field.

Right?

In her mind she peeked at Sibylla. The woman refused to believe she was there, as if ignoring Chloe would work. "I must beat Ileana," her host-body wailed. "This is my only chance. If not, we'll all still be ruled by her! Each summer she grows worse, people mean even less to her, she hurts and maims more freely!"

"I thought the Golden ruled," Chloe said.

"Aye. She rules through him, however," Sibylla responded. "Nay! I cannot speak to myself! I am not going mad!"

"'Behind every strong man is a stronger woman'?" Chloe asked.

Sibylla ignored her. "She's moved beyond self-centeredness. She is a killer. We're all in danger."

"What can she really do?" Chloe asked, scoffing.

"She is Kela-Ileana, she can destroy Aztlan if she chooses."

"If those visions don't get you first," Chloe reminded Sibylla.

The coach had walked off, and Chloe saw the other runners leaving in twos and threes. The January wind cut through her light tunic, and she shivered. The feeling of loneliness surrounded her again, and she walked slowly back to the palace complex. If only Cheftu were there.

Well, this race wasn't Chloe's problem. In her mind Sibylla was repeating, "I must win, I must win. We'll all be in danger. I must win.
We're in danger. . . ."

EGYPT

THE WORDS POUNDED THROUGH HIS BRAIN. "She is in danger, she is
in danger, she is in danger sheisindangersheisindanger," running together into a litany of fear that drilled through his aching, weary mind
and poked the place where the real man slept, wrapped in grief and
sorrow, unwilling to awaken. As sharp and deadly delicate as the blade
of a rapier, it pierced—"Sheisindangersheisindangersheisindanger"—
the man within, on the remotest possibility that the "she" was *his* she,
forced his mind forward.

Up through the tunnel of blissful forgetfulness and into the pain
of his body: legs that were swollen, a chest that ached, and breathing
that caught and rasped on each exhalation. "She is in danger She is in
danger . . ." the words became more precise as his mind stepped into
the harness of consciousness. A lightness glowed around him, and he
opened his eyes. His lashes made whispery sounds as he blinked, and
he realized his eyes were bandaged.

A deep breath caught in his chest, and he doubled over, coughing.
Hands quickly removed the linen from his eyes, a voice cried out, and
he blinked, clearing sudden tears. Incense stung his nostrils and
throat. Through the grayish smoke he saw vibrant paintings on the
walls; Osiris and Thoth and Ma'at . . . The door opened and a bald
man rushed into the room.

His clean-shaven pate identified him as a priest. He was of
medium height, his shoulders stooped like a scribe. Gold hung from
his ears and wrapped around his scrawny upper arms. As he stepped
to the couch, the patient flinched and withdrew. "You are stronger
now?" the priest asked.

The man blinked. The language felt . . . awkward. He licked dry lips and nodded. "Aye, my lord." His voice was ragged, as though his vocal cords had rotted from inactivity. The priest clapped, and the young boy who'd unbandaged the man left and returned with a tray. The boy was skeletally thin: the man could count his ribs.

"You are in Noph," the priest said. "Take this and eat. . . ."

"Take and eat, take and eat . . ." Another litany, but one that brought a sense of welcome, salvation, rapture. The man picked up the dish and put the mixture of grain and fish into his mouth. The meat was stringy and dry. Had the man not been starving, he would have thrown away such swill. Did Pharaoh, living forever! know what the priests were eating? Or not eating, the man thought, watching as the young boy's eyes followed his every movement. He set down the dish, searching for a finger bowl. How uncivilized this temple was!

"What is the date, my lord?" the man asked.

The priest looked surprised, then pleased. "The second month of *per-t*, third summer of Many-Teared Inundation."

For some reason, the man felt panicked. "Many-Teared Inundation?"

"Aye, my lord," the priest responded, frowning slightly. "The famine is under control, though, administered by Vizier Ipiankhu himself for Pharaoh, living forever!."

The man felt his heart race. Sweat broke out on his forehead and back. He was suddenly chilled and shaking. The priest stepped closer, tucking a linen sheet tightly around the man's body. Expertly the priest checked his temperature and the swelling. The man relaxed as the pressure around his chest eased.

"You are healing well, my lord, I shall call the *hemu neter*," the priest said, his eyes bloodshot from keeping vigil. "First, may I ask a question, er . . . my lord?"

"Aye?"

"Who are you?"

The man opened his mouth . . . and no answer came.

He saw visions in his head, confused flashes of a life he recognized as his own. Women and men in black wigs and elaborate kilts, wearing collars of exquisite beauty and construction around their necks. He saw multitudes of *rekkit*, commoners, stretched before a parted sea.

The face of a woman, eyes as green as grass, hovered before him. Her lips formed a word, a name, but he couldn't read it. Then he saw her again, bedraggled and weeping. Kneeling, her hand across her breast, the other outstretched. A blinding light obliterated her . . . and the man was lying on the couch again.

"My lord? Who are you?"

The man blinked against gathering tears. *"Je ne sais pas."*

The priest stepped back. "Who, my lord?"

The man realized that he had spoken words he should never say, that he had a great secret he must not share. He licked his lips and forced himself to concentrate, to speak the language the priest spoke.

"Who are you?"

"I know not, my lord."

The priest pursed his lips, then nodded. "Rest, it will come to you."

He left and the man lay back, panting as though he'd run a great distance. A ring was fitted onto the small finger of his right hand. His left being bandaged, he put his finger into his mouth, pulling off the ring and then holding it in his right hand. His stomach clenched as he stared at it.

It was small, made for a graceful finger. Staring at the ring of silver and gold with amber chips, he heard words in a different language from the one he'd just used, spoken in his own voice, rough with tears.

"As unbreakable is this circle, so is my love for you. As pure as the metal, so do I love you. Like the silver and gold, our lives are woven together, forever binding us, even though we now take separate paths." Separate paths . . . He felt such an ache inside, such emptiness. His chest heaved, each breath agony. The priest returned, admonishing him to drink from an alabaster cup and rest again.

Floating in a sea of disconnected memories, the man felt bandages being replaced over his eyes. They prevented his *ka* from fleeing the virulent *ukhedu* that must be in his body. Protect me, he thought as the sleeping draught seduced him into darkness.

STILL CLAMMY FROM HIS BATH, Imhotep was ushered into the darkness of the sleeping chamber. Senwosret lay on the couch, his shaved head covered, his large hands clenched on the linen covers. Ipiankhu, in full court attire, stood by his side, a phalanx of priests to his right.

Imhotep looked at the vizier, and he nodded slightly. Senwosret's condition had not improved. Pharaoh, living forever!, was losing his sight. After the appropriate greetings, Imhotep performed the examination he did each morning.

Each day was dimmer for Pharaoh and grimmer for Egypt.

"Can you count my fingers, My Majesty?" Imhotep held his two fingers above Senwosret's face. The room was silent. "My Majesty?"

"Hold them up and I will count them!"

Imhotep slowly lowered his hand. Pharaoh was blind. Blind Horus. It was not a good omen.

Imhotep turned to Ipiankhu, trying to hide the fear in his expression. The vizier spoke quickly. "Nay, My Majesty, this exam is unnecessary today. Tomorrow we will do it." He gestured uselessly to Imhotep. "*Hemu neter* Imhotep has returned from Avaris. Perhaps he has heard of some medicament with which to return My Majesty's sight?"

It was important that Pharaoh not lose hope. Meanwhile he and Ipiankhu would scour the courts of Egypt and every other land, searching for some, *any*, remedy. Pharaoh must not grow discouraged. If the *rekkit* knew what was happening, there would be mass hysteria in addition to the famine. A hungry people were an intemperate people. Add to that the watchful presence of the Aztlantu envoy and military, and Egypt would know the gods were against them.

"How was your trip to Noph?" Senwosret asked. "Did you find a remedy?"

Imhotep ran his tongue over his teeth, rattling the looser ones. "I have a poultice to try on My Majesty," he said. "To have its greatest effect, though, it must be taken at the full of the moon."

"As you know, the last full moon is just past, My Majesty. You have more than a week before the next," Ipiankhu offered before Pharaoh asked.

"What of the man you brought back?" Senwosret asked.

Ipiankhu looked at Imhotep, curious. "Merely a patient, My Majesty," Imhotep hedged. "He was found trampled in the Apis chambers. I am trying to nurse him to health, though he seems to care not if he lives or dies."

"Who is he?"

"*Aii* . . . I do not know. Due to the nature of his wounds, My Majesty, he awakened only once while my staff attended him. He fell back into an unwakable sleep almost instantly. By Isis, I have the smallest hope for his survival."

"What color are his eyes?"

"His eyes?" Imhotep repeated in surprise, looking to Ipiankhu.

"Pharaoh, living forever! has dreamed a golden-eyed man will restore his sight," the vizier said. "My Majesty knows no person with these strange gold eyes."

"His eyes are bandaged, My Majesty," Imhotep answered.

"His sight is also damaged?"

"Nay, My Majesty, but you well know that one's eyes are the windows to one's *ka*. Consequently, we seek to keep the patient's eyes closed. If he wakes healthy enough to merit their being unbandaged, I will check their color."

Pharaoh beckoned the scribe. "I will offer prayers to Thoth and HatHor for him."

Imhotep paced impatiently. The man was neither dead nor alive. He might not win the wager from that aged physician in Noph! The patient lay like a corpse, and Imhotep still hadn't gotten a glimpse of his eyes to see their color. Would the patient's spirit fly away if Imhotep forced his eyes open? It was forbidden in the House of Life. Even if his eyes were the right color, the man would be dead, useless to Pharaoh, without his *ka*.

A knock heralded the vizier, and Imhotep bowed automatically. "Life, health, and prosperity."

"Aye, may your gods smile on you." The words were hurried, and Imhotep dismissed the slaves. Ipiankhu walked to the side of the couch, looking down on the bandaged man. "How is he?"

"Deaf to our words," Imhotep said. "What did the envoy say?"

Ipiankhu sighed and swallowed his cup of beer in one gulp. He'd forsaken a wig today and instead wore a headcloth. He pinched the bridge of his nose and sighed again. "Envoy Nestor seems sympathetic that we cannot pay the fifty percent tribute. After much haggling, he said that less grain is acceptable, but the Aztlantu want hostages and twice as many Apis bulls."

"Hostages?"

"Aye, though of course they were called 'guests for the goodwill of our empires.'" Ipiankhu quoted bitterly.

"Rekkit?"

The vizier snorted. "Nay. Our finest. Magi and noblemen."

"So how many *kur* of grain is a nobleman worth?"

He smiled, a curious, rare curving of his thick lips. "Seven."

"Seven *kur?*"

"Nay, seven hostages. Three children, preferably."

Imhotep rose and stomped to the balcony, where the huge carcass of the Aztlantu ship floated. "If only we could just destroy the ship and the envoy, then maybe—"

"You know better. They would send a dozen more. Every day Nestor releases birds." Ipiankhu shrugged. "Presumably they report on his day's work."

"Aye." Imhotep sighed. "Aztlantu train birds as couriers. The empire's spies from around the nations keep the clan chieftains aware of events. It is an unbeatable form of communication. They know the spy's thoughts within days of his thinking them."

"It is very nearly magic," Ipiankhu muttered.

"So we give them the bulls, the grain, and the hostages?" Imhotep asked.

"What choice have we?" Ipiankhu asked. "Though the bulls are quite sickly, I fear."

"If the Apis bulls are not on Egypt's shore, we will not be held responsible for their starvation," Imhotep said.

"If they demand twice as many bulls, they will get some that are sick," Ipiankhu said. "Livestock are victims of the famine, just as the *rekkit* are."

"When does the envoy plan on leaving?" Imhotep asked.

"He needs to have the bulls in Aztlan shortly. If he sets sail at week's end, all should be well."

Imhotep sat down. "Who goes as hostages?"

Ipiankhu joined him. "I will ask the Unknown to show me."

Imhotep sighed, weary. "I was born in Aztlan," he mused. "A more beautiful land, a more industrious people, you cannot imagine. Justice, honor, discipline, such were the standards of the day." He shook his head. "*Haii,* apparently no more."

"Will you send greetings to your father?"

Imhotep stiffened. Ipiankhu knew his father was the Grand Spiralmaster of Aztlan, even though Imhotep never mentioned him. Imhotep's gray eyes narrowed. "I have no father. Only sons."

It was dark and late; wine and curiosity were flaying Imhotep. With a decisive motion he ripped the bandage off the victim's eyes. If the man died, it would be his secret. If he lived and his eyes were golden, Imhotep would forever after be known as the *neter* who gave Senwosret his sight. If they were not, then Imhotep would sell the man and make quite a profit.

Either that, or the man could be one of the four adults required by the Aztlantu. Imhotep ran his tongue over his loose teeth, thinking. The man had been bitten, possibly by one of the bulls. It would be Ma'at if one of the Aztlantu hostages sickened and died from blood poisoning, stolen, as they were, from their homeland.

The man inhaled deeply and opened his eyes. Breath caught in

Imhotep's throat. The man's eyes were gold, like a cat's. He blinked, focused, and raised himself up, wincing slightly. "Where am I?"

His Egyptian was perfect, his gaze clear.

"Noph."

The man glanced around, his gaze going from the woven mats on the floor to the low tables and chairs scattered throughout the room. "Egypt, again. *Haii,* what time?"

Imhotep glanced up at the clerestory window. "Nearly dawn."

"Nay . . ." A tone of impatient command crept into his voice. "Who is on the throne?"

"Pharaoh Senwosret, living forever!"

The man blanched, falling back on his elbows. Suddenly his skin was gray and his eyes looked hollow. He muttered the pharaoh's name like an incantation, and Imhotep straightened his amulet against the Evil Eye. "How long have I been ill?"

Watching the man, Imhotep calculated the time. "Slightly less than two weeks." He smiled as he called for a scribe. "Send to Noph, one User-Amun. Tell him the patient lives and he owes me our agreed stakes." The young scribe sleepily marked a piece of *ostraca* and stumbled from the room. Imhotep turned back to the patient. "You were found in the Apis chamber. Do you remember anything?"

The man laughed, a raspy sound tinged with despair and a little madness. He looked at his still bandaged hand and quickly stripped away the linen. Using his teeth to rip off the restraints and splint, he held up his hand, looking at it fearfully, touching the tips of his fingers. They remained immobile and awkward. "My hand," he said softly.

"It still needs a bit more time. It was broken in several places."

"I know, I got caught and the bull drag—" He swallowed and exhaled. "It is not perfect, but I can still use it. Thank you, God," he said in an undertone, and Imhotep wondered which god he was thanking. Apis? Ptah?

"Who are you, my lord?"

"Cheftu *sa'a* Khamese."

Imhotep frowned. "Which Khamese? Where are you from? How did you come to be in the chamber of the Apis bull?"

The man stared at him, silent. Imhotep waited: silence often produced the most truthful of truths. Nervous sweat beaded Cheftu's brow and upper lip and he looked fearful again.

Imhotep turned at a slave's quiet cough. "The vizier awaits you, my lord."

Imhotep hid his surprise. How had Ipiankhu known? He glanced at the nervous Egyptian Cheftu. "Bring the vizier here," he commanded. "Bring us beer and the patient some mashed grain." The servant bowed, and Imhotep turned to Cheftu. "What ailment clouds a man's vision more each day, like a disturbed pond, until finally he is blind?"

The man blinked, his expression blank, and Imhotep almost laughed. Pharaoh's dream! *Haii!* Twice he had foretold accurately, but this time it was nothing more than the wishes of an aging ruler! Imhotep should have wagered on it! He heard Ipiankhu's steps, yet he could not take his eyes off the sweating Egyptian. For once, Ipiankhu was wrong! Imhotep rattled his teeth in joy and began to turn—

"Cataracts, my lord, though I would need to examine the patient," Cheftu said.

Ipiankhu stepped closer and looked intently into the patient's face as Imhotep stared, motionless as a granite *ushebti* funeral statue.

"The only cataracts I know are rough spots in the Nile," Ipiankhu said.

The patient smiled, and suddenly Imhotep sensed in his bones that Ipiankhu and his god had won again. Somehow, birthed by the Apis bull himself, perhaps, this man with the manners of a courtier had been created to heal Pharaoh's eyesight. "A cataract is also the cloud you are describing," he said. "It layers day after day until the patient can see nothing except gray."

Ipiankhu gasped, and Imhotep met his questioning glance. Still, Imhotep wanted to be sure. "Is there any remedy?"

Cheftu chewed on his upper lip with strong teeth that Imhotep instantly envied. "Surgery."

Ipiankhu recoiled. "You would cut Pharaoh, living forever's! eyes?" He looked at Imhotep, the message clear. Not possible!

The patient nodded. "Without cutting there is no way to remove the cataracts."

"Have you done this before?"

He hesitated a moment. "Dozens of times."

"My lord," Ipiankhu said politely. "A moment of your time, please?"

Imhotep bowed slightly to Cheftu and joined Ipiankhu in the adjacent room. "Have you taken leave of your senses?" the vizier hissed.

"Pharaoh's dream said a man with golden eyes! The man has golden eyes!"

"Aye, he does! But does he know what he's doing? To let him cut Senwosret? How can you even consider it?"

Imhotep turned impatiently. "I cannot. But I am curious to hear what he says. You know Pharaoh must be told."

"Aye, his spies have probably already informed him. To dally will be to undermine the trust he has in us. How will you present it?"

"*Me?*"

"You *are* his chief physician and mage."

Imhotep groaned.

Ipiankhu continued. "He will not go against your recommendation. Advise against it; has he refused you before?"

"Nay, never." Imhotep ran a hand over his shaved head and heavy collar. "I will go now. Stay with the man Cheftu and tell me what you learn."

"Senwosret will listen to you. He always does."

Imhotep nodded and left, crossing his chest, muttering the ritual blessing of farewell. Then he clapped for his standard-bearers and litter carriers.

IPIANKHU RETURNED TO THE PATIENT. "Pardon me, my lord?" Cheftu asked. The vizier turned to him. His hazel eyes were unreadable. "I would you answer a question," Cheftu asked, his voice steady.

"If I can, my lord," the vizier said.

"Was anyone, uh, with me?"

"With you?"

"Found with me, where I was."

"This was found," Ipiankhu said, clapping for a servant. They brought in a small package, and Cheftu remembered the last time he'd seen it.

Chloe had been lying next to him when he'd awoken. He'd turned to her, disturbed when she did not awake. He'd run his hands over her body, searching for broken bones. He'd felt the lump and pulled it out—the parcel from the market in Pharaoh Hatshepsut's Egypt, given to her just hours before they'd left that time period. Was that weeks or centuries ago? Cheftu didn't know.

When he got no response from her, he had panicked. Laying his head on her chest, he'd hoped for a slight movement, any indication that she was yet alive. No breath, no movement. Her body was granite cold. Had her spirit never traveled here? Holding his breath, he'd listened for her heart again. There was no sound from her body, but the rumble of approaching bulls had quickly become deafening. He grabbed her hand to pull her out of the way, and her ring, the wedding ring he'd given her, had slipped off her cold fingers. Dragging her corpse, he'd stumbled toward the far wall. The animals had rounded the bend, and Cheftu had looked up into the murderous gaze of the Apis bulls, the white markings on their foreheads almost glowing in the faint light.

Chloe's body had caught on something, and Cheftu had tried to work her free, the bulls pounding toward him. She wouldn't move! At the last moment he'd thrown himself flat against the wall. He'd screamed, felt the hooves on her body as though they were on his. Pressing as flat as possible, he'd heard the bulls run past him. The healthiest were first. Then came those that had been used in temple ritual. They'd hobbled, their forelegs cropped, the calves and cows lowing in the whitewashed cavern.

Cheftu had waited until it sounded clear and then stepped back. He'd turned and seen Chloe. Pulverized. Her beautiful face was a mash of flesh and bone, her body broken and torn. She'd been dead, he knew that, but the destruction of her corpse made him mad for a few moments. He'd kissed her bloodied hands, smoothed away her matted hair, covered her face with cloth as best he could. It was unreal. She had to be alive. Yet she wasn't; even the blood from her body was stagnated and dead.

At some point he'd looked up and seen a lone bull running toward him. Unable to bear the thought of Chloe's body being trampled again, he'd run, inciting the bull to chase. It had cornered him, and though Cheftu had no desire to live, he'd unconsciously turned away and flung himself in piles of manure, protecting his face and groin. The bull had run over him; Cheftu remembered the blinding agony of his hand being crushed, his difficulty breathing.

Then nothing.

No one had been found with him. Chloe had already been dead, he comforted himself. She was gone before the first bull. She had felt no pain, she'd already been with *le bon Dieu.* Why hadn't he been allowed to join them?

"My lord?" The vizier's tone was impatient. Cheftu blinked. He had been ignoring the second most powerful man in Egypt.

"My apologies," he said. "It is just . . . that . . . ," Cheftu inhaled sharply as the reality came crashing in. Chloe was dead! It couldn't be true! It couldn't be! But it was. He'd seen her body. He'd touched her corpse-cold hands. *Mon Dieu!* "What . . . happened to her . . . remains?" Was she . . . ? Had they . . . ? Cheftu couldn't bring himself to ask of her burial.

Ipiankhu looked away. "I know not, but I will ask."

Cheftu looked at the delicate ring on his finger. The memory of her trampled body filled his mind and he doubled over, relieved for the pain of his cracked ribs. It kept him from feeling his broken heart so strongly. "My lord—," Ipiankhu began, then he placed his hand on Cheftu's shoulder. Cheftu froze, fighting the tears inside. Chloe was gone? How could such a life be gone? The first sob caught in his chest as he heard Ipiankhu leave.

"Chloe," he whispered brokenly. "*Mon Dieu,* Chloe!"

CHLOE TURNED IN HER SLEEP, the woolen sheet tangling around her waist, long hair tying around her neck. Long hair? Why long hair? The thought was lost as her dreams swept her away again. . . .

Dreams? Or memories?

The ship moved gently beneath them, and Chloe tossed the throwing sticks and landed in the net, which meant she had to go back at least half the senet board. Cheftu got two more pieces into eternity. His tossing of the sticks had become a sensual act, his long fingers moving over the carved bone pieces with slow grace.

She felt heat in her cheeks and looked away. There were so many things they weren't speaking of, so many painful topics they were avoiding. She looked at him, his amber eyes narrowed against Ra's light. Shadows sculpted his chest and arms, highlighting the sweat-sheened muscle, delineating the cut of ab, delt, and bicep. At least fifty people were easily a glance away. "If you had to lose a physical sense, which would it be?" she asked.

Cheftu tossed the sticks; for once his throw was bad. Chloe kept her gaze focused on the wooden deck, not on his sinful hands.

"A sense?"

"Aye. Sight, sound, smell, touch, taste, hearing."

"Which for you?" he asked.

"Anything but sight. If I couldn't see color, or texture, differentiate between the sky's blue and sea's blue . . ." She trailed off, watching his hands. Such long, beautiful fingers, square nails—masculine hands, but not harsh. "I think I would die if I couldn't see. My world has always been in color, in shape and perspective. To have that taken away would be to kill the core of me." Chloe tossed the sticks. Finally, a decent roll!

"To pick a sense means I would lose one of my ways of loving you," Cheftu said. He stretched out, laying his head on her linen-covered thigh. In the way of dreams, his touch melted away her linen and his bronzed hand lay on her naked, quivering leg.

"I wouldn't be able to hear your cries of pleasure, or I wouldn't be capable of feeling the satin of your skin or I wouldn't recognize the perfume of your arousal . . ."

His hands suddenly caressed her everywhere, stroking, touching, teasing. His voice was in her ear, inciting her.

"Or I couldn't see your hair like a sheet of night, around me, black and shining. Or your eyes, green and full of life. Ma belle," *he murmured. He picked up her hand, still clasping the throwing sticks, and brought it to his mouth. "To forfeit taste would mean the sweetness of your body"—he sucked on one fingertip—"would be lost to me." He sucked on another. "To lose my speech would mean I could only tell you with my body"—he sucked the tip of her ring finger, tightly, almost stinging— "how much I love you and worship you with my soul." He took the length of her index finger into his mouth, and Chloe inhaled sharply as he closed his eyes in pleasure.*

He tossed the sticks and moved his man. "I won."

Then they were rolling on the deck, not only linked by flesh, but linked by soul. She felt her skin melt into his, heard him begging . . . begging . . .

Chloe, don't be dead!

DARKNESS ENGULFED HER. It was pitch, like night. She sat up slowly, her hand to her pounding head, where it felt slightly disconnected. Her sense of direction was shot; she had no clue of where she might be. The silence was consuming as the last images of an ancient temple played back in her mind . . . with the viewing came searing pain. *Haii,* Cheftu! Oh God, Cheftu!

She froze as the ghost of a voice echoed, rich and velvety in the blackness around her.

"Chloe? Chloe, don't be dead!"

Sibylla jerked awake, sweating and shaking. Fear. She was deathly afraid. Something sought to take her over, to subject her! No one has the power, she thought calmly. I am the oracle, I am a priestess, I am in control. Breathing deeply, she steadied herself.

She had looked forward to the solitude of the Daedaledion. Once here, once purged of the shadow-infested cave, she'd thought all would be well. Her mind flashed images of burned fields, the young bride's death. Sibylla flinched. Cigarette, she wanted a cigarette.

What was a cigarette?

Her tormentor had come with her, was living here with her. Recoiling from herself, Sibylla ran to the outside balcony, trailing her linen sheet. Cold rain lashed the sleeping countryside, and she let the steady sound soothe her nerves. It was the not sleeping, she reasoned. Every night threw her into a frenzy of emotion. She felt battered within and without. Sometimes the voices were almost audible, screaming in fury, weeping in agony. Sibylla smoothed her hair over her shoulders. She hated to face the possibility of no longer prophesying. . . .

So she wouldn't consider it. Kela was trying to tell her something; she only needed to be aware, to not fear and to not run. Breathing deeply, she let the cool breeze soothe her. Calm once more, she returned to her bed, lit by the oil lamp. She opened a small leather bag and poured the few stones into her palm. Opal, lapis lazuli, turquoise, red agate, and tiger's eye. She wanted to purge herself of mental conflict, of this oppression, so she slipped the others into the bag and placed the tiger's eye on her right elbow. Still breathing deeply, Sibylla willed herself the calm of the Great Goddess to pour into her veins through the stone. She visualized the words in a dance of pattern, backward and forward, twisting and turning.

Sibylla's eyes closed.

"We need to talk," Chloe addressed the resting mind of her host, Sibylla. "Though it's not possible, both of us are in this body. We need some rules."

"It's *my* body," Sibylla said. "You are only here because you took advantage. My *psyche* had not left, it was merely traveling."

"Your body should be like an American Express card. Don't leave home without it."

Sibylla groaned. "You fill my mind with this meaningless chatter all the time! What are you? Who are you? Why are you here?"

Chloe had an immediate cartoon visual: a miniature of her, with green eyes, and a miniature Sibylla with blue eyes, sitting on the shoulders of the life-size body of Sibylla. The question was, who was the devil and who was the angel? "A disaster is coming. I can help you."

"You are a manifestation of the Great Goddess and can calm the earth and soothe the sea?" The sarcasm was apparent, though thousands of years separated their minds.

"Actually more like a manifestation of the Federal Emergency Management Agency," Chloe snapped. "Look, we have to share this body. Let's do it in peace." She waited in silence. "Or we can continue to battle it out every moment of every day. After all, you do have to sleep sometime."

"My reasoning must be trapped out of my body, along with my memories!" Sibylla snarled. "I am loath to agree to this. These disasters you see are allegories, metaphors. The gods would never destroy their faithful supplicants."

"Then why did you tell that young woman to move to Phaistos?"

"I didn't," Sibylla said archly. "You interfered. The gods can be placated, they always have been, time before mind."

"You can't reason with nature," Chloe said. "I can help these people, your people." She was silent a moment. "I tell you what—you can do all of your priestess activities. I will act as your nonpublic persona."

"How benevolent of you to grant me control of my own body. At least now I won't have to confess that I'm bartering with a *skia*."

Because the communication seemed to be on visual and verbal levels, Chloe knew that a *skia* was a ghost, a fanged shadow, to be exact. The equivalent of an Egyptian *khaibit*. Just once I would like to live in a nonsuperstitious time, Chloe thought. Why can't I, just once, step into the future; into a world of silver-and-glass structures, female urinals, and everyone wearing Saran Wrap? "In return, I get to make the decisions about the disaster, the prophecies."

Sibylla shuddered. "Aye! The visions are horrible. Never before has Kela communicated such terrors to me."

Chloe had serious doubts about Kela communicating anything, but she kept her mouth shut. Metaphorically speaking. This wouldn't last more than a year, right? She'd been in Egypt for only a year. What was one more year?

"In payment you will have to run the race," Sibylla said.

"The race?"

"Aye. Contending for the position of Queen of Heaven."

"I hate running."

"I hate to share my body," Sibylla said tersely. Both women were silent for a moment. "May I sleep in comfort now?" she asked with knife-edged courtesy.

"I'd say it's a free country, but it's not," Chloe said.

Sibylla's spirit quieted, and Chloe looked around at *the body*, quickly checking for the identifying marks that made it hers. Scar from the dog bite on her palm, slash across her knee from Camille's motorcycle accident. Her body was shaved smooth, in the same fashion as the Egyptians. It seemed familiar, though: long, lean, muscled. Her hands looked the same. But she had this *hair!* Long hair! Black and curly! She finally had the hair she'd always dreamed of.

Immediately Chloe decided she liked this body.

Touching her face, she felt the bridge of her nose, the tiny cleft in her chin. She ran her tongue over her teeth. All present, though she would kill for a toothbrush. Still no movement from Sibylla. Mentally Chloe slipped into the caverns of the woman's knowledge.

It was sneaky, it was guerrilla warfare, but Chloe had to learn more about this woman and the world she inhabited. She was going to have to use every skill and bit of wisdom to prevent these disasters from wiping these people off the planet. If need be, she would have to invade Sibylla's mind, take over completely. She had to save these people. Otherwise, what was she here for? What could be vital enough to separate her from Cheftu?

CHAPTER 5

AZTLAN

THEY PULLED AWAY FROM EACH OTHER, sticky with sweat. Ileana was shaking; she'd never given or taken like this before. Priamos was a tidal wave of passion, and she'd been swept along, unwilling to seek help. She rolled over, looking at the young man whose gaze was focused on the ceiling. He seemed completely awake and *henti* away.

"I must leave," he said.

Ileana struggled to focus her thoughts. "Why?"

"I do not want to," he said, ignoring her question. "But I fear to stay."

"I find it hard to imagine you fear anyone or anything," she said, smiling.

Priamos rolled on top of her in one quick, fierce motion. "I fear I will kill Zelos when I think of him in your bed."

She stared into his eyes: they burned with anger and hate. "You dislike Zelos so?"

"He has you. I do not."

"You just had me, Priamos," she said with a coquettish smile. "You forget too quickly."

"I want you for always, Ileana. You are my sun, my moon, my stars at night."

How stunningly trite, Ileana thought. She pushed him away, covering her shoulders. "I must leave for the temple," she said.

"Phoebus despises you, Ileana." He caressed her nape, ignoring her stiffening. "He would rather kill you than fulfill his duty toward you. I would adore you, live to serve you." He kissed her neck as a petition. A peacock screamed outside her door.

What a nuisance, Ileana thought. She didn't want to offend the handsome boy, she might need him later, but this affection was time-consuming, time she didn't have. She'd picked him because he seemed self-contained, too proud to fall in love. She didn't want emotions. "Priamos, love"—she grimaced inwardly—"I must go to the temple. You need to leave so I can send for my serfs."

"I will be your serf, Ileana. Let me dress you, wash you—"

She stood up. "Now, Priamos."

He blushed prettily and dressed, his back to her. *Please, Kela, tell me I haven't wounded his fragile ego.* The set of his shoulders was tense, and she turned him around, kissing him with all her technique. He was a glorious lover, he just needed to learn when to leave. "Come to me tonight," she whispered in his ear, then swatted his firm buttocks in farewell. The peacock screamed again.

"Until my eyes hold you again," he began.

"Aye. Until then."

She closed the double doors behind him, letting in her pet, and snapped for her serf. Had Priamos' seed taken root inside her? Was she even now fertile ground? With a modicum of her usual toilette, Ileana was hustled into a covered traveling chair and was carried down the flagged stones to the Kela-Ata high priestess.

Signs of spring, the Season of the Bull, were everywhere. The hint of green on the hills, the budding flowers. Oh, let Priamos' seed make me like the spring, she thought. Let me be full of fruit and fertility! Once inside the sprawling red-columned temple complex, Ileana alighted, drawing a finely woven scarf over her hair and face. She would be as nameless as the hundreds of women who sought Kela daily.

She stood in line with the others, watching the women, young and old, disperse. Those who sought medical care through the hands of the Kela-Tenata were dispatched to examination rooms and apothecaries in the farthest third of the temple. Those who needed to be reminded of their sexuality, or craved a release their spouse or lover didn't provide, were sent to the small, plain chambers where the Coil Dancers administered their skills. Shell Seekers ran back and forth through the temple, carrying their catch, the stench of fish heads and salt water following them. It was hard to believe that pampered, perfumed Vena once was brown and hardy like these girls.

Ileana deliberately relaxed her jaw so as not to grind her teeth at the thought of Vena. The woman was a strong contender for Ileana's role. Was she training for the race?

Ileana was next in line.

"My mistress, how may Kela minister to you?"

In response, Ileana parted her scarf, showing the girl the golden seal of the Clan Olimpi. The young woman swallowed, uncertain whether to bow or salute, and settled for a hesitant smile. "She awaits you," she said. Ileana heard her questioning the next supplicant as she walked into the narrow hallway that branched between two sections of the temple.

The Kela-Ata was hers. The woman owed her position to Ileana, and the Queen of Heaven never let her forget it. When Ileana had been the mother-goddess for only two summers, the then reigning Kela-Ata had confronted her. She'd had a vision: she knew Ileana had killed Rhea.

Thinking quickly, Ileana had confessed and played the part of a penitent. After swearing on the Triton and Shell, she had poured them both wine. She'd poisoned one rhyton and watched the Kela-Ata switch rhytons when Ileana's back was turned. So the wily *skeela* had been expecting it! What she didn't know was that Ileana had anticipated the high priestess's suspicions and had served herself the poisoned wine.

A Shell Seeker had entered the room moments later. With a knife at her throat, Ileana had offered her the position. In exchange for silence and duplicity forever, Ileana would make her the Kela-Ata. She would never want for anything again. Though the Council had been divided, the succession had been approved. That was many summers ago, yet the relationship had not changed.

"I may be with child," Ileana announced.

Embla, the Kela-Ata, turned slowly. She was so grossly obese, her every movement was labored. Ileana controlled her through food; Kela-Ata was eating herself to death. Ileana wondered briefly if she had made Kela-Ata hate herself, if bending this woman had unleashed some specter within her. However, this slow suicide was useful.

"Seduced Phoebus early, did you?" the high priestess asked.

"You fool. You know he hates me." Ileana sat down. "Give me an elixir, a potion. Help me fertilize my lover's seed!"

"You have had two children, Ileana. You know that you cannot be certain if you are with child for moons yet!"

"My youngest daughter is seventeen summers, Embla."

"Aye, but since her birth we have used herbs to prevent conception."

"What if they have made seed reluctant to settle in me? What if Phoebus uses herbs and withholds himself? This is the *Megaloshana'a*. I must be big with child by harvest! My . . ." Ileana bit her lip and sat back. "Do something."

Embla lumbered to her feet. "You just left the couch of your lover?"

Ileana refrained from reminding her that she never shared lover's couches, they came to her.

"The seed needs to stay in you. Turn around."

"Around?"

"Aye. Your head to the ground, your feet in the air."

Ileana hesitated, and Embla shrugged. "*Eee*, you must not be as anxious as you said."

Fuming quietly, Ileana turned on the stone bench, resting her head against the floor, raising her legs high. Blood rushed to her brain, and she hoped the sacrifice of dignity was worth it. *Please, Kela. Let me be pregnant.* "How soon can you tell?"

Embla nibbled a shrimp. "Nothing is certain until your next season of menses."

"So I sit upside-down until then?" Ileana asked, outraged.

"I will give you mandrake root to drink. Eat an egg with every meal. Those will increase your lover's fertility."

"Embla," Ileana said, her voice strained, "are you aware of how many young women will challenge me this summer? You should know, because I am the only one who still believes you are an adequate Kela-Ata. If I am cast out, so are you."

"So, we eliminate your contenders."

Ileana sat up. "I cannot murder every qualifying cousin." She rubbed her neck. "I may be the Queen of Heaven, but I am not above the Council. Not in this."

The Kela-Ata smiled. "Not murder. Elimination need not be so extreme."

Ileana's gaze narrowed. "It's a race, first."

"Whom do you fear most, my mistress?"

"Vena. Sibylla. Selena."

Embla's jaw tightened, a ripple running through her multiple chins. "Selena is the inheritor for Kela-Ata. She is very qualified."

"There are others, but those three are my strongest competition."

"They are all powerful with the spirit of Kela, my mistress."

"Surely not more powerful than you?"

"Nay, nay," Embla said, a little too quickly, Ileana thought. "I will consult my tablets, see what can be done."

"Do this first. Prevent all other women from competing. These three I will race at the midsummer fest. Just assure me that there will be no surprises."

Embla smiled. "Chieftain Sibylla runs in a festival next week. Shall her competition lose?"

"Aye, my Kela-Ata. Give her a sense of speed and agility that is faulty. Build her up, so I can enjoy breaking her down."

"Would a broken ankle be too much?"

Ileana picked up one of Embla's shrimp. "I think it would be perfect."

PHOEBUS RAN, DUCKING THE SWINGING BAR, feinting to the left of the knee-length blade, and vaulting tightly over the shoulder-height spikes. He rolled and turned.

"Too late," said Garu, his trainer.

Phoebus turned. "Why!"

"He gored your abdomen while you were turning."

Grudgingly Phoebus shook his head in agreement. The twelve-year-old boy smiled. "It is easy for you," Phoebus said. "You barely reach my chest. I have a lot more length to protect."

"Truth, my master. However, you need do this only once." The boy looked away, instructing the attendants to move the obstacles into new positions. Aye, Phoebus thought. I do this once, you do this until you die. Bull dancing had been so much easier as a child—jumping, dodging, riding.

Phoebus stood and walked back to his mark. It was mere moons before Becoming Golden. In this, as in each aspect of his life, he must prove himself superior to every other man in Aztlan. Sound of body, agile of mind and limb. His birthright demanded that he be as limber as a twelve-year-old with the mind of a Scholomancer. Every facet of his personality would be tested. Then self-control: a year-long test.

He grimaced and knelt.

"Now!"

Phoebus jumped over the bar leveled at his knees, then rolled under the one swinging at his shoulders. Spikes came from both left and right, and he froze as they passed within a finger's width of him. Alerted by a roar, he propelled himself forward, curling tightly between the fake bulls' horns. He was thrown and rolled. Phoebus knew he was dead.

Garu called a halt and knelt beside him. The Rising Golden was breathing hard, sweat gluing his hair to his back.

"You have one main flaw," his trainer offered. "You do not tumble quickly enough."

"Aye. But how can I improve?"

"Think of your limbs as liquid, each muscle moving into the other with no stress, no strain. Your movements must flow like a wave. As the bull approaches, throw your bulk forward, and pull the rest of your liquid body in a curving arc. Think of this as you practice, my master." Garu faced him, his somber expression disconcerting in his boyish face. "You have neglected this practicing. If you do not improve, you will be buried and mourned the day you should be crowned."

Phoebus didn't need to hear that his name would also be reviled as the first Olimpi who had failed. How had the weeks and moons passed so quickly? "When may I meet the Apis?"

"They are due from Egypt, my master. You will know of their arrival before I do." The trainer rose to his feet. "Practice, Golden One. There is no other way to avoid death, save practice." Gesturing to the rest of the serfs, he left Phoebus standing alone.

Garu had not answered his question.

Scowling, Phoebus approached the hanging rings. He pulled himself up, then brought his knees to his chin. A wave, he was a wave. He turned in a ball, then straightened. Too slow.

He straightened, pulled tight, and turned again. In his mind he saw the sea churn into curving shapes, then flatten out again. Phoebus straightened, then pulled tight and turned. *A wave.* And again. *The sea.* By the stones of Apis, he had done this perfectly before and would do so again! He pulled his legs up and turned.

Straight. Turn. Straight. Turn. *Waves coiling and flattening on the shore.*

Sweat ran down his arms, slick on the soft leather handles. Straight, turn, straight, turn . . . He felt his movements begin to slide into each other. With each try, the motions became smoother, one flowing into another. *I will become the Golden One.* He refused to think of missing Zelos, of the dark mystery of the day. He would rule. He would Become *Hreesos.*

It was his destiny, just as certain as the tides.

THE SPIRALMASTER OPENED THE INSCRIBED RECORD. The language written on these leather pages was in his native tongue, Egyptian. His grandfather had translated the contents of this tablet from an earlier account written by the hand and in the language of the founders of Aztlan.

The Clan Olimpi had stepped into power only a hundred summers ago, but the founders of these islands had lived here time before mind. When the earth had been one sea, a man and his wife had come to this land. The man's grandfather, Noach, had walked with a sole god, who had given him some mystical stones. Noach passed these stones to Iapheth, and Iapheth passed them to his son Iavan, who set-tled on these isles.

These stones had offered direct communication with their one god. In his protection, the people thrived: the god showed them where the springs were, taught them about the plants, the sea, and the stones. Spiralmaster's trembling hand followed the text roughly.

"In justice and mercy the One God spoke. Light illuminated our way, and we were guided by the clicking of the stones."

The stones. All the references he'd found claimed they were con-nected to this one god. Spasms racked Spiralmaster's body, and he dropped the tablet. The leather fell to the ground, and Spiralmaster cursed; how was he supposed to get it? He could barely walk, and bending was impossible!

Narrowing his gaze, he studied the fallen tablet. Each missive was made of inscribed leather, two pieces fitted together and sewn, then attached to the next section in reversing folds. Something was hidden between the two sections.

Adrenaline raced through his old body, and he fumbled for a stick, clumsily dragging the leather folder closer. Two specters appeared be-fore him. *Skia.* Both were tall, to appearances male. One appeared limned in light, radiating warmth and compassion. The other seemed dark, forbidding and solemn. Words whispered through his mind, a language he didn't know but intonation he recognized. Then they were gone, and the tablet was in his hands.

Though his movements were awkward, Spiralmaster managed to extract the narrow piece of papyrus from between the leaves of leather. Egyptian hieroglyphs, mixed with the strange scratchings of Aztlan's first language, crossed the page, right to left. He read quickly, his lips pressed together tightly lest he accidentally whisper some word and give it life. Like Egyptian spells, the articulation was left out of the original language—a protection against anyone save the initiated speaking this magic.

The fold of papyrus fluttered to his feet as pain beat against his skull. Iavan's stone-borne warning was explicit: "Three times will Aztlan be raised up. She will wound herself, then maim herself, then destroy herself." Was this the first time? or the third? Spiralmaster wondered through his agony. He called for help, his vision clouding as an adept carried him to his couch. I cannot die, he thought fiercely. There is much to be done. Oh gods, help me.

EGYPT

THE MAGE WALKED SLOWLY, easing his weight onto a cane. His light eyes reflected more than they revealed. His body, though scarred from his recent encounter with the Apis bull, showed no telltale signs of famine: loose teeth, hair loss, flaccidity, dull skin. He looked as though he'd stepped into court from the Egypt of three Inundations ago. Deadly Inundations, Ipiankhu thought. The mage moved stiffly, regally, his jaw set.

Imhotep said he'd virtually refused to speak, to explain anything, which made both Ipiankhu and Imhotep nervous. Cheftu was deeply angry, grieving. Telling him about the body of the woman had unleashed a monster who had destroyed a room and sent slaves cower-ing. To let such a man close to Pharaoh was grossly irresponsible, yet even they could not disobey a direct command. Who could have guessed that Pharaoh would demand this surgery? Senwosret's advisers' pleas had gone unheard. Ipiankhu sighed heavily.

Pharaoh was immobile, his open eyes unseeing. Ipiankhu held his breath along with the rest of the court. Had the dream been right? Was this golden-eyed man the cat Pharaoh had seen heal him?

"It is as I feared," the mage said slowly. "The scales are in his eyes."

Imhotep's glance touched Ipiankhu before moving to the mage. "Can you heal him?"

Incredibly, the man shrugged. "I can try. Only God heals."

Ipiankhu felt a touch of fire trace through his body. "God," spoken in the singular. Did this man refer to Amun-Ra? Yet his tone . . . Ipiankhu swallowed and stepped closer.

"Do it now!" Senwosret commanded. Ipiankhu watched emotions cross the mage's face, then he inclined his head and turned to Imhotep, whispering and gesturing. Tools, implements, Ipiankhu guessed, were presented to the mage. Slaves passed among the company, offering wine and beer, honey cakes and sickly fruit. The crowd pressed closer until the mage turned and glared at them.

"This is not a wrestling match. I need complete silence in order to perform this procedure. You would serve Pharaoh, living forever! and Egypt best by leaving." Ipiankhu motioned to a guard, who ushered out the protesting courtiers and ladies. The mage picked up a bronze blade. Ipiankhu flinched and wondered again if this were the only, the best, alternative. With his hand bandaged could the man even manage surgery?

CHEFTU PERUSED THE TRAY. Lancet, ties, honey, fat, and three more blades, should they prove necessary. One to use on himself, he thought wryly. If this operation were less than successful, he was a dead man. Maybe that would be for the best? He looked up, gauging the best light, then asked for Pharaoh to be moved.

Senwosret, he thought. The pharaoh in the last dynasty before the Hyksos, known in French as Sesostris. How would this man, whose careworn face testified to his worry over Egypt, feel to know that centuries of subjugation would be his people's lot, until Hatshepsut's grandfather Ahmose conquered the invaders and ascended the throne? Would he consider the hardships of the past Inundations a worthy price? Or would he retreat into his own palace, gleaning from the masses' fields and ignoring their problems? God knew, pharaohs had done that before. Nay, Egypt was protected by a father in Senwosret, even if Pharaoh could glimpse the red and black lands' future.

Cheftu leaned over the man, forcing himself to regard Pharaoh as merely another patient. He stood to the side, allowing the sun to light the area, seeking his best angle. At Cheftu's request, the patient had consumed copious amounts of beer with poppy juice; he was conscious but numb. Cheftu motioned for the priests to tie the patient's hands to the armrests and hold his head steady on the headrest.

Cheftu wouldn't actually remove the cataract. He would simply break it into tiny, unobtrusive pieces and scatter them in the eye, so vision would once more be complete. Cheftu reached for the delicate knife with his right hand and sent a quick prayer to *le bon Dieu* for dexterity and nerve. He'd been trained in the House of Life to use both hands with equal skill, but he preferred his left hand. Though the splint had been removed, his fingers still wouldn't bend fully.

He closed his eyes, focused all his strength and energy onto the patient, then carefully inserted the lancet into the milky white between the corner of the man's eye and his iris. Cheftu blocked out all other sound, listening for the slight crack and watching for the tears that would indicate he had the cataract. With quick, precise movements, he sliced the covering into pieces. Finally he laid a linen soaked in honey and fat on the eye and turned his attention to the other.

IPIANKHU WATCHED THE MAGE'S HAND as he moved over the still face of Pharaoh. Except for the unconscious gestures of his left hand, the mage's movements were artistry. Where did this skill come from? How did he know what to do? Egypt had the world's finest physicians; the man *was* Egyptian, yet some unnamable flavor of foreignness hung about him. It was as though he were playing a role. This Ipiankhu understood, having played many roles in his own life. He had yet to figure out the motive behind Cheftu's careful behavior. A patch was put on Senwosret's other eye, and the mage looked up.

"It will be several days before we are certain, but I feel, gods willing, that the surgery has gone well." The cumulative exhalation of those watching brought a faint smile to his lips. Ipiankhu stepped forward; Cheftu would be his guest until Pharaoh was healed. With the appropriate bows and phrases, they left the palace and headed into the city of Avaris. Though Ipiankhu's house could be reached by a private thoroughfare from the palace, he enjoyed milling with the *rekkit*. If the mage was surprised, he hid it well.

Mud-brick houses, slanting toward each other and whitewashed time and again, formed archways, pockets of shade for children to play in during the summer and old men to rest in during the winter. The streets, stone paved in the more affluent parts of town, were still muddy here. Scrawny fowl pecked at the muck at their feet. Tired housewives ground meal into powder. Children, their eyes black with flies, romped in the courtyards to the music of slowly dripping water.

Ipiankhu ground his teeth, recalling a verdant, fertile Egypt. It would be so again, this he knew; he just wondered how many would die while waiting. They walked through the marketplace. Jewelry was cheap, bread expensive. He watched two *rekkit* boys attempt to steal from a fishmonger. They were quick and sly, but the man was angry, and his wrath made him fierce. As the fishmonger brandished his knife at the skinny, filthy children, Ipiankhu moved instantly to intervene. The vizier of all Egypt was once again a child, wondering if he would be killed or sold into slavery. At the cost of a month's wages to satisfy the fishmonger, Ipiankhu bought the children's lives. He pressed his lips together tightly. Once again, the Unknown took what was meant for evil and redirected it for good.

CHEFTU WATCHED AS THE TWO BEDRAGGLED BOYS followed the vizier. He didn't understand him. Until Ipiankhu's last action, Cheftu hadn't even tried. At least the mysterious Ipiankhu provided some distraction from the ache with which Cheftu had awoken, the ache that lasted through every day and into his dreams. Chloe, Chloe—so vibrantly alive—it was not possible that such a life was gone. He could not think of it, the pain was too exquisite. Even her body hadn't been saved, no way to build her a tomb and spend the remainder of his days waiting to join her.

Why had he gone *back* in time? If he were whisked from Thut's hands, shouldn't he have arrived in the future, in his real body? With his real name?

Cheftu was baffled. Not that it mattered, any of it. He was in the wrong time. Wrong place. The Egypt that had been the mistress of his heart was centuries away. The nobles, houses, and nomes he'd known did not exist. Pharaoh ruled and the priesthood prayed and each family sought to scratch a living from the sickly soil. In Hatshepsut's time Pharaoh owned most of the arable land; in this time even Pharaoh was poor. Cheftu didn't even *know* Egypt anymore.

Why the stampede had not killed him, he couldn't imagine. What had he sacrificed for this shadowy world? The stench of the dying marketplace brought him out of his reverie, and he surveyed the broken stalls and refuse standing in the open, gathering flies. Senwosret's Egypt with its disease and filth bore a resemblance to the Egypt of Cheftu's modern time instead of the glorious Egypt of Hatshepsut, with its sewage systems, temple distribution centers, and education.

He stepped over an indistinguishable rotting carcass and averted his eyes from the thin women nursing from sagging breasts.

Ipiankhu changed direction, and the whitewash grew whiter, the streets wider, and the people healthier. The air cleared, and Cheftu saw sandbags protecting the larger estates. Three Inundations of over-flooding had brought the famine, he'd learned. Egypt had been pre-pared, however, stockpiling seeds, grains, and dried produce from Inundations before. Cheftu shrugged. The events sounded familiar, but he didn't care enough to pursue it.

After entering a low doorway, Cheftu followed Ipiankhu into a court-yard. He knew that once it had been beautiful. Now mud bricks shored up the house against stagnant green water. A dying tree stood in a mos-quito-covered pool, and the stink of rotting vegetation hung thickly over the estate. Servants moved slowly before the oven, its gray smoke fading beneath the blue sky. Fowl was roasting; Cheftu's stomach rumbled, and Ipiankhu turned. "My servants will show you to your quarters," he said. "Bid them anything, anything you desire, and it is yours."

"Save my freedom?" Although he knew the answer, Cheftu per-versely wanted confirmation.

Ipiankhu smiled, a politician's smile that stretched his lips and nar-rowed his eyes. "I would wish for this famine to end at dawn, yet my wish is also impossible."

Cheftu nodded and followed a wraith of a slave through the sun-lit chambers of banquet hall and baths, up several flights of narrow steps to a doorway. She opened it, and Cheftu stepped into the Egypt he'd once known.

Walls painted with flowering vines and multitudes of birds pro-vided a brilliant backdrop to a footed couch and trunk. Cheftu pushed aside a curtain and found the bathing alcove. No plumbing, he noted. He stepped to the balcony door, halting when he saw the guard. The man saluted politely enough, yet his gaze never moved from Cheftu.

Weary and head aching, Cheftu sank onto the couch. The woven mattress creaked beneath his weight. Three days to wait. Would Pharaoh see? Would Cheftu live?

Did he care?

Three days.

CAPHTOR

"IN THREE HOURS, THE MOON WILL BE IN POSITION," observed the Daedaledai, a student of the Daedaledion. Chloe looked up at the sky. The ancients were obsessed with astronomy and astrology. Chloe had occasionally checked her horoscope in *TV Guide* or read her "animal" off the Zodiac in a Chinese restaurant, but these people ordered their lives around the stars.

What did they do on a cloudy day?

"I wish you luck," said the scrawny, cloaked boy. With a gentle push Chloe found herself standing inside an alcove. "Sibylla," she called inside, "is this ritual?"

"Aye," Sibylla answered tersely. "It is, but I am too tired to do it." Hanging a mental "Do Not Disturb" sign, Sibylla left Chloe alone.

Alone had grown to have many meanings for Chloe. But this "alone," away from Sibylla's controlling consciousness, was really eerie. Where was she? What was she supposed to do? Sibylla's door cracked open. "It's the Daedaledion Pavement. It's a training ground for your race with Ileana." She shut the door firmly, and Chloe was certain that if mental door chains existed, Sibylla had used one.

Chloe stepped farther into the darkness. Three hours until the moon was in position. Just so. Position for what, she had no idea, but obviously getting to the other side was the point. Walls ran on both sides, and she followed them, walking determinedly until she walked into a dead end.

Cursing, Chloe turned around. Where had she missed a turn? Retracing her steps, she discovered she was farther than she thought. She ran into another dead end.

Clenching her fists against unreasonable, growing panic, Chloe fought not to scream. She was in a maze of some kind. She'd been to

Kew Gardens, those playful twists of yew; it couldn't be more complex than that. Where's the cheese? she wondered.

Okay. Mazes are often motifs. Patterns employed by the Aztlantu flickered through her mind. Spirals, Greek keys, stars . . . a dozen others that didn't have easy names. She turned around, looking at the walls. Long, straight, built at angles. Chloe narrowed her eyes, intent on the opposite wall. She crossed to it, running her hands over it carefully.

A passageway. Narrow, but deliberate. Was this a pattern within a pattern? How could she find her way out? "Where is a skein of yarn when you need one?" she murmured. With a last backward glance, she stepped into the adjoining pathway. She walked straight, crossing two intersections that ran at near right angles. The path turned sharply left, and she walked straight for what seemed like an even longer time.

Moonlight painted the maze with shadow and silver. It was a waning moon, the goddess was in her blood, her phase as midwife, before she died as hag. Another sharp turn, also left. Chloe raced down the straight passage, turning sharply left again. She was trapped in the same pattern.

Somewhere, in one of these lengths, there must be a doorway to the other path. Looking left, then right—there was no discernible difference, so she opted for the right. I've been going left all night, she thought. Her breath was loud as she ran her hands over the wall. There!

Chloe stepped back into the other section of the maze. Had she been here before? I'm going to carry chalk from now on, Chloe announced in her mind. Sibylla was silent.

The paths were longer, the turns not so extreme. Chloe kept turning left, the distances growing shorter and shorter. It's a Greek key, she thought with relief. Running the last few passages, pushing herself off the walls into the next turn, she arrived at the center just as the small clearing was flooded in moonlight.

Sweat clung to her, more from fear and nerves than exertion. She looked over her shoulders. She was alone. Stepping up to the pavement, she saw the formula of the maze written in colored stone in the pavement. A Greek key around a five-pointed star, the end of the key between the legs of the star.

That's fitting, Chloe thought. The key is between the legs. Kela was definitely a fertility goddess. With a low laugh she sank onto the cool grass.

She didn't have to get back out, did she?

CHEFTU SCHOOLED HIS FEATURES TO BETRAY NOTHING. The court would be watching as he pulled away Senwosret's bandages. This time he could not banish the observers. Everyone would see. Or not, as the case may be. Swallowing carefully, he pulled back a layer of linen, thankful for the heavy shadow. Reaching for a small lamp, its flame no bigger than his thumbnail, Cheftu waved the light before Pharaoh. Several swathes of linen were still in place.

"Tell me what you see."

"Brightness . . . flickers before me." Praise Thoth, at least the surgery had not blinded him further! But had it healed him?

Cheftu held the light still. "Now, My Majesty?"

"It is before me. Standing."

Cheftu knew the scales that had grown in Pharaoh's eyes had thickened until his vision had narrowed into one small tunnel of clarity. Finally the tunnel had closed, and Pharaoh had seen nothing. The tunnel was the vital part; the surgery should have cleared and widened it, gods willing.

Ignoring the cold sweat trickling down his temples, Cheftu removed several more layers of linen. He tested again. The final bandage dropped to the floor, and the light was extinguished. The court waited in breathless silence. "My Majesty, open your eyes very slowly, very carefully." He watched as the caked eyelids rose, revealing dark eyes.

Senwosret's gaze was unfocused, his pupils dilated. Cheftu felt sweat run down his back. By the gods! What could he do?

"You are a young man, mage."

Pharaoh could see!

The court erupted in sound. "Silence!" Cheftu shouted. "My Majesty, it will be several more days before your sight is clear enough to stand Ra's full power. You must keep in the shadows. You must not bend, or move your head rapidly."

Senwosret smiled, his sagging jowls lifted slightly by the action. "So I live as a *kheft* for a few days! No matter. You have given me sight, mage!"

Cheftu allowed himself a relieved smile.

"In this court you have a new title, an honor and responsibility." Senwosret lifted his hands, and the chamberlain handed him the symbols of Egypt, the crook and flail. "From henceforth, this mage will be known as Necht-mer, Protector of Sight! I vow, on the sacred head of Apis, that any desire of Necht-mer, up to a third of my kingdom, is his for the asking."

Cheftu bowed, then thanked Pharaoh.

Senwosret took his hands, blinking back tears. "To see the faces of my grandchildren, this is a gift beyond understanding! The gods' blessings on you."

Speared by the humility of the monarch, Cheftu could only nod as he turned and was greeted by the hordes of shaven and perfumed courtiers.

Tonight Pharaoh was hosting a feast for the mage who had returned his sight. Cheftu, Necht-mer, had been awarded palace apartments and given his choice of maidens. Even the perfumed limbs of a dozen different women couldn't raise his attention. He had smiled and thanked and sought blessed solitude. Imhotep came to see him, but Cheftu claimed to be resting. Ipiankhu invited him for a stroll through the menagerie, but Cheftu declined.

Another time, another court. Cheftu sighed as he fingered the marks on his shoulder. The wound was not healing, and it hurt. He drank another cup of wine. "Why" seemed so pointless to ask. Why here? Why trampled? Why apart from Chloe?

Why did he feel so ill at ease?

In disgust he threw his cup at the wall, watching the fragile alabaster shatter, staining the whitewash. The one moment of gratification melted into a deep sense of regret, shame that he would treat his good fortune so callously. After tying on his sandals, he left the palace, refusing guards, slaves, and bearers.

His steps took him through the rank gardens, past mosquito breeding pools and rotting flower beds. The gates from the palace to the city were open, two young sentries on duty. They saluted him, and he felt a pang; even the Egyptian salute was different.

The road branched. He could walk toward the noblemen's houses on the waterfront, or to the market clustered in the poorer sections of town, with its sales of slaves and animals, fruits, vegetables, and goods, or toward the harbor. Cheftu set off for the harbor, watching as the Egyptians haggled for fish, prostitutes flashed their wares with black-toothed smiles, and children begged. His leg ached, yet his heart ached more. This was *not* Egypt.

Chaos ruled the waterfront. Men, cats, and children all raised their voices to Ra as they bargained and bartered and cheated. Pulling his cloak over his head, Cheftu leaned against a wall, watching.

Papyrus boats bobbed in the water next to the riverboats with towering masts and center cabins. A nobleman's barge, identifiable by its gold-plated oars—what a ridiculous waste of gold—pulled in to dock. It was immediately surrounded with hawkers selling overpriced food and pleasure, and children whose long black eyes camouflaged their plans to steal. Dockhands lowered a ramp, and the party began to disembark.

The women came first, surely this generation's flowers of Egypt, Cheftu thought. Their linen was finely woven, their faces protected by the sunshades and fans of their trailing slaves. Though they were beautiful, they were cold, aloof, and Cheftu had no desire to see beyond their painted masks. A group of men followed; the famine had scarcely touched their toned, brown, hairless bodies.

The owner of the ship, Cheftu guessed from the deference shown him, debarked last. He was a beautiful boy, a man, really, but he walked with the hope of untried youth. Cheftu wondered if he'd ever been that young, that hopeful. Though he was only thirty-two, he felt a thousand.

Only thirty-two in three time periods, he reminded himself; France, Hatshepsut's Egypt, and now Senwosret's Egypt.

Cheftu was sitting in a tavern, cringing at the bad beer, when the Aztlantu ships sailed in. The docks filled with silent watchers as the huge, purple-sailed vessels dropped anchor and the Mariners came on shore.

Cheftu stared in astonishment at the ship. It was obviously not Egyptian design, nor did it resemble paintings he'd seen of Greek triremes. Twenty oarsmen covered each side, and from the towering mast a square purple sail was now being lowered. The prow and bow rose high out of the water at almost a ninety-degree angle. Along the waterline an artist had painted a wave rippled with red and gold. Tritons of gold rose from the prow and stern. Shields rimmed the edge of the ship, the fronts now turned inward as a sign of peace. Still, there was something familiar about the shields. Two circles atop each other, covered in cow's hide. Tall enough to cover a man even six feet in height.

Accustomed to being one of the tallest men in any time, Cheftu was surprised to see the Mariners were his height and taller. Meat: they eat a lot of meat, Cheftu thought. They were built differently from the Egyptians, too: wasp-waisted and broad shouldered with much larger bones. Next to them, the Egyptians looked like dainty children.

The Mariners marched in an orderly fashion. Their uniform seemed to be long braided hair, brief, brightly patterned kilts, and codpieces. They wore strange boots that laced up to their knees.

Four of the black-haired Mariners carried a litter down the ramp. Cheftu swallowed hard when he saw the passenger. He was white. Not just in skin color, but Anglo-Saxon in features, with a large bumpy nose and receding chin. Blond hair flowed over the back of his chair, and his eyes were so intensely blue that Cheftu could see them from this distance. He was young, his mostly bared body firm and golden skinned. He scanned the crowd coolly.

Cheftu had seen blonds in Egypt. Usually they were highly priced concubines from Hattai. But this man, with his sharp features and prominent nose, he looked savagely English. "Who is that?" Cheftu asked the fishmonger standing next to him.

"Nestor, envoy from the empire," the man said. "He was here a few weeks ago, and Isis knows why he's back."

"There is no famine in the empire?"

The fishmonger honked, a sound Cheftu took to be a laugh. "Nay. Aztlan's streets are covered in gold, and they have a pyramid that reaches the sky and blinds a man with its beauty."

"Egypt too has gold," Cheftu murmured. "It is not nutritious, however."

"Aye, my lord. But in Aztlan they have fields that stretch for *henti*, as far as a man can see, waving with grain twice a year. They have orchards heavy with fruit, and the state gives every man a concubine for a year."

Cheftu grinned. Food and women, quite the fantastical empire. "If they have all of that, why is Nestor here?"

The man's face grew solemn. "Pharaoh, living forever! alone knows." He looked at Cheftu, noticing for the first time his fine linen and muscled body. "Long may Senwosret live!" the fishmonger said, then scampered away.

Cheftu returned to the tavern and drank a few more cups of beer, his tongue numb to the taste now. In payment for his beer he checked one of the children's sores, rebandaged it, and bade the tavernkeeper's family farewell. Walking through the courtyard, he was surprised to see that stars were out. Another day and night alone in Egypt, he thought, and began making his way back to the palace.

He needed to talk to Ipiankhu tomorrow.

Cheftu was ushered into the vizier's chamber. Ipiankhu sat by a small table washed in sunshine from the clerestory windows. Cheftu took the proffered seat and accepted a cup of beer.

The light glinted off the vizier's chin and eyelashes. The man had auburn hair, Cheftu thought with astonishment. He had never seen him without his full court attire, and now, sitting here with the barest of cosmetics, Cheftu could tell he wasn't a native Egyptian. "You asked to see me, my lord?" the vizier said.

Cheftu placed the ring on the man's table. Ipiankhu frowned slightly, then picked it up. It was a two-sided swirl of pearl and obsidian, inscribed in characters Cheftu had never seen. It had been in the parcel Chloe had received in Hatshepsut's Egypt, and he'd taken it from her . . . her corpse, he forced himself to think.

"Where did you get this?"

"It was a gift," or a curse, he thought. "My wife, the woman found with me, received it before we arrived here." Some crazed witch in the market of Noph placed it in Chloe's hands, he thought. She never even had time to open it. Perhaps that was an omen?

Ipiankhu looked at him through narrowed eyes. He rose and walked to a tiny balcony overlooking Avaris's harbor. Cheftu followed him.

"Behold the purple-sailed ships." Ipiankhu said, pointing to the enormous vessels Cheftu had seen sail in yesterday. "They are Aztlantu." Ipiankhu returned to his chair.

"What has that to do with my ring?"

"Your ring is Aztlantu," Ipiankhu said. "Now would you care to tell me how you came to have it?"

Was this a sign? Cheftu wondered. "Does Egypt trade with Aztlan?"

Ipiankhu's gaze grew more intent. "We supply their Apis bulls for rituals. Now they are demanding more from us."

"Demanding what?"

"Political prisoners. 'Guests of the empire,' the envoy calls them. But in this time of hardship I find it even harder to ask an Egyptian to forsake family and friends and go to live in a strange culture."

Cheftu's stomach tightened, and he felt a tinge of excitement. Was this his destiny? The reason for his being in this time and place? "I will go."

The vizier said nothing, watching. Cheftu picked up the ring—it slid perfectly on his finger. "I have no wife," he said coolly. "I have no position, no fields, no home. There is nothing for me on these shores." He glanced into Ipiankhu's hazel eyes. "Indeed, it is an agony to see Egypt this way and know I cannot heal her." He shifted his hand, watching as the strange symbols took fire when the sun hit them. "You need Egyptians, you said."

Ipiankhu templed his fingers. "You are loyal to Egypt, are you not?"

"I have given my life in her service," he said. *In more ways than you can know.*

"How is your shoulder?"

Cheftu touched his left shoulder. He could move his arm with no difficulty, merely the occasional twinge. His left hand concerned him most. It would take practice for him to fully regain his dexterity. "It is well enough."

The vizier opened his mouth to speak, then shut it. "I will inform Pharaoh, living forever! and Imhotep that this is your wish."

Cheftu rose at the dismissal and walked back to his apartments. Feeling disoriented, he lay down on the couch, enjoying the warm sunlight falling across his legs.

"My lord?" A slave shook him awake. "The vizier asks for you."

Hurriedly Cheftu donned kilt and collar, repaired his kohl, and tucked his stubby hair beneath a headcloth.

Imhotep and Ipiankhu were seated on a back balcony. Mosquitoes clambered along the edge, but slaves with fans and switches kept them away. Cheftu hadn't seen Imhotep since Pharaoh's surgery. A slave brought a chair, and Cheftu sat opposite them.

"Do you know the Aztlantu?" Imhotep asked.

Cheftu shook his head.

"Well, that is one of the most annoying things about them," Imhotep said.

Cheftu frowned. "What is, my lord?"

"Every other people shake their head negatively and nod in agreement. The reverse is true in Aztlan."

"They nod in disagreement?"

"Aye." Imhotep rubbed his bulbous nose. "It is disagreeable."

Cheftu smiled politely.

"So why do you seek to abandon Egypt?"

"It is not abandonment, my lord, I merely seek to aid Egypt."

"Why?"

Cheftu took a deep breath, sending a prayer to *le bon Dieu* for assistance. "My lords, I tell you a grave secret. For reasons I do not understand, I am a tool, or was a tool, for the most high God." Imhotep blanched, but Ipiankhu watched him knowingly. "The woman found dead at my side was my wife." He swallowed his tears. "We married four hundred years hence. Let me tell you of the chamber we knew. . . ."

The lords' faces took on the smooth facades of those who are dealing with a madman, yet they nodded politely, not quite meeting his eyes. "You found us in the Apis bull run, but in the time we left, it was a secret chamber with painted walls portraying the story."

"What story?" Imhotep asked.

"How we came to be there, what our destiny was while we were there." Cheftu focused on Imhotep. "A man, an old man named Imhotep, found us in the desert, four hundred years hence, and saved our lives. He had a scroll with our tale, a prediction of the exact day we would be rescued. You must have written it, passed it down to him. The family resemblance is unmistakable. He was your blood."

Their attention was piqued. Cheftu laid his hand, with the Aztlantu ring, on the table between the two cups of beer. "Send me to Aztlan. Let me serve Egypt this way."

"Senwosret has welcomed you to court," Ipiankhu said.

"My skill as a physician would make me a better marker with which to barter, *haii?*"

Reluctantly both men nodded. "We must seek approval from Pharaoh, living forever! but I think My Majesty will embrace this solution."

Would the Aztlantu bring him back? Cheftu wondered. He crossed his chest and made his way back to his apartments. He was doing as destiny bade, following the sparse clues he'd been given. Aii, *Chloe, if you are watching, if you can see me, tell me what to do.*

Senwosret turned in the room. He stood in a painted alcove, a sandstone lintel above him, a tale painted on the back wall in brilliant colors. Amid finely rendered hieroglyphs was the figure of a woman, surely a goddess or priestess from the size of the picture. He saw her long, turned fingers and straight-nosed profile, her skintight sheath and ankle bracelets—and her green eyes.

Her green eyes seemed to burn with an unearthly fire. Senwosret's gaze dropped to the words "a priestess of an unknown god, sent to be a scribe to his wonder and then returned to the Otherworld."

Pharaoh's skin prickled and he turned away. To his right the wall was black, carefully covered with stars in an uneven pattern. To his left he saw a phrase, the hieroglyphs seemingly formed of fire.

Then the wall melted and he saw destruction, the terror of which he'd never known existed: blood-filled lakes; fire falling from the sky; a cloying darkness that seemed to have fangs and reach into his throat; then a specter so fierce, he screamed, and screamed . . .

He awoke, shaking, sweating, and gasping for breath. Slaves stood in an anxious semicircle around his couch. "Water," he croaked, and put the cup to his lips, feeling it soothe his throat, dribble down his chin and chest. He was panting as though he'd run through the marshes. "Ipiankhu," he said. "And Imhotep!" The slaves stared, their black eyes full of fear. "At once!"

Both men stood before him in a matter of moments. Ipiankhu's chin glinted ruddy in the light of the torches, and Imhotep winced when one of the slaves dropped a flagon. They listened as Senwosret related his dream. He noticed them exchanging glances and finally burst out, "What? What have I said that makes you look at each other with understanding?"

Ipiankhu spoke, his voice trembling. "My Majesty, living forever! You have just told the same tale the mage Necht-mer, *aii,* Cheftu did." He looked at Imhotep. "This green-eyed woman was his wife. She died in the Apis bull run. Cheftu told us of these plagues that you saw."

"What does it mean?"

"It means the words the man spoke, for all their incomprehensibility, are the truth."

Senwosret smiled wistfully. "What is truth?"

Assuming the question was rhetorical, the vizier and the mage were silent. Senwosret twisted his earlobe with his fingers. "Where is this room supposed to be?"

"In the bowels of the Apis chambers."

"Move the bulls."

"What?"

"Are you deaf? Remove the bulls to another area, make a new temple for Apis. Then build this chamber, exactly."

"My Majesty," Imhotep sputtered, "that means transporting thousands of bulls to a yet unknown location and rebuilding the temple, the priests' rooms. Egypt cannot afford this extravagance."

Senwosret stood, his large, bony body covered only by a flimsy kilt. "Egypt can afford to thank this physician for restoring my sight, and Egypt can afford to make this small room as a thanks to this unknown god. What Egypt *cannot* afford are disobedient, questioning courtiers." He turned to Ipiankhu. "What say you?"

The vizier looked away. "I am still seeking wisdom, My Majesty."

"Let me know when you find it. Begone."

TAKING HIS NEWFOUND PLACE OF HONOR at the right of Pharaoh, Cheftu stared blankly at the court. Blazing white shifts and kilts clothed the women and men standing about. The audience chamber was wide and long, with Senwosret on a raised dais at the end. Pharaoh's enormous ears stuck out from the red-and-white crown of upper and lower Egypt, and loose skin sagged over his golden sash. But his eyes were kind.

More important, he could see.

Nestor, the Aztlantu envoy, stood next to the nobles. Today he wore a purple kilt that wrapped tightly around his body and fell below his knees in front. Feathers stuck out of the knot of blond hair twisted atop his head, and gold—pendants, armbands, and anklets—made him blinding. He looked like a peacock among swallows.

The envoy's blue gaze met Cheftu's, and he inclined his head slightly, then focused on the doors at the end of the chamber.

The chamberlain admitted a group of men. Judging from their clothing, a variety of kilts and collars, Cheftu guessed they were merchants. The formal Egyptian dialect was difficult to follow, but Cheftu was intrigued.

"My Majesty," one of the men said, "we, the elders of Gebtu, have come to ask for your mercy."

Cheftu watched Ipiankhu's eyes narrow.

"My Majesty is all that is merciful," Senwosret answered.

"Aye, and for this we are grateful to Amun-Ra." The man twisted his hands before him. "However, we cannot pay our taxes this year. The Inundation flooded us, and in our whole village we have barely enough to feed our children, much less to pay thy noble self."

Senwosret pulled at one of his large ears. "How am I to feed the priesthood without the people's support?"

The elder drew up. "Amun-Ra will take care of his own. As men, we must provide for our families. It is the way of Ma'at."

Ipiankhu leaned forward and whispered to Pharaoh. The royal brows rose, then Senwosret looked meditatively over the group of men. Pharaoh narrowed his eyes and crossed his chest with the crook and flail. "The way of Ma'at is to do as Pharaoh, living forever! commands."

The elder stepped back and swallowed. "Aye, My Majesty."

"Pharaoh is merciful, however. I offer you this penalty in exchange for not paying your taxes. The lands you own will become the property of the double crown. You will live there, till the land, and bring it to fruition once the gods see fit to send us a healthy Inundation. For the remainder of the famine, you will pay no taxes. However, once the river returns to normal, forty percent of all your harvest shall come to me. In perpetuity."

Cheftu watched the carefully painted faces of the elders. Confusion warred with anger. "My Majesty," another man said, "we are of the land. What is there for our children to inherit if not our property?"

"You will *be* of the land, you and your children and your children's children. You may work and live on the land, but forty percent of everything harvested will come into my coffers. In this way you thank Pharaoh for rescuing you in a time when you surely would have died."

They were caught. The penalty for evading taxes was slavery. Families could be broken apart and sold. Ipiankhu leaned forward again, whispering to Senwosret.

"Additionally," Pharaoh said, "I will grant one from your village a special accord to visit in my palace and to serve as a representative of your village here in Avaris."

Cheftu's lips twitched. Wily old man! Divide and conquer. Make each man so determined to win this new place that he fails to notice he has sold himself for all time. Was this the beginning of Pharaoh's economic power? Cheftu wondered. This man? If Senwosret offered this assistance agreement to just half of the nobles, that would account for the size of Pharaoh's estates in generations to come. Cheftu remained expressionless.

"What say you?"

The elders glanced at each other. "My Majesty, whom will you choose?"

"No one, until I know we have a bargain."

They huddled, arguing silently. You have no choice, Cheftu thought.

"Aye, we accept, My Majesty," an older man said. "And I nominate—"

"Tell it to the scribe," Pharoah cut him off. "One of you will sit at my table tonight. Life, health, and prosperity to you and your beloved ones."

They backed toward another door as the chamberlain announced the next request.

Cheftu watched with glazed eyes as petitioners came before Pharaoh. Men, women, everyone from the highest priest to the lowest beer maid had the right to seek an audience with Amun-Ra incarnate in Pharaoh.

The courtroom finally cleared of petitioners and the scribe rose, for Pharaoh was going to review the paltry troops immediately afterward. The courtiers shifted, weary from the ritual. "Is there something My Majesty has forgotten?" said Nestor, the envoy.

Cheftu watched Imhotep and Ipiankhu exchange glances. He felt his throat tighten. His thumb brushed over the Aztlantu ring, turned on his finger.

"Have you a petition, foreigner?" the chamberlain asked.

Nestor smiled, a predatory smile, Cheftu thought. "Greetings from *Hreesos* Zelos," he said, walking forward, the feathers in his hair trembling with momentum. At the snap of his fingers, the chamber doors opened. The courtiers exclaimed at the parade of gifts.

"Embroidered linens from Arachne, Clan of the Muse!" Nestor cried as vibrant bolts of cloth were unrolled at Pharaoh's feet.

"Supple furs from Kouvari, Clan of the Horn!" Leopard, zebra, and lion skins were draped on the steps to the dais.

"Secrets of the sea, from Ariadne, Clan of the Wave!" A conch shell the size of a large cat, overflowing with pearls, was laid at Pharaoh's feet.

"Jewels from the catacombs of Pluto, Clan of the Stone!" A wooden box was handed to Pharaoh. Ipiankhu opened it cautiously, and Cheftu almost whistled. Precious stones of tourmaline, turquoise, sapphire, citrine, and onyx filled the box.

"Delicacies from the Clan of the Vine!" Slaves carrying pointed flasks of alabaster and shell placed them in gold stands around Pharaoh. Baskets of dried fruit were set at his feet.

Nestor paused, smiling. "Now, My Majesty, I present the empire's most precious mystery, most luscious export." He chuckled, a hint of the ribald in his tone. "From the Cult of the Snake I gift you with Pythia, a Coil Dancer!"

Flutes began to play, and a woman glided in. Her body was completely covered . . . in sheer veiling. Hair the color of ripe berries fell to her knees, and Cheftu saw courtiers recoil and touch their amulets.

Not only was she redheaded, her eyes were deep blue. Nestor had erred greatly, Cheftu thought. Though there was no doubting the seduction of her movements, the Egyptians believed that redheads were synonymous with Set, the destroyer god. Set had murdered his brother Osiris, and only through the diligence of Osiris' wife was the king reassembled and resurrected. In Egyptian eyes, this red-haired dancing woman was kin to a demon. She was a *kheft*-maiden.

Having blue eyes made her even more alien and demonic.

She whirled, gyrated, spun, and finally flung herself panting onto the furs. Her hair brushed Pharaoh's foot, and Ipiankhu quickly moved it away. It was customary at the end of gift giving for the receiver to reciprocate. This was how the bulls and Cheftu himself would be transferred. However, Pharaoh was greatly displeased. Would he flout tradition?

"Remove this woman," Pharaoh commanded tersely. The court tensed visibly, and Nestor's eyes glittered.

"She is a nymph, a maid, as you say," he explained.

"Her appearance offends me!"

Nestor snapped his fingers, and the Aztlantu slaves led her away. The envoy stood stiffly, an offended peacock. "In honor of our Becoming Golden ceremony this year, we offer the bounty of our land."

Ipiankhu leaned forward, whispering in Senwosret's ear. Cheftu saw Pharaoh's fingers tighten on his emblems of office. "We gift *Hreesos* with Apis bulls."

Nestor turned around, as though looking for them.

"They will be delivered at dawn, before you catch the morning tide," Senwosret said. His meaning was lost on no one, and the envoy's face reddened.

"My gratitude," he said shortly.

"My Majesty also shares with *Hreesos* our most valuable asset. Our people."

"We shall endeavor to be gracious hosts."

Ipiankhu clapped, and the people walked in. Cheftu forced himself to stare straight ahead. He needed to be one of them! A lord and lady, to judge from their clothing, twin boys of ten Inundations, a girl just entering puberty, and an older man, a merchant judging by his un-Egyptian beard. All were thin, fragile. Products of the famine, Cheftu thought. Senwosret spoke. "They too will arrive at your ships at dawn tomorrow."

Nestor was furious. He stepped closer, and the guards around Pharaoh drew to attention, shifting their weapons slightly. "You shame Egypt and Aztlan," he hissed. Though the room strained to hear, only the five on the dais did. "These people are sick! They are of no worth to Aztlan."

Senwosret spoke, his mouth barely moving. "We are in a famine, my lord envoy. Perhaps next time your mighty empire chooses to rape and pillage, you will choose another land?"

Nestor blanched, apparently realizing what he'd said. "Nay, My Majesty, of course not. Egypt has been, and always will be, our sister, raised alongside and loved by the same gods." Nestor's left hand played nervously with the edge of his kilt. "If, in a show of good favor, I could have just one guest with a . . ."

"Title?" Ipiankhu suggested.

The envoy smiled. "A title would be graciousness itself. I am sure My Majesty, in his . . . wisdom . . . understands the folly of my returning with such paltry specimens of Egypt. I fear the Council would . . . wish to speak to you on these shores."

The threat was clear: hand over someone else or Aztlan would invade.

"Take me, my lord," Cheftu said.

Nestor turned to him abruptly. "Who are you?"

"He is the foremost mage of our court," Imhotep said. "My father, your Spiralmaster, would be pleased with his wisdom."

"Your name?"

"He is Cheftu Necht-mer, first physician of the Eye, beloved of Thoth, chosen of Nephthys, and hearer of the god," Ipiankhu answered. Cheftu crossed his chest with his arm, a sketchy bow, listening to the vizier craft his tale.

"Why would you give him up, My Majesty?" Nestor asked Senwosret.

"Horus-on-the-Throne has yet to speak."

The court gasped at Pharaoh's words. Cheftu dared not look at the two lords; they carried his fate in their hands. Senwosret clapped, summoning wine, and the clenched group at the dais unbent enough to sip from alabaster cups.

"Step away, my lord envoy," Senwosret said over his cup. The envoy moved away, and Senwosret turned to Cheftu. "You are Egyptian, a friend to this court. I would know why you choose to be with foreigners."

"It is my destiny, My Majesty. Written for me by the hands of Thoth and HatHor."

"I forbid it," Senwosret said.

"My Majesty's oath means so little?" Cheftu knew by Imhotep's hiss that he had gone too far, but by the horns of HatHor, he must get to Aztlan!

Senwosret's gaze was cutting. "I am Pharaoh, my word is Ma'at. I vowed you any boon." He gestured with his chin, and the scribe hurried to Nestor's side. Senwosret spoke to the envoy. "My lord is your gift. Leave the others here. They are ill and need the red and black lands of Kemt to heal them." Pharaoh's tone brooked no argument.

Nestor glared at Cheftu. "By dawn, Egyptian lord."

Senwosret rose, and the group on the dais left in his wake. Surprised that his legs even worked, Cheftu walked down the stone steps.

Dawn stained the sky as Cheftu watched the sails unfurl. The wind snapped the huge purple woven sheets, finely embroidered with a crab, triton, and shell. The ship dwarfed the Egyptian boats. On the other Aztlantu ship men took their places at the oars.

Each of the three ships carried forty bulls; in the event a mishap befell any one ship, the sacred Aztlantu ritual could still be consummated. Though Egypt had promised only one hundred bulls, Ipiankhu had apparently decided it worthwhile to add the other twenty.

The first ship began to move away from the docks. The bow was the same height as the back of the ship, so the rowers sat facing the opposite direction. There was no need to back out of the harbor or turn the massive ship. Sunlight warmed their straining muscles as the rowers pulled, in rhythm to the low beat Cheftu heard from across the waters.

"My lord?" Ipiankhu stood by the rail. He smiled and bowed. "I wanted to wish you a good journey. Are you certain this is what you want?"

Cheftu nodded. He had to be certain; it was done.

The vizier gripped Cheftu's arms. "May Shu blow you safely to your destination. May Ra shine on your journey. May Nuit kiss your dreams every night until you return to Egypt."

"Life, health, and prosperity," Cheftu said slowly, debating his next words. Why not? "Will you tell Imhotep this? 'Your teeth bring you pain. Teach your children to sift their bread flour ten times, and chew mint with each meal.'" Ipiankhu smiled and began to turn, but Cheftu laid a hand on his arm. "One more thing, my lord . . ." He leaned closer, his words lost beneath the beat of the timekeeper's drum.

Ipiankhu sat down heavily in his chair and commanded the slaves to run immediately to his home. His hands were trembling and his throat felt closed. He looked at himself. Egyptianized. Shaven like a priest, clothed in the finest kilt, and draped with gold necklaces portraying a pantheon of gods and goddesses. His hands were soft, no calluses, no marks. The hands of a nobleman.

Closing his eyes, Ipiankhu thanked his god, the God of his tribe, for the sign he had received. *Cheftu's tale was true!* It was the will of the Unknown that Senwosret build the chamber. Why, Ipiankhu did not know. The sun shone without his understanding, but it shone. He ran his hand over his chin, a habit he'd acquired from his tribe, though he had never had a beard to know the feeling. In the silence of the traveling chair, the words Cheftu had spoken echoed in his head.

"Shalom, Yosef ben Y'srael. You shall be a great nation."

PART III

CHAPTER 6

CAPHTOR

CHLOE WAS BEYOND REGRETTING that she had agreed to be the "driver" for all of the race-related activities. Her legs hurt, her arms hurt, her breasts really hurt, and her feet were covered in bruises and blisters.

Sibylla reclined on the edge of her consciousness, like Jeannie in her pink velvet bottle. *While I am busting my keister for a race I don't want to run*, Chloe thought with a sigh.

Today was the first of a series of qualifying races. If she lost here, Sibylla wouldn't have to continue racing. *Which means I wouldn't have to continue racing.* She winced as Sibylla, previously silent, began to accuse her of having no honor, no integrity . . . *Yadda, yadda yadda*, Chloe thought.

She began her stretches, exchanging small talk with the other women. Twenty-five contenders were in this competition. Chloe scrutinized them and realized that, like Cinderella's slipper, most weren't going to fit. Three were lean and muscled; those three she'd have to keep an eye on.

The runners moved into their starting positions, and Chloe furtively tied her breasts into a halter with the sash from her skirt. It was hardly a sport bra, but it worked and it wasn't visible beneath the thin woolen shift the racers wore.

"*Yazzo!*" the timekeeper cried. They were off.

The Aztlantu hadn't quite grasped the concept of distance vs. sprint, so the race was in fact a long-distance sprint. About four miles' worth. I hate running, pounded through Chloe's mind in time to her footsteps.

She focused on breathing and not wrenching her ankle as she began to break from the pack. As expected, two of the lean, fit women were leading. Chloe and the other lean woman were edging their way through the mass of huffing and puffing women. Chloe veered slightly, avoiding an overzealous elbow in her gut.

The path turned, narrowed, and Chloe put on an extra burst of energy, leaving the pack and the third runner behind.

At least she thought they were behind. It was surprisingly quiet, only the sound of the wind and her breathing. Dappled sunlight fell on her, and Chloe watched her legs, in Sibylla's skin, pump and step through the leaf-covered path.

Then she was in a clearing, gaining on the other two runners. One was hobbling, losing ground rapidly, and Chloe realized she must have twisted her ankle. She focused on the ground again, wary of small depressions and stones. The woman finally gave up, falling to the ground. Chloe slowed. "Are you well?"

"My ankle, mistress," the girl said, panting. "Run on, I will be well."

Chloe was past, the words floating after her like a benediction. One more runner, she thought. Sibylla was growing excited, and Chloe glared at her. Sweat matted her hair, trickled between her bound breasts, and soaked her woolen shift. She kept running.

Ahead she saw the lead runner. How close were they to the finish line? Chloe wondered. Photo finishes might be fun and glamorous looking, but she wanted to win, no question, leaving the contender in her dust.

You are quite competitive, Sibylla observed.

Ignoring the oracle, Chloe commanded her legs to move faster, her strides to lengthen, her blood to pump more. The first runner was a blonde, a tiny thing, but light and fast. Chloe gritted her teeth and ran faster. Her body ached, but now there was an edge, an exhilaration, she'd not felt before. She pounded up behind the blonde, who turned her head just a little.

Seeing the finish line, Chloe felt adrenaline surge through her. This one is for the USAF, she thought. The small grouping of people grew more distinct, then closer to life size, and then she was across the burn mark in the grass, her ears ringing, sweat pouring off her body.

The blonde was two steps behind, two steps too few. Chloe submitted to a crown of bay leaves thrust on her head, and her hot, shaky body was doused with wine.

We won! Sibylla cried inside.

One down, a dozen more to go.

AZTLAN

"I THOUGHT I'D FIND YOU HERE," Phoebus said. Niko looked up from the stack of scrolls and tablets. Dust and dirt marked his face, and a dustball clung to the side of his head. Phoebus smiled. "How does your search go?"

With a sly grin, Niko held up a rectangle of leather. Aztlantu had kept their legends pressed into folded leather tablets since time before mind. The leather was hard, cracked, and brittle, a hundred tiny lines obscuring the text. Niko handed him a vial of oil. "I am down to two tablets; be useful."

Phoebus threw his cloak to the floor and sat on it, smearing the oil on the leather to reveal the image. Because the writing tiles cut into the leather, or impressed into the gold, there was no fear of water damage. A useful feature when one lived on an island, Phoebus thought.

"Do you know how Aztlan was founded?" Niko asked.

Phoebus shrugged. He knew Aztlan was older than the reign of the Clan Olimpi, but he'd never learned the earlier history. It wasn't taught, it wasn't mentioned. How could anything surpass the glories of the clan? I will, he thought. "I know what we were taught. Judging from your question, I would guess there is more?" He continued to rub oil into the hide. Thus far there seemed to be nothing on it.

"What a reasoned response," Niko said. "Now listen to this." He opened a newly oiled scroll. " 'Time before mind, a man and his wife were shipwrecked on this island. Though they were alone, they walked with a great God. He gave them secrets in the stones. There were only two laws: A life must be given for a life taken in violence; the energy of life was in the blood and must not be consumed in any form.' "

Phoebus interrupted. "Those cannot have been the laws! That must be a myth!"

"I am not finished. The writings claim that this couple begat a numerous people. They began to move to the other islands, spreading their name and skills across the sea. This people walked with a great, unknown god, and he communicated to them through some stones. Then, the patriarch Iavan was lost at sea. The people turned from the god. The challenge to worship what they could not see was too great."

"Do you think Apis is this god?"

Niko folded the tablet to the next partition. "You do not believe that any more than I do. Worshiping a bull is but a symbol for worshiping the strength of nature. Someone *does* shake the earth, but it is not a giant bull on whose back we rest. A bull did not settle this land, teach us how to farm or sail."

Reading from the page, Niko quoted, " 'The people said, "Look at the sky! Listen to the hills, how they roar! Hear the sea, how she sings! How can this be only one god? There are many!" So they took the knowledge the great God had taught them and turned from him. They refused to listen to him, and finally destruction ripped the land apart, separating it into vast islands, filling it with snaking streams.' Phoebus, that is what we have now."

Phoebus continued to massage the oil into the leather. A line finally appeared along the right-hand side of the page. As the oil was absorbed, all but the deepest marks were smoothed away. He opened the next section, poured more oil on it, and wiped away the grime. There were a lot of markings here, but not letters. "Continue."

"After the destruction, the people were invaded and they absorbed the invaders. Civil war ensued. That was when the Council rose. People fled the Council's rulings, the new laws. In our history classes we were told colonists left Aztlan to establish outposts. This document denies they were colonists. Phoebus, it claims they were outlaws."

The Rising Golden stopped, listening to his friend, comparing what he said to the legends on which they'd been reared. "We were told they were colonists, going north, south, east, and west. They brought back the secrets of two growing seasons, how to form stone and the tides." Phoebus looked up. "Why would they flee?"

"They rejected the Council's ruling about families. They wanted their blood relation to stay with them. They resisted becoming clans."

"But the clan structure is what makes Aztlan work," Phoebus said, fingering the gold medallion around his neck. "It grants equality and balance among citizens. It maintains a stable economy. Marriages are strong, as are children, for their blood is varied." He shrugged. "Why would anyone oppose that? We have peace and plenty. Clans *are* Aztlan." He watched Niko in silence. "What is it, my friend?" he whispered. "Your thoughts are like smoke in the air."

"Spiralmaster wants these stones."

"What stones?"

"The stones that allowed our forebears an audience with this god."

Phoebus looked up. "He believes these tales?"

"Apparently the stones were lost with the man Iavan, the patriarch. He died on a small island. Some of the followers of the god went after him and built a tomb for him. They left the communication stones there."

"But no one knows where they are or has used them since?"

He nodded his head. "I think Spiralmaster is purely hoping now, though. I've been through all of these. There is not one map."

Phoebus unfolded the next page of the tablet. Impatiently, he rubbed the oil into the brittle leather, then stopped. Finally, some letters. Letters marking an island in a massive sea. "You said we were working on the last two? What was yours?"

Niko picked up the oil-slick leather. "Recipes for childbirth."

Phoebus winced. "What would be the reward for finding your tablet?"

"A night with that red-haired Coil Da—" Niko leaped over a stack of papyri and leather to crouch by Phoebus.

Phoebus handed the tablet to him. "Aye. You pay for the dancer. That is the map!"

Light flickered around the edges of Phoebus' eyes, and he winced. "Was she worth my humble, hard-earned pay?" Niko asked.

"*Okh!* By the horns of Apis, what are you doing here?" Phoebus groaned, rolling over onto his stomach.

Niko sat on the couch. "Spiralmaster has chosen to send me," he said.

Phoebus, his head buried beneath a pillow, lay quiet. "Send you where?" he asked as the words penetrated.

"Dion wanted to go, but Spiralmaster persuaded him that he could make more progress with his air-sailing device if he didn't take time away from it."

The Rising Golden sat up, pulling the linen over him. Niko sat on the end of the bed, his violet eyes ringed with kohl, his white hair braided and twisted. "Did I miss a feast?" Phoebus asked.

"Aye," Niko said. "Spiralmaster would like me to leave on the next tide."

The sexual haze vanished. "Next tide? You mean tonight?"

Niko shook his head, delighted.

"This is madness!"

"Phoebus, Spiralmaster believes if we get these stones, we can ask this god how to help our people. He can give Spiralmaster the missing ingredient the elixir needs."

"You crazed scholars!" Phoebus said. "You read an ancient, nonsensical myth in one decrepit tablet that no one has ever heard of, and decide an unknown god will aid us? How? He will tell the mountains to throw themselves into the sea? This is a legend, my friend! A story! We are the only gods in these lands; tales of our daring will become a religion!"

"Phoebus, if he exists, he was the one who founded Aztlan. That being the case, we have forsaken him. Daily we use these gifts he's given us. We forgot who the gift giver is."

Phoebus studied his friend carefully. "You are quite serious about this, are you not?"

"Knowledge is my deity, this you know. However, I feel we need to try, to reason and reacquaint ourselves with Iavan's god. I know seeking the god is the right answer. It is the only answer to this question."

"You, who claim we cannot truly know anything? You know what you are doing is right?"

Niko's gaze focused inward. "I hear a call, a cry in my *psyche*, Phoebus. I must follow it. Only once before have I known such a passion. . . ."

"You are a brilliant fool!" Phoebus shouted.

Niko's smile was wistful. "Perhaps only fools are foolish enough to understand truth."

"Truth is what we make it." Phoebus frowned, pleating the linen sheet. "Who travels with you?"

"Three Mariners. Even Spiralmaster doesn't trust my ability to take care of myself," Niko grumbled. He gripped Phoebus' wrist. "I will be back before you miss me."

You cannot leave me, Phoebus thought. You are my dearest friend, reared since birth to be my mage. But the words would not come. This could not be happening. "Do you follow the directions on the map? Are there any landmarks still? How long will it take?"

Niko smiled. "You sound like a clan mother." His gaze turned solemn. "Until my eyes hold you again, Phoebus."

The men embraced, and Niko left, closing the double doors behind him.

AZTLAN

MOUNT CALLIOPE BURNED WITH RAGE. She was smaller, her channels shallower and weaker, than her brother Krion to the south. Unaware of the danger, people scaled up her sides, living in two-, three- and four-story houses, planting small gardens of herbs and vegetables, orchards of fruit. This was the Clan of the Muse, whose main industry was cloth.

Cloth from Delos, the Clan of the Muse, was exported all over the empire and her vassals. The clanspeople were famous for sails, whose interlacing woven strips could hold the wind, tightly controlling the direction of the ship. They fashioned fabric, some made from Egyptian flax, some from local wool, and others from the fine stuff traded in Caphtor and Kos, into garments.

A village of blue-tiled houses clustered within the narrow, winding streets of Delos's main city, Arachne. The stench that rose from this section of town was carried away by a saltwater river that poured directly into the sea. The dyers who lived here were instantly recognizable. They alone of all Aztlantu did not bear the tattoo of their clan. They wore its brand.

Each man's, woman's, and child's hands were purple-blue, a color painstakingly extracted from the murex shell. In its deepest hue, it was the color of Theros Sea. The color was so intense, it made one's eyes ache, and so eerily beautiful that it was impossible to look away.

In normal strength, it was the color of lupine flowers that grew in scattered clumps across the mountains. Tinted, it was a blue between Egyptian lapis and turquoise, most often used as a pottery glaze. At its lightest, the color was so pale and pure, it was reserved exclusively for children, a color so fragile that a bird's eggshell looked weighty by comparison.

Because of the stink and markings, those who worked the Azure married only among themselves. They birthed children and waited impatiently until the firstborn was weaned, and then set him or her to work, staining young hands with the badge of blue.

Beneath the cobbled and dirt-packed streets of Arachne, beneath the smoking vats of color and the looms of linen and wool, the mountain heated. Within its lava chambers, molten rock bulged against the weight of stone, soil, person, and beast.

In the fields, the sheep bleated unceasingly, and the dogs and donkeys that lived alongside them grew panicked. Birds flew nervously in wide circles, wary of perching.

Neotne stood in the shadow of the mountain at the wharf. The sun had pierced the gray clouds. She tugged at her belled skirt, clenching it in her blue-nailed fists. Saltwater spray spattered her face and body, and she wondered about her clan brother Y'carus, a Mariner sailing far beyond the Breakwater.

His last message said he was for Knossos, on Caphtor. She'd never been to Caphtor, never even been to Aztlan Island. He was seeing the world. She was always bidding him farewell, until her eyes held him again. Whenever he returned to his bloodparents, her clansmen, he brought tales of exotic ports, little gifts from places she would never see. She would love to sail anywhere, if he were at her side.

She touched one of the earrings from Alayshiya that dangled against her cheeks, wondering where he was. Did he get frightened when no land was in sight? With a prayer to Kela for his safety, she turned back to the town. Goat cheese was on her list, in addition to cucumbers and Caphtori honey. Clan sister Sela was expecting her firstborn, and after much prompting from the Kela-Tenata, she had finally taken to her couch. The whole Azure community waited in joyful impatience for another to join their numbers.

When a low rumble shook the earth, Neotne dropped into a crouch. The Earthshaker's dance had become so frequent, it was commonplace. The ground stilled, and Neotne walked through the market. Banners of finest cloth advertised the skill of the weavers in Arachne. Paintings on the sides of houses, children at play, swallows over lilies, the courtship of a young man and woman, indicated the interests and talents of the artisans within. The market tables glittered with jewelry. Perfume bottled in exquisite alabaster vials tempted the buyer to try and buy. Neotne exchanged greetings with the *parfumier* and uncorked one.

A strong draft of rotten eggs blew over her. *"Okh!"*

"That odor is not my perfume!" the woman protested.

"Then what is it, mistress?" Neotne asked. The perfume stank. The stink still filled the air. She looked at the other shoppers. Everyone had stopped; many had pinched their noses, frowning at the stench. Maybe it wasn't the perfume, but what could cause such a horrid smell? Neotne left the market and walked uphill to the temple. She would pick up some fresh fish for the noonday meal and go home. The rest of her list could be purchased later.

The red-columned building was empty of buyers, and Neotne sighed in relief. She hated to wait. Inside, the Shell Seekers had laid out the day's catch—fish, shrimp, and octopus. Fresh vegetables and fruits from the Clan of the Vine and spiced meat from the Clan of the Horn were attractively arranged in baskets.

The earth moved again, and Neotne caught herself against a table. She watched as a pomegranate crashed to the ground, splitting and spilling seeds the color of blood. *Please Kela, let that not be an omen!* The shudder continued, and pieces of whitewashed ceiling fell. Neotne raised her arm, shielding herself. Beneath the roar of the Earthshaker, she heard human cries. She tried to look up, but a fog of white powder hung in the room. Crouched next to a column, she felt a crack begin beneath her palm. The column would fall. She would be crushed!

Dodging and jumping pieces of building falling around her, Neotne ran in the direction of the door. The temple steps had cracked down the middle; this was the worst Earthshaker had ever been.

A burning powder fell, stinging her bare breasts and face. The smell of sulfur was strong in the air, and panicked people ran through the streets to the harbor. Caught up in the mass, Neotne was pushed along. Sela, she thought, what about Sela? Her clan sister could scarcely move, she was so full of child.

People shoved at her back, and Neotne shoved at the people ahead of her. What she had thought was a powder were tiny, hot, stinging pellets, falling from the sky. Neotne couldn't turn, couldn't break from the crowd. On all sides she saw broken buildings and fires. Bright pieces of fresco lay shattered on the ground, quickly being covered by gray. A weaver's house had fallen in on itself, the cloth still on the loom scarlet as a splash of blood.

What was happening?

The sound struck like a blow, and Neotne was felled, people beneath her and atop her. She felt the ground shudder as though it longed to birth, and Neotne struggled away, terrified.

With strength prompted by fear, she wrestled out of the group and got to her feet. They were at the harbor, except the sea had vanished! Ships and boats sat mired in sand. A crack seemed to rip from behind her, a deafening sound that threw her to her knees. Neotne turned and saw fire shoot from Apis' Nostril.

The Bull roared!

Only a few people still stood. Buildings had fallen, bodies lay in the mucky seabed like swathes of drying linen. She watched as streaks of red and green and orange shot into the sky. Lightning glowed in the gathering darkness, and Neotne knew that Arachne was doomed. Sela, could she get to Sela?

She turned to the sea. Where were the waves? Was there no escape? A low sound, like hordes of buzzing bees, grew louder, closer. Mount Calliope began to bleed, red and black smoke billowing from the smoking Nostril. The blood moved fast, and Neotne jumped off the pier, onto the wet sand. A tiny boat listed to one side, stranded on the sand but small enough for her to push. Neotne grabbed at it and it moved.

A little.

The blood had reached the outer edge of Arachne. The beautiful nobles' homes built high on the cliff's edge were swept under in the blink of an eye. Neotne got in front of the boat and pulled. It moved more.

Other people moved and screamed and ran, but Neotne felt as though she alone faced the fury of the Bull. What had they done that Apis would destroy them? The boat slid farther out. Neotne grabbed the anchor rope and twisted it around her wrist, granting more leverage to her pull, tossing the anchor end inside the boat.

People's screams tore through the air, and Neotne ran, the hot breath of Apis on her back. The boat dragged behind her as the sand grew wetter and it grew harder to gain footing. Beached octopus and fish lay dead all around her. Darkness approached, and the falling ash seemed to gouge her everywhere it touched.

A crack of wood sounded behind her, and Neotne turned, watching the Bull's blood crush the wooden pier. She saw people vanish under its deadly wave. Arachne was gone. Sela, the child, her clan, her family. The Bull despised them! She felt the heat of its power but could no longer move. A rush behind her made her turn again.

The sea!

A wave higher than Arachne's cliffs approached. Neotne looked at the fiery blood about to embrace her and then at the churning white waves. She dove into the sand as the sea crashed into the lava, jerking Neotne with violent force.

It ripped her blue-stained hand off her arm like the snap of a thread.

AN ICY COLD WAVE WASHED OVER HIM and Niko sat up, clutching the prow of the boat. A cloying darkness surrounded him and he coughed, heaving ocean water and gritty phlegm from his chest. He watched as the Mariners fought with the sail and the wind. The air stank of sulfur. Niko's skin itched, but that thought was lost as the boat rose high in the air, almost tossing them out. Lightning and thunder flashed in the distance, momentarily illuminating the night.

In a glimpse he saw orange and red glowing in the distance. His boat was caught in the waves again. He began bailing water. The boat was sinking, water was up to his knees and Niko could see nothing except a furnacelike glow on the horizon. The sail ripped away and Niko heard the finely woven Aztlantu cloth flap in the wind like a Coil Dancer's skirt.

The boat turned and Niko hung on for blessed life as he felt them spin in an eddy. The deck tilted and Niko heard a man cry out, then a loud splash. Through the flashes of lightning Niko could see the Mariner's dark head in the white-capped waves. The boat pitched again and Niko felt his body lift completely from the deck, then crash down again.

Utterly disoriented, Niko squinted through the whipping wind to get his bearings, landmarks. Before he'd fallen asleep they were supposed to pass into the narrow channel between Delos and Paros. That was the location of the stone's island, according to the map. Was that fiery, angry mass Delos?

The island glowed as though it were in Talos' forge. Red, orange, yellow, and black covered the side of the mountain, and there was no sign of Arachne. The boat bounced on the water. Niko was certain he was going to die.

Niko had never contemplated death before. It happened to the aged, the infirm. He was the brightest student ever to sit in the Scholomance. And he was going to die. Little use all his knowledge was now, he fumed.

The boat was whirled by the winds and the waves and the blackness of whatever was coming from the sky. "Help me!" he cried, his words eerily distorted on the rising wind. The echoing cries bounced around him. Knowing that they were merely a trick of nature did not dissuade him from the possibility that a wandering *skia* was torturing him. Ocean spray and falling ash mixed on his cheeks, and Niko resisted forbidden tears. Was this his answer to searching for the great god's stones? You deserve to die?

Or was this storm a product of Apis' jealousy? For the Bull did seem an entity now, a bucking, frothing-mad creature bent on destruction.

He pulled an oar flush against his body. The Mariners had disappeared. Was he alone? Niko used his sash to tie the oar to him. The wood should help keep him afloat when his boat broke up. "Please help me!" he whispered as he watched the burning mountain stretch fingers of fire into the sea.

The boat spun again and Niko fell to the deck, clinging to the oar as he slid back and forth on the slick wood. Lightning flashed and ash fell on him, his face, into his eyes. Niko curled into himself, groaning as his sliding body was battered. The wind was a live thing, and Niko begged for mercy.

The sea calmed. Niko sat up, dazed. The waters were placid. The island was to his back, the unearthly glow cast on the sea in reflection. Frantically Niko began to row, pulling his boat into the deeper water as quickly as he could.

It began as a low rush, a reverberation that ran up his spine and made the oar tremble. He pushed deeper and yelled as the oar was torn from his hands. Bracing on both arms, he held himself in the boat as the oar, still tied to him, danced on the waters. In another eyeblink he knew it would pull him down with it. Suddenly a sucking sound followed and Niko turned, splashed with water. The power of the crests raised the boat, but kept it in one place as the sea roared beneath him, across the murky night, to crash on the shore of the flaming mountain.

He pulled out the oar and began paddling furiously, begging whatever, whoever had saved him, to save him just a little further.

Just a little further . . . The wave knocked him over, sucking him from the boat. Niko felt his waist tighten almost unbearably as he was pulled along by the weightless oar. Impact to his head . . .

Niko opened his eyes. Grit clustered at the edges of his vision and he blinked, trying to move it away. His cheek felt abraded. He looked about: the east side of the world was slick black, the west was rushing waves to the sky.

It took a moment, then he realized he was lying on a beach, the waves appearing horizontal. Wincing, he sat up, the cold air chilling the side of his body he'd kept warm against the black pumice.

Where was he? Shaking, he rose to his feet—noticing the cuts and abrasions covering his body. Yet he was alive. He scanned the shoreline for his boat, his map, food, clothing. The beach was empty.

The tide was coming in, rising from his ankles to his knees. His tender feet were cut by the rough rock, but he had to walk.

Apparently he'd washed up on a small island, densely covered with trees and foliage. How far had he been blown off course? The volcano had erupted on Delos, that was certain. Why and how—he didn't know. Had the inhabitants managed to send off birds to Kallistae? Had the clansmen at Paros summoned aid? Had those at Tinos? A gray smoke fog still hung over the sky, casting the day into false twilight.

Niko began walking, listening for sounds of people or animals. The quiet was ominous, no birds called, no *maeemus* chattered. No wind, either. He stepped into the trees and saw what appeared to be an overgrown path.

Pine trees grew beside bougainvillea that had not yet been killed by winter frost. Basil rose in bushes as high as his chest. Roses grew wild, their petals sprinkling the black soil with yellow, red, pink, and peach spots.

What was this place? A sense of reverence hung as thickly as the smoke covering the treetops.

Niko kept walking, his breath coming faster. The path twisted and wove, overhung with grapevines, fig trees, pomegranate bushes, and a grassy covering of oregano and hardy thyme, hyssop, and rosemary.

At least he wouldn't starve.

He walked for hours yet felt as though he traveled nowhere. Niko began to tire. His legs ached from the unaccustomed activity. It was getting darker, and he ate the grapes he'd picked along the trail.

Pine needles poked his bare feet as Niko headed in one direction, paused, turned around, and ran in another. Cold sweat glazed his body. Where was he?

The thirst that had appeared from time to time now manifested itself fully, and he found he could barely swallow. He tried to calm himself, but Niko was a man of civilization. Water was simply a matter of drawing it from the clay pipes that wove like threads through the walls of the palace. He was a refined man. He could speak all known languages. The formulae for Aztlan's greatest accomplishments were buried in his brain. Like all courtiers, he could dance, he could ride, and he could sail.

But in the wildness of this island, he was blind and mute, ignorant as a child and as vulnerable as a hatchling. Despairing, fearful of the growing darkness, he looked frantically for a place to hide. Wind began rustling in the trees, raining tiny needles onto his bare skin.

He hunched down beneath the spreading lower limbs of a pine, shivering. After surviving so much, would he die here? Would his bones eventually become one with the roots of this huge tree?

Would all he'd hoped for come to naught? He thought of those he would miss: Phoebus, Spiralmaster, his students, his *maeemu*. He'd never know if Dion perfected his air sail; if Irmentis and Phoebus finally consummated their love; he'd miss Phoebus' Becoming Golden.

He would break his word to the person dearest to him. "All I wanted were the stones," he pleaded in a whisper. "Just a chance to talk to the first god of this land. Maybe apologize for forsaking him? Intervene and ask him to heal Aztlan?" Was that so wrong?

As darkness threw the trees into wicked, shifting horrors, Niko, feet bleeding, throat swollen, and eyes red, slept.

AT SEA

THE BULLS' RUMBLING ROCKED THE DECK beneath his feet. Mariner Batus raced for the hatch before the commander could send him; he had no taste for a lashing. After his eyes adjusted to the darkness, he ducked under the beam that ran the length of the ship.

The bulls were unhappy. They were making odd noises. Of the forty that had been loaded in Avaris, not many were standing.

Mariner Cynaris hissed from the darkness.

Batus knelt. "What are you doing?"

"One of the bulls is dead!"

"By the gods, say it isn't so!" he cried, pushing between the hot bodies of the animals. Lying on its side, the bull was still. Several others lay around it, but they all were breathing, hot, fetid breath in the close darkness. "What happened?"

"I know not," Cynaris said. He moved his hand over the still flank of the animal. It had no smell. It appeared to be resting.

"It's dead?" Batus asked, kneeling beside the animal.

"It was lowing. I reached to touch it and the cursed thing collapsed and died right before me."

An omen of the Apis god? What did this mean? "We must tell the commander."

"How many bulls were there altogether?"

"One hundred twenty."

"Who knows that number, save you, me, and the Egyptian priests?"

"Maybe that Egyptian on board!" Batus was silent a moment. "You think to deceive the high priest? The Minos?"

"*Eee*, well . . ." Cynaris grew silent. "Nay, it will not be deception, for he will not ask us."

"We should just confess."

"We could be blamed!"

"For what? Sick Egyptian bulls?"

"These are Apis bulls," Cynaris said. "This mark of the inverted pyramid makes them more than just cattle. Dare we offend the gods like this?"

Batus snorted. "Either offend the gods or be punished! Our choices are grim."

Cynaris stopped patting the animal and stood. "What will we do with the carcass?"

Batus looked at the dead bull, debating. "Who is in the galley?"

"An Alayshiyu serf. Why?"

"We shall dine well on this journey," he said with a smile.

"Feed the sacred bull to Mariners?"

"We serve the gods as much as or more so than any of the priesthood," Batus protested. "Our lives are subject to the whim of the Olimpi. We have earned the right to eat this sacred meat."

"Just so," Cynaris said. "But how will we get it to the cook?"

Batus knelt. "Pull out your blade, we must work quickly."

"What of the other bulls?"

"They are well. See, they stand in silence and watch us."

Cynaris knelt, blade in hand. "Just so, they watch us blaspheme."

THE MIST CLEARED AROUND HIM, and Niko saw two flickers of light. One after the other lit in an awkward rhythm. He moved without walking, drawing closer to the lights.

A low clicking noise grew louder, emanating from the flashes of color. He stood, looking down on an oddly shaped two-sided box. Its sides were curved into a point at either end. The top consisted of two pieces joined at an angle on the long sides.

His hands, the color of bleached linen, touched it, and he marveled at the smoothness of the wood. The clicking was growing louder, the flashes of color brighter.

He set aside the lid and looked in.

Niko shielded his eyes from the blinding contents.

Two rocks lay inside, each throbbing with color after color. One stone flashed in a continual spectrum of black to deep purple, blood red, clear red, orange, yellow; the colors were beautiful but inexplicably tragic, and Niko felt melancholy. The other stone flashed from purest piercing white through a range of blues and greens so indescribably rich that Niko blinked back tears.

Like living things, they flipped again and again, clattering against the sides of the smooth wooden box. The clear rhythm penetrated through to his bones. When Niko reached for them his hands exploded into flames.

Exquisite fire.

The pleasure was soul searing, his head filled with the song, the call, the clicking of the stones. Louder and louder . . .

He woke to see a bird pecking away at the tree, just next to his ear. Niko sat up, so thirsty he ached, disoriented from his dream. He rose to his feet, angry and confused. The Scholomance had taught that many times one's dreams were hidden truths.

Of course, such dreams could also come from eating undercooked squid.

In contrast with the previous day's silence, the island was brimming with life. Birds filled the trees, small animals poked their heads out of their holes, noses twitching. The woodlands were coming alive. Niko felt watched.

He ate what fruits he could gather, hoping the rich, juicy flesh would help him swallow, his mouth was so dry. He slept again, within the protection of the trees.

The next time he woke, he vomited. His head hurt and when he touched the back of it, he found a huge scab on his scalp, matted blood snarling his hair. He had a head wound? No wonder he'd been disoriented and sleepy. He needed water. Head pounding, he stumbled to his feet and began walking. Fallen needles and plants formed a springy pathway beneath his feet as Niko concentrated on moving one battered foot after another, forward.

The ground changed some time later; fine pebbles were laid in elaborate patterns of creatures and vines. Niko looked up in surprise. In the center of the clearing a pile of stones formed a table of sorts. An archway rose over it, standing fifteen, maybe eighteen cubits in the air. Niko walked forward.

The table's top was an obsidian slab that rested on two mounds of smooth river rocks the width of Niko's waist. The archway was formed of red sandstone. As Niko studied the odd structures, he became aware of a presence, as tangible as the smell of flowers or the low bellow of approaching cattle.

Niko saw no one. Terrified and awed beyond his understanding, Niko knelt. It was arrogance to come here and make demands, he realized. What had seemed a thoughtless matter, like feeding the Apis bull, suddenly expanded in difficulty. The thing that dwelt here would never be caged, could never be, he thought. It had no need for his food, or care. It was far more fearsome than any being Aztlan knew.

"I apologize," he whispered into the wind and rocks. The Aztlantu had forsaken their right to ask for anything. Niko realized he should leave. This god was too powerful, too terrifying, to confer with. Again Niko tried to force himself up, and again he stayed kneeling, head bowed, eyes closed. He couldn't make himself move.

Peace ruled here; no questions, no answers, a sense that none of it truly mattered.

A soothing, gentle breeze teased his hair, stinging the wound on his head. His eyes burned beneath his lids, yet he hesitated to open them. The sense of presence had grown stronger, and Niko felt if he just reached out he would touch . . . It.

He began to tremble.

Images flashed through his mind: his careworn parents, who had given their son the best life they could by giving him away; the young woman who had sweetly offered her body to him as a youth, whom he'd reduced to tears with a callous rejection; the fellow students he'd prided himself on surpassing and delighted in subtly humiliating. Finally, Phoebus, whom he had loved and hated in ways he dared not consider.

For the first time since stepping into the red-columned halls of the Scholomance, Niko broke down and wept. His secret shame, hidden pride, and fear—always fear—bubbled out. His tears slipped between the tiny patterned pebbles as he lay, twisted into a ball, sobbing.

When he opened his eyes later, the clearing was hazy with rose, gold, and purple light. Sunset, Niko thought. He heard rushing water and followed the sound to a stream. After rinsing his face and head wound and drinking till his belly felt tight, he leaned against the stone cliff, trying to gauge where he was.

A sound made him turn his head—and Niko shouted.

Not a hand's width from his nose was a grinning skeleton. He backed away like a crab, resisting the urge to run.

He'd been sitting at the entrance to a cave. A cave filled with skeletons.

They were not decently buried in *tholoi* beneath the earth with golden butterflies and octopus funeral symbols, but shelved here, like papyri scrolls, one beside the other. They wore pendants instead of death masks, their features melted away by time. What defilement was this?

Shivering, Niko leaned over one of the skeletons and blew at the dust that covered a medallion. The first part was impossible to read, but the latter part, written in the ancient Aztlantu script, was legible: "Resting Iavan son of Iapheth, son of Noach Who Tamed the Waters."

He blinked, his fingers tracing the letters. *A sole man, Iavan and his wife shipwrecked.* Had he found the burial island? Were these the earthly remains of Iavan? Gritting his teeth, Niko moved the bones around, looking over the other skeletons. No communication stones.

But he had found the right island!

Slowly he walked back to the clearing, the night sky blacked out by the haze from Mount Calliope. Where would the stones be? Leaning against the center altar, Niko felt very alone. There were no night sounds, but the hair on the back of his neck stood up.

Something was out there. Shuddering with fear, he hunched closer to the altar, his eyes tightly closed.

The breeze seemed to speak to him. "You asked, you shall receive. You sought, I have helped you find." The rhythmic beat of blood in his veins was nearly deafening until Niko realized he was hearing something else entirely.

The noise in his dream!

Beneath the altar was the odd-shaped box. Gently he lifted the peaked lid: the stones were inside. They were not imbued with actual color, but Niko could see the dark judgment of the one and the light mercy of the other. They were etched with the symbols of ancient Aztlan, the archaic text used before the Council decided the language needed to be symbols: skins, fish, men, instead of just arranged marks. But Niko knew these letters, the sacred letters.

In the mysterious glow of the box, he reached for the stones. Shaking them together in his hand and tossing them against the box, he saw them flash as they turned while they fell. On each throw, light caught certain characters. Eventually he could read words, and chains of words, spelled out.

"T-e-l-l-t-h-e-p-e-o-p-l-e-t-o-f-l-e-e-t-h-e-y-h-a-v-e-f-o-r-g-o-t-t-e-n."

"Forgotten what?" Niko asked, then tossed the stones.

"T-h-a-t-I-A-M-h-e-w-h-o-g-i-v-e-s-a-n-d-p-r-o-t-e-c-t-s."

Niko felt pierced to his very core. The god who had given them all the secrets of the earth and the sea, which Aztlan had forgotten, just as the tale said. Only two laws, and Aztlan had broken them both. Niko laid the stones inside the box and put the cover on it. They clattered riotously inside. Following the bidding he felt in his mind, he took them from the box and slipped them into his sash. They continued to move.

Aztlan had been forgiven. This great god who'd showed them everything and had been forsaken had given them another chance. Niko realized it took more strength to be gentle than harsh. It took more control and power to forgive than to punish, more character to be kind, especially to one who had erred. The mission he'd been entrusted with had been completed. This god wanted communication with them. He would save them. Niko need only believe.

CHAPTER 7

CAPHTOR

SIBYLLA SMILED AT THE PETITIONER. It was nice to have her body back. She was glad that the *skia*, the interloper, was resting. This was the world she knew, a world where the words made sense and her mind was not bludgeoned with strange images of silver birds, their bellies full of people, tablets with no folds, or a prediction box that never stayed focused for more than a few heartbeats.

Aye, here in Eleuthia Sibylla was at peace.

The meadow before the cave was bright green with new grass. She'd just walked the few *henti* from Knossos, through the fields. Caphtori were nudging the final olives from the trees, the fruit landing onto a cushion of sheepskin before it was gathered, bruised, crushed, and made into oil.

Spring was coming; the Season of the Bull was almost upon them. Vintners were busy cultivating the vines, trimming old growth away with sharp bronze blades, and burning the dead vines as an offering to Kela for allowing the roots to survive the winter. Golden stalks of winter wheat caught the brighter light, contrasting with the groves of almond trees, hinting pink with blossoms. Red and white anemones, yellow oxalis, and blue lupines were scattered across the fields.

Leaving her cloak at the guardian's small dwelling outside the cavern's entrance, Sibylla stepped into the cave. It was long, with fairly even ground and ceiling. Spots of light showed her where the petitioners stood, votives held like fallen stars. Amid whispers of "the Sibylla!" "the priestess of the winds," and her other titles, Sibylla walked carefully to the cave's center.

The earth's phallus in the cavern was a shoulder-high stalagmite as thick around as she was. Sibylla placed a piece of poppy gum on her tongue as she leaned against the stone. Within moments she felt a delicious lethargy steal through her body.

Come to me, Kela, she thought. I am open; let me see your divine loom. Let me foretell the futures of these children! The darkness that filled the cave seemed to fade, and she could see the faces of the petitioners.

Most petitioners were women; they came to learn when they would get with child, what they should name the child they carried, or what to do with the child they had. Sibylla spoke slowly, her words forming calm, ordered statements. The petitioners left gifts for her at the mouth of the maze enclosure.

Sleep licked at the edges of her mind, and Sibylla rested on the stalagmite, feeling the stone cradle her, comfort her. Her answers became less distinct.

Speak to me, she asked. Let me know.

Like a fine blade ripping a hide, knowledge sliced through her drug-induced stupor.

Fire. Blood. Dust.

Sibylla saw mountains black and red with lava. Trees that had been lush and green were charred stalks. Flowers were withered, birds lay dead, blackened, fruit was carbonized into lumps on the ground. Nothing moved. Nothing breathed.

Against her will she was pulled forward. Sibylla couldn't get her bearings, the sea had vanished beneath a mass of gray stone. The air was thick with sulfur. Bits of humanity—a broken pot, a scrap of cloth, a wooden doll—scattered the earth like macabre seeds.

Sibylla stood at the edge of a cliff and looked down.

Where a mountain had once stood, a gaping hole let her see into the wound of the earth. She turned away, looking back at the fields. But there were no fields, no orchards, no homes, no people. It was a wasteland; nothing moved, not a snake, not a spider.

Tell them. The words reverberated through her bones.

This couldn't be the future, Sibylla thought. It couldn't be her land.

Tell them.

Let me go! Sibylla cried. Leave me alone.

Tell them.

She opened her eyes to an audience of wide-eyed, openmouthed women.

The cave was too close. She needed air, she had to breathe. Pushing her way through the women, stumbling over the clay votives of birds, bulls, butterflies, and men, Sibylla fled through the cavern.

For an eyeblink she hesitated on the threshold, terrified that her vision was reality.

Sunlight blinded her, and she rubbed her eyes, looking around.

Green fields, the cry of a father to his daughter, the muted bleating of sheep.

Sibylla fell to her knees, shaking.

Relief or fear?

BELIEF WAS MORE DIFFICULT FOR NIKO when two days later he was still stranded. He walked along the shoreline, picking through driftwood and blocks of pumice in search of usable material. If he could just find a big enough piece of wood, he could hew a boat.

Provided he could find a blade, he amended.

Other pieces of the clansmen's lives had washed up: metal pots, linen sheeting, even a broken table. Try as he might, Niko could not recall where this island was in relation to Arachne. His tablet did not appear.

The stones were stowed safely in their box, silent once distance separated them. Still, in his mind he could hear the stones turning. Don't turn too much, he thought. You are needed for important questions.

If you are going to save me, he told the god irritably, please make it soon. I have done what I came to do; I am ready to leave.

So engrossed was he in searching the horizon for a ship and the shore for wood that he missed the sound. He attributed it to an animal or the waters themselves. A sound, a cry of pain, separated itself from the rush of the water, pulling him to awareness. Niko turned, trying to isolate the direction. There! Another cry!

Niko ran down the beach, following the sound, which grew louder with every step. He almost tripped over what he thought was a large black stone. *A woman.* Her body was badly burned: long singed hair shielded part of her body as she rolled back and forth, moaning. She must be in agony.

"Mistress?" Niko reached out toward her, recoiling when he saw her face. Lava burns. By the stones of Apis, was she dying? Her whole eye was glazed with fever, the other burned shut. Niko hoped his Scholomance education would be enough. When he lifted her into his arms, she screamed as her blistered skin pressed against him. She thrashed violently, upsetting his balance and tumbling them both into the surf.

Water washed over her. She didn't move. Ignoring her wounds, Niko turned her over, pounding the center of her back until she sputtered and coughed. He carried her to the clearing.

He dribbled fresh water into her mouth and tried to rinse her wounds. More than half of her body was scorched, as though she had been laid onto a sheet of scalding lava for just a few moments. One arm crossed her chest, her hand protected beneath her opposite arm. Despite his efforts, Niko could not get her to remove it. Fever gave her strength and she curled up, ripping at the sores swelling on her side and front.

After spending countless gray decans fighting her fever, Niko realized he had spent more time with this injured woman than he had with anyone in his life. He estimated she was younger than he, judging from what remained of her features. He tried to guess what she had looked like. She'd been a dyer, her hand was blue. Had she once been pretty? She never would be again. He traced one finger over an arched brow, down the healthy half of her face, circling a round cheek and dimple, feeling sorrow for her. Would it have been better to let her die?

On Niko's fifth night on the island, her fever soared. He soaked his kilt in an icy well and draped it over her, but her fever dried it faster than he could wet it. Stars were out when he fell asleep at her side, only to awaken from the heat of her body.

Half-awake, Niko carried her to the stream. He laid her in the shallows, holding her shoulders steady as the icy water flowed over her body. When he was shivering and sniffling, he pulled her back out, relieved that her body felt cooler. Lying her on the stone-paved ground, he poured bucket after bucket of cold water over her until she was shivering and chilled.

Afraid he'd gone too far, Niko bundled her in some of the linens he'd found on the beach and held her close. Her body had become as familiar to him as his own, and he was filled with a sensation he'd never felt before. She was his. He'd found her, restored her, she belonged to him. Cradling her to his side, he lay down.

"Master Niko?"

Was he dreaming? Niko moved but felt weight holding him down. His arm was numb. "Master Niko?" the voice repeated. Niko's throat felt as though he'd dined on sand, and he swallowed gingerly before opening his eyes.

Mariners. They stood politely in a circle around him with their pressed green kilts and clean hair blowing in the wind. His ship must have freed birds before they went down, so the Mariners knew where to search. Niko was very conscious of being naked. The cool, soft body next to him made him very aware of his own body. "Her fever!" he croaked, rolling the woman flat on her back, peeling his kilt off her. "It is down!"

She was still asleep, but her body felt cooler and her wounds were weeping. "Sheets," he commanded one of the Mariners. "Wine. Herbs." He noticed the men look away from her damaged face and body. "Contact Spiralmaster, she will need immediate care."

"She will have to wait, master," a Mariner said. "We are treating the survivors, the few there are, of Delos first."

"She is mine. That gives her precedence." The Mariner didn't argue and another gave Niko sheets. Gingerly he wrapped her, then gave her drink. Despite his exhaustion Niko would not allow anyone else to carry her. Once aboard he remembered the stones.

Back at the clearing, he found the box where he had left it, the white and black stones safe inside. He couldn't risk dropping the box in the sea or someone stealing it. He ripped the hem of his kilt, then tied one palm-size stone into each side of the makeshift sash and wrapped it around his waist. The stones thudded against his thighs as he walked, but they didn't turn. The boat was already in the shallows, crowded with the survivors of the Clan of the Muse. Niko pulled himself onto the deck as the Mariners rowed to the ship. The blue-purple sail of Aztlan caught the wind, taking them home.

THE GREAT GREEN

THE RUSH OF WAVES WOKE HIM, and Cheftu jerked alert. A north-western, cutting wind pulled at the ship. He tightened his kilt and lurched toward the mast. Lightning struck in the distance, and he could see the white froth of angry, churning waves. Thunder sounded around them, and Cheftu held on to the ropes as he made his way back to his scarce possessions.

He sank down on the deck, wincing at his sore leg, clutching his cloak around him. The waves rocked the ship, and lightning flashed again. The sailors' shouts carried on the wild wind that whipped first from the west, then from the north, pushing them farther away from Aztlan. From their direction, due north, he guessed this mysterious kingdom was close to Greece; maybe it even was Greece. He'd never heard of Aztlan, except when he was in Hatshepsut's Egypt. This clothing, this language, none of it was familiar. He shivered.

Cheftu doubted they would arrive within five days, as the captain had claimed. The captain of the *Krybdys* had chosen to sail directly across the Great Green from Egypt to Caphtor, then on to Aztlan. Nestor and his shipment of cattle were out of sight, aboard the *Cybella.*

Sailing across the Great Green in wintertime was unheard of in Egypt. The few times the Egyptians sailed at all, they always stayed within sight of land. The Arabs, Turks and Greeks of Cheftu's century did the same, tacking up the coast of the Holy Land, then over to Turkey and into the Aegean Sea. The winds were too unpredictable, too many people had died on the Mediterranean in the winter. Most ships docked until spring.

The Aztlantu sailed the sea year round, the feat that made them a powerful, intimidating thalassocracy. Water splashed Cheftu, cold in sudden twilight. He huddled in his cloak, staring at the grayish substance sifting down from the sky. Warm and gray.

He'd seen this before.

Cheftu closed his eyes, reliving the pain and pleasure of that moment. *He and Chloe, together on their wedding couch, savoring the newness of each other. Skin sliding on skin, their mingled scents . . . then the knock at the door and his loyal slave holding out a handful of this stuff. A powder was falling, he'd said, causing weeping wounds.*

Volcanic ash.

Cheftu blinked as his vision became flat, filled with the falling gray. He could feel it accumulating on the deck around his sandal-shod feet. It retained a small element of heat, and he heard the Mariners mumbling among themselves. They had quickly adjusted their shields so that the rowers were protected.

He wished he understood Aztlantu.

Soon he was pressed into service, helping to clear the deck so the weight of the ash didn't send them to the bottom of the sea. It was too dense to see, and Cheftu blindly scooped and threw—over the side, he hoped. The wind was so loud, licking the ash into dervishes, that he could hear nothing.

Except the crack of wood shattering as the mast was struck by lightning.

The thunder masked the cries of sailors crushed beneath the flaming upper mast. Fire consumed the wooden ship in a terrible frenzy. They were going down.

Tongues of flame engulfed the deck, and the wind carried away both cries and commands. Cheftu looked around for escape. The rest of the mast fell, creating a curtain of fire dividing the ship and casting a hellish glow on the screaming sailors and tossing waves. Men jumped overboard, their bodies living torches. Others hacked away madly at the wooden planks. Cheftu grabbed his bitumen-covered reed trunk.

The sound of splintering wood muffled the whip of waves, wind, and the boom of thunder. Cheftu felt the deck shift beneath him, and he fell, sliding for cubits. He reached out for something to grab, but the ship was tilting too quickly. The roars of the bulls in the hold made the boat vibrate.

Another crack and the ship split in two. The ash was blinding, clogging his throat and nose. As he covered his mouth, the ship shifted and Cheftu was thrown from the deck into the sea.

White water closed over his head.

Cheftu came up gasping, coughing, narrowly missing being hit by a plank. With powerful kicks he swam away from the burning wreckage, hauling the few bodies he saw onto his piece of wood. He pounded backs and breathed into men's mouths, making them cough and sputter and come back to life. He'd been a physician before, but the modern skills he'd learned from Chloe gave him the appearance of a god now.

Relinquishing his piece of wood to the four men clutching it, Cheftu swam across the dark sea toward the other bobbing heads.

It was raining paste made of ash and water, and Cheftu knew they wouldn't be able to breathe for long. The night was black, pelting them, and Cheftu couldn't even see the horizon. Would they just let the tide take them? Holding on to a new buoy, Cheftu joined the Mariners in kicking away from the wreckage and heading gods only knew where.

They sighted land about the time the sky began to lighten. Cheftu's legs trembled when they finally walked up on the beach. For decans, they fished people from the sea.

Cheftu pounded another Mariner's back until he vomited up seawater, coughing and wheezing. He'd just washed in on the tide. Cheftu next walked down the hard pebbled beach and assisted some other sailors. No one had seen the commander, and seven others were still missing. Aztlantu Mariners trained well, though. The men knew these waters and could easily find an island with fresh water. Unless of course, they were wounded. Cheftu learned through halting Aztlantu that if a Mariner could not swim back to his ship, he was declared dead.

Cheftu masked his expression at this statement of Aztlantu callousness.

Ignoring the thanks he received, he moved to the next group, setting a broken arm and checking on the unconscious cabin boy.

Cheftu climbed up to the cliff that overlooked the beach and the rest of the island, a cheerless expanse of gray. He stared out at the water. Ash floated atop the waves, obscuring their brilliant blue. He knew of no term for "volcano" in Egyptian or in Aztlantu. Where was the eruption?

The birds in which the Aztlantu put so much store had been released as the ship was hit. Even now, the Mariners assured him, Aztlantu were on their way to rescue them. A group of men had hiked into the interior of the island in search of fresh water. Another contingent had begun repairing the small boat that buoyed many of them up last night.

The bulls were lost. Cheftu winced as he thought of the terrified animals fighting against their greater weight, going down in the hull of the ship. He hoped the Aztlantu Council would not hold Egypt responsible. The ship they'd been sailing on was Aztlantu, the storm was no one's fault, but it was impossible to predict the Aztlantu reaction.

Cheftu watched as one of the men staggered to his feet. Several of them seemed to have seawater in their ears; their balance was uncertain. One seaman seemed on the verge of collapse. Cheftu frowned; perhaps the Mariner had received some type of blow during the wreck and it had . . . had what? Those who were disoriented had neither wounds nor any other visible injuries.

Dehydration, Cheftu surmised, looking out on the beach. The sun was almost obscured by clouds of ash, and each man had tied a cloth over his nose and mouth to breathe. His gaze moved over the laid-out bodies of the sick. Cheftu closed his eyes as a wave of dizziness swept over him. Deliberately he swallowed, intent on staying upright. Dehydration and exhaustion. The dizziness passed and Cheftu tried to concentrate.

Why was he here? If his calculations were correct, he was in the Middle Kingdom. Why?

He stretched. Why here, in the Aegean Sea? With this Aztlan empire he'd never heard of outside Egypt? A missing culture. The idea was somehow familiar, but he was too weary to pursue it. Slowly he clambered down the bluff, brushed off his dingy kilt, and adjusted the pack on his back.

Frantic shouts drew his attention, and he ran around the foot of the bluff to the open beach. Two of the sick Mariners were fighting, their hands locked around each other's throats. Cheftu shouted for assistance as he tried to pull them apart. The one being attacked was blue, unable to breathe, but holding his hands around the other's throat with an uncanny, fever-driven strength. Both were big, sinewy men, and Cheftu couldn't break their grips.

"Somebody help me!" he shouted, looking for a way to separate them. "You idiots!" he yelled in Egyptian. "You kill yourselves on your deathbeds? What madness is this?" He raised a piece of drift-wood and brought it down on both their heads.

Hands still around each other's throats, the men fell, unconscious. The other Mariners watched wide-eyed, muttering about Cynaris and Batus. Cheftu gestured for the men to be laid on the sand. With a grim expression, Cheftu lashed their hands and feet together. If they died, they would be freed, but they were not allowed to kill each other. Not in his infirmary—even if it *was* just a beach!

Niko stood outside Spiralmaster's laboratory door. His hands were clammy, he couldn't ever recall being so excited. He'd run to his mentor as soon as he'd been assured that the young woman would survive. Blood poisoning had set in through her wound, and Niko was ashamed to admit he'd not seen her hand. Or, rather, not seen the stub where her hand had been. Now she slept easily. She had fought the infection well, and Niko had finally felt free to leave her side.

What would the Spiralmaster say about the stones? What myster-ies could they learn from this god, together? Niko stepped in, and Imhotep turned to him. In these past weeks, the Spiralmaster had aged a dozen summers. The normally well-groomed man was in stained linen, his face unshaven. "My master?" Niko said question-ingly.

Spiralmaster's side seemed twisted, and Niko was dismayed at how slowly and awkwardly the man moved. Niko took a deep breath, then announced, "My master, I found the stones." From each side of his kilt he pulled a stone.

The white one.

The black one.

Spiralmaster looked at each one, rubbing bent fingers over the etched letters.

"Do you know how they work?" Spiralmaster's words were so

slurred that Niko had to ask three times before he could understand his mentor's query. What in the name of Apis had happened?

"Aye," Niko said, shaking his head. "If you look closely, you see that each mark is lined with gold, to catch the light. Ask the question and the answer is spelled out." He assumed Spiralmaster knew the ancient language, though Daedalus had been Niko's instructor.

Imhotep looked at the stones. "The elixir," he mumbled.

Niko tossed the stones. No light caught the engraved letters. "Perhaps the question needs to be rephrased," he suggested.

Imhotep leaned against the table, muttering about the elixir.

Niko was shocked to see his master, his clan chieftain, so helpless. What had happened? What went wrong? Imhotep was shouting, "Elixir!" and Niko threw the stones. Again, no answer.

"Is there an elixir?" he asked.

Nothing. Perhaps the question wasn't specific enough.

Be specific, Niko thought. "Is there an elixir for immortality?"

He threw the stones and frowned at the response before remembering to translate it into the common language. He looked up at Imhotep, his face frozen with incredulity. "There *is* an elixir," he said.

"Ingredients," Imhotep mumbled.

"What are the ingredients?" Yet what good was this question without a literal and fluent understanding of the ancient tongue? As he expected, the stones gave no answer but lay silent.

A summons at the door, and Niko hid the stones. A serf informed them that another of Zelos' *hequetai* were ill.

Imhotep paled and Niko led the elderly man to his bed, appalled at the fragility of bones he felt beneath Imhotep's clothing. What was happening to his master? The Spiralmaster was muttering, agitated, yet Niko couldn't understand a word he said. He put the stones within reach of Spiralmaster, one on each side of his couch.

"Ingredients!" the older man shrieked.

"Ask the stones, my master. I do not know what they are. Two clicks will be nay, three will be aye."

"You know this how?"

"It is the language, my master. Three consonants and a vowel are an aye, two consonants only for nay. Count the clicks for the answer."

Niko closed the door at Spiralmaster's command to be left alone. Something was wrong with him; gods knew what it was.

Young sea urchin, Imhotep thought, listening to the boy's steps on the staircase. So these were the great legacy of Iavan's god? Imhotep squinted, trying to make out the letters. He bellowed for a serf to get him more light. Even with a torch above him, Imhotep could not read the sacred writing.

Should he take them to Kela's temple? Or perhaps the Pyramid of Days? His mind was cloudy. Imhotep touched the glass vial before him. A liquid moved in it, an important liquid, but he couldn't remember what it was.

He scooped up the stones in one trembling, lined hand and was slowly putting them in his side pouch when they began to move. Imhotep opened his palm and saw them twisting and turning, blinding him as light caught the silver-and-gold letters.

"What is in the recipe?" he asked the stones. He tossed them and got no answer. "Is water in the recipe?"

Nay.

Okh! This was how to do it! He had to pose aye/nay questions. Imhotep snapped for a scribe and began to ask the stones about ingredients.

Decans later Spiralmaster glared at the stones, frustrated by their apparent inability to speak beyond "aye" or "nay." Time was running short for *Hreesos,* for Imhotep, for them all. He needed the answers the stones could give him.

Through the stones, he now knew his elixir was one ingredient short.

Which ingredient was the query.

Painstakingly Imhotep listed every element he had, rolling the stones and reading the answer. "Nay. Nay. Nay. Nay." His scribe long since dismissed, Imhotep racked his tired brain. So close, by Kela, so close! Wearily the old man tossed the stones again.

Nay.

He named another herb.

Nay.

Another.

Nay.

Another.

Nay.

Spiralmaster sighed and moved on to another list. He must find the last ingredient! They could not fail this close to the finish! He turned the leather page and resumed his questioning.

The stones resumed their negative responses.

Nay.

Nay.

Nay.

"What can we do to save our people?" he asked rhetorically, throwing the stones. They clattered repeatedly. What did that mean, *eee?*

Numbness stole his breath and pain squeezed his head. Imhotep's hand went slack, the stones sliding across the painted floor in two directions, the imprinted letters dancing on the tiles.

"F-L-E-E!"

Y'CARUS MOVED STIFFLY ACROSS THE SLOPING DECK. Without thought he helped raise the sail, the nearby conversations and time-keeper's drum low throbs against his pain. *Neotne.* Just saying her name was like the scrape of a blade. He looked across the sea. Though it was far away, the vision of the smoldering island was clear in his head.

As though a giant had cleaved it with a blade from above, Delos Island was torn in half. Where once the main street had run past the shops of weavers, dyers, and merchants, now a deep, jagged hole, half-filled with houses and bodies, cut through town. Lashed to flood levels by the sea, the river had submerged those who did not die in the quake.

Or in the fires.

Y'carus shook his head in absentminded agreement with some lesser Mariner's inquiry, the man's words lost in Y'carus' memory of the lava flows. Like uncoiling serpents, streams of molten rock had slithered from the peak to the shore. When Y'carus had first heard of the eruption, he'd pushed himself, his ship, and his crew to the farthest reaches of their endurance.

Still, he had arrived too late.

They'd landed on the island at night, shocked silent by the view of the mountain, glowing red and black like the wood of a banked fire. They couldn't get to the shore; the harbor was clogged with debris, including bodies.

With a small rowboat he'd landed, commanding his men to pick up any survivors and take them to safety on the neighboring island of Paros. Y'carus couldn't help but think the safest place of all was the sea. The islands were suspect now; friend or foe?

Past sea skirmishes had not prepared him for the sights of destruction and loss. Though lava had ceased to flow, it covered everything, so hot that the hairs on his legs were singed from walking by it.

Shapes bulged out from the mixture of mud and rock. Y'carus could make out the forms of women and children—caught in the savage rush to the sea. The stink of roasted meat hung in the air. Above it all was silence.

Nothing lived in this once crowded city.

He'd gone toward the house of his bloodparents, but he could not get close. The building was indiscernible from another dozen like it. All of them had been flattened, moved, and submerged by heated earth. Y'carus roamed past lush green gardens now buried under glowing red rocks; a river silted motionless by ash and debris. He stumbled silently, hurting so badly that he could do no more than put one foot before the other.

After his search he walked to the tip of the island, the last spot of green—the meeting point with his ship.

The few who'd survived the horror were gathered there. Most were naked, some burned so badly that they glistened as though covered in oil or grape juice. These people were dying slowly, their mouths, tongues, and throats so burned, they could scarcely breathe and swallow. One person, he couldn't identify gender, had rasped, "Thirsty, thirsty, thirsty." When Y'carus brought water from a nearby well the person had choked on it and died in Y'carus' arms.

He tightened the appropriate ropes, his thoughts on Arachne. Help had arrived from the empire—a belated sacrifice of men and material. Four ships of fleeing survivors had made it to Naxos, Clan of the Vine, nearby, and another three shiploads of Arachne survivors had been pulled from the sea.

No dyers among them.

Y'carus answered questions from the crew, doing his tasks while inside he smoldered just as the city now did. *Hreesos* Zelos had declared the clan dead—for certainly the sheep, the looms, the ships, and most of the citizens who worked them were dead. And that was that. Thousands were lost, and the empire tallied, weighed, and sailed past. Now it appeared the island was falling into the sea. His precious Neotne, encased in a sarcophagus of angry rock, would sink beneath the waves.

The Scholomance must have realized the eruption was coming. The Cult of the Snake oracles must have known! Obviously neither cared about a small clan—not enough to warn the clansmen.

He pulled out his blade, polishing the bronze with the edge of his cloak. The empire was falling. It had forsaken him. He'd spent his life at sea, trusting that the empire would care for his family while he was away, protect his loved ones even as Y'carus protected the empire.

He had been deceived.

"Master?"

Y'carus looked up. His second in command stood next to a tall man whose features were nearly indistinguishable beneath a covering of ash. Poor shipwrecked fools, he thought.

"Who are you?" he asked.

The man frowned slightly, then spoke in broken Aztlantu. He introduced himself as Cheftu, an Egyptian guest. Y'carus called for the fleet log and saw that Cheftu had been on one of the three boats sailing to Kallistae from Egypt. A guest? Y'carus realized the man was a hostage.

"The Apis bulls, they were drowned?" he asked.

It took the Egyptian a moment to reply.

"Send a swallow, find out if the other two shipments arrived," Y'carus instructed his scribe. "I am Y'carus, commander of this ship," he said. "Welcome."

The Egyptian bowed in his foreign way, and Y'carus began to move away.

"My . . . master," the Egyptian said.

"Aye?"

"This ash, do you know where the eruption was?"

Y'carus looked away, blinking rapidly. "Aye."

"Are there survivors? I am a mage, a physician."

His Aztlantu was painful to listen to, but he seemed earnest.

"Those who lived are beyond aid. In the end, there will be no . . . survivors."

"I am sorry," he said in Egyptian, one of the few phrases Y'carus knew. "Did you have family there?"

"I did."

The two men stared at each other, then turned away. The Egyptian made his way to the prow, and Y'carus called after him, "Egyptian, you will dine with me tonight." The man made his funny bow again, and Y'carus turned back to the business of sailing. He checked his log.

Knossos tomorrow, the Greeting Kela Ceremony.

WAS SHE SLEEPING OR AWAKE? The room was dark, and for a moment Chloe was afraid, disoriented. However, there was no sense of oppression here as in the cave. Something brushed her waist, and she turned sharply. Her hair? A mass of curls hung down her back. She leaned against a wall, struggling to get her bearings.

Sharing a body with Sibylla was like trying to control a Chinese dragon, Chloe thought. One person could see out the front, the rest had to follow and trust the consciousness in command. When Sibylla was in control, Chloe saw only bits and pieces, not a complete picture. She was glad they had come to a "driving" agreement.

Hearing noises outside her chamber, Chloe fumbled for clothing. Clumsily she lit the alabaster oil lamp. A skirt hung on a peg on the wall, and Chloe slipped it over her head, shimmying so it fell to her waist. It was a riot of pattern, five ruffled tiers, each different, though in the same saffron-and-crimson color scheme. A jacket, the sleeves padded so that they were stiff and very fitted, hung next to the skirt. Chloe slipped it on. It wouldn't meet in the middle. The elbow-length sleeves fit, the waist was in the proper place, but it tied *beneath* her breasts. No coverage.

She stared at her breasts and suddenly knew this was normal. Breasts were not erotic, they were nursing bottles. Her back and shoulders, *they* were sexy. Breasts, no. A red leather belt wrapped twice around her waist and tied in back.

Her hair was everywhere, long, curly strands caught in her clothing and in her mouth. She felt like a molting bird. Spitting out her errant hair, she picked up the heavy pendant that hung between her very bare breasts.

Her mind felt clearer than it had since she'd woken in Sibylla's body, she realized as she read the symbols easily. She was Sibylla Sirsa Olimpi, chieftain of the Clan of the Horn, born in the Season of the Snake . . . the equivalent of December 23. Chloe felt chilled. The symbols on the disk looked vaguely familiar, even from her modern perspective.

Very familiar. She'd seen them on her mother's desk her entire life. They covered a duplicate of the Phaistos disk, an as yet undeciphered clue about the pre-Greek culture in Crete and Santorini.

Chloe sat down, her head with its wealth of black curls in her hands.

This was unbelievable. Was she dreaming? Sir Arthur Evans had discovered the palace of Knossos and named the wisps of culture he found there after Greek mythology. Her own mother had worked on one of their ash-covered towns.

Minoans.

Mom's specialization. The mysterious, lost race of the Aegean.

Chloe snapped up, grabbing the oil lamp with trembling hands and pacing the perimeter of the room. Where was she? This wasn't Santorini, that was certain. So it must be Crete? "Oh God, Mom, why didn't I pay more attention," she muttered.

In modern Crete she'd gone shopping and wind surfing while the rest of the family hung out in the museum and the archaeological sites. She'd never been to Knossos before. It was no surprise if she didn't recognize it. Was this Knossos?

Setting the lamp down before she dropped it and made the question moot, Chloe racked her brain. Her mother's specialty was Santorini. She'd been working there when she met Chloe's father.

Someone knocked and Chloe froze, staring at the door.

"My mistress?"

"Enter," she called with Sibylla's understanding of the language. A nymph came into the room. Her costume was similar to Chloe's, though not as finely crafted, and her skirt had only three tiers. She held her arms at right angles to her body, then bent at the elbow for right angles again.

"The sun rises, mistress. Kela comes!"

Chloe listened intently for a clue from Sibylla, but the voice was silent. Was she asleep? I could use some hints, Chloe thought. Like what the hell do I do? Priestess ritual stuff is your job!

Nothing.

The girl repeated her strange salute and held the door open. Presumably for Chloe—Sibylla—whoever I am, Chloe thought. The hallway was so narrow and dark, she could barely see the edge of the girl's skirt. Then light flooded them and Chloe looked up. They stood at the edge of a huge staircase, the roof above cut through so a well of light fell to the bottom floor. While the rooms and corridors had been plain, this chamber was not.

Chloe looked around as unobtrusively as possible. Pattern on pattern on pattern. It was like a Todd Oldham visual cacophony in a four-color palette: spirals, squares, circles, diamonds, and stars. A painted procession of life-size gift bearers walked down the steps with them, carrying fruit and grain, boxes filled with spices, rhytons with wine. Punctuating the artwork were piano-legged columns in red, black, and gold.

Chloe swayed. She knew that column! A thousand images crowded in her mind: an interior design class examining the columns of ancient people. "In Crete we find the first examples of many design motifs. First, they crafted a piano-leg-style column that had a simplistic capital and base. They also are the first civilization who used the wave, the Greek key, and various other repeating designs. The main color scheme of goldenrod, carnelian, and Mars black was probably inspired by the building materials available to them."

She was a Minoan!

A refrain of "Ohmigod, ohmigod, ohmigod" followed her until they reached the ground floor. Chloe had to stifle an astonished whistle. The room was enormous, brilliantly colored pattern covering every inch of the place: floor, roof, doorways. Paintings were featured on each wall, framed in black and red.

People milled about, handsome men in very brief kilts with long hair, women, also with long hair, in the same costume as Chloe. Most wore high-heeled sandals. The scents of perfume, sweat, and cooking permeated the room, and Chloe was grateful to follow the nymph out into a garden.

Sibylla had never given her such control before. Usually by the time she was dressing, the other woman informed her it was time to "move over" and let the professional handle it. Where was Sibylla?

Nevertheless, this was cool. She was a Minoan. Man, the life I lead, she thought.

The sun shone dimly, and Chloe reminded her cold nipples that it couldn't be much into February. In Crete, but when? Asking Sibylla would do no good. Her concept of time was not measured in terms of A.D. and B.C.E. Preclassical Greece, she knew that, but that information only narrowed the search by two thousand years. Why was she here in ancient Crete?

It seemed rather elaborate for her to travel through time just to help with natural disasters. Wasn't she a little arrogant to think time would be arranged because she was so good at emergency management? It didn't seem as though she were going to get her hands on any paint in this lifetime, so what was her purpose? Her thoughts were like a hamster in a cage. Run run run run run—going nowhere.

The two women continued down the stairs, through another tunnel, down another set of stairs, a left turn, a right turn, up stairs, turn again. A portico, a hallway, another series of artistically chaotic rooms.

These people were fixated on labyrinths, another Minoan motif.

When they walked into one more room the women saluted her immediately, with the right-angle gesture. "The Sibylla," the nymph said, and left.

A woman with a protrusion of feathers poking from her hair came forward. "Greetings, mistress. We are honored you would dance with us today. We trust that Kela will speak through you?"

Chloe felt as though she'd swallowed a porcupine, but Sibylla woke up and answered appropriately and graciously. Chloe watched uneasily. Dancing, *more* dancing! What was it with ancient cultures and dancing?

Someone put kohl on her eyes, drawing the lines up and out, not in the Egyptian style, but still very exotic. Red cream was brushed over her lips, and her hair was tied back in pieces, topped with a flat-crowned hat adorned with feathers. Following the other women, she walked down to the lowest level.

The room was quiet, yet thick with presence. Chloe braced herself. The silence seemed ominous, but Sibylla was completely comfortable. The floor was sunken in the middle, and the sunken portion seemed to writhe. A woman waded through the shifting, slithering mass and lit the raised oil lamp.

Snakes! My God, millions of snakes! Minoans also had a thing for snakes, she suddenly recalled. Chloe cringed, but Sibylla calmly accepted a few serpents, winding them around her arms as living bracelets. A priestess wrapped a snake around Sibylla's hat and another serpent around her waist. Chloe completely withdrew; Sibylla could handle today. If *this* wasn't ritual, then she couldn't guess what would be. She'd have to trust Sibylla. Reluctantly Chloe stepped into the darkness of the mind. Wow, she was in Crete.

Her mind clearer than it had felt since she woke in the cave, Sibylla asked the names of her snakes and spent a few moments petting them, growing accustomed to the dry weight that tightened and loosened around her arms and waist.

Music prompted them from above, to a worship ritual of the goddess Kela. When the first butterflies returned to Knossos, it was time to greet Kela and welcome her back to life. The goddess of the earth died every year when the winds rose and was reborn with the butterflies and the snakes. People came from all over Caphtor to participate in welcoming Kela. Already crowds gathered, a good omen. The Shell Seekers had prepared a feast, and the smell of broiling fish, fresh mussel stew, and grilled shrimp hung on the morning air.

AZTLAN

"WAKE UP, MISTRESS! WE GREET KELA TODAY!"

Ileana rose up on her elbows, trying to open her eyes. Wine from the night before pounded in her head, and her mouth was fleecy. By Kela, what had she done? Even the cry of her pets was annoying. She buried her head in the linens, trying to recall the night before.

Bedded Priamos while eating *kreenos*, she recalled.

Oh, Kela!

Weary and aching, Ileana allowed herself to be carried to the bath, then slowly massaged with warm water and oil until she was awake. The serf's hands were gentle and knowing, and Ileana felt herself drifting and peaceful.

She needed to wake up! This was an important day! A day of dancing and joy, in which she was the centerpiece. For the first time in her life, Ileana cringed at the idea of being the focus of the hundreds and thousands who would come to the island's cave sanctuary to see her.

The door that adjoined her apartments with Zelos' burst open. With a snap he dismissed her serfs and sank heavily onto the edge of her bath. Though *Hreesos* was still golden, still desirable, lines tugged his face earthward and sorrow clouded his eyes.

"Another of my *hequetai* is dead, Ileana."

"Another?"

"That makes seven in the past twenty days."

"They were all older men, Zelos."

He looked away, and Ileana recalled that his cabinet were all his age. Just a few years older than she was, Ileana thought distastefully. "Do you suspect something?"

"What would be the point? Phoebus will rule, instate his own *hequetai*. Save to hurt Aztlan, what would be the motive?"

"I know not," Ileana said impatiently. "I must prepare for today, though."

"*Eee* . . . one of your favorite days, mother-goddess? When you are worshiped and adored? How you live for that."

Too weary to fight, Ileana just glared. Zelos rose and walked back to his open doorway, stumbling into the frame. Ileana watched in shock as he grabbed the door for balance and tore it off the hinges. The sound brought serfs running, but none dared approach *Hreesos*. With deliberate moves he pulled himself up, threw the door aside, and stalked into his chambers without a backward glance.

Ileana rose from her bath and stood while her serf dried her body and oiled it. She snapped for feathers to adorn her hair.

What had the *hequetai* died from?

Could Phoebus have it and be dying?

Please Kela!

CAPHTOR

CHEFTU LOOKED AT THE JUMBLE OF EMPTY BOATS in the harbor of Amnisos. Where were the people? He turned to Y'carus. "Is something wrong?"

"Nay, Egyptian. Just the start of the growing year. Everyone is in Knossos." With sharp commands, the Mariners slid the Aztlantu ship into place, dropping her sails and anchor at the same time. There was a nervous excitement about the men, and Cheftu noticed they all kept glancing hopefully toward the land. Strangely, no ash had fallen here.

He could see Caphtor was a beautiful country. Caphtor was the root of the word "column." Biblically, Caphtor was Greece and the islands around her. This wasn't Greece; they hadn't sailed long enough. Looking over the perfect natural harbor, snow-covered mountains on the distant horizon, cypress and fir towering over the white, gold, red, and black buildings, he surmised this was a Greek island. The purple blue of the Aegean contrasted sharply with the spring green. Cheftu pressed his lips together, the scholar retreating as the aching man advanced. How Chloe would have loved to see this. Her artist's mind would have reveled in the colors, the contrasts—

Cheftu forced away the thought and helped one Mariner as he straightened some lines. Why were the sailor's hands trembling? Y'carus walked around the deck, checking everything before commanding the men to disembark.

Never before had Cheftu seen any military group scramble to get in line with the enthusiasm these men did! They stood at sharp attention, the wind blowing their short green kilts and long hair. Y'carus turned to Cheftu and beckoned. Pulling at the tie of his Egyptian kilt, Cheftu walked down the plank to the dock.

Their pace through town allowed little time for observation. Nothing was open, anyway. Through closed markets and stalls they walked, fast. Cheftu felt his lack of exercise, the ache of his ankle, but he was determined not to fall behind. Y'carus strode easily, his stocky legs eating up the *henti*.

The sun rose higher, and they began to see more people. Dressed in their finest, families with children young and old were striding up the same paved road. Arching trees filtered the sunlight, and periodically Cheftu saw an altar of horns on the side of the path.

"They are places for petitioners to refresh themselves before they reach Kela," Y'carus explained.

"As a resting place?"

"Aye, but also because that is where water is pumped. They can have a drink, maybe even a little wash, before they reach the pavement."

The closer they got to the pavement, the more people Cheftu saw. Men, older women, and children. Where were the young women in this society? They trooped under an archway of stones and up a set of shallow steps. Cheftu stumbled when he saw the first young woman.

He didn't notice her face, just her clothing. Or rather, the lack thereof. He looked away quickly, his cheeks heated. He'd seen many dresses that revealed as much, but never displayed so provocatively. He saw another woman, and another. "Y'carus," he said, his voice strained, "are these all, umm . . ." He looked at the young commander.

"Nay," Y'carus said, clapping Cheftu's shoulder. "The Coil Dancers are the ones who dress alluringly. They show shoulder." His tone was aloof, though it deepened on the word "shoulder." Cheftu had to bite his lip to keep from laughing. A woman who showed her shoulders was more alluring than these dark-eyed, small-waisted women, whose breasts pushed forward like offerings?

Their steps slowed when they reached the mass of people. Hawkers walked through the crowd, offering skewered shrimp, oranges, goat cheese balls rolled in fresh herbs, sesame and honey strips, wine, votive statues, and flower rings. The air of festivity was contagious, and the Mariners eased their stance.

No one trespassed onto the enormous pavement opposite the steps and the tree-shaded gardens. Rising three stories above the pavement was a small portico, with a solitary red column tapering from floor to roof. On the shaded wall behind it Cheftu could barely glimpse a painting.

The portico was part of the palace, constructed as a series of saffron and white boxes stacked on each other, different levels at different points. Red-columned porches and balconies were crowded with people, tiny figures from this distance. All of Caphtor watched today, it seemed.

A jangle, like that of a sistrum, quieted the crowd. Cheftu saw the rapt expression on the Mariners' faces. Tritons held in one hand, the other hand on their hip, they stared in fascination at the empty pavement. The sound of pipes rose on the air, a plaintive minor note that brought utter silence.

The dancers came out, spinning recklessly, rapidly, and Cheftu held his breath, the tension of the crowd infectious. Could he forget Chloe for just a few hours? He was weary with sorrow. Dozens of dancers filled the pavement, then stopped altogether, forming a striking tableau of bright reds, blues, gold against the white stone. Some of the women wore hats, others' hair was unbound.

Every last one of them had upthrust, beckoning breasts. Cheftu closed his eyes. What manner of man—nay, beast—could lust after another woman's body so soon after losing his wife? He opened his eyes again and recoiled. Snakes were draped over the women.

The music started again, slowly, and the dancers divided into groups.

"They will reenact the legend of the first coming of Kela," Y'carus whispered.

Cheftu watched as one group of women pretended to toil at the earth, wiping their brow and grimacing at the hard work. Another group of women descended on them, stomping on the fields, lashing out at the first group. "Savage winter, the Season of the Serpent," Y'carus explained. The first group of women mourned, tearing at their hair and rubbing imaginary ash on their heads. As the music deepened a woman emerged from the building. Obviously she was representative of Kela.

The moment she appeared, Cheftu ceased to follow the plot. She struck a chord so deep within him that he fisted his hands to keep from reaching toward her. Her features were indistinguishable at this distance, but her grace was apparent. With slow, sinuous movements she coaxed the fruits from the earth. Cheftu guessed the "fruits" were the temple prostitutes, for they flashed their shoulders and the crowd literally groaned.

Arousal stirred the warming air as the dance became provocative. Another woman danced with Kela.

"She is the bull god," Y'carus whispered. "She wears the boot."

The dancer used a snake and a lot of imagination to impregnate the earth mother. Cheftu shifted positions, trying not to stare at her, want her. She was not Chloe. He looked at the palace instead. It was big, made of hard stone . . . hard . . . He swallowed and looked back at the woman.

They danced in a circle now, an elaborate pattern that first moved forward, then backtracked, like a potter's wheel. Cheftu noted their motions as he fought the irrational lust he felt for the unknown dancer. He had no idea why, he just knew he desired that woman. Desperately. Using gestures that needed no explanation, the women danced with the snakes. *His* woman's snake was slithering over her breasts, and her dance grew more frenzied, more erotic. Hands on each other's wrists, the priestesses were running lightly, spiraling in and out, creating elaborate designs. Cheftu couldn't pull his eyes away.

The Coil Dancers lay on the pavement, writhing in an imitation of ecstasy that was driving the crowd mad. Summer had never been so alluring.

Suddenly a woman screamed, and they all froze.

"I am Kela!" she cried. Cheftu was relieved it was not *his* woman. "I bring fertility, fecundity. Celebrate with me!"

Five men from the crowd darted onto the pavement to the Kela woman. She danced with them, her quick movements leading them closer. One by one the steps of the dance confounded them, and they returned to the crowd. Finally the fifth kept her pace, until he was dancing with his hands on her waist. The crowd cheered as the two danced into the building.

The other dancers began to move closer to the crowd. Each seemed to be selecting a partner, and Cheftu opened his mouth to ease the sound of his breathing. Whom would *his* dancer choose?

Her steps brought her close to where he stood, and he finally saw the woman's face. Beautiful. Her glance flashed over him, and he groaned aloud. The noise was lost in the heat of the moment, and she moved on.

Moans and gasps carried clearly from the one-columned portico. Cheftu was appalled; he was inflamed. His dancer still sought a partner, and he focused on her, willing her to him. He caught her glance again. Her expression, her eyes, made his blood pound.

"The Sibylla wants you," Y'carus said, pushing Cheftu forward. "She will not choose you unless you extend your hand."

That's not all that is extended, Cheftu thought. Stepping forward, cold sweat on his back, he thrust out his hand. A hundred men stood with outstretched hands and tented kilts. Me, Cheftu thought. Me. Pick me.

Her look met his, and he felt a touch on his hand. He clamped his fingers around hers. She pulled and he followed, a wake of disappointed Caphtori behind him. The dance steps were easy, all he had to do was mirror her movements. It was a slow seduction, a taste of the reciprocity that more intimate partnership promised.

The couple in the balcony were nearing their conclusion. Cheftu watched the woman in front of him, her breasts moving with the dance, each tier of her skirt alive with her energy and passion. He saw no signs of snakes—a relief. His hands were finally on her waist as they stepped into shadow.

They entered a hallway and she stopped, her heated body against his.

With no invitation he kissed her, his mouth open, his heart racing. Her nails scored his chest delicately, and then she gripped him, hard. He groaned against her mouth, his eyes wide. A door opened somewhere. His hands touched her skin, soft, her breasts filled his hands, the peaks hard against his palms.

She untied his kilt as though she'd done it a thousand times, following its slide to the floor. Cheftu fumbled with her belt, and with a low laugh she undid it, her jacket opening, her skirts loosening.

Outside, the death-throe ecstasy of the priestess rose. Kela was welcomed back; the snake lived, the butterfly flew, harvest would come. The Season of the Bull was begun.

The woman abandoned undressing herself and straddled him, slowly joining their bodies. Cheftu closed his eyes, the reality of what he was doing finally penetrating, even as his flesh entered hers.

Like this, he could imagine she was Chloe. Like this, it seemed every muscle in his body, every particle of his being, recognized her. She rode him hard. Coherent thought was impossible as her unrestrained cries and pleas drove him wild, holding her to him tightly.

He felt tears on his face and he rolled over, her long legs wrapped tightly around him, her back arching as she accepted and taunted him. With a swallowed shout, Cheftu climaxed, his face pressed into her neck. Her pleasure began as his ended, and Cheftu felt her body milk him again.

They lay in silence. Two strangers, intimately intertwined. He couldn't bear to open his eyes and not see Chloe. He drifted for a while, lost in a sea of satiation, a morass of guilt.

SIBYLLA STARED AT THE CEILING. The quiescent man lay on her, pressing her to the floor, imprinting the pattern of shells on her back. He felt good, though, a welcome weight. More than that, she craved him: his skin, his scent, his touch. From the moment her gaze had locked with this golden-eyed man she knew that if she chose him, it would not be just for ritual mating.

This could not happen only once.

His short hair was damp against her cheek, and she felt more wetness against her neck. Did he weep with pleasure? She closed her eyes, wondering how her decision to forsake the Caphtori in favor of a foreigner would be perceived. He was definitely not Aztlantu. From his plain white kilt, now crumpled beneath them, to the pendant he'd thrown off after it hit her in the chin, he was Egyptian. She shifted positions and he sat up, pulling away abruptly, his face averted.

He looked toward the door, his legs crossed at the ankle, his arms resting on his knees. He cleared his throat and spoke. "I am Cheftu Necht-mer. From Egypt." His Aztlantu was simplistic.

Sibylla sat up, too, pushing her skirt down, throwing her hair over her shoulder. "I am Sibylla."

They sat in awkward silence. Sibylla wanted to hear his passion rise again. Though he was turned away she remembered his face. He had strong features: heavy dark brows arching over his eyes, a straight nose, and high cheekbones. His body was strong, though scarred. Frowning at herself, Sibylla got to her feet, walking toward the rattan couch. "A rest, Cheftu?"

He bowed his head, silent and removed. A few moments later he answered, "I think not. My gratitude." He stretched a long-fingered hand back for his kilt, and Sibylla felt panicked. He was leaving; he couldn't leave! She thought quickly.

"As you are a foreigner, you may not realize that your service to Kela is not complete."

He turned around and looked at her for the first time since touching her hand. Sibylla felt his gaze caress every part of her. She was astonished to see how looking at her had an immediate effect. "Take off your tunic," he said.

Obviously he didn't know the word for outer garment, but his intention was clear. Sibylla slowly eased the jacket off her shoulders. Cheftu stood, legs braced, his hands clenching and unclenching. "Now your—" He gestured at her skirt, and Sibylla slithered out of it, like a snake from its skin. Cheftu's breath was harsh as he raised his eyes to hers.

He touched his belly with his hand, then he touched his sex, and Sibylla inhaled sharply. With slow steps he approached her, his chest rising and falling rapidly. "Are you one of those Coil Dancers?"

Sibylla smiled. Nay, she wasn't, it was an insult even to ask her, but for him, for him she would do anything, be anything. "If the Egyptian wishes it, aye."

He licked his lips, swallowed, and then spoke. "I have not been with a woman—" His expression altered, and Sibylla reached for him, kissing him, trying to erase the pain in his eyes.

She tongued his ear, his responses driving her further. "What do you want, Egyptian?" she whispered. "Anything you ask is yours."

He pulled her flush against him, his erection pressed between them. "Touch me," he said, his voice cracking. "I starve for touch."

In truth the ritual mating consisted of one coupling. Any foreplay was for Kela, the pleasure was for Kela, embodied in the priestess. There was nothing for the male; he was simply the contributing seed in the equation. Sibylla ignored these thoughts as she picked up a small flask of hyacinth-scented oil, a gift from Dion.

Sibylla pushed the Egyptian onto the bed, then poured the oil into her hands. His face was turned away from her, he seemed to hate looking at her, but she felt his skin melt into her hands when she touched him. He wanted her, or her body by proxy. Sibylla didn't know which and didn't really care.

With slow strokes she rubbed in the oil, feeling the texture of his skin, the firm muscle and sinew. Rubbing his back, shoulders, and arms, she moved farther down his body, settling herself on his thigh. His buttocks were round and tight, the skin lighter here than anywhere else. He sighed into the linens, his words cutting her before she realized she shouldn't understand them. "Chloe," he whispered. "My beloved."

Sibylla froze.

CHEFTU AWOKE SLOWLY, not the horrified jolting awake to which he had become accustomed, but with a sense of peace. The tang of sex was in the air, and he felt the slick cement of his skin against Chloe's.

Chloe!

He opened his eyes and blinked at the sunlight. Curled inside the cradle of his arms and legs was a woman. Black curly hair covered them both, and Cheftu felt equal parts grief, shame, and lust. Lust was winning as the soft heat of her seduced him. His hand felt the heaviness of her breast, his other cupped her flat belly.

Tears pricked his eyes again. If I didn't open my eyes, would I think she was Chloe? Would this pain go away? It was too late for that. He should leave, go to Aztlan or wherever, fulfill whatever destiny the ring foretold, and then . . . what? He wanted this woman once more. He wanted to close his eyes and imagine his wife with him one last time.

He slid his hand lower and felt fire run through him. Kissing her cheek, neck, and shoulder, he felt her pleasure rise. Her body tightened around him, and she rubbed against his chest like a cat. In seconds they were face-to-face and he begged her, in some language, to look at him. He wrapped his fingers in her hair, holding her head still, forcing her gaze to his.

Green eyes, glazed with pleasure but nothing more. She held him tightly, her forehead wrinkled as she fought toward him for release.

Cheftu closed his eyes, suddenly unwilling to share the intimacy of his gaze with her, then opened them when she moaned.

He saw into the green shadows of her eyes as if he'd been plunged like hot metal through flesh. Behind the bars of culture and circumstance, he saw Chloe. He pulled the woman's hair tight and stared deep into her eyes, pounding his flesh into hers. Chloe was there! He saw her!

With a howl of fury, frustration, and release, Cheftu poured into Sibylla's body. She was weeping, kissing him, and caressing him, and Cheftu rolled off her, his mind suddenly clear.

Sibylla lay gulping for breath. He leaned over her, looking into her eyes, searching. Was it possible? Was he dreaming? Green eyes. Warm, but not Chloe's. Cheftu turned away. Just accept your adultery, he told himself. Do not lie to make your action less reprehensible. Chloe is not here. You saw her broken body. Sate your lust if you must, but don't envision Chloe in every green-eyed woman you meet. Sibylla rolled over, already asleep, and Cheftu lay back, staring at the ceiling.

Disgusted with himself, he crawled over her, retrieved his kilt, left his Eye of Horus–inlaid pendant as payment, and slipped into his sandals. She lay in a mass of dark curls, the mysteries of her body shielded in sleep. Kohl smeared her face, reminding him of his own, and he went to the water mirror to repair his eye makeup. She didn't stir.

The sun testified it was late afternoon. He was tired, starving, and what could he say to her, anyway? He was a prisoner, however well he was treated, a man with nothing left to lose. *But you saw Chloe.*

He turned away from the sleeping woman and his thoughts of Chloe. She was dead. If he dwelt on his loss, he would go mad. Never think her name again, he thought. Please, God, let that ease the pain. Quietly he let himself out the door, wandered around until he found the pavement and the food hawkers, then walked back to the ship.

CHAPTER 8

AZTLAN

Y OU OWE ME," SHE SAID, her voice low and throaty. Zelos looked at his daughter and felt a shiver of revulsion. The first glance was always the hardest. Pale skin, so fair and translucent that it looked like the underbelly of a fish. He could see the faint lines of blue in her throat and in the fragile skin of her temple. She had dark blue eyes, long lashed but cold and predatory like those of a hungry animal.

"I am the Golden Bull," Zelos said harshly. "I owe you nothing."

Irmentis grabbed his wrist with strong fingers. "You know what Ileana did. She did it because of you! If you could have kept your kilt on, she would not have seen the need to make both her daughters pure."

Zelos pulled away. "Ileana knew me, how our marriage would be, long before we were wed." Unconsciously he looked at his left hand and arm. The symbol was faded, but still visible. Vines of green wound around his fingers, over the back of his hand and around his wrist. The Aztlantu symbol of marriage: a tattooed arm. How very long ago it all seemed. Zelos was suddenly filled with a fierce will to live, but he squelched it and turned to his daughter. "She would have me anyway."

"Did she really know how being wed to you would be, *Pateeras?* Did she know the lengths to which you would go?"

"She knew I was a man, with a man's needs."

"A conniving, fornicating man who drove her mad. She feared you'd seduce your own daughters."

Dizziness assaulted Zelos, and his tongue felt thick. Or she feared you would seduce me, he thought.

"Do you know what she did to us?"

He tried to think, to speak, but his mouth wouldn't obey him. In detached horror he watched as his youngest daughter began to raise her tunic.

"Ileana did this. But did it keep you from masquerading as a bull at that feast in order to seduce Yuropa?" Irmentis' white cheeks burned with spots of red. "Did it keep you from training a swan to charm and seduce Letas? How many children did she give you besides Phoebus?" Irmentis was untying her sash. "What of Daneaia, the Mycenaen? How much gold dust did you rain on her before she took you to her bed?" She grabbed his chin, glaring at him. "Ileana may have directed the knife, Zelos, but you drove her to it! See the results of your faithlessness? See how you ruined my life?"

Zelos had seen hundreds of nymphs intimately. He knew the female body almost better than his own. He felt his gorge rise when he saw his daughter's mutilated sex. *Everything* had been carved away, and only a series of tuckered pink scars remained.

Through tears he looked at Irmentis. How could he explain? The passion and lust that had so often seized him was something she would never know. Never know because of him; because of Ileana. "What do you want?" he asked slowly.

Irmentis dropped her gown. "I cannot bear to leave Aztlan, *Pateeras.* Neither can I endure seeing Phoebus with another." The ache in her voice made Zelos wonder if maybe this strange woman really did understand passion.

"Aye."

She knelt before him. "Give me an island, let me take my dogs and some nymphs with me. I will leave Phoebus and spend the rest of my days hunting and fishing. I will never return here." She glanced away. "Until he dies; his Great Year."

Zelos had never felt kinship with his dark daughter. Her head was bowed, her dark hair curling over her shoulders and spilling across her covered breasts. "You will leave Phoebus?"

"Aye." She didn't look up. "When he learns, I will be anathema to him."

Zelos had seen his son with Irmentis. She was not anathema to Phoebus, but if she thought she was, so be it. He sighed. Why not please, unselfishly, at least one woman in his life? "By the Triton and Shell, I swear it."

She presented the haft of her knife. Offended, yet strangely sympathetic, Zelos cut his finger, smearing blood across the blade, then over his lips. "I swear it on the Triton and Shell and on my honor as Golden Bull Zelos Zeus of the Clan Olimpi," he vowed.

She kissed his mouth hard.

"*Kalo taxidi, Pateeras.* I shall eat the funeral *kollyva* for you."

SPIRALMASTER'S WRISTS ACHED from tossing the stones. He'd gone through almost everything in his storerooms, yet nothing had received approval from the stones. He'd tried asking the stones to tell him what was necessary for the elixir, but he could not understand the response.

He sighed. He should bring in someone else, tell them about the stones, someone who could read . . . yet he dared not. He'd refused to see Niko; even now the boy might be carrying the illness that was killing Zelos' *hequetai*. Aztlan needed a Spiralmaster who was not a confidant of *Hreesos*, who was not infected with this disease, who had no political aspirations.

What tragic days for the empire! They needed this elixir! They needed to rise above this disease, the disasters. Immortality could achieve that for them, yet the cursed stones would not help. Irritated beyond understanding, Imhotep began to name items for the final ingredient, anything he could think of, from kohl powder, to the kiss of a nymph, to what he had for dinner the night before.

The stones said aye.

Spiralmaster felt his breath shorten and the pain in his head begin again. Nay, nay. He must stay calm and coherent. What had he said? "Kohl." He threw the stones.

Nay.

"A nymph's kiss."

Nay.

"Lettuce and onion salad."

Nay.

"Figs."

Nay.

"Orange."

Nay.

"Crab."

Aye.

"Crab."

Aye.

Crab was the missing ingredient? There were dozens of types of crabs! What kind of crab? What part of the crab? He snapped for a serf and sent him for a Shell Seeker. Surely she would know what kinds of crabs there were? Imhotep grinned, self-consciously wiping drool from his cheek.

They would be like gods!

Decans later Spiralmaster knew what needed to be done. Who was brave enough? Reckless enough? It was a rare type of crab, one that regenerated itself. The crab would give its essence to the elixir, combine with the other herbs and elements, to regenerate, to maintain life! It had been eaten time before mind for its healing powers; consequently only a few remained, hidden in caves beneath the sea.

Who could go? Who would go?

CAPHTOR

CHLOE AWOKE IN THE SUNSHINE, achy and deliciously rested. For three days Sibylla had had the body. Apparently now she was willing to share. Wow! What did she do while I was gone? Chloe thought, sitting up gingerly.

Her skin was scented, musk so familiar that Chloe's throat tightened. *She's been having sex with my body! Did she even use protection? Please God, don't let me wind up pregnant in this ancient time. Please, don't let that happen!*

Sibylla was silent, and for that matter, so was God.

Needing a bath desperately, she snapped for her serf, who filled the cramped stone bath with warm water.

So Sibylla had fooled around, the festival was over, and Chloe ... Chloe what? What was the point? The water in her tub sloshed over the side in a violent stirring of the ground. It lasted only seconds, but it seemed like forever.

A divine answer?

The serf wiped up the spilled water and helped Chloe out, dressing her and leading her down to the main chamber to dine. Exchanging greetings with those Sibylla knew, and Chloe knew from her late night excursions into Sibylla's consciousness, Chloe listened to see if anyone mentioned the tremor they'd experienced this morning.

She accepted bread, cheese, and fruit—European breakfasts hadn't changed in four thousand years, she thought—and took a bench seat along one wall. If only they had coffee.

"My mistress," a clansman in a cowskin cloak said, "we will be ready to sail in a matter of days. Would you care to travel to Aztlan proper first? Or the clan?"

The clan. Green fields torched. Marble covered in soot. Bodies rooted in mud?

The vision was like electricity through her body, a shock that made every hair stand on end, from the stubble on her knees to the waist-length locks flowing from her scalp. Some place, some people, destruction; Chloe concentrated. She felt as though she were a tuning fork for better reception. Terror, not for self but for others, seized her. It was too late! They were too late! She fought to reconcile her vision with Sibylla's memories.

Velvet fields were torn in half. Buildings fell into gurgling pools of slime. People fought to climb up, out, only to be engulfed in flames. No! Chloe thought. Don't make it too late!

"Birds," Chloe said aloud, her grip strong around the clansman's wrist, her eyes wide and staring. "Now. Get me birds." He backed away, and she noticed people were staring. It didn't matter. What had she seen?

Sibylla! she screamed in her mind. Wake up. Tell me, what island is verdant and has lots of marble? Tell me, damn you. The shouting and sheer panic woke Sibylla, who answered tersely.

Naxos.

NAXOS, CLAN OF THE VINE, was the greenest, lushest island in the Aztlan empire. It provided not only wine, but vegetables and grains to every clan in the empire. The island was well protected, watchtowers built from peak to peak, guarded by clansmen who defended the island with their lives. If even one of them lit the bonfires already laid out on the many stone roofs, the island would mobilize to fight against fire, insect swarms, or invasion. Naxos was the market basket of the empire.

To the north was Delos, or what remained of the smoldering land. Ash still fogged the air, and the Naxos clanspeople had spent decans dusting off the plants to make sure they got sun and water. The aqueducts that laced the terrain of Naxos brought fresh water from the main reservoir to the many small tracts and fields stretched along and up the hills' sides.

Natural coves on marble beaches made it easy for ships to anchor, and many of the days on Naxos began with merchants meeting and greeting, bartering and stealing from each other over rhytons of watered wine and fresh fruit. The spine of the island, peak after mountain peak, ran in a jagged line from north to south. A fertile valley lay between the coastal cities and the ridge of mountains, filled with budding orchards and climbing vines.

Above the city of Demeter, the clan chieftain Bacchi's villa cascaded down levels, each terrace filled with a profusion of flowers, overlooking the channel to Delos and Paros. It was evening now, all the homes lit with the warmth of oil lamps, the chieftain's no exception.

A clansman brought him a rhyton of wine and a message from Caphtor. "Open it," Bacchi said.

" 'The Sibylla oracle warns of a disaster here,' " the clansman read from the slip of papyrus.

Disaster? The chieftain looked out over his clan. The air was scented with growing things, oregano and thyme overlaying the smell of a thousand women preparing dinner. The sea was calm, the white ruffle of waves crashing against the rocks below, jostling the ships in the harbor gently.

His gaze fell to the cats that treated his terraces like personal sleeping porches. Not a feline stirred, absorbing the stones' remaining warmth from the sun.

Disaster?

Never before had the orchards been so heavy with blossom. Prices were better than they'd ever been. The Clan of the Vine was developing into a substantial community with a great deal of say in the workings of the Council.

"Perhaps Sibylla was forecasting the eruption on Delos," Bacchi said. "There is nothing to fear here."

"Should I send a warning to my clansmen, my master?"

The chieftain looked at the sturdy man. "Go take a walk along the shoreline if you need to. Rest between the thighs of a Coil Dancer, but do not alarm the clansmen." He shrugged. "Sibylla's timing is inaccurate. Bring me more wine and light a few more lamps."

The air was still around the port of Demeter. Men stumbled

home, rotten with drink; water slapped against the hulls of hundreds of ships; and the occasional yowl of a male cat mingled with drifts of laughter as doors opened and closed.

The clansman walked his lonely pathway, looking out to sea. Delos still glowed faintly red and orange on the northern horizon, and he felt pain for the loss of a clan. A little ash still powdered the harbor, but the clanspeople claimed that this would be the most abundant growing season Naxos had ever seen. Could the Sibylla be wrong?

An archway rose from Naxos to a tiny islet. Ships coming to harbor frequently sailed beneath it. The Scholomancers built an archway here first, demonstrating the design before the expense of building a larger one on the Breakwater. The clansman paused suddenly, the hair on the back of his neck rising. Slowly, he looked over his shoulder.

The town was silent, too silent. He lifted his gaze to the mountains. Unable to shake his sense of unease, he continued walking, a bit faster, toward the steps that led to the islet.

Beneath the islet, beneath the lace of the waves on the shore, the faint coating of ash on the sea, beneath the level of fish and squid, beneath the wreckage of ancient ships, their lichen-covered wealth scattered on the ocean floor, the earth trembled.

It trembled again, then convulsed, the Aegean microplate nudging its African brother, the brother sliding beneath the smaller plate, buckling and rending the earth. Throughout the empire of islands, life changed.

Channels brewing with lava began to boil.

Chambers of magma that had been content resting deep within the mountains began to push up, building pressure.

The water table shifted, and ground that had been floating on a mixture of pressurized soil and water sank. Some places quickly, some slowly.

Fractures the size of hairs widened, letting the sulfuric stink waft upward, a signal to the animals, to the fowl. The wispy, discerning stamen of spiderwort flowers changed from a safe blue to a deadly pink.

Nature's countdown had begun.

The epicenter of the quake was out to sea, strategically placed along the underlying plate of land that comprised Naxos island. A seismic pebble was dropped, and Naxos was in the path of the resultant wave. No wining, dining, and laughing human felt the shot running through the island.

The clansman jumped in surprise as the cats of Demeter began howling, the mules kicking, and thousands upon thousands of rats came running toward the water.

Before the clansman understood that anything was happening, the primary wave shook Naxos.

Walls wobbled, roofs collapsed. Breakables stored on shelves teetered and fell, dinnerware, still slick with olive oil and the remnants of the meal, slid off the tables and smashed on the floor.

Lamps, the hundreds and thousands of oil lamps, rocked, turned over, or fell.

The shock lasted only heartbeats, giving the clanspeople time to reach for the hands of their loved ones and duck.

The second wave was the killer.

Naxos gyrated, rattling the walls until they fell or exploded with pressure. The ground was a live thing, bucking beneath those who tried in vain to flee. Roofs caved in, objects seemed inhabited by *skia* as they flew through the room, felling people, bursting midair.

Those clanspeople who had sensibly fled to the safety of a doorway were crushed as the power of the quake shook even the resilient wood into splinters. Rocks shattered and rained down from the cliffs, smothering and killing. The quake lasted only eleven seconds yet left little alive.

The third wave was gentler, though most of the island's inhabitants were already dead or dying beneath their stone walls, impaled by their own handiwork or trampled by their own animals. Yet the third wave touched what the others had not.

Aqueducts that stretched across the island met at the central point of the dammed river, forming a reservoir. The Scholomance had invested summers of work and had poured *kur* upon *kur* of stone before the waters of the lake could be restrained. During the first quake a few stones slipped.

A few more.

During the second quake, an agitated wave of water hit the weakened wall, but the Scholomance's stones held. Then the third quake hit. The stones shifted and the roiling water burst free, leaping the rest of the dam, flowing down the hillside from Mount Zelos, overflowing the ditches and aqueducts, carving new channels of fury, mixing with dirt and ash, flowing downhill, gaining momentum. Unleashed.

Bruised and bloody, the clansman rose to his knees. Pain filled his body; he was hemorrhaging internally, though all he knew was agony. He feared he was the only person alive on Naxos, though something else lived.

Fire.

His only thoughts were for his clan, the empire, the fields that fed the thousands. Had birds been freed? Was there any hope of rescue? He ran.

The air was dense with noise and the smell of burning. His sandals slipped on the slick stone, and he braced himself before the sharp turn.

Gasping with pain, he stumbled, falling the last few steps. Salt water stung his wound, bringing him sharply alert, and he fought with the door that led to the tunnel.

Steps. He paused, trying to still his breathing, aching with pain. He felt blood streaming down his back, soaking his loincloth. He opened the door and stepped into the tunnel.

The tunnel was another experiment of the Scholomance. He ran through the mold-scented darkness to the island and the archway. He ran faster, each step more difficult than before, each step taking longer. Only a few more steps to the other doorway.

Hands slippery with blood, he wrenched open the door and ran up into the night air. A brief glance over his shoulder confirmed his worst fears.

While the towers remained dark, fire raged in the fields. He ran up the archway steps, weeping and groaning. He fumbled for the small torch, left always burning. He could hear nothing except his own body begging for the release of death. Tears wet his cheeks as he witnessed the conflagration of Naxos.

The deliverance bonfire was laid out. All he need do was throw the torch onto the tinder.

Paros was barely visible through the darkness. He knew if they did not see a watchtower aflame, they would not summon help. They would assume the fields were being burned as a farming practice or ritual. They were idiots, working beneath the earth instead of in the sunshine.

A sudden blast of heat made him look down in horror. His kilt was on fire. "For the Triton and the Vine!" he mumbled. Staggering forward, with all his weight, strength, and love of his clan, he threw himself on the prepared bonfire.

The Sibylla was right; disaster had come.

"THE WATERS ARE CHOPPY," DION SAID. It was dawn, the only time Spiralmaster claimed that the elixir-saving crab could be found.

"Spiralmaster said it glows, *eee?*" Nestor asked, newly arrived from Egypt and unwilling to face Vena.

"It will be in a cavern, just beneath the surface," Dion said. "It glows purple."

"Should be easy to see," Nestor reasoned.

Dion looked at the diving shell. Though Mariners and Shell Seekers used them often, Spiralmaster wanted a member of the Clan Olimpi to do this, seek this crab. He claimed it was a sacred task, fit only for the Golden. He's getting paranoid in his old age, Dion thought. He looks his age and then some. Dion noticed Nestor staring in horror at the shell and remembered that Nestor didn't like going underwater.

Okh, *it's the coin you pay for being Golden, clan brother.*

The diving shell was approximately seven cubits tall, formed of pottery clay and designed to hang in the water by ropes, secured to the ship above. A person could swim inside it, rise to the top and get fresh air, then dive out. The shell eliminated the swimmer's need to rise to the surface when diving. Posidios, chieftain of Clan of the Wave, was designing a shell that could be worn *on* the swimmer. Dion chuckled at his uncle's imagination.

The only dangers of the diving shell were that the air would become stale and poisonous or that the swimmer would stay down too long.

"It does work, Nestor," Dion said with a smile. "Surely you have submerged a cup beneath wine or beer?"

"Aye, but I was interested in returning it to the surface full rather than empty," he said with a twist of his lips.

Dion laughed. "Just so." He knelt beside the huge shell, pointing to the metal drops hanging from holes in the lip. "These weights will hold the shell evenly in the water. Inside the shell, the water level will rise." He touched a point on the shell about the height of Nestor's chest. "Above this level will be air for you to breathe. Then you can swim out, search, and swim back for a breath of clean air."

"When you come up, do so slowly." Dion pulled off one of the weights. "Keep hold of these—they won't weigh you down, but when you remove them, the shell will rise higher, giving you air to breathe. Go slowly."

"What happens if I go quickly?"

Dion looked away. "You will not be deep enough to truly hurt yourself."

"How deep is 'deep enough'?" Nestor asked nervously.

"We will hang a rope, weighted, beside the diving shell, marked with depths. Do not go lower than the level of the rope."

"Is that deep enough to find this crab?"

"Since the caves are fairly shallow, the crabs should be there." Dion smiled. "I will be right with you. Besides, you were the one who wanted to hide where Vena couldn't find you to mourn your broken liaison."

"I was hoping that would be in a tavern," Nestor muttered.

THE MARINERS BEGAN LOWERING THE SHELLS. Nestor sat on the edge of the boat, watching as Dion stripped off his kilt, the feathers in his hair, and the many bands around his arms. Only his seal was left. Nestor took off his clothing, leaving just the bag around his waist.

"Your air time has begun, my master," the Mariner said as the men slipped into the cold water.

"By the horns of the bull, I cannot believe I am willingly swimming this early in the season," Nestor said.

"Already we have welcomed Kela," Dion said. "You are acting like a child."

"We will keep an eye on you, my masters," the Mariner called, pointing to the dyed cork that would indicate where the men were. The Mariner handed them bronze mirrors "for light."

Nestor greatly disliked floating naked in the salt water. He felt exposed and disconnected. Touching the dagger tied to his arm, the other one on his calf, and the third in a hilt around his waist comforted him little. He had a decan to search. After that he would be too weak to come back up or he would be struck by the infant's death, as the illness was called. Victims died in a fetal position, wailing, as helpless as an infant. Vena would definitely not be impressed by that.

Dion shouted to him and dove, his feet breaking the surface of the water a heartbeat later.

Nestor swallowed and beseeched protection from Kela. After breathing deeply several times, he dove. Amazed, he looked around slowly.

Schools of fish swam beside him, turning as a unit to the command of an unheard voice. He swam down farther. Pressure built in his ears, and his chest began to hurt. His eyes finally adjusted to the dim light and he swam in the direction of the hulking shell hanging in the water. The weights caught at the bag around his waist and he spent precious moments untangling himself, then rose up, up.

Air! Nestor breathed deeply in the darkness, smelling the slightly mildewed odor of the pottery shell, the briny scent of the sea. Rubbing his face, he readied himself to go back down.

He dove beneath the lip, holding the bag close to his side. Swimming cautiously, avoiding the jutting coral that could shred him, keeping his eyes open for those creatures of the deep that were dangerous, he moved toward the caves. They would be to his right, he recalled.

Dion swam in the distance, a paler, larger-limbed figure than the surrounding fish. Had he found these mythical crabs?

The water was darker closer to the caves, and Nestor angled the mirror, reflecting the sunlight streaming through the sea. Fish scurried away as Nestor forced himself farther. He felt a pull against his legs and moved cautiously.

A cavern! After swimming rapidly back to the shell, he got a good gulp of air and then swam quickly back to the site. Cautiously he floated toward the cavern's mouth. The darkness was complete, and he blinked a few times before the glowing brilliance of the vegetation came clear. In utter darkness he saw orange, pink, green, and yellow so bright, he felt his pupils dilate. They moved, like specters, in the unseen currents.

Nothing purple.

He swam back to the shell, breathing shallowly to save air. Another deep dive and he was in the sea again. Not that cave, he thought, and turned his head slowly, searching for the glowing purple decapod crab. Within the crab's body was a component that gave the crab the ability to renew itself perpetually. The decapod crab could regrow any part of its body. It was most rare—a creature that had eternal youth and life.

Okh, the crab wasn't here. Another cave, but first he needed air. He backed out of the cave and felt something flick the back of his neck.

Turning as fast as he could, he saw the huge shape swimming away from him. A flat, gray thing, its tail a whip, lashing the water side to side. Nestor swam on, wondering how much of a decan had elapsed.

Three caves later he found them. The luminescence of the crabs brightened the entire cave, flickering off the sides of fish, blinding among the glowing corals, seaweed, and plankton. The creatures must be alive to be most effective. He tucked three into his bag and moved to the diving shell. He gulped for breath, and again. The air was thin, and Nestor's head began to ache.

What was the next step? Weights, remove the weights, he told himself, ducking beneath the level of water and fumbling for the weight's wires. He could barely feel their shapes in his tingling hands.

He needed to wait at each step of his ascent, take time for his body to regain itself or suffer. His air depleting rapidly, Nestor forced himself to breathe slowly. He could see nothing save the fading purple glow that lit up the water before him.

Finally he broke the surface of the water and heard the cheers. Arms trembling, he crawled into the boat. Dion stood in the first rays of sunrise, holding aloft his woven bag full of crabs.

"You did well," Dion said, draping him with a sheet. Nestor shook his head. He'd survived. Man should not live in water; it wasn't natural. The world beneath the waves was eerie and fantastic, but he preferred air.

The men uncorked a flagon of wine and passed it around. "We give these to Spiralmaster, and then we celebrate tonight," Dion shouted. The Mariners lifted the sail and they tacked around the edge of Kallistae and back into the lagoon of Aztlan.

SHE WAS TOO LATE, Chloe knew it in her bones. Had the clanspeople of Naxos paid any attention to her messenger bird? She'd been horrified at how much time it took to extricate herself from Knossos. Apparently no one, not even clan chieftains, bailed when the mood suited them.

Despite her warnings of major disaster, evil portents, the whole nine yards, the Caphtori had hung on to her like leeches, her ship, and her men. They didn't want the oracle to leave, they wanted her blessings on the new crops. We're too late, Chloe thought. Please don't let us be too late! Last night they sailed through the gateway to Aztlan, the ship's horn-embroidered sails working as effectively as a diplomatic passport in Saudi. Mist was heavy on the sea this morning, and Chloe wondered, though she didn't dare ask, how they could see to get through it.

Ash from the eruption still coated the water in places. Chloe's skin prickled at the thoughts of what a volcanic eruption must be like. Very few of her clanspeople were actually up to talking with her, so she didn't ask. The Mariners were scrupulously polite, but everyone watched her as though she were a madwoman.

You *share a body with an oracular priestess who doesn't believe her own words and see how you feel!*

It was cold this morning, and her sense of dread multiplied with every hard-won *henti.* Out of the mist, two ships converged on them. Drawing on part of Sibylla's knowledge that she had swiped, Chloe recognized the triton on the sails and breathed a sigh of relief.

She also shuddered; Zelos Olimpi was sailing toward Naxos, too. Her fears were justified. *Eee,* those poor people, Chloe thought. What had happened? Her vision had faded rapidly, leaving only a feeling of doom. She gestured to the ship's commander to allow Zelos' ship first. The azure-and-goldenrod sails filled with wind, and Zelos' ship streaked out before them.

Chloe chewed her lip, thinking about relief programming. Food, water, shelter, clothing. Her Sibylla-snatched memory told her whom to contact on each of Naxos's neighboring islands. "Bring me some messenger birds and a scribe," she commanded. While Sibylla herself might not arrive momentarily, help certainly would in the form of other clanspeople.

CHEFTU WAS ON DECK FOR THE FIRST SIGHTING of the Breakwater. Islets arching from one side of the empire's islands to the other formed a natural barrier, the skeleton of a greater landmass. In some areas they were but a dark stain in the water, but high enough to rip hulls from unsuspecting ships. Cheftu just stared. He'd seen many of the wonders of the ancient world; surely this was the unknown Eighth? Atop the islets, rising from the sea to a height twenty cubits above the ship, was the gateway to Aztlan. They approached an entryway, and Cheftu was staggered.

Two enormous pylons topped with carved griffins guarded the archway that Mariners in green swarmed across. Y'carus ordered the sails down, and the rowers' pace slowed. They halted before the entrance, where several other Mariners came on board who talked to Y'carus, went below decks, and finally granted approval. The ship moved beneath the stone arch, Mariners on either side saluting. Then they were through and in the bluest, most vibrant water Cheftu had ever seen.

His head was swimming; who were these people? Where was this land?

"This is the beginning of the sea that becomes the lagoon around Aztlan," Y'carus said beside him. He handed Cheftu a roll of bread with a vegetable paste inside it. "It is called Theros Sea. In Aztlantu, 'Theros' means summertime." Y'carus made a production of wiping his brow. "Regardless of the weather elsewhere, sailing is always hot. The sun boils us on the water."

Islands began to smudge the horizon. With evident pride, Y'carus pointed out the various clans. "East, you see Kallistae. Mount Apollo is that mountain on the edge of the island, one of the sites for Apis' temple. To your west"—he pointed with his chin—"that is Folegandros." Cheftu nodded, then corrected himself and shook his head in agreement. Y'carus pointed straight ahead of them. "See that glimmer on the horizon? That is the Pyramid of Days, on Aztlan."

Cheftu was almost choking. "Pyramid?"

"Aye, where do you think you Egyptians learned to build them?"

"Just so," Cheftu said slowly. "What is over there?" He pointed to the horizon, where the sky was gray.

"That was Delos, the city of Arachne, the Clan of the Muse," Y'carus whispered.

"Your family?"

"Aye, and my beloved. She was killed."

Cheftu bowed his head in sympathy. "My sorrow for you," he said in Aztlantu.

Y'carus stared at the sea. "There was no warning," he murmured.

"It is most painful when you cannot say good-bye."

Y'carus turned and looked at him. "You sound as though you know . . . ?"

"My wife," Cheftu said shortly.

"Then the Sibylla . . . ?"

Cheftu clenched his jaw. He couldn't regret his actions; still, he was ashamed of them. "She bears a striking resemblance."

"Your wife was very beautiful, then."

"Aye, and strong, and intelligent and passionate and vibran—" His voice broke. "However, I was able to bid her farewell." Cheftu looked away, muttering in Egyptian, "Then, in a cruel jest, I thought we'd been given another chance to be together, only to have my hopes trampled. Literally."

Y'carus ignored him, staring out at the water. "In Aztlan, we don't bid farewell, but rather *Kalo taxidi*, Good journey. As the dead travel and submit to trials, they are strong because they know they are loved." It was silent on the sea, only the rush of waves around them.

"We are now entering the current that will carry us into the lagoon of Kallistae, surrounding Aztlan Island."

"I am confused," Cheftu said, grateful for something to think about other than Chloe and how he had betrayed her with Sibylla. His body tightened—don't think about Sibylla at all. "How is Aztlan governed?"

"By clans. Each one has a chieftain, and the chieftains assemble in Council every nine summers. There they discuss and debate, negotiating policies for goods and services that will stay in place for the next nine summers."

"Do men and women rule?"

Y'carus shook his head. "In the eyes of the clan, there are no gender differences. Each gender has his or her own god, each is born and given to their clan—"

"Born and given to their clan?"

"Aye." Y'carus drew a deep breath. "You really know nothing about us, do you? Just so. Aztlan is built not on blood connections, but on birth order."

"Aye?" Cheftu said, prompting him.

"The firstborn, male or female, inherits the clan position of the parents. The second-born joins the defense clans: mining, or as a Mariner, or an engineer. Also, there are those who supply weapons, armor. They are the Clans of the Stone, the Wave, or the Flame."

"Just so."

"Third-born go to the cults. We have the Cult of the Bull, Apis.

Or the Cult of the Snake with Kela, the earth goddess. She is the patron of women."

"She was the one honored . . ."

"Aye." Y'carus grinned. "You worshiped her in Knossos."

Adultery *and* idolatry, Cheftu thought. He was going to be in purgatory for a *very* long time.

"Within the priesthood are many different factions. The Apis priesthood are the builders. They make the stones and pave the walkways. The Kela priesthood are the fishers, the Shell Seekers. In fact, it is against the law to fish without permission from the cult."

"Why is that?"

"You deprive them of their labor." He grinned. "We find great satisfaction in our work. Our clans are everything to us: our family, our occupations, our identities."

"Your beloved was . . . ?"

"My clan sister. I was second-born, destined for the sea in defense. My bloodparents were dyers in the Clan of the Muse." He swallowed. "Neotne came to foster with my family at age five. I was ten the summer before I left to foster. I knew even then, as soon as I saw her. . . ." They stood, the salty breeze blowing over them. "Just so," Y'carus said, his voice thick. "The fourth-born go to the land. Olives, fruits, vegetables, vines, they keep the empire green."

"Those would be the clan of . . . ?"

"Clan of the Vine. If it grows, they nurture it. The Clan of the Horn raises animals, both for food and products. Fifth-born are the artisans. We are—were—proud of our creative skills: textiles, ceramics, painting. They are the Clan of the Muse."

"Arachne was the city there? The city that was destroyed?"

"Aye. Arachne was. I grew up there; it was my home."

"What of the Scholomance?"

"*Eee.* It is for the brightest minds, regardless of their birth order. Parents bring their children to foster with the greatest intellects of Aztlan. They learn everything—medicine, arts, science, architecture, mathematics, astronomy, and astrology. They guide us. Are you going to the Scholomance?"

"I know not." Though if that was where the medical arts were headquartered, Cheftu guessed he'd be there. "My gratitude for your helpful words," he said, stumbling a little. "Where are your magi?"

"In Aztlan?" Y'carus shrugged. "The medical skills are administered by our Kela-Tenata priestesses."

Women in medicine? In Egypt women were healers only in small, poor villages. In France? Cheftu almost laughed. "I know not this word."

"Kela, the goddess, and Tenata, her working arm. Each village and town has its own temple, with Shell Seekers—"

"For fish."

"Aye and Kela-Tenata—"

"For medical care."

"You learn quickly. Also Coil Dancers."

Cheftu blinked. "State-regulated . . . ?"

"Temple prostitutes." Y'carus frowned. "I forget how restrained you Egyptians are. Aye, each village has temple prostitutes. Marriage is a sacred undertaking here, since the clans are woven so tightly together. The Coil Dancers ease the needs of men and women, so that they approach Kela's altar with the intention of being forever unified."

Cheftu thought back to his own world, the facades of marriage and the promiscuity that was still such a vivid memory. Marriage was a business contract. Once an heir was born, both parties, provided they were discreet, were free to take lovers. "So once people are wed, they no longer go to the Coil Dancers?"

"Nay!" Y'carus laughed. "Nay, a man or woman may visit anytime they need to. Men do so often when their wives are with child. However, it is only a release of the body. A worship act to Kela."

"No attachment of the heart, then?"

"With a Coil Dancer?" Y'carus sounded appalled. "They are sworn to Kela! She is their husband."

"They never marry?"

"Their initiation is marriage to her." Y'carus pointed. "Behold! The beginning of the lagoon!"

They were moving rapidly now, the timekeeper singing a bawdy tune that made Cheftu blush even though he understood only one or two words in every line. He was reminded uncomfortably of the green-eyed priestess.

"We come to the mouth of Theros lagoon and Aztlan Island," Y'carus shouted over the rising noise. They entered a narrow canyon whose walls grew steeper with every cubit. The sound of rushing water was deafening now, and Y'carus gestured for Cheftu to tie himself to the boat with one of the embroidered straps. They were moving rapidly through part of a massive river.

The cliffs surrounding them were striated and so high that the sun had yet to touch the water. Like an ancient legend, the city rose from the sea, perched above on colored cliffs. Houses and villas in white, red, black, and yellow, intricately designed and painted, hung over the cerulean water. Beyond was the glint of gold, topping everything. Terraces covered the hillsides. "That is the city of Hyacinth!" Y'carus shouted.

Cheftu glanced at the sun and saw they were coming in from the southwest. Two arms of land embraced them, well populated and verdant. Cheftu saw bustling ports, tiny in comparison with the striated cliffs.

They reached a curve where the islands, the bridges, and the harbor were visible. Aztlan Island towered above the islands that surrounded it. Atop the mountain sat a jewel-toned pyramid. It was smaller than an Egyptian one, sans capstone, but identifiably a pyramid. The flat gold top blinded them, even at this distance, with the sun's reflection.

The currents pushed and pulled as they passed beneath the first bridge that attached Aztlan Island to Kallistae. "That bridge will take you to Hyacinth. On the other side of the land bridge is another crossing that will take you into the main street of Echo."

The harbor was filled with brilliantly patterned boats. A mixture of languages rose on the midmorning air. Astonished at how quickly they had arrived, Cheftu stepped out of the way as the Mariners lowered the sails, hauled in the lines, and dropped anchor.

On to Aztlan.

CHAPTER 9

PAROS

Zelos and his brothers Nekros and Posidios stood in the torchlit darkness. On the island of Paros, where Nekros was chieftain, many of the dwellings and buildings were underground. Huge caverns for both clan administration and citizens' housing alternated between quarries on this island where most men and women worked beneath the earth.

Nekros' white skin glowed unnaturally in the shrouded chamber. Zelos, still slightly dizzy from the quick journey, looked around the cavern. The walls were damp—indeed, the whole place was cool, like a winter night without the wind. He wondered with a shudder where the bodies were interred. In addition to being the maintenance clan for the many caves and coves throughout the empire, quarrying, mining for precious stones and metals, Paros was also the land of the dead.

While most chieftains had luxurious estates or commanded the best views, Nekros lived alone on this islet Antiparos, journeying out only at night and spending his days ruling the clan from this dank room.

Nekros' belongings were scarce and elementary. Zelos imagined his brother had even less female company than he had possessions. Who would want the cold hands of the lord of the dead on her body?

Posidios was studying the map laid on a flat-topped stalagmite, its carved markings faint in the torchlight.

"What is left of Naxos?" Zelos asked.

Nekros leaned back against another stalagmite. "Not much. My clanspeople are seeking out the dead, to bring them here and inter them with all other generations on Paros. Thus far the account is no survivors."

Zelos closed his eyes in pain. "Chieftain Bacchi?"

"The clan chieftain is dead. His body has been found."

Snapping for a serf, Zelos demanded a note be flown to Aztlan. Dion, the inheritor, was the new chieftain. "Can anyone guess what this inferno has done to the produce?"

"As of this moment, there is no produce. There are no people."

"By Apis stones, brother, 23,000 people dwelt on that island! Do you tell me that not even one person still lives?"

Nekros shrugged. "The reports are preliminary. I can tell you no more."

Zelos raked a hand through his hair. This was the worst imaginable disaster. Two clans wiped from the face of the empire within weeks. Please do not let this be an omen, he thought.

The sound of footsteps echoed in the archway of the cavern. The brothers turned as one and stared at the woman who was standing there. "I thought I saw your ship," Zelos said.

"I sent a warning to Chieftain Bacchi," she said. "He chose to ignore it."

"He may have received it too late," Posidios said, turning to the woman. "Greetings, daughter."

Sibylla halted, her green eyes widening for a moment. "Greetings, uh, Posidios," she said quickly. "Bacchi ignored me."

"Welcome to Paros, niece," Nekros said. "You honor us with your presence this black day."

She snapped her fingers and a scribe ran forward, offering a clay tablet to each of the three men. "Based on preliminary reports, most of the island is either ravaged by fire, which is still burning on the northeastern side, or is submerged in mud slides, which ran from the reservoir on the slopes of Mount Zelos to the valley, washing out hundreds of homes, produce, and most important, people."

The three men exchanged glances.

"Where are you getting your information?" Posidios asked.

She stepped closer, and Zelos noted with appreciation that his niece Sibylla had become a desirable woman. Her glance was anything but warm, however, and she seemed discomfited beneath her capable veneer. "When I realized that the chieftain had ignored my request, I inquired of Atenis owing to her proximity."

Nekros laid his tablet on the stalagmite that served as a table. "This is a thorough inquiry. It is a great sorrow that Bacchi did not heed your word," he said gravely.

"Regardless of what Bacchi did or did not do, people are trapped, homeless, starving, and dying of thirst. We need to get to them."

"The island is dead," Zelos said.

"It is not."

Posidios and Nekros both looked at her as though she'd lost her wits. To contradict Zelos, *Hreesos?* "You are the clan chieftain and ruler of the empire," she said to Zelos. "You must certainly realize that the most vital possession these clansmen had was knowledge. If the vines are demolished and the fields laid waste, still, with the experience these people have, you can reclaim some of what has been lost. Quickly." Sibylla was now almost face-to-face with Zelos. Her voice sharpened. "However, if these people die, their expertise will be buried with them."

"It would be an expensive salvage operation," Zelos said.

"Not to mention dangerous," Posidios added.

She turned to him. "I am willing to take that risk, but time is essential." She looked back at Zelos. "May I get started?"

"Tell my scribes what you need," Zelos said. "Report to me tonight with the results." He caught Posidios' disturbed expression and wondered what it meant. Zelos might have to endure his arrogant niece's demands about this, but he would see that she was properly humbled on his couch. Posidios grinned farewell as Zelos dismissed her. "Until our eyes hold you again, dear Sibylla."

She looked uneasy, and Zelos laughed.

DION SHIFTED. The woman's bony hip dug into his side and he turned over, catching the other woman's hair, his fingers still twined in it. The boy had fallen asleep at his feet, his hands cupping the redhead's breasts, his mouth open and warm breathed on Dion's thigh.

Unwilling to awaken his partners, unsure as to what had happened, Dion gingerly pulled away from the three sleeping figures. His mouth felt as though it were filled with sheep's fleece, and the top of it zinged with pricks that both tickled and hurt. Flagons of wine, empty, some overturned, were scattered on the floor and tables. Pots of poppy had turned to gray ash, and the *kreenos* pods that . . . he couldn't remember her name or title, had brought, were piled into a pyramid.

Okh, by the stones of Apis, being decadent was hard work.

Unsteadily he got to his feet. Bodies—dancers, students, clansmen and others whose clothing was missing, making them hard to identify—sprawled around the perimeter of the room. The smell of vomit reeked as he rubbed a hand over his face and hair, and he realized it was himself.

Dion picked up a cloth from the floor and wrapped up in it, dizzy and nauseated from bending over. His head throbbed and his nostrils felt as though an Egyptian had tried to embalm him, pulling his brains out through the passages.

Sunlight pierced the linens on the windows, and Dion turned, feeling watched. He waved at the woman in the doorway, then remembered he was holding his kilt on and grabbed for it. Selena smiled and nodded her head.

"A curse on you for looking so alive this morning," Dion grumbled, wincing as the words banged in his head, making it ache more.

"How many times have I seen you like this?" his clan sister Selena responded. "You have entertained and woken with the scent of a thousand men and women. What are you seeking, Dion?" The differences between them seemed amplified and unfairly exaggerated this morning.

Unlike him, filthy and fog headed, Selena was responsible, the inheritor to the Cult of the Snake. One of his sisters by Zelos, she served reason where he served passion. *Her* only lusts seemed to be power and knowledge. Though she was strikingly attractive, she was also strangely asexual. It was an irritating trait this early in the morning, especially when he couldn't even recall the night before. Dion groaned and deliberately dropped the kilt. "No rebuke this morning, Selena. I cannot bear it." He glanced behind her. "Is the passageway clear?"

"Given your present appearance, I doubt even you would be chased and adored," Selena said. She held out the hooded robe draped over her arm. "Nevertheless, I am prepared." Dion stepped over a sleeping girl and let Selena settle the robe over him. "Zelos has sent you a message."

Dion halted, nausea, headache, and nakedness forgotten. "Zelos? What does *Pateeras* want? Where is he?" Dion was certain the Golden Bull had been at the feast the night before, but feasts often seemed one long meal with only breaks in between, rather than separate days.

"Bathe and dress first," she said, leading him out of the chamber.

The sun was only slightly farther in its journey when Dion emerged from his chambers, clean, shaven, coiffed, and dressed. Selena sat in a stone wave-backed chair, staring out the window and eating nuts, one after the other, as though she were in a trance. Her eyes were enormous in the pallor of her face. "Selena? Sister?" She turned, and he saw that tears had streaked the kohl around her eyes, that nail marks marred her cheeks with angry stripes.

"It is gone, Dion," she said brokenly. "The clan is destroyed."

Dion tried to smile; surely it was a jest. Another attempt to get him to accept the responsibility of his clan and stop acting as if every woman were his first Coil Dancer. Another attempt at persuading Dion to leave Daedalus and his wild inventions alone. To embrace his heritage, which meant concentrating on the sugar level of the grapes, the necessary mulches for the vegetables; negotiating and selling within Aztlan. Yet he was chilled. "Tell me."

"I read a message addressed to you. It said there were fires in every field. Thousands of homes burned, the aqueducts smashed and left to flood those fields lying fallow. Cities flattened."

He sat down slowly. Naxos. "The clanspeople?"

Selena chewed on her lip, shaking her head soundlessly. "Submerged, devoured by Apis. Men, women, children." She paused. "The chieftain is dead."

As if he were looking through a prism, Dion saw the man he had been forever altered. With dizzying speed the existence he had known was mutating like one of Spiralmaster's experiments. For just a moment, he saw his whole life.

Fathered by Zelos, his mother murdered by Ileana. His infant self had been taken to a remote cave on Nysa, an islet off Tinos. He'd been raised by the wolves expected to devour him. Sibylla had found him, more than half-wild, and tamed him. As they matured, they had journeyed to Caphtor, Alayshiya, Troi, Hattai, and beyond. He had reveled in every pleasure he could imagine. Finally he had returned to Aztlan, accepted to wife golden-haired Kassia and the seal of his authority.

Her death had reduced the tattooed lines around his fingers and wrist to fruitless decoration. The death of his son, a tiny babe unable to breathe, had rendered all else pointless. He had rejected everything, leaping back into physical pleasure. Best to enjoy life while one could, for it ended brutally, he reasoned. At the end, you held nothing. His cousin Bacchi had taken his place as chieftain.

Now, the destruction of "his" people, a term he'd not considered for summers. "How many survive?"

"I know not."

"Who did this?"

Selena rose. "The earth. Apis leapt, destroying everything."

"Why do we worship such a brutal god?" Dion whispered. Selena cried quietly. He blinked and snapped for bearers. "I go to Naxos."

"First, Zelos would want you to have this." Selena picked up a cloth-wrapped parcel. Heart beating unsteadily, Dion knelt before her. The heavy gold seemed like fetters. The seal of the Clan of the Vine: his seal, his birthdate, his birthright.

"You are entrusted with the life, welfare, and productivity of the Clan of the Vine," Selena intoned. "Their blood is yours; you are defender and cultivator, you are mentor and chief. Seek the welfare of your people, your land, and the betterment of Aztlan."

Dion stared at her bare feet, the tips of her toes painted scarlet.

"What say you, Dion Dionysus, Clan of the Vine?"

He fumbled for the blade at his waist. He'd made vows before and broken them. However, he had not made them in blood. This action would irrevocably change his life. He rose to his feet and drew the knife across his palm, a slash of fire. But it was nothing compared to the flames that had consumed his land. He rubbed blood on both sides of the black blade, then swiped a streak across Selena's dry lips. "I swear to be defender and cultivator, I swear to be mentor and chief. I swear by the Triton and the Vine."

After rubbing his own blood across his lips, he and Selena kissed. A sacred vow; he would be accountable to her, and she would be his conscience. She wrapped his hand in linen as he washed his blade.

"May Kela's grace guide you until my eyes hold you again," she said as he ran down the hallway to summon a ship.

SPIRALMASTER POURED CAREFULLY, steadying his arm as he forced his limbs to measure the liquid and powders. The disk mold was shallow and round, a common shape in Aztlan. Annual charts were scored on disks, tile typing in clay. Astrological charts, farmers' almanacs, and simple things like recipes were kept in this fashion. This disk was a recipe of sorts, he thought with a low chuckle.

A recipe for life. His eyes filled with tears, the symbols of man, plant, and animal indistinct. It was too late for so many; and this would be the end of Zelos, too. How Spiralmaster had hoped to change things. Perhaps Apis had read his intentions and thus the plague?

But it wasn't a plague. It didn't strike indiscriminately, it didn't appear to be infectious. It was methodically picking out Zelos' *hequetai*, the Clan Olimpi. Who knew how many of the Scholomancers had it? He thought of those he considered sons. Were they ill? Would they be able to survive this and see Aztlan through to another time?

With a twitch of muscle, Spiralmaster turned to the table on which the disk rested. There, hidden among the signs in the sky, rising from the end of the Great Year and through the seasons, he hid the formula. His legacy to Aztlan.

Who could succeed him?

Whom could he trust with this? Who had no clan allegiance, no stakes in the internal rumblings of the empire? He turned the wheel again, his palsied fingers slow to press the characters into the drying clay.

"My master?" a woman asked.

Spiralmaster dismissed the Kela-Tenata. She left reluctantly, vowing he would do himself harm. Silly nymph, did she not realize he wouldn't survive the day? He pressed the figures in.

Fumbling within his sash, Imhotep pulled out the stones. With trembling fingers he asked the question foremost in his mind and tossed them. His rheumy eyes couldn't catch the rapidly flashing letters. But he felt them pierce his soul, a fatal blade.

"F-L-E-E-D-E-S-T-R-U-C-T-I-O-N."

His fluttering hands stopped the stones, sending one skittering across the floor, the other clenched tightly in his fist.

"My master?" an unfamiliar voice said.

Imhotep jerked, lifting his finger just in time to not ruin his disk. "What do you want?" he asked, glaring over his shoulder.

An Egyptian faced him.

Imhotep had fond recollections of Egypt, a world so different yet similar to the one in which he'd chosen to live. The pristine white clothing and carefully ordered paintings of his heritage were far removed from the chaos of Aztlantu art and costume. The many gods, the hierarchies of priests, the society's rigidity, compared to Aztlan's two gods, the clarity of the clan structure . . . he would have said the purity of the people, but it was no longer the truth.

Spiralmaster studied the Egyptian before him. He was an unlikely specimen of a land crippled by famine; he was tall, healthy, and his eyes were clear yet strangely vulnerable.

This man had nothing to gain, and nothing could be taken away. He'd lost everything; it was written in his gaze.

"Who are you?" Spiralmaster asked.

The Egyptian crossed his chest and began to speak in Aztlantu. Fluently. The words he said were arrows, sinking deeply in Imhotep's mind.

"For many generations, as long as Aztlan followed the divine nature within, you were obedient to the laws and well affectioned toward the God who gifted you, whose seed you were, for you possessed true and in every way great psyches, uniting gentleness with wisdom in the various chances of life and in your interaction with each other."

Imhotep hardly dared to breathe.

"But when you began to ignore the divine laws within you, and your base nature gained the upper hand, you then, being unable to bear your fortune, behaved unseemingly, and grew visibly debased, for you are losing the fairest of your precious gifts; and to those who have no eye to discern true happiness, you appear glorious and blessed at the very time when you are full of avarice and unrighteous power."

"How can you say these things? What do you know?"

"They were revealed to me. Warnings have fallen on deaf ears repeatedly. I am but another cautionary word from a *Pateeras* who seeks your best future," he said, inclining his head.

Pain seized Spiralmaster's skull, a vise tightening over his ears and temples. He held out his shaking hand. "Put on the tiles! Quickly! Type what I say! I have waited for you!" The Egyptian placed the tiles on his fingers. "The swallow," Imhotep said. It took the man a moment to find it, but he did, pressing it firmly into the clay. "The leopard skin." The Egyptian found one tile. "Nay! That is the bear skin. The leopard skin." Laboriously Cheftu typed in the remaining few symbols needed for the disk.

"Where did you come from?" Spiralmaster whispered. He could feel his lungs congesting.

"Egypt."

He looked at the man more closely. "Where did you truly come from?"

The Egyptian's expression faltered, and he spoke slowly, as if realizing the words as he said them. "I am a student of the Scholomance's legacy."

"Be certain the library is saved," Imhotep said. Loss of the knowledge was his worst fear. "We are a rotting corpse in Aztlan, only our bones will tell our story. Help me to my couch."

The Egyptian's hands were sure as he led the Spiralmaster to lie down. He gave him some water, checking for temperature, swelling. His questions were intelligent, but so misguided. "This is how it strikes," the Spiralmaster wheezed. "The body does not rally. Where did you learn Aztlantu?"

"I do not know it," he said defensively.

"Then what are you speaking?" The color drained from the man's face. Imhotep chortled. Aye, this was the one. As Spiralmaster he had no more time. Already delirium ate at his mind. "Take the disk and guard it with your life. It carries the answers," he gasped out around his pain. His throat was closing, and he felt his lungs stretching for air, even as his legs began spasming. "It will be a sign that you are the new Spiralmaster, inheritor to the Clan of the Spiral."

"My master—"

"Help us outlive the prophecy, survive these trials. Save Aztlan from ignominious destruction. We are dancing into our graves."

"What prophecy? Who will believe me? I am a foreigner."

Spiralmaster snapped weakly for a serf. "A quorum! Now!"

"My master, the brothers, chieftains Sibylla, Atenis, all are away at Naxos," the serf said.

"Find everyone else. I need them here immediately," Imhotep said, and Cheftu heard the metal of command in his voice.

He was speaking, understanding, Aztlantu? Cheftu shivered. He'd just started speaking, repeating the words flowing from the scroll in his mind. He'd given no thought to language. What had made him quote Plato he didn't know. His words to the citizens of mythical Atlantis applied to this culture and time, even though Cheftu had read them three lifetimes ago.

Imhotep's words finally penetrated. "Did, did you say Sibylla?"

Cheftu asked, unable to help himself. Surely, please God, in this scattered country Sibylla was a common name?

"Aye. Chieftain of the Clan of the Horns and an oracle, also."

Mon Dieu, please, no! Cheftu thought. She was the first, the only woman he had heartlessly *left* after loving. His stomach tightened, and he feared he would regret his behavior. "What prophecy?" he asked the aged man as he rested.

"The prophecy of our downfall. Take the disk," Spiralmaster whispered. "Never let it from your sight. The wisdom of this empire is there."

The next decans were a mist for Cheftu. He could not believe what he was doing, yet his intuition told him to do it, accept the honor, the position, and responsibility Imhotep was offering.

He found himself on his knees, the Minos from the Cult of the Bull, the Kela-Ata from the Clan of the Snake, lame Talos from the Clan of the Flame, and others gathered around him, watching with outraged eyes. "You are entrusted with the life, welfare, and productivity of the Clan of the Spiral," Imhotep whispered. "Their blood is yours; you are defender and cultivator, you are mentor and chief. Seek the welfare of your people, your land, and the betterment of Aztlan.

"What say you, Cheftu Necht-mer, Clan of the Spiral?"

Someone handed Cheftu a blade, thick and black. Once his vow was made, he was linked to this land and people until he died. Or until they did, he realized with sadness. As instructed, Cheftu drew his own blood, rubbing the blade on both sides, then swiping Imhotep's drooping mouth. "I swear to be defender and cultivator, I swear to be mentor and chief. I swear by the Spiral and the Crab."

He kissed the man's blood-wet lips even as a scream echoed through the chamber.

"Nay!"

Everyone turned as a white-haired, lavender-eyed man ran in. He stopped short when he saw the stains on Cheftu's and Imhotep's mouths. "Are you mad?" he yelled at the room. "I am the inheritor! I know Spiralmaster! This man, he is, he is . . . ," the towhead sputtered, and Spiralmaster spoke softly.

"Niko, greet Cheftu, the new Spiralmaster."

Cheftu watched as blood suffused the man's face and chest, mottling his skin with rage and embarrassment. He shook his head curtly at Cheftu. The clan seal's new weight on Cheftu's chest felt like lead when Niko knelt next to Imhotep's couch. "It was for me," he whispered. "All these summers, that is what I thought."

"Come away, Niko," another man said. "It is Spiralmaster's decision. You were never named inheritor." The room emptied of Council members quickly.

Imhotep laid a trembling hand on Niko's shoulder. "We need new blood. New ideas, new perspectives. The Egyptian is an answer to my prayers."

Niko's gaze met Cheftu's, and Cheftu knew that the man hated him; if he had been promised this position and then had it taken away by someone who could barely speak the language—but I *am* speaking the language, and understanding it, fluently, Cheftu thought.

Imhotep's breath was racked and wheezing. His eyes went wild suddenly, his gaze unfocused, and he began to jerk and twitch.

"His journey begins," Niko said in a voice thick with tears. *"Kalo taxidi,"* he whispered. Niko and Cheftu stared at the couch. Complete silence, no breathing. "He had changed and come to hate me, I think," Niko whispered. "Why? Why would he cut me so?"

Cheftu debated on what to say, on the wisdom of saying anything. "Often with the aged the shield of tact is thrown away and they speak exactly what is on their mind." He fingered the seal around his neck. Was that what Imhotep had done? Chosen Cheftu just to hurt this young man? Nay, there was more at work here. He could sense it. "My sorrow for your loss."

Leaning over the couch, Cheftu closed the old man's eyes and frowned at his expression. Denial, anger, fear—forever carved on his features. "Call Nekros," Niko instructed the serf. Cheftu heard the door close and began to move the old man's hands into position for burial. After much prying, he was able to lay them flat. A stone fell from the deceased's palm.

He laid it on the table, then continued to straighten in readiness for whoever prepared the bodies here. Leaving the quiet room, he saw Niko, now standing in the dark hallway. "Go in and speak to him," Cheftu said. "The dead need to hear the words we need to say before their *kas* find security." Shaking his head, Niko walked through the doors, closing them firmly behind him.

Cheftu could hear him crying. "Leave be," he instructed the attendants. "Now we have time." The serfs, clansmen, and Kela-Tenata healing priestess left. Cheftu looked back at the door; but mourning should be done alone.

"Shall I take you to your laboratory, Spiralmaster?" a serf asked. Cheftu was startled, then realized he *was* Spiralmaster. He started to nod, then remembered to shake his head in assent.

NIKO STARED INTO THE FACE of the man who had been his father, his mentor, his guide, his idol. The man who had betrayed him, choosing another. Did this Cheftu know the secrets of Aztlan? Did he know the formulae and the powers the Scholomancers controlled? "Why not me?" Niko whispered to the face of the corpse. "What did I do wrong?"

Sitting back on the couch's edge, Niko gazed around the room, then suddenly returned his attention to the table. The stone! The new Spiralmaster knew nothing of the stones! Niko picked up the black stone and looked around frantically for the white one. There! Under the edge of the couch. He had them both. They seemed to burn his hands.

The clansmen of the Stone soon entered to prepare Spiralmaster's body. First an artisan sat down, laying a thin sheet of gold on Imhotep's face. He looked up at Niko. "Did Spiralmaster want to be interred on Paros or in the land of the pharaohs?"

They had discussed this many times, Niko recalled. Imhotep loved Aztlan, had spent his life with her, but his final request was to join his forebears in a tomb in Egypt.

Niko smiled. "He requested an Aztlantu burial, but he wanted his body to be burned before interred." The clansman was shocked but turned back to his exacting work, fitting the sheet of gold to the man's face, drawing his impressions of life from Imhotep's skin.

How does it feel to have your requests and needs and rights ignored?

Niko thought, his fingers caressing the stones. Even though the Spiralmaster had betrayed him, the Egyptian did not know about the stones. In spite of Imhotep's wishes, Niko would be inheritor of his power.

He quit the room; he needed to see Phoebus.

CHLOE COULD DO NOTHING EXCEPT STARE. She'd seen artwork by modern artists that looked like this—a swathe of gray, murky with hints of green and brown, laid over the entire canvas in forbidding, all-encompassing strokes.

This was not art, however. This had once been an island. A beautiful place; she knew because she'd been rifling through Sibylla's memory again. Now—devastation. What the fire had not consumed, the mud had embalmed. The few high points that had been spared were desolate islands in a sea of chaos.

How had anyone survived?

Chloe directed the few men she'd managed to bribe, cajole, or bully into assisting her. Apparently the ancients weren't big on recovery. Their reaction to disaster consisted of, "Oops! The gods got angry. Better leave it alone." She shuddered when she thought of the many people who were probably trapped, hoping to be rescued. Without her intervention, they would die with that hope.

"Over there," she said, pointing to a small, still existing cove. The silence was eerie as they stepped from the small boat onto the shore. Using Sibylla's memory, she could imagine where the areas of greatest need were. What remained of Demeter was to her left. A tiny pass cut through the beach cliffs before her. She nudged her reluctant volunteers, and they agreed to meet on the shore before dark. No one wanted to be here alone with the uninterred.

Taking the youngest man, actually named Thom, by the arm, she propelled him toward Demeter. The residents had erected what appeared to be the prototype for an apartment building. Stacks of buildings housed families who hired themselves out to the farmers farther inland.

As though cement had been poured over the whole scene, everything in Demeter was frozen in motion. The mud had had the effect of stopping the action in freeze frame. Chloe shuddered as she looked at collapsed homes. Some areas had been flattened into slabs of dried gray mud as impersonal as a foundation. Bodies, like half-carved statues, were gray coated and immobile, running, ducking, lying down.

Shivering despite the sunshine, Chloe walked on, wishing she had a search dog. Of course, when she'd suggested this to the clansmen, they had not understood. Apparently dogs were slightly above wolves on the karmic chain, and only Irmentis knew how to control them. Man's best friend had yet to be recognized. Chloe had given up hope of finding anyone alive when she heard an animal chirp—a zoo sound.

A monkey?

They both stopped; in this shattered place the sound of life was eerie, uncanny. Thom was already calling for the monkey, looking around for it. It would be able to seek out the living. Not as fuzzy as a dog, but it didn't need walks, either. Chloe marched to the first multistory dwelling, calling out. The mud had swept around it, drenching the fire that had been burning. Parts of it were undamaged by fire or mud; were there survivors? Chloe called out.

"Me," a thin voice responded, "help me . . ."

"Thom, here!" Chloe said, stepping toward the voice. Mud brick felt like concrete, and Chloe tested the charred wooden door frame before stepping into the house. Shabby in any time, it smelled of urine and rancid grease. "Where are you?" she called out.

"Me!" the voice said, and Chloe feared the owner was too far gone to be much assistance. It seemed to be coming from above her. Biting her lip, she tried the stairs—so far, so good. She ran up them and found herself in a smoke-stained hallway. "I'm coming!" she called out, listening for the voice to guide her. Don't give up yet, Chloe thought.

She fumbled with one door, then the next. They were hard to open, the normal width of a door divided lengthwise to make sure the two sections fit together. Fire and mud had swelled the wood, jamming the two parts together. Chloe threw her body weight at the door closest to the whimpering voice.

Thom joined her, and they crashed into a room whose outside wall was burned away. Underneath the couch, open to the gray-blue sky, was an old woman, wheezing and wide-eyed. Listening to her breathe, Chloe guessed she had a pierced lung or a broken rib. As gently as they could, Chloe and Thom moved her on the top of the couch, then tied a linen to the window so they would know where to find her when they returned.

Fortifying her with wine and bread, the two left again, hurrying this time, calling out to those who struggled beneath the deadly ooze. Bodies were locked in action everywhere or charred bones poking through the gray ooze. Fire and mud, Chloe thought. Dear God!

The sun was low. Among the eight of them, they had found twenty people. Hundreds of corpses, but only twenty people. The waters had swept many away, the fires had taken thousands. Rescue efforts had not extended to the interior of the island where the damage was worst. The bulk of the clanspeople would never be found.

Chloe relinquished her charges into the medical care of the Kela-Tenata on Paros and stumbled back to her ship, her mind swimming with the image of a woman's arm, waving above the sea of mud, down for the count, crying to heaven for help.

Not being answered.

She shivered and forced herself up the gangplank. Bed, she thought. I just want to slee—"Greetings, Sibylla."

Chloe blinked, focusing on the man who sat regally in the center of her deck. Even through her exhaustion, Chloe's body zinged. He was gorgeous. Drop-dead, Calvin Klein underwear–model dazzling. Who was he?

The magnificent creature stepped to her and took her in his arms, nuzzling her neck and ear. "My poor Sib, you are exhausted! How hard you have worked today. Let me relax you, Sib." He kissed her cheeks, then her mouth, before holding her close. Chloe prodded the sleeping Sibylla, Who is this?

"Do you feel me, Sib?"

Chloe's eyes popped wide open. The man's fragrance was musky, dark, and erotic, and her heart pounded. His voice was low pitched, rumbling through her nerves like distant thunder. Who was he? "Do you feel that against you?" he whispered in her ear. "Do you know what I learned today? Apart from you, I sorrow to say."

Running her tongue over dry lips, Chloe tried to think of a response. Obviously she was well-, make that intimately, known by this man. "It's harder than I remember," he said, and she wriggled free of his embrace.

Ohhh, my gosh, she thought, looking up into his eyes. For one, looking *up* was a new thing. At her height she'd not looked up to many men, particularly since she'd been masquerading in ancient times. Then his eyes; this boy could have such a future with the Ford Modeling Agency! He was too beautiful for words, he was—

He's gotta be gay.

"See!" he said, touching his throat. Chloe dropped her gaze from his face to his bronzed, muscular throat. Finally she focused on the pendant. *That* was what was hard, what was new! A flicker of a stolen memory fit the pieces together.

"You have accepted your clan again, Dion?"

He smiled sadly, gesturing to the piece of rock across the strait from them: the once fertile and lush rock. "There is not much of a clan anymore, Sib."

"Zelos sanctioned the rescue team."

"For today," Dion said. "The twenty you found will be the twenty with whom I renew the Clan of the Vine." He glanced at her. "Tell me, there are both men and women?"

"Even a few children," she said, vaguely repulsed at his attitude. Was it all about profit with these people?

He took her arm and pulled her into the tent she'd slept in last night, erected against the main mast. "I thought you might be hungry," he said. A feast steamed on a tiny table, and Chloe was instantly starving. Yet before the first piece of bread touched her lips, she saw

the hand again, frozen as it reached, begged, pleaded . . . and was
unanswered.

What more could I have done?

Chloe laid the bread down and accepted the wine Dion handed
her. "We have a new Spiralmaster," he said. "Imhotep began his journey and the inheritor was sworn in."

"Niko?"

Dion grinned. "Nay. The new Spiralmaster is not even Aztlantu,"
he said in the international, trans-time tone of a gossip. Make that a
Ford model with a tabloid talk show, Chloe thought.

Her cup of wine finished, she leaned back onto the pillows scattered on the floor. *Eee!* This felt so good! Now if she could just get a
bath—"

"—so this Egyptian," Dion was saying.

She sat up abruptly. "What Egyptian?"

"The one Spiralmaster made the chieftain of his clan! Haven't you
been listening?"

It's not possible, she thought. Don't go there, you will only be disappointed. It can't be, not in a thousand years! Oh please, oh please . . .
Chloe swallowed, her voice strained. "What is his name?"

"*Eee,* well, he is now the Spiralmaster, though already they are referring to him as the Egyptian Spiralmaster, which is silly since we all
know that Spiralmaster was Egyptian, he has those Egyptian tattoos,
but we never called hi—"

"What is the new Spiralmaster's name?"

"Something foreign—"

"What!"

Dion closed his eyes. "Ch-something. I only just received the message. In fact, you probably have one, too."

Chloe was outside, demanding her bird-delivered messages before
Dion finished the sentence. Hands trembling, she looked through the
tiny slips of paper that had come from all over the empire that day.
Prices on beef, on skins; weather reports from Hydroussa . . . She in-
haled sharply as she read the next note. "New SM Cheftu at
Imhotep's demise."

Oh God. Cheftu!!

CHEFTU AND Y'CARUS STOOD ON A BALCONY, looking north to the sea.

The island of Aztlan was stunning. Though they'd sailed north, toward Greece, this was *not* classical Greece. This was no culture he'd ever read about, save perhaps in myths. Who were these people? He had no idea why so many Egyptian-flavored rituals, symbols, and buildings were used. Was Aztlan an ancient Egyptian outpost? But that made no sense, for Egyptians' concern was maintaining Ma'at. No true Egyptian would seek to leave the Nile. Conquer, aye; colonize, never. Cheftu felt tired to his very bones, bewildered by this strange land.

Though he'd been here almost a week, he'd yet to adjust. Lack of sleep and copious amounts of sexual guilt will do that to you. He could hear Chloe in his mind, quipping with a sardonic smile and raised brow. By the gods! Would he ever stop thinking of her, longing for her? She flowed through his veins, and he wondered if he would ever be free.

Ships of a dozen different sizes and models crowded the lagoon to their south.

"Apis stones!" Y'carus said suddenly.

Cheftu followed his gaze and saw two ships on the horizon. Both were flying red sails. "Is it code? What does it mean?"

"A Golden is wounded."

One of the ruling class, Cheftu recalled.

"There you are!"

The two men turned, and Cheftu frowned when he recognized Nestor. Without his peacock's dress and bearing, he looked very young and gravely concerned. Y'carus immediately crossed his chest in respect, and Cheftu did the same. "Spiralmaster?"

"Aye."

"Posidios Olimpi is wounded; he arrives now."

"I am a Mariner," Y'carus said quickly. "Posidios is my chieftain. Pray, what happened?"

"Naxos claimed another life," Nestor said. "Lands the gods have forsaken should be left alone!" He sighed. "It's the chieftain of the Horn's fault. Sibylla is such an interfering woman," Nestor groused. "While seeking to free those still alive from Naxos, Posidios was hit during another earthwave." Nestor looked over their shoulders, and they all turned. The red-sailed ships were pulling into the tunnel beneath Aztlan Island.

Y'carus saluted and then turned to Cheftu as Nestor walked on. "My ship is due in for maintenance," he said. "It has been my pleasure to know you, Egyptian. We are brothers of sorrow, you and I. Call on me if you need anything." He grinned. "Though, being the new chieftain, and so young, I daresay you will have more than enough company during your days and nights." Y'carus and he embraced. "Until our eyes hold each other again," the commander said, walking away.

Cheftu crossed his breast in respect, honored that Y'carus would speak so to him, a foreigner. He ran to catch up with Nestor. Within ten minutes he was grateful he had a guide to the palace. Within a half decan he was convinced he would never find his way around. After an hour of touring passages, tunnels, dark hallways, light wells, large grand rooms, tiny staircases, and ramps, he was certain he would die en route. Never had anything been as poorly planned as this sprawling complex.

A headache was starting on the left side of his head when they stepped into a well-lit corridor where men lined the walls. Their bloodstained kilts identified them as Mariners who'd just returned from a skirmish with death. Cheftu was ushered through the door.

A strapping man with a belly wound lay on a woven couch, a rotten piece of wood still protruding from his flesh. Without invitation Cheftu moved forward, observing. The man was severely chilled, and the wound was seeping. The injury was a death sentence; it was a wonder that he still breathed. If Cheftu were in Egypt, he would say the prescribed formula: "Man with fatal wound to belly, this is not a wound I will treat." Then he would see that the man was fed and cared for while he sent for the priests.

"Your patient, Egyptian," the towheaded man said. Niko. The man was always underfoot!

A quick touch told Cheftu the patient was burning with fever. Methodically he named the implements he would require and then stepped to the side of the room where a serf pumped up hot, sulfuric water and rinsed Cheftu's hands while he intoned the wisdom of Thoth, patron god of healers. Then, at his request, wine was poured over his hands.

It was a smooth extraction, but the resulting gush of blood was life-threatening. Shouts brought more cloths to stem it, and Cheftu soaked them in wine before placing them in the wound. While they stanched the flow, Cheftu shaved the man's body. Only an eloquent plea kept the man's long blond hair. After the rest of him was shaved he was wrapped in cold, wet cloths.

When the wound had stopped bleeding Cheftu carefully pulled away the cloths and studied it. The aperture of the wound would almost fit his hand; fortunately Posidios' blood clotted quickly. More wine splashed inside the wound made Posidios come around and then pass out. After it was clean, Cheftu applied a paste of honey and fat, then drew the edges of the wound together. With chewed *mastic* paste from the lentisk tree, he affixed linen strips over the wound. Dismissing the Kela-Tenata priestesses, he said he would stay and watch his patient. He was left in peace.

Posidios was breathing shallowly. Cheftu wrapped new, cold-water sheets around him. He looked out the window; dawn was just a decan or two away. The *ka* of man was most likely to flee the body in these darkest hours. Out of rote, Cheftu recited prayers against the *khaibits* of the night, and in his heart he asked for the protection and assistance of the One God. Then he waited.

Decans later, someone entered the room and Cheftu sat up abruptly, his heart pounding. Standing before him was a wraith of a man. Extremely tall, and slender with wiry strength. His features were bold—a large nose, shapely lips, a pointed chin, eyebrows that rose into sharp angles. His hair was dark, cut short, and he wore a goatee. . . . His eyes were black as night and his skin parchment white.

He looks the very image of a devil in a painting, Cheftu thought. The tall man didn't spare a glance for Cheftu but went to the patient's side. With narrow white hands he touched the man's brow, then his wound. "How does he fare?" The man's voice was as dark toned as his appearance. He didn't even wear the bright colors of Aztlan, but instead a solid blue kilt and shirt that reminded Cheftu uncomfortably of the blue mourning worn in Egypt.

"Not well."

"What more can be done?"

Cheftu sniffed at his patient's wound, for though the man was no longer burning with fever, he was hot. Dry. *Ukhedu* was being battled. "I am preparing a physic," Cheftu said, gesturing to his arrangement in the corner. "My master, who are you?"

The tall man opened the throat of his shirt. A heavy gold seal lay there, incomprehensible characters inscribed on it. "I am Nekros, clan chieftain of the Stone and priest of the dead. Posidios is my brother." He walked to Cheftu's makeshift lab. "Tell me what you are doing, Egyptian."

Cheftu showed him the prepared medicine. During the night he'd hung a piece of copper over a vial of vinegar and covered the whole thing with a linen. Now, the metal was tinted with a faint turquoise growth, with hints of rust. Nekros looked skeptical but watched as Cheftu took the tape off the wound and scraped in the growth.

The chieftain watched over his shoulder and chewed without question when Cheftu needed more *mastic* to attach the linen. "What will that do?"

"It will purify the blood," he said. "If in a day's time the wound is not red, clear blood, the patient will die." As he spoke, he mixed cinnamon and olive oil, then capped it and set it aside. "First, we observe what happens with the medication."

"I wish you could have been with us in Naxos," Nekros said. "So much death, so many bodies, so many lost. I will send a lustral bath in. My brother must be bathed next." His head bowed, Nekros left, and Cheftu leaned against the wall, breathing deeply.

"You did a splendid job."

He turned and saw the envoy Nestor. "Are you a physician?"

"Nay, though I have studied doctoring."

Without warning, the floor moved. Cheftu staggered toward his patient, shielding his wound from the falling ceiling. A low roar was the counterpoint to the sound of shattering pottery and screaming people. Cheftu felt pieces of plaster hit his back. With Nestor's help they maneuvered Posidios into the doorway, leaning over him protectively. It was a brief shock, but it had opened Posidios' wound.

The room was uncommonly still, absent even of the labored breathing of the patient. Panicked, Cheftu felt for the man's pulse, the voice of his heart. Avoiding the gaze of Nestor, he waited for the faint throb that would signify the man lived.

He waited in vain.

"His bath," Nestor said. "He needs his bath!"

With a jerk of his head, he and Nestor carried the man to a stone tub, immersing him and covering his face with linen. Nestor summoned a serf to return with Nekros, then Nestor joined Cheftu at the window and clasped Cheftu's shoulder. "You did all you could. It was in the hands of the gods. We will trust Kela that he got to the bath in time."

"If only we could have stopped the bleeding," Cheftu said, anguished.

Nestor dropped his hand. "You are merely a mortal, a man. You cannot know the minds of the gods." He was silent for a moment. "It is not a good omen for your chieftainship, however."

As if Cheftu cared.

Their conversation was interrupted by the entrance of Nekros and his minions. They removed the body from the bath and laid it back on the bed. The chieftain sat down and placed a piece of gold over

Posidios' face. Tears streaming down his cheeks, his hands faintly trembling, he conformed the gold to the dead man's features.

"It is our custom," Nestor explained. "A mask to identify him in later generations." The gold was frail, fine stuff, and Nekros pinched and pressed it, imprinting it with the image of Posidios' nose and chin, his deep-set eyes, and even his ears. Then carefully Nekros lifted it away, a rough imitation of the man. "The workers will give him more distinct features," Nestor said. "This, however, will capture the essence of his *psyche*."

The priest of the dead rose, and his minions wrapped the body in lengths of cloth. "We bury our dead in the ground," Nestor explained. "They stay there until they become desiccated. Then they are moved to a burial sarcophagus and filed in the *tholoi* beneath the Clan of the Stone."

"You do not preserve your dead?" Cheftu asked with the horror of an Egyptian.

"The soil here is enough embalming. Indeed, for moons the bodies appear to still be alive. If they are bathed before death, they will reach the Isles of the Blessed, so no more need be done."

Cheftu shuddered.

Nekros was sobbing openly now, and Cheftu felt guilt weighing on him. He turned to the window; what should he have done? How could he have saved this man's life? Finally the corpse of Posidios was carried away.

"Come, Egyptian, I will walk you to your apartments," Nestor said.

Wearily Cheftu followed the golden man out into a corridor. "I sometimes doubt I will ever learn my way around here," he said. "I keep finding myself in the storerooms."

Nestor chuckled. "It is good to know where the olive oil is."

Cheftu smiled wryly. It was the only area he'd found repeatedly. This maze confused him the rest of the time. Once he'd found the ominous archway leading into the Labyrinth; another time he'd found a long tunnel with dozens of doors leading away, through the bowels of the mountain. It was an amazing place, an architectural feat. If only he could see a map of the building.

Cheftu cheered as he began to recognize the hallways.

They climbed several flights of stairs and through another long, wider corridor. Periodically the wall was interrupted by alcoves, painted and fitted with horned altars. Cheftu watched as Nestor walked from altar to altar, turning the axes. What a strange custom! They walked on until Nestor stopped before a brightly painted door. He snapped his fingers, and it was opened.

Cheftu stepped in and stared. In less than twenty-four decans from his landing here, he had changed from being a guest—a prisoner—of the empire to being a chieftain of a clan. In title, at least. He was not used to the idea yet, or to the chambers. Already his personal belongings, gifts from Pharaoh that Nestor had brought, cluttered the room. Kohl pots, tweezers, a small statue of the god Thoth. A few pure white linen kilts were pressed and laid on the end of his couch.

Through a doorway he could see the scroll room. Tablets, scrolls, and papyri filled the cubbyholes in the wall. A chair and desk, both carved from gypsum, sat in the path of the sun. Fresh flower garlands hung over the window, filling the room with the scent of hyacinths.

The exact fragrance the green-eyed priestess wore. He was suddenly, pleasantly aroused.

Then all thoughts ceased as he halted in total shock before the object on the edge of the desk. His lungs felt squeezed as he approached it warily. It was not possible! This was the wrong time! Such things did not exist until the Renaissance!

Layers of disks were connected by a shaft, surmounted by two spheres on metal arms for movement, and controlled by a crank handle to one side: an astrolabe? Cheftu stepped closer. The two spheres were differing sizes, one made of gold, one silver. He inhaled sharply, gazing at the first of the disks. It was painted in a distinct pattern with green and blue, and he recognized the shapes. Continents. "What is this?"

Nestor's steps seemed uncommonly loud, the room very close and hot. "Unlike you Egyptians, we think the world is a sphere and thus have sent our ships every conceivable direction to give us the truth of the matter. This device tells the motions of the sun and moon, past and future, determines the altitude of stars and constellations. Useful when one is at sea, *eee?*"

"The gears," he choked out. What ancient culture had gears? Even the Egyptians, as sophisticated as they were, had no knowledge of this. He picked it up.

"See this," Nestor said, turning the crank. Cheftu watched as the disks realigned themselves, then stopped. Nestor, smiling, took the back off it and cranked it again. They watched the gears, operating at different speeds, catch and release. Involuntarily Cheftu stepped back, stunned. Who were these people?

Cheftu picked it up, scrutinizing the little shapes of blue and green. He walked to the window, his back to the foreigner. Breath rasping, he searched for his homeland, France. It was there! The details of the coastline were indistinct, but the shape of it, and Spain, were unmistakable.

He looked back at France.

Memories of his childhood hit him like a physical blow, and he leaned against the window frame, staring blankly. Figeac with its green parks and nearby river, the crowded marketplace, and the squalor, had been his world. Memories of his home, his family . . . his brother Jean-Jacques, who so patiently taught him alphabet after alphabet, giving him the foundation to learn so many languages.

How France had reeked! How infrequently they had bathed! How bitterly cold the winters were and how ill prepared France was to feed and clothe all her children. He turned; the man Nestor had been speaking.

"You are well, my master?"

"What? Aye, of course."

"You are pale. Please, sit. I will have a serf prepare you a bath and some food."

Cheftu sat obediently, the astrolabe still clutched in his hand. "How do you know about these, uh, places?" he asked, indicating the astrolabe.

Nestor leaned against the wall, narrowing his eyes. "The Golden came from there. Still our cousins come and bring us news from beyond the Great Green. They travel rivers from here to their white lands."

"The Golden?"

"The Clan Olimpi. My family." Nestor laughed at Cheftu's startled expression.

"So are you a clan chieftain?"

"I am inheritor to the Rising Golden," Nestor explained. "Apis forbid, should Phoebus die, I would rule until another Golden was born from the mother-goddess."

Cheftu turned the astrolabe over again and again, dizzy with information. Nestor excused himself so Cheftu could rest.

Nestor was sitting in the library, playing a set of pipes, when Cheftu awoke. Nestor set them down and rose to his feet. "Your new clothing has arrived. Aztlantu clothing," he said with emphasis.

Cheftu smiled grimly. His pressed white kilt was a stark contrast to the bright patterns that everyone, even the serfs, wore. His wide Egyptian collar was unlike the necklaces and pendants the other men wore, and his headcloth covered hair that was unfashionably short in contrast with the flowing locks of the Aztlantu men. Apparently the Spiralmaster needed to adapt more.

"When you are changed we will go dine. The rest of the Olimpi are returned, and it is time for you to meet them."

After the elaborate toilette was completed, Cheftu followed Nestor silently through the corridors, light wells, and hallways. Cheftu ignored the stares and whispers of those around him as they passed through a series of wide, busy chambers. The aroma of cooked meat hung in the air, compounded by a mixture of perfumes, body odors, and fire.

He followed Nestor thoughtlessly. The western-angled sun shone in the light wells, and Cheftu realized the day was almost gone. He was exhausted, lonely. He wanted to tell Chloe about his experiences today, whisper his wonder of what had happened against her skin before he—Cheftu closed his eyes at the thought of Chloe; his thoughts alone were betrayals. A serf offered a rhyton of sweet, peppery wine. He drank, then drank more, and still more.

Maybe he could drown his thoughts of green-eyed women. Living and dead.

Chapter 10

CHLOE, FOR THE FIRST TIME since she'd heard Cheftu was alive and was here, was not thinking of him. A zigzag path rose before her, climbing to the sprawling metropolis on the hills. She stared at Sibylla's city in wonder. If she'd been in Crete, then where was she now? Sailing to Naxos first had confused her even more.

Surely this was not Santorini?

Though it was a hike, they walked up the hill. Chloe felt her weary muscles screaming in protest and sweat gathering between her waist cincher and skin. They turned onto a flatter pathway, and Chloe hissed. *This can't be real. Has Disney taken over ancient times?* Dominating all was an enormous pyramid in a rainbow of colors with a flat top of gold. A pyramid? A *pyramid?*

The Minoans didn't have pyramids, of that she was certain. Well, as certain as modern archaeology was, she amended. Who, then, were these people?

Behind the pyramid was a palace, or meeting hall, with acres of painted walls and columned corridors. To the east and west of the pyramid were graceful gold-and-red temples, with pylons, columns, and flat roofs. A deep channel cut between the two islands, a channel bridged by suspension bridges, and in the middle, the islands were attached by land. Her brain was in overdrive. Where was this?

The walkway was steep and difficult to manage in sandals. Chloe stumbled, wondering how the Mariners, some barefoot, walked with the security of mountain goats. Of course, Camille had been that way. She was almost roachlike in her ability to climb anything. *Oh, Cammy; oh, Mom,* Chloe thought. *Y'all would sell your souls to see this now!*

People bustled all around them, and Chloe just kept staring. Women were bare breasted and tightly corseted, with long black hair flowing around them. They walked on high heels that looked almost like platform wedges from the 1970s. *So this is where European women got the ability to scale mountains in heels—their ancestors have been doing it for centuries!*

The men were also corseted, with very short kilts and, again, long hair. Most everyone Chloe saw was young, fit, attractive. Where were the elders?

They walked along, jostled by the citizens of this place, carrying market baskets, towing along children, bartering. It seemed like almost any other city, except Chloe couldn't stop staring at the multitudes of bare breasts and the men who ignored them. Women nursed in the street, and the men just walked by.

And Muslims thought Westerners were wild.

Nearby, a woman approached, and the people stepped back. She was dressed the same as Chloe and everyone else, though she wore far more jewelry and a cloak. As she swept past a group of men, teetering on her high heels, she slipped off the cloak, showing a bit of shoulder. A Coil Dancer with very little style, Chloe thought through Sibylla's perception. Two men followed the woman, and all three entered one of the white-and-red-columned buildings.

Chloe entered the heart of the town, and the noise was deafening. Buildings, some four stories high, lined both sides of the street, with occasional hanging balconies. Businesses with swinging signs were sprinkled in between the town houses. She glimpsed narrow courtyards and blooming gardens. Up and down, up and down. Her legs were screaming with pain. She really should have taken at least a week to train before coming here. Even slogging through mud—Don't think about Naxos, she reminded herself. You could do no more, not without bulldozers, EMT professionals, and antibiotics.

The final count on the rescue of Naxos had been thirty-five people. Thirty-five out of 23,000. The numbers alone shook Chloe, but when she began attaching names and faces and belongings—cornhusk dolls, painted pottery, tools—it became overwhelming.

She'd failed.

They continued walking. The Mariner's fast pace made her sweat, even in the cool air. They turned and twisted, each street a snare for the senses. Brightly colored buildings painted in the now familiar shades of goldenrod, crimson, and black, shouts of children, neighing of donkeys, and cries of women; food, a dozen different aromas rising on the air to mingle with the perfumes and herbs of the people around them.

Daphne was chaos, as crowded as any modern city. As they walked under two overhanging balconies, Chloe watched the women string a laundry line, gossiping as they completed their afternoon chores. Seated outside at a ground-level door, a young girl with an elaborate tattoo beat grain with a pestle. She's a young bride, Chloe realized.

They left the residential section and began walking down. Chloe caught glimpses of the mountain before them. The reflected sunlight from the gold-topped pyramid—unbelievable that there was a pyramid at all—obscured the rest of the hill.

The populace was becoming rarefied. Chloe saw more and more traveling chairs, more serfs tagging along, as they approached Aztlan Island proper. They reached the edge of the lagoon that encircled the mountain, and Chloe saw a suspension bridge before them, hanging 1,200 feet above the indigo sea. Holding on to the railings, people were crossing. Oh, my God, Chloe thought. I really don't want to do this!

Normally she didn't mind heights. But this, this was a long, surprisingly narrow bridge. And the fall was straight . . . she couldn't look. "How many people fall off here annually?" she asked Thom.

He scoffed with all the arrogance of adolescence. "Only those who are fool enough to stand in the way. Go forward, my mistress." Sibylla had done this a hundred times, a thousand. It was safe, and only a short distance. To her left she could see the land bridge, a wider, olive- and grape-covered pathway. Why didn't they take that?

"My mistress?" Thom inquired. "Is anything the matter?"

Other than I'm not your mistress and this bridge is scarier than anything in any amusement park, no, Chloe thought. Stiffening her spine, she stepped forward. The bridge felt mostly solid though how it could be before the invention of concrete and steel, she didn't know. Don't ask, just walk, she told herself. Look to the opposite side, and for God's sake, do *not* look down!

She focused on the back of the stranger in front of her, taking one step at a time, her other hand sliding in a stranglehold along the rail- ing. Shouts rang out ahead of her, and Chloe feared the worst.

Two kids, apparently playing chase, ran past her, shoving Chloe against the railing. She reached out to catch herself. Screams filled her ears as her foot slid, hanging a thousand feet over churning waters. She felt hands trying to help her up, and she was vaguely aware of people around her, but Chloe couldn't move her gaze from her dirty foot in its ankle-tie sandal, suspended in space.

A hand grasped her waist, her wrist, easing her up. Focus on the end and do not look away, she hissed at herself. Her grasp on Thom's arm was white knuckled. Then they were safe on land again. Aztlan Island, Sibylla's home, she thought. Within her, Sibylla stirred. But the oracle was contributing less and less. . . . Chloe guessed that her raids on the woman's memory were depleting her. What had hap- pened to the rest of Sibylla, the part that was out at a virtual cocktail party when Chloe commandeered her body? Had she been left in the cave?

As they progressed toward the sprawling multihued palace, Chloe had to remind herself to turn when she heard Sibylla's name called. Men, women, mostly her clanspeople, called out greetings. She watched from the corner of her eye while listening to an elaborate tale about cows that weren't eating and had lost their coordination. Chloe saw that gorgeous man, Dion, approach her.

After another effusive salutation and thorough once-over he gave the blushing Thom, Chloe found herself invited to a feast. A feast to meet the new Spiralmaster.

Giddiness bubbled inside Chloe. Scarlett O'Hara's "tomorrow" had never sounded so good.

Chloe woke up in a white-shrouded room. *Not again.* Not another white room that could be anywhere in any time. Quickly she checked: same long hair. She'd gone to bed early last night *hoping* the day would get here faster.

Wherever *here* was. She wasn't so sure she knew anymore.

Cheftu was on this island somewhere; she didn't want to miss him.

Her room was spacious with many windows. Heart pounding from those few terrorizing seconds when she feared she'd returned to her own time, she slipped out from under the soft sheets and ran to the window. The view of the pyramid, the sea, the connecting island, was spectacular. Stunning and completely foreign.

This place couldn't be Minoan, which left her with few known cultural choices.

She was looking directly down onto another building with the same flat roof and red pillars. Lush vines covered the grounds and hung from the many squared doorways that connected this building to others. Chloe turned at the sound of someone entering the room.

"A bath, please," she responded to the serf's request. The sunlight was just now falling onto the buildings. Such an incredible shade of light, Chloe thought. She was definitely in Greece. The light was utterly unforgettable. But where? How did this relate to her world? Did it matter? Cheftu was here, at least. Heart in her throat, Chloe turned toward the room.

The serf had stepped into an alcove, and the sound of rushing water filled the room. A bathroom? Chloe poked her head in, bug-eyed in astonishment. *Running water?* These people had running water? "My mistress, what temperature?"

"Warm," Chloe said without thinking, and watched the girl adjust the two pipes so there was more hot water than cold. Hot and cold running water? What age was this? The science-fiction age? Chloe stepped back into the main room, her mind racing. Some things were so recognizable as Minoan, some so alien. Chloe shivered.

The pyramid was a complete surprise. Its sides were brightly colored in a rainbow array, culminating in the flat gold-covered top. Yet the colors had depth, almost as though they were jewels. *Yeah, right, Chloe. A sapphire that doubles as a two-by-four.*

The girl called her, and Chloe, anticipating her first warm bath in over a year, had to keep from running. The fragrance of hyacinths filled the air, and she saw the tiny flowers floating atop the water. With a sigh she didn't bother hiding, Chloe stepped down. Warmth . . . this was almost better than sex.

Sex.

Cheftu.

She sat down rather hard on the submerged bench, trying to sort the memories she had stolen from Sibylla. With a snap she dismissed the girl and washed, the water sluicing over her tawny skin. Shampooing her new long hair took forever, and Chloe realized why she had always kept hers shoulder length or shorter. This was a pain.

Finally, certain she had everything rinsed, she stood up, wrapping herself in a sun-warmed sheet. *I could get used to this,* Chloe thought, inhaling the scent of the hyacinths. She poked her head into the main room. A partition had been set up, covered with some kind of metal that reflected the sun. A low mat and a basket of fruit had been prepared, and Chloe wondered who was going to invade her bedroom.

"My mistress, would you care to sun?"

The girl indicated the mat in the sun, and Chloe lowered herself, grabbing a handful of grapes. First the girl brushed her hair, then laid the heavy mass in the sunshine, over Chloe's shoulder, while she massaged and prodded Chloe's body into a state of blissful relaxation.

"*Okh!* There you are," a woman said. Chloe's eyes popped open. "You are running behind, Sib. The Council is holding an impromptu meeting in a little over a decan. My sorrow for your *pateeras*, though I know you didn't know him. Out of forty-five siblings, how could you?" Chloe heard the woman sit on a stone bench, talking a mile a minute.

Chloe had heard of Posidios' death but had gotten no response from Sibylla. "The work you did in Naxos is well on its way to becoming myth," the chatty woman said. Chloe tried desperately to place the voice, to get Sibylla to offer something—a name, a title—honestly, the woman was useless! "It is astounding what can happen when the Bull roars." The woman crunched grapes noisily. "Sib, are you ever going to say anything?"

"Just waiting for my chance," Chloe said jokingly. Fortunately the other woman laughed.

"Embla and Ileana have been closeted together almost every day for decans," the woman said. "I have become very careful about what I eat; Embla would not be above disposing of her inheritor if it would win the favor of the Queen of Heaven."

Inheritor! Cult of the Snake! This was Selena, Sibylla's closest friend. Oh Kela, Chloe thought. What if she realizes that I'm an impostor? The serf finished the massage and wrapped a cloak over Chloe's shoulders, easing her up.

"Are you going to dress?" Selena asked. "The meeting convenes shortly, Sib."

Chloe tried to keep a tremble out of her voice. "Will the new Spiralmaster be present?"

Selena laughed. "You will have to go to know."

Chloe turned around and watched as Selena's eyes widened and narrowed at her changed appearance. "By the skirts of Kela, what happened to you?"

My eyes, she thought. "Wha-what do you mean?"

"Your face is . . . Well, Sibylla, I don't intend rudeness, but it seems flatter."

"Flatter?"

"Aye, your nose is . . . well, it looks smaller." Selena approached her, a frown on her not-so-flat features. "Where did you get that mark on your chin?" Self-consciously Chloe touched the tiny cleft in her chin. "I thought your eyes were blue. They look green now." Selena crossed her arms over her ample bare breasts. "Forgive me, my friend, but you look distinctly ill favored."

Stung, the real Sibylla rose inside her, and Chloe understood suddenly. In this empire, big bumpy noses and receding chins were all the rage. Neither of which she had. Though she'd always thought her nose big, it was straight and long, not a single bump in sight. On a good day her chin could pass for merely aggressive; never receding. She stared at Selena's nose and felt herself blush.

Akra was the word for both nose and tip. In Aztlan, one's nose size was analogous to one's sexual prowess. "The bigger the better" suddenly took on all new meaning. She blinked at the large but beautifully modeled example on Selena's face. All the paintings, all the pictures, *that* was why everyone was wearing honkers.

"You poor dear," Selena said, embracing Chloe. "I am heartless! Let us see what we can do, what dressing you need to take everyone's attention off your . . . well, off your face."

Chloe wasn't offended. Not much, anyway. Sibylla, after cursing her former friend, returned to her room with a slam of the mental door. Not a good sign, Chloe thought. Selena snapped for the serf. "I heard your predictions this year were extreme. Perhaps your dreams have done this to your face?"

Rhinoplasty while you sleep.

Resisting the urge to testify that she was considered quite appealing when she was in her own skin and time, and that not all civilizations thought weak chins and huge beaks were attractive, Chloe focused on the ritual of dressing. Between the two of them they settled on a white, blue, and saffron skirt. Four of the layers were embroidered straight across, the fifth dipped into a point around her knees, and a quilted apron of blue with gold threads wrapped tightly over her hips and waist. Selena scoffed at the sheer shirt and declared that since Kela had arrived, no one was wearing those silly things. Chloe found herself staring into a mirror in a jacket with blue-and-gold-threaded quilted sleeves that bared both breasts. Selena turned her around and laced a waist cincher, which had the combined effect of a WonderBra and girdle and was about as comfortable as a straitjacket.

Her breasts seemed obscene, especially once they were tipped with gold paint. The heavy clan medallion hung right above their swell, and the serf selected several other necklaces and an anklet or two of the same matte gold.

The serf played with Chloe's hair for what seemed like aeons. The final arrangement was pulled away from her face, with two long tendrils curling over her ears. A band of matte gold crossed her forehead, allowing another, shorter curl or two to fall over it onto her face. The rest of it was interlaced with blue and gold beads, twisted and braided. By the time the girl was finished Chloe felt as though her hair alone weighed ten pounds. The Egyptians were right; wigs were definitely easier.

On the other hand, she was wearing her own hair, as opposed to the baldness factor in Egyptian culture. Besides, all the other women she'd seen were wearing a similar hairstyle.

Did everyone have naturally curly hair here?

Like most sun-dwelling peoples, the Aztlantu wore protective kohl around their eyes. Chloe stared in the water mirror. Bumpy nose or not, she looked fabulous. How vain, she thought to herself, but it was true. The clothing, at least, was Minoan.

"If you are through admiring yourself, Narcissus," Selena said, "perhaps you can manage to make it to the Council?"

The Council, Chloe thought. "No need for the sharp side of your tongue," she said. "I only want to look my best because . . ." Because why? "Because I need to negotiate that transfer at Milos."

"Because you have heard the new Spiralmaster is built like Apis and has eyes like saffron, more likely," Selena said.

That, too, Chloe thought, her knees feeling a little weak.

Arm in arm they walked through the palace, greeting and waving along the way. The garden was gorgeous, red and gold flowers blooming in swarms over the ripple-backed settees scattered here and there. The sound of rushing water was soothing, and she saw a graduated series of pools, linked by a miniature waterfall. The main pool was a mosaic of stylized fish, octopus, and other sea creatures. They walked past it and up over a stone bridge. Sibylla looked over her shoulder and saw the hulking pyramid, the sunlight deepening its rainbow sides. What building material was that?

The women stepped down into a large room, and Chloe smothered a yelp. This was real—it seemed unreal, but it *was* real. Hundreds of people filled the chamber, all clad in clothing as colorful and revealing as her own. Rapidly purloining Sibylla's understanding, Chloe went mentally around the table.

For one thing, there was only one table. That was extraordinary in itself. Remembering one of her few interior design classes, Chloe recalled that long feasting tables were an invention of the Greeks, as in Plato, Sappho, Pericles. The Egyptians feasted on small tables that sat one or two.

Then she realized this was not a feasting table, but a gathering table. Before each of the ten seats was a mosaic design. The artist in her itched for a sketch pad. A faceted stone, a stylized wave, a tritone flame, a lush vine with grapes, the inside of a conch shell, a butterfly, a serpent, a set of horns, a triton, and a column. It was the same-styled column she'd seen throughout the palace. It was wider on the top than the bottom, slightly awkward in appearance but striking when painted crimson.

Again, Minoan.

She looked again at the people: Nekros, frosted white skin and eyes as limitless as hell. Iason, Posidios' inheritor and new chieftain of the Clan of the Wave. His eyes were red rimmed and his hands shook in the presence of this company. Talos, as dark as the soot he worked with, and lame. Her cousin Dion, gray-eyed Atenis, the Kela-Ata Embla, herself, the Minos of Apis, and the blond giant who was *Hreesos*. Behind each of them stood the inheritors to their position. Scowling fiercely at the empty Spiralmaster chair stood an albino man with eyes of Elizabeth Taylor purple.

It was like Holland. The average for beauty was so high that even the ugly people were gorgeous.

Chloe sat down on her chair and waited for the meeting to start.

Swallowing, she recited her ritual lines, and *Hreesos* brought the meeting to order. Contracts needed renegotiating; bartering needed to be done—both of which Chloe was lamentably ill equipped to handle. In any time period. She sat back and begged the Minoan, Aztlantu, she reminded herself, Sibylla to control this event. If you don't, you are going to lose money, she chided the woman. Wearily Sibylla took over.

Chloe concentrated, trying to recall what she knew of the Minoans. What had Mom said those many times? Why hadn't she listened? If only I'd known archaeology was going to be so important a subject in my life, Chloe thought. I would have accepted the genetic obsession and studied it.

A new entry into the room brought Chloe out of her reverie. The Rising Golden Bull swaggered into the room, saluted them all respectfully, and moved to stand behind *Hreesos*.

The family resemblance could not be more pronounced. The Golden they were indeed. Jutting noses, receding chins, thin-lipped wide mouths and glorious, flowing blond hair. Phoebus' eyes were a shade darker than *Hreesos'*, but they had the same strapping build and the same easy sense of command.

"I wanted Phoebus to address us today since soon, *eee* soon he will be in this chair," Zelos said. The group murmured.

"Clansmen," Phoebus said. "Prostatevo is nearly complete. Due to the recent misfortune at the Clan of the Muse"—he inclined his head to Atenis—"we are running behind schedule."

Sibylla was appalled at the Rising Golden's callousness—and Chloe had to agree. To call a monumental volcanic eruption a misfortune seemed a horrible understatement. Either that or the man redefined self-absorption.

"Nevertheless, Prostatevo should be ready for the Council to view by midsummer festival." He licked his lips and braced on the table. "On other matters, as Rising Golden, I must lodge a complaint with this body. More specifically, with the quorum of this body."

Fidgeting, cold silence.

"Spiralmaster is a vital position in Aztlan. It takes summers of training for a candidate even to be considered worthy to learn from Imhotep. Niko was the most brilliant student Imhotep ever had." Phoebus looked at them. "You and I heard the Spiralmaster say those exact words countless times."

Chloe's gaze went around the room. The tension among the Council was frightening. For some reason she was able to see and hear, even though Sibylla was "driving." There seemed to be less and less of Sibylla to argue with.

"The blood vows have long been held—"

"Time before mind," the Minos interjected.

"Inviolable," Phoebus continued, "but I submit that Spiralmaster was beyond reason and would not have inducted a foreigner, an unknown, into the Council. I further submit for consideration that this

Cheftu be stripped of his position and it be rightfully conferred on Niko."

The ensuing babble proved that *Robert's Rules of Order* were not established in the Minoan—Aztlantu—world. The group seemed evenly split, half screaming that Imhotep had chosen and sworn the man in, the other half blaming the death of Posidios on the missing Spiralmaster.

The argument was cut short as the floor rippled, raining plaster on the Council's heads. The quake lasted for only three seconds, but it had shaken them all. *Hreesos* called for an adjournment, and Chloe stumbled out the door with the others.

Fresh air, solid ground, that was what she needed. Desperately!

When they reconvened it was obvious wheeling and dealing had taken place during the break. Chloe watched as glances were exchanged. Phoebus reiterated his concerns about the new Spiralmaster, and Nekros rose to his feet.

"I was there when Posidios began his journey," he said. "This new man, whether clan blood flows in his veins or not, is well skilled. Imhotep was discerning—"

"He was mad!" Phoebus shouted.

Nekros glared at the Rising Golden. "Imhotep could measure a man's worth in less time than it takes to pick up a nugget of copper." He held up his hand at the rise of argument. "Therefore, before we break sacred vows, I propose we let this Egyptian Cheftu prove himself."

Everyone stiffened.

"Test him in the pyramid."

The Council was silent. Chloe knew nothing about the pyramid testing and no one else offered an explanation. *Sibylla? Hello?*

"It is how Phoebus will prove himself in a few moons," Nekros said. "It is how Spiralmaster proved himself summers ago. It is fitting that since Cheftu is an unknown, we should try him. The Rising Golden is wise in this. However, Cheftu should be allowed to defend himself in action."

Dion rose. "I agree with Nekros."

"If you favor the chieftain of the Clan of the Stone's view, raise your staff," *Hreesos* said.

Six were raised, and Chloe scrambled to raise hers. She hoped it was the right thing to do.

"A feast is already under way to welcome the Spiralmaster," Zelos said. "His examination shall begin at dawn the day after."

"Better not to test with fumes of the grape about one's head," Talos commented. The group laughed, except for Phoebus, and moved on to debate something else.

Cheftu, oh my love, I cannot wait to see you!

Chloe slipped on the fitted jacket, touching the pendant of her clan, wondering if this Egyptian Cheftu was *her* Egyptian Cheftu. Hope pounded through her veins, and she spoke to herself, trying to quiet her anticipation. For all she knew, Cheftu was as common a name in Egypt as John or David was in the States. He could be some old man with rheumy eyes and a wart on his nose!

Considering what she had heard, though, she was certain Cheftu was hers.

Because if he were her Cheftu—would he be surprised to have her back? Shocked? Happy? Don't be silly, she thought. He loved you, he loves you. It will be paradise! Chloe shook her head, clearing it, and began applying kohl to her eyes.

She was shaking too much and had to wipe it off and try again. *Cheftu was here.* Chloe rubbed ocher on her lips. The flounced skirt, quilted apron, and open bodice made her look so foreign, she didn't recognize herself. Even though she wore Sibylla's skin, her body moved beneath it. Light-colored eyes were not as rare here as in Egypt, so there were more green-eyed women. Would Cheftu recognize her? She would be introduced as Sibylla, but would he see her as Chloe?

A woman was announced; Chloe turned and had a hard time keeping her mouth shut. With chestnut hair and fair skin, she was striking. Chloe had always hated her own parchment white skin, but on this woman it really was the color of milk, and glowed like alabaster.

Her most stunning feature were her violet eyes; they had the same far-away-in-mystical-lands look that Boticelli's women had.

Sibylla peeked around the door of her mind, took one look at the woman, and said, *Vena. Okh!* and slammed the door.

Apparently the two women were not friends. So why was she here?

"How was your cavern this Snake's Season, Sibylla?" Vena said.

"It was . . . fine," Chloe said lamely. Sibylla's mental door was barricaded shut, so she assumed it really was fine. Vena sauntered into the room, running her hands over everything. She's like a cat marking my stuff, Chloe thought.

"I suppose you know that I left Nestor," she said.

"My, uh, sorrow," Chloe said, guessing.

"So I will be competing with you in the race, *eee?*"

"*Eee*, the race."

"Aye. The race." She smiled, a beautiful, dreamy, white-toothed smile. "Phoebus has grown into quite the stag. Have you seen him? Pity he can't forget Irmentis." Vena turned to her. "Are you ready to go dine? The new Spiralmaster is being feted tonight. Though he's a foreigner, I understand he is also—"

"A stag?"

"*Eee*, Sibylla, have you seen him?" Vena was all but purring.

"Let us go, then," Chloe said. She was as ready as she was going to be. And she didn't think she could take much more of Vena. The woman oozed . . . something. Sex appeal so noxious that Chloe wanted to scratch her eyes out, then toss them to a cat for a play toy.

As they walked down the wide steps together, Chloe noted they were good contrasts for each other. In addition to her amazing eyes and cascading curls, Vena had eyelashes about five inches long and a bustline that a Victoria's Secret model would covet.

Still, Chloe thought, Sibylla is no slouch. Chloe had seen her own features beneath caramel-colored skin; she had masses of ebony hair with a hint of red and thankfully! her own green eyes. Though she wasn't exactly voluptuous, she certainly did justice to the barebreasted fashions.

Would Cheftu recognize her?

The sounds of the feast reached them before they arrived. Chloe licked her lips, threw her shoulders back, and prepared to remeet her husband. Reseduce and remarry him, if necessary.

They joined others, a gaggle of young women, all perfumed and painted, dressed in their finest. Despite herself, the excitement of actually going to a party pricked Chloe and she smiled. Tonight she would be with Cheftu, even if she had to entice him under Ileana's table!

Comments and looks decipherable in any language were thrown their way, and Chloe stuck close to the other women, avoiding the gaze and grasp of the broad-shouldered, long-haired men. The smell of roasting meat and wine surrounded her. Lost somewhere in the chaos of thousands was the melodious plink of strings and the calling of the flutes.

As her bodyguard of ladies was absorbed into the mass, Chloe found a wall to stand against, her gaze roaming over the group. A mosaic of colors and patterns filled her vision. The floors and walls and ceilings were painted gaily, and women and men in the same bright blue, red, and saffron grouped before them. Men with mohawks, dressed in the codpiece and kilt of Mariners, grouped before one doorway—*Hreesos'* guards. A huge hearth provided a center for the room, and beside it stood an enormous vat, where a young nymph, up to her knees in wine, scooped rhytons of the fruit of the vine and gave kisses.

Slowly, avoiding the caresses and once or twice delivering casual slaps, Chloe made her way across this room into the next. If possible, it was even more crowded. She could barely move and was unpleasantly reminded of college parties. Hands outstretched, Chloe pushed through into another room. Low tables for three were scattered throughout the room. On the dais she saw the various thrones of the Clan Olimpi.

"Are you going to sit with the clan?" Vena asked.

A familiar laugh froze her blood, and Chloe turned. It was true, then, he was here. *In this time.* She was so overcome, she forgot to breathe. They could be together again. Her eyes filled with tears as she watched him.

He looked so distinctly Minoan, she wondered for an instant if it really were Cheftu. However, every cell in her body stood up and gave a marching band salute. Somehow his hair was long, the kilt he wore was tight and bright, and gold glistened on his chest, upper arms, and ankles. A pendant hung around his throat, and another disk swung from a chain against his thigh.

His legs. Oh Kela!

His eyes were still the color of warm honey, ringed with black. Despite his smiles, he wore a whipped look. He longs for me, she thought, tears spilling over her lower lashes. It was all Chloe could do not to run to him, wrap her arms, legs, and lips around him. I'm Sibylla, she reminded herself. Calm. He'll know me, he must know me!

Cheftu was seated next to Dion. Dion, who would most definitely recognize her as Sibylla. Next she noticed that the most beautiful women on the island were clustered around the men, touching their knees, legs, shoulders. Chloe felt her blood pressure rise and fought the urge to strangle all of them, including Cheftu. His words were slurred, and she realized he was drunk.

Cheftu was *drunk?* That was a first.

Vena laid a hand, cool and plumply feminine, on Chloe's arm. "Come along, cousin, the Spiralmaster awaits." *She's not my cousin,* Sibylla hissed. Chloe shook her head and they pushed forward. Compared to the rigidity of Egyptian court protocol, this was a free-for-all. Dion saw them first, and smiled, beckoning.

"Spiralmaster Cheftu," he said, touching Cheftu's shoulder, "I present you with my cousin Vena and clan sister Sibylla. Vena is a she-dog in heat; beware the teeth beneath her painted lips. Sibylla is an oracle, so she will know what you think of her."

Vena glared at Dion, and Cheftu looked at her, mumbling greetings, then looked at Chloe.

Cheftu's expression froze, and Chloe thought, Yessss! Then he turned away and focused on Vena.

Chloe felt slapped, then realized he probably was concerned about appearances. It would not do for two strangers to start making love in the middle of the floor; it might draw questions. Of course, she thought, he's just being wary.

She clenched her jaw as Cheftu drew Vena onto his lap, claiming he could think of places to be bitten that weren't so bad. Livid, nearly crying, Chloe let herself be seated by Dion. "What is wrong, Sib?" Dion whispered. "The color is gone from your face, and I would swear by the horns of Apis that your eyes are green!"

Though she wasn't looking, Chloe knew, she could *feel* Cheftu nuzzling Vena, his long-fingered hands on Vena's waist. Trembling with anger and hurt, Chloe accepted a rhyton and drained it. She was shaken to her very core. Cheftu had recognized her, she was certain of it! Was this—

"Do not weep, Sib," Dion said, pulling her closer. "Come, eat the *kollyva* funeral dinner with me for your *pateeras*, Posidios."

Shaking her head wordlessly, Chloe leaned against Dion as they crossed the room.

Leaving Cheftu behind.

HE WATCHED HER MOVE AWAY, attached to Dion as though he were a boat and she were a barnacle. Even now, even in the heat of this room, he remembered her body, the way it held him. Vena squirmed on his lap, and Cheftu wished desperately for more wine.

She was so beautiful . . . so . . . familiar.

It's the green eyes and black hair, he told himself. You are searching for Chloe. She's not here! Move on. I do not want to, he thought. God forgive me, but I would bury my body in Sibylla just to feel close to Chloe.

How perverse he had become.

Vena left to mingle with other long-haired, painted eye Aztlantu, and Cheftu watched the people walk by. They greeted him, introduced themselves, but he found himself looking past them for Sibylla. The oracle.

I asked if she was a Coil Dancer. She said if I wanted her to be. By the gods, that must have been an insult! He looked into the wine of his cup, debating whether or not to finish it. Why not? What did it matter? He'd given her the cut direct; she wouldn't speak to him again.

It was either that or pull her from this overcrowded room of peacocks into the first garden he could find and . . . He drank the wine.

"So you supplanted my friend Niko," a slurred voice said. Cheftu turned toward a sharp-faced blond in his cups. A quick glance at his throat and Cheftu realized this was Phoebus, the Rising Golden.

"It was Imhotep's decision," Cheftu said.

"It was your choice to accept," Phoebus countered.

"Aye. For the reasons Imhotep mentioned I felt I was the right person."

Phoebus kissed the mouth of a red-haired girl, then had his cup refilled, dismissing her with a snap of his fingers. "The *hequetai* illness?"

"Aye." Cheftu looked at the young man. "I understand that you were present during several of the deaths?"

Phoebus shivered. "A horrible thing. Ofttimes the beginning of one's spirit journey is a joyful occasion. These were . . . unsavory," he said after a moment. The music and noise ceased, and Phoebus looked toward a set of closed doors. "Ileana and her grand entrances," he muttered.

The double doors opened, and peacocks, their tails spread, strutted into the room. A high-pitched voice began to sing, announcing *Hreesos* Zelos and Kela-Ileana. Everyone, with the exception of Phoebus, raised their arms and hands, saluting the rulers of the Clan Olimpi, the embodiment of gods on earth. As they approached, Phoebus raised his hands, too.

"So you are the choice of Imhotep," Zelos said, his voice gruff. He was an impressive man, tall, barrel-chested, his hair long and still blond, his eyes cornflower blue and intense. Cheftu acknowledged he was and then met Ileana. She weighed him with her eyes until he felt like berries before a hungry crow. The couple swept on, and the rest of the room relaxed.

Dion sat down next to him, greeting Phoebus and asking after Niko. With a glance at Cheftu, Phoebus said Niko had gone in search of some privacy, some time for meditation. He was probably at the temple. The feast was served, most of it still in its shell, and Cheftu sat silently while the two men discussed Dion's air sail. Cheftu's gaze searched restlessly for Sibylla until Dion's words recalled him.

"You think Sibylla will run?" Dion asked Phoebus.

"I have heard she is already training," Phoebus said, licking his fingers.

"You should see her," Dion murmured. He slapped Cheftu's back. "Our Egyptian friend was slain by Vena—"

"A ritual here in Aztlan," Phoebus said. "Vena offers every newcomer her favors. We should leave her on the Breakwater for the purpose of serving traveling ships!" Dion laughed, and Cheftu tried to smile. "You were saying about Sibylla?" Phoebus asked Dion when they had stopped laughing.

"I know you have always cared for Irmentis—"

Phoebus' face darkened. "It is no matter."

"Aye, well, Sibylla has matured greatly this past Snake Season. You would not know her to look at her. She is beautiful."

"Always Sibylla has been beautiful," Phoebus said.

"There is something more now," Dion mused. "I am the closest man to her, and it is very clear."

"You only wish she were not such a good friend, so you could rut with her," Phoebus said.

Dion shrugged, and Cheftu clenched his fists. They were discussing her as though she were a plot of land! A goat, to be bartered over! "She lacks," Dion said slowly, "some things that I find attractive." His glance met Cheftu's, and Cheftu looked away. In his mind he could see Dion and Sibylla linked together, breathing and basking in—

"Look at her!" Dion said, nudging him in the ribs, muddying his stream of thought. It was the same dancer Nestor had tried to give to Senwosret.

The music got louder, and as the guests finished eating, they began to dance. Linking into lines, they formed elaborate patterns that brought them close together, so that breasts brushed bare chests, and then far apart. They danced halfway through a pattern and then reversed direction.

Cheftu's head began to ache. The woman who had caught Dion's eye was even now rubbing against him as they danced together. Phoebus had left, stony faced, and Cheftu sat alone, watching the dark-haired women, wondering who was holding Sibylla. He snapped for more wine and looked around the room.

Compared to the Aztlantu, the Egyptians were absolutely reserved.

Within a few more cups of wine, Cheftu imagined this feast would become an orgy. Already he had stopped a few southerly moving hands.

Half the line was turned away from him, and Cheftu's gaze skimmed over the hourglass shape of the women, long black curls dancing on their ruffled rears. Then he felt his body tighten. He knew it was she, he could sense it, even though she was turned away. Her feet moved swiftly in the pattern, coming around to face him. As she danced he could see the flush of exertion on her skin, the glow in her green eyes.

She met his gaze for a moment, then curtained her face behind the dark veil of her hair. He downed his cup and snapped for another. His head would ache horribly come dawn, but perhaps this would soften the ache he felt elsewhere, now.

CHLOE WAS HAVING FUN in this ancient version of a conga line. Cheftu, whom she'd not seen for a while, was leaning against a male companion, a voluptuous redhead sitting on his lap. Chloe stared hard at him. *Look at me!* she thought. *Get your hands and mind off that woman and look up!* The conga line moved closer, and the redhead was pulled off his lap by some guy. Cheftu looked up, his eyes seeming dark in the muted light. The line moved closer, and Chloe danced over to her husband, taking his hand and pulling him.

He didn't move. He didn't look at her. He just sat. Chloe tugged and he jerked away, continuing his conversation with the other man. Three women came up to the other guy and towed him along, rubbing their hands on his body, making the invitation quite clear.

Still Cheftu sat. He was ignoring her? Boldly Chloe brought his hand to her breast. He looked up, his fingers already caressing her, and stared. *Guiltily,* Chloe thought. He blinked a few times, and Chloe grabbed his other hand and dragged him into the line.

It was not an easy dance, but Cheftu matched her steps. She felt the heat of his body, smelled the blend of his skin and unguents and wine. After a while the line turned directions, each person holding tight to the partners before them, while those behind them moved very closely. The music took on a primal, seductive beat. Chloe was flushed—the feel of Cheftu against her, hot and aroused, was sexier than imagination. The circle grew smaller as couples broke away. She was just deciding to pull Cheftu into a darker corner when she was lifted and kissed.

He tasted like wine and hunger and Cheftu, and Chloe could barely breathe for wanting him. She heard voices, felt a very cold wind, but his body, scorching, was against hers. His hands moved beneath her skirt, his mouth laved her exposed breasts. Tears streamed from the corners of her eyes as he whispered to her. She was with Cheftu, finally! He knew her! He loved her!

The contrast of his black hair against her paler skin was visible even in the darkness. He kissed her stomach, the insides of her thighs, and Chloe fell back with a low moan. She became nothing but sense and felt as though she were laid bare to the bone with electricity jagging through her body. He pressed his fingers into her mouth and she sucked on them, imitating the actions that were shattering her. Chloe was whimpering, alternating hot and cold until her body was reduced to shudders and tears.

He pulled her onto his thighs, entering in one slow movement. Chloe draped her arms around his neck and absorbed his thrusts, still reeling from the magic he'd worked on her. His lips were pressed against her neck, her skin muffling his panting and final stillness.

They fell back as one body. Her love was back, here in her arms. Chloe was so happy, she wanted to cry. "*Eee*, Cheftu," she whispered, her hands in his hair.

His lips were against her ear, his voice husky and wine scented. "So you craved me again, Sibylla?"

Again?

Chloe's eyes popped open.

"I apologize for leaving the way I did," he said. "I did not know you were a chieftain." He kissed her ear. "It was not intended to be disrespectful."

What the hell was he talking about? Chloe banged on Sibylla's mental door, demanding a response.

He kissed her, *Sibylla's*, shoulder. "You are magnificent, my mistress."

Chloe couldn't think. Her body was still trembling from him, yet he didn't know who she was? He didn't recognize her? How had he known Sibylla? He made love this passionately, this *graphically*, to a woman he'd known only . . . only . . . she didn't know how long.

Chloe wondered if she could kick in Sibylla's mental door. *Cheftu slept with another woman? Well, with me inside another woman? But I wasn't there!* With a last defiant battering of the door—unanswered—Chloe searched Sibylla's memory.

Knossos. Rituals. *Yeah, right!*

She couldn't decide if she felt more pain or anger. She knew she wanted to kill him. She also wanted to run. Far, far away. He didn't know her? The man who'd promised to find her in any century, in any body, and he didn't recognize her when they were making love? *Twice?*

He pulled away from her, lying on his back, apparently dozing. Her Cheftu had always been a chatterbox after lovemaking. How could he not know her? Chloe sat up, pulling down her skirt and tucking it around her cold feet, straightening her jacket. This was the last, the *very* last, time Cheftu would touch her until he knew whom he was touching!

"This cannot happen again," he said, his words slurred. "After tonight, although I crave you, I cannot . . ."

"Trust me, abstinence will not be an issue," she said coldly.

He opened his eyes at her response and raised up on an elbow. His hair was just as mussed as hers, and he hadn't yet bothered to straighten his kilt. "Do I detect anger? Have I left you less than satisfied?"

Much less, she thought. "Your skills are worthy of a Coil Dancer."

Eyes narrowing, Cheftu sat up. "Your manners are not."

Chloe stood up, furious and blinking back tears. Was their love affair just for Egypt? Was he not attracted when she wasn't Egyptian? Were their souls really *not* connected? Had she been lying to herself?

Cheftu stood up, grabbing her wrists with one hand, adjusting his kilt with the other. "I do not appreciate lovers who leave without even a word of kindness."

Like you left Sibylla, *me*, in Knossos, she thought. "Perhaps you are reaping as you sow?"

He dropped his hand. "I see you do not easily forgive."

"You *more* than easily forget, though!" Chloe said, fighting back tears. He frowned at her and rubbed his face, gestures that were so Cheftu they hurt. What had happened? He touched her face, frowning when she pulled away.

"I want you again, Sibylla. Gods help me, I do."

She watched the face she'd memorized, detail by detail, from eyebrows to the fine lines around his mouth and eyes, draw nearer. His pupils were dilated, and she knew his expression of desire so well.

For another.

"Go to hell," she said in English. Lifting her skirt, she ran away, weeping.

CHAPTER II

I T TOOK A MOMENT FOR CHEFTU TO REALIZE she'd spoken to him in English.

English!

Green eyes, black hair, skin that received him eagerly, a spirit that left him buoyant to behold. Cheftu pressed his hand to his chest, feeling the thundering of his heart. He couldn't catch his breath, he didn't dare even think it. He'd seen her body, her dead body! The Egyptians had told him she was gone.

Gone into another body!

It explained so much! Why hadn't she told him in Knossos, though? Why let him believe she was dead and that he would spend his life mourning her? Why flee him now? His heart slowed, and Cheftu wondered if she was happy he was here. She'd bedded him willingly enough, but . . .

He ran after her, stumbling, drunk on sex and wine, almost sick with apprehension. "Chloe!" he cried out. "Chloe! Sibylla!" The

moon gave some light, but he didn't know the gardens, and like everything else on Aztlan, they were labyrinthine. He had to find her! *Mon
Dieu*, he'd committed adultery with his own wife. Was that even possible? The thought made him stumble, and he cursed, then swore
again as clouds skittered across the moon. "Chloe," he called out in
French. "Chloe, my love, I am such a blind man. Please, Chloe!"

Silence answered him, and he stopped, gulping for breath, fighting
against the alcohol in his veins to stay upright. She wasn't dead, she
was alive! She was here! Even if she hated him now, he had a chance,
he could win her back. He could see her, touch her. The tears he had
stifled for so many lost, aching weeks began to flow down his face.
His love was alive, she was here. Cheftu sank to his knees, weeping.
Thank God! *Grâce à Dieu!*

Her hand touched his shoulder, and Cheftu brought it to his
mouth, kissing and crying on her long, clever fingers. So blind! She
stood, resisting him, but Cheftu didn't care. She was here! She lived.
He buried his face against her skirt, the scent of them commingled
on the brightly patterned wool. His body had known her, recognized
her, even though his mind had not.

He cried with relief, then froze when she touched his hair, cautiously running her fingers along his scalp and hairline. "How did it
get so long?" Her voice was soft, and Cheftu smiled through his tears.
The questions, the hows and whys, what light she brought to him!

"It is braided into mine," he said, his voice muffled against her
skirt, his arms aching with his grip around her. "*Eee*, Chloe, my love,
my heart. Forgive me." She stiffened. "I—I did not dare to hope."

"Oh, Cheftu," she said, then slipped bonelessly through his grasp,
so that her mouth was on his, and Cheftu tasted her, his Chloe,
through his tears. The desire was so strong, so elemental, they simply
lifted their clothing, joining, staring at each other as completion came
quickly.

Gently he held her body against him, marveling that it was Chloe
he held.

"*Grâce à Dieu,*" he whispered against her neck.

"Amen," Chloe said.

PREDAWN CHILL WOKE HER and Chloe opened her eyes, staring at the tinted clouds, holding her breath for fear she was wrong. Cheftu turned in his sleep, shivering, trying to get closer. "It's cold," she said. Her hands and feet were numb. It obviously wasn't summertime yet. His arms tightened around her, and Chloe submitted to being cold on one side and melting from contact with his hot skin on the other.

She sighed, contented.

How was it that he was always so warm? He was a space heater on legs! She cuddled tighter to him, fitting her body against the solid strength of his. One arm pillowed her head, his fingers resting lightly on her side. The other crossed over her hips, holding them together snugly.

What an amazing thing to sleep with a man, Chloe thought. She was certain the little refrain of happiness that she heard was her blood singing. How had this happened, how had they gotten together? It was a miracle! Nothing short!

She looked above them. The gold and orange of the clouds had turned to pink and lavender with the rising sun's reflection. It was a perfect morning, they had a perfect day—Chloe froze. Dawn. Cheftu was going to be tested at dawn. Was that today? No, they had made allowances for hangovers, Chloe recalled.

The pyramid tests, what were they?

"You are thinking so loudly, I cannot sleep," Cheftu rumbled in her ear. The tiny hairs on her neck and ear rose on end as she shivered. "You like?" he said softly, then began to follow the curve of her ear with his tongue. Chloe felt her body heat and turned to him, arching to receive him, holding him close, not moving, just savoring.

Then, with a groan, Cheftu began to move slowly. He drew so far away, the cool air rushing against her hot skin, the contact almost breaking, then straight, deep, inch by inch, as though he were drawn magnetically, until they were hipbone to hipbone. Chloe watched as her body swallowed his wholly, as they became one.

High golden light fell across the tops of the garden trees, and Chloe rolled beneath him, her hips rising to keep the contact, their fingers laced, white knuckled, riding the rising waves. Cheftu began to pound into her, his jaw set, his eyes dark. "I almost lost you," he said hoarsely. "You are mine!"

Chloe's legs began to ache, rubbed raw, and she winced, then begged for more as he raised her hips, going deeper, harder, faster. Her breath was loud in the birdsong morning, and she ran her hands over his back, feeling the power, the need, the benign threat of his body.

It didn't begin or end, just flowed like waves on the shore, cresting higher and higher, her cries muffled by his mouth, his teeth stroking her tongue, sucking on it, his sweat slippery against her skin. Cheftu bit the nape of her neck with his final thrust, holding her close and tight, grinding against her, and Chloe felt herself burst on an almost molecular level, bucking off the ground, trying to get closer, get more . . .

"I cannot move," he said after a while.

"Why not?" Chloe murmured, half-asleep.

"I think my seed was a fast-growing vine that holds me within you now."

Chloe smiled against his shoulder. "That sounds nice. Like a watermelon."

He was silent a moment. "A what?" Cheftu was sounding a little more awake.

"When I was a little kid my Mimi would say that if we ate watermelon seeds, we would grow watermelons in our tummies. I used to think that pregnant women had swallowed watermelon seeds." She licked at his skin and felt him shudder instantly. "It scared me to death."

Chloe recalled with horror that they'd made love with no protection. If she reminded Cheftu of that, he was likely to pull away. His feelings about parenting were set in concrete and didn't include trysts beneath trees. Please, don't let me be pregnant, she prayed quickly.

Cheftu pushed himself up on his forearms, staring at her. He looked as if it had been a rough night, Chloe thought. Leaves and twigs and all manner of outdoorsy stuff decorated his hair where once it was neatly plaited and curled. His eyes were red and bleary, razor stubble dotted his somewhat blotched skin. However, the love pouring from his bloodshot eyes, his expression telling her she was the most beautiful sight to him, this made him gorgeous. Especially when he looked well used. Especially when she'd been the user. Chloe arched against him, and Cheftu groaned.

They froze at the sound of voices. The sun was higher now, coming through the trees that had sheltered them all night. Cheftu ran a hand through her hair, touching her cheekbones and nose, the flat of his thumb running over the arch of her brow, the tips of her lashes.

He gazed at her mouth, and Chloe felt her lips part. Cheftu followed the bow of her upper lip, the fullness of her lower lip with the tip of his pinky. "I dreamed of you," he whispered. "Every morning I woke up, remembered you were dead, and it was like hearing it for the first time." She saw the muscle in his jaw flex. "There was no color without you. Food was tasteless because all I could think was Baskin-Robbins—"

Chloe laughed. In Egypt they had likened lovemaking to ice cream. All the many different "flavors" they could explore together. We came pretty close to a menu of thirty-one, she thought.

His eyes were smiling. "So what flavor, *eee*, Chieftain?" He raised his brow, and Chloe thought of pirates and bikers and masquerading Frenchmen. His eyes darkened as she clenched him deeply. "This," she said, turning her face into his palm and kissing it, "was as far beyond ice cream as water from coffee."

Cheftu's face, lean and hard, was turning gaunt with desire before her eyes. "So then?" he asked, his voice low and filling every syllable with seduction.

I am insane, Chloe thought, to classify "So then?" as seduction. But with Cheftu, it was.

"Crème brûleé," she said. He cocked his head, asking wordlessly for an explanation. "It's hard"—Cheftu inhaled sharply at her softly undulating body—"and crunchy and sweet on top."

Her husband half laughed and half groaned. "You think so, *ma chérie?*"

"*Eee*, I know so," she answered with a smile. "And beneath is—"

"Soft and creamy and melts on my tongue," he whispered, and Chloe heard no more, her blood pounded too loudly.

"Take me," she whimpered.

"*Toi aussi.*"

Finally someone answered the pounding at the door. About time! Chloe thought, hiding her head beneath the pillow. She'd slipped into bed about the time the palace was stirring. These crazed Aztlantu, didn't they realize when you party all night you sleep until noon?

Apparently not.

Of course, she reasoned, not all of them were in the garden making it like mink all night. She smiled against the bedclothes. By Kela, she ached and was bruised and would probably walk funny for a while, but to be with Cheftu—They'd hated to part but, uncertain of Aztlantu etiquette, had deemed it best.

Cheftu had left her at her door and run back to kiss her no less than five times, each kiss longer and more involved, though he swore he was exhausted beyond mortal range. Good, Chloe thought.

Heaven knew she was!

Dozing had just turned to REM sleep when she was jolted awake by a hand on her shoulder. Chloe jerked upright, heart pounding, confused. She blinked at the owner of the hand, trying to place her.

"I called you thrice," the woman said. She was tall and plain. Except for her eyes, which were large, thickly lashed, and a shade of gray that looked almost silver, she was just . . . there. Her bright clothing hung like sackcloth. Her long hair, streaked with gray, was wrapped around her head, styled like that of a traditional German waitress. "Sibylla?" she asked again.

Right! Cover her with mud and tears and blood, and it was the woman who'd loaned her people to operate on Naxos.

"My apology, Atenis," Chloe said. "I was sleeping too hard, I fear." Atenis sat on the edge of the bed. "You got to your couch late?"

"Aye. Very late."

The woman smiled. Goodwill and kindness transformed her features so that she glowed, light seeming to pour from her like a prism. "Very early this morning, more like. I came by at dawn, but you were not here and your serf said you hadn't come back yet."

Chloe felt herself blushing.

"Should I check to see who else was late in returning?" Chloe got even rosier, and Atenis laughed. "Just a jest this morning, my sister. I have not felt like laughing much since Arachne—" She broke off and looked away, her hand touching the clan seal at her throat. "I came to offer my services, in truth."

Oh, Kela, I want some coffee! "Your services?"

"I will not be running against Ileana, but I do know how to run and how to win. I can train you."

"Why me?"

Frowning a little with confusion, Atenis shrugged. "Vena is . . . unbearable to me. Her frivolity reminds me of a saline bath on abraded skin." That would be grim, Chloe conceded. "Selena is a good friend, but her mother is a grasping, dishonest creature." She smiled again. "You and Phoebus would make a beautiful baby."

Baby.

Was she even now carrying Cheftu's baby? She hadn't taken any birth control seeds this morning. Did these people, these quasi Minoans, even have birth control? Chloe blushed again.

"I've heard you won the first four races you were in. I know a few of those runners, by reputation at least, and am quite impressed. You have never shown an aptitude for physical activity before."

Living in a world where distance was measured by how the crow flies *and* how the goat climbs up and down, up and down, how could Sibylla have been less than physical? Chloe stifled a yawn. "Sounds good. Thank you." Slowly she began inching back down, yelping when Atenis yanked off the covers.

"Come along, then."

"*Now?*"

"You have less than three moon-cycles to learn how to win, to beat Ileana. I assure you, she is out training this morning and will spend part of the afternoon at it also. Now."

I hate running, Chloe thought, wincing as she stood. I really, *really* do!

CHEFTU HAD BEEN UNABLE TO SLEEP, so after a bath and shave, his body silent and sated, he had broken his fast in the scroll room. He was just finishing a treatise on the human circulatory system when Dion was announced.

After traditional greetings (Cheftu still didn't know where these language skills had come from; a sign of approval from the One God?), the two men sat down. Cheftu waited expectantly. Dion was formally dressed, and only a smudge or two beneath his eyes betrayed the grape and dance he had reveled in the night before.

"Egyptian, the Council has decided, and I have been chosen to convey, the need for you to undergo some testing."

"Of what sort?"

"Spiralmaster was expert in all the fields, including: *mnasonry, al-khem,* medicine, astronomy, mathematics, physics, geometry, biology, spirit travel." Dion licked his lips and smiled sheepishly. "Because you are an unknown and seek this position, the Council would like you to undergo the testing that Spiralmaster would have required of any inheritor."

"When?" Cheftu asked. He dared not even voice the fear that he would fail. Some of the things mentioned by Dion were unknown to him, at least named as such.

"Dawn tomorrow."

"I have no time to prepare?" I've been ordained to fail, Cheftu thought.

Dion shrugged. "You have today. I—" He held out a hand to still Cheftu's response. "I am a Scholomancer myself. I can assist you in anything you want to know."

Why am I here? Cheftu thought. Can you assist me with that? Why have I been placed in this position of power? Any illumination there?

Unable to sit, he walked to the window, looking out across the sea. Delphiniums, a shade lighter than the waters, waved in the breeze below. Cheftu breathed deeply, trying to calm himself. Chloe was here, they had positions in society, he had to succeed this testing or he might not be able to be with her.

His resolve now iron, Cheftu turned to Dion. He was looking at an Egyptian papyrus illustration of the human body. "What is this?" the chieftain asked.

Relieved to speak of something of which he was actually a master—anatomy—Cheftu explained the Egyptian understanding that all vessels came from the heart, in the center of one's chest, but assembled again around the rectum. Hence, all healing required purging first.

"How is that? You should give a sick person an enema first?"

"Aye. Anything that breaches the anus vessels can be carried anywhere in the body, poisoning the entire body with *ukhedu*."

"*Ukhedu?*" Dion repeated slowly.

"Poison, vitriol, the power of *khefts* and *khaibits*. It can infect man and lead him to intemperate behavior, illness or insanity." Cheftu realized as he spoke that the Aztlantu didn't share the Egyptian ideals of calm and balance.

"Enemas flush this out?"

"Aye, only for a short period of time; but during those moments the body is pure and medicaments can be administered effectively."

"So what of intercourse?"

Cheftu turned back from the view. "My friend, intercourse is not with a woman's anus. There is no fear of *ukhedu* from coupling."

"What about sex with a man?"

Blinking, Cheftu tried to discern what the man was asking. He wanted to be certain, to not offend. "A man . . . and a man?" he asked cautiously.

"Aye. Equals. Brothers. Comrades." Dion crossed his arms. "There are many things women cannot know or understand. Only a man can truly be the equal heartlove of another man."

A man and a man. In Egypt, homosexuality was virtually unheard of. The gods—Isis and Osiris, Amun-Ra and Mut, Geb and Nuit— all showed the pathway to fruitful, marital love. A man and woman producing a child. That was Ma'at, the universal fulcrum that each Egyptian sought to keep stable.

In other courts, Mesopotamia, Canaan, even the strange land of Punt, men might have been lovers of men, but Cheftu had never participated and was uneasy speaking of it. "I . . . have not thought about it," he stuttered. During his childhood in France, there was hushed gossip about men who preferred the love of other men. As one who appreciated the differences between the sexes, two men seemed one man too many to him.

Dion rose. "I gathered from your silence that you had not." He stepped closer, and Cheftu felt himself drawing taller, defensive. "What do you find so distasteful, Cheftu? Is not a mouth a mouth and a receptacle a receptacle?"

Cheftu had the sudden urge to laugh, imagining Chloe's response to being called a "receptacle." It restored his equilibrium. "I doubt any of this will be in my Spiralmaster testing," he said with a smile. "Perhaps we could discuss those things that might be?" Looking out the window, he gauged his time. "I have less than twenty decans to learn all that Spiralmaster spent his life studying. I confess I feel a little overwhelmed."

Dion laughed and clapped Cheftu on the shoulder. "Let us go to the library first, then the laboratory!"

CHLOE WAITED PATIENTLY, SHE THOUGHT, to hear from Cheftu.

Nothing.

She returned from her training with Atenis, threw herself into the bath, rushed through the massage/dressing phase, and made sure wine and fruit were cooling and on call. The sun sailed farther and farther west, and Chloe sat looking out the window, drumming her fingers on the window ledge and waiting.

By the time the sun was setting she was fuming. Selena brought her wine and sat with her. "I hear the new Spiralmaster has been closeted with Dion all since dawn."

Chloe could have smacked herself for being so dense! He was tested tomorrow! Suddenly her irritation melted into fear for him.

"I hope for the Egyptian's sake that they really were studying," Selena said coyly.

"What happens if he, uh, doesn't pass?"

"You know, Sibylla. Death in the Labyrinth."

Oh my God. "That seems unfair, one day to study for a position he didn't request, then a death penalty if he errs."

Selena shrugged. "The priests at the pyramid are jealous of their secrets. You cannot go inside and hope to live without becoming one of them."

Cheftu once said he'd been inducted into the secrets of Amun in Karnak, hush-hush priesthood rituals. Maybe they were the same? Please, God, please help him, she thought. Does he need me?

The answer didn't come from without, it came from within. In her heart Chloe knew that she gave strength to Cheftu, gave him drive and confidence. Call it chemistry, soulmates, or just lucky, nevertheless they needed each other. He needed her to survive this. In microseconds Sibylla was complaining of a headache, refusing Selena's offers of infusions and herbs and locking the door behind her well-meaning friend and the serf.

Swiping the palace's floor plan from Sibylla's mind, Chloe slipped into the corridor. Cheftu might as well be on the moon for the sense the directions made, but she would find him, she would get there. To think I used to complain about the one-way streets in Dallas, she thought to herself.

A decan later, she was tapping on his door.

A serf opened it, and Chloe found herself at a loss for words. With a shawl over her head and most of her face, she blinked at the serf. "Tell Lord Cheftu that his *chérie* is here," she said, hoping she sounded foreign.

He was at the door in seconds, and Chloe smiled behind her costume as she saw the pulse in his throat beat faster. He dismissed the serf without even looking at him and pulled Chloe into the room, closing and locking the double doors behind her.

"My *chérie, eee?*" he said, kissing her softly.

"I have been led to believe so," she said.

He took her hand and led her into the adjoining room. Scrolls and booklike pieces of leather and papyri were open everywhere. "My preparation," he said.

"Do you need me to help?"

He sighed. "I can only hope that Imhotep taught Egyptian skills. I do not know what secrets Aztlan guards."

Rifling through Sibylla's memory, puzzled, Chloe repeated the answers to herself. "They are these: pouring stone, shaping rock, and transforming."

"Where did you learn that?"

Chloe touched her forehead.

"*Eee,* you have a spy." He glanced away. "Do you have her memory?"

"Actually, I think I *am* the spy," she said. "I only remember a few things. Why?" Sibylla hadn't spoken in days, and the space felt very . . . open. Was Sibylla even there? *If she isn't, did I kill her off?* But her knowledge was there, intrinsically.

"Pouring stone, shaping rock, and transforming," Cheftu repeated. "By the gods! I know how to embalm, to do surgery, to pray to a dozen deities. These skills . . ." He bowed his head, his hands hanging loosely between his kilted thighs.

"You are tired, beloved," Chloe said, slipping to kneel before him. "Did you get any sleep?"

"Nay. I cannot sleep now."

"Do you feel prepared?"

"As prepared as I can get in one day," he said bitterly. "It is . . ." Cheftu sighed. "I fear losing the privilege of being with you. Nor do I want to fail in my duties here."

"Which are?" she asked, stroking his legs gently.

Cheftu shrugged. "I am not certain."

"God will help you. Hell, Cheftu, he brought us together in a whole other time! Other bodies. What time is it, by the way?"

He squinted out the window.

"Nay, the time in history. Chronological time," she clarified.

"Middle Kingdom. The Hyksos will invade Egypt shortly."

"What years are those?"

He gazed at her, his golden eyes glittering. "The 1850s Before Christ."

"Holy shit." Back almost four hundred years? Chloe sat beside him on the stone sofa, staring and wondering. "Sleep, beloved," he said, picking up a scroll and bending over it. Chloe watched him, his finger moving over the page, his concentration tangible, until her eyes closed.

THE PYRAMID GRACED THE NOSTRIL OF THE BULL, the largest of the volcanoes scattered through the islands of Aztlan. Priests and priestesses lined the causeway that ran up at a nearly forty-five-degree angle.

Cheftu would walk the three hundred and sixty-five steps, alone. A step for each day, giving the temple its name. The flat gold top reflected the limitless turquoise sky. Far below, the water shifted from dark blue, almost black, to silver-crested waves. Fortunately Cheftu was not required to recite the prayers for each day as he walked up the steps. Phoebus would do that when it was his turn to submit to the pyramid testing.

He'd had nineteen years to prepare, Cheftu thought, mounting them. I had one day. Licking his lips, he continued walking.

The Council stood near the top of the flight. Atenis, Talos, Iason, Dion, Embla, Minos, Chloe—he didn't dare let their gazes touch for more than a moment; still, his heart swelled. She was so beautiful, so magnificent in her passion, her care, and her talent. Zelos and Nekros bade him Apis' wisdom. With a last glance toward the sun and Chloe, Cheftu stepped down into the shadows of the pyramid.

The Minos touched his arm and Cheftu followed him, listening to the crunch of the high priest's sandals on the shell-strewn floor. He felt, rather than saw, a wall loom before him. Without hesitation he walked to the left and, after a sharp turn, entered the room. For a moment breath left him. In more than a decade of dwelling amid Egypt's gilded splendor he had never seen such opulence. Again he asked, Who were these people?

The walls were covered in a mosaic of gold, silver, and bronze, depicting scenes of the founding of Aztlan by Atlas Olimpi. As Dion had told him, everything was written in the ancient tongue, scratchings and symbols that had no meaning outside of the priesthood and the Scholomance.

However, they were decipherable to Cheftu. He'd learned this language, along with a host of others, in order to unravel the mystery of Egyptian hieroglyphs. It was a proto-Hebrew. *Mon Dieu!* Cheftu stepped closer, reading the legacy of these people. The text contained innumerable references to "stones." Communicating stones.

Turning to check that the door was open, Cheftu was shocked to realize it was gone. He scrutinized all the walls, the stories marching seamlessly down one long wall and onto another. He could find no way out. He looked up. Even the ceiling, covered with the same precious metal mosaic, offered no exit. He stalked through the room, calming himself. Measure the paces, he thought. Here, as in Egypt, numbers are very significant.

It measured sixty-six by sixty-six paces. Thank God he'd learned the exact measure of an Aztlantu pace yesterday. Cheftu stared at the floor. It was abstractly patterned hammered gold. If there were any more light in this room, he would be blinded.

He glanced up, a shimmer unlike silver or gold having caught his eye. He scanned the far wall, moving his head slowly until he saw it again. He crossed the room and stared into the crystalline eye of the Bull.

Cheftu reached up and pried at the crystal. A loud groaning filled his ears, then was gone. The crystal pulled forward, extending a full cubit, then halted. He stepped back, looking at the crystal and knowing there had to be logic behind it. Were there more?

For a decan he searched the room, finding two more crystals that extended from the wall. Three, the mystery number. Dion said it was odd, consequently sacred to the goddess, just as sixty-six was an even number and would be sacred, doubly so, to Apis.

Now what? Cheftu had already taken off the gold links he'd been wearing, so he stripped off the elaborate belled skirt and loosened his corselet. The three crystals formed a triangle of sorts. Triangles were sacred; any mage knew that. But there wouldn't be just one. There had to be at least two more.

The ceiling! The floor!

After decans of searching he found another triangle, formed by shards of black obsidian. He pushed against it until stone ground against stone. The room sounded as though it would shatter as the mechanism outside it shifted.

The third triangle was simple to find. Cheftu leaned against the wall and tried to put himself into the mind of the builder. What was the purpose of this exercise? He'd dealt with the three dimensions of creation: width, depth, height. The only other dimension was time.

Time? He stood up and walked around the room again, searching for some symbol of time. Find an ankh. He turned back to the room, mentally imposing the triangles he'd created on the ceiling, floor, and walls. There, at the joining of the three dimensions, was the key of life for millions of years; a more potent symbol for time did not exist. Looking down at the floor, he smiled. An ankh-shaped depression.

Now where was the ankh that fit there? Again he perused the chamber. Stepping closer, he noticed an ankh that was made of a metal other than the silver in which it was set. The difference was subtle but noticeable.

It jiggled in its setting, and Cheftu tried to slide something beneath it, but his nails were short. Think, he told himself. He walked back to the center of the room, looking again at the hollow, approximately where the three triangles intersected.

Using the post of his earring, he pried the ankh from its resting place and put it in the shaped hollow. The ensuing noise shook the walls. He watched the room change. With great shrieks the walls moved, portions levering and sliding, until at the end he was in a triangular room.

By the stones of Apis, this was incredible!

The gold-and-silver narrative had been replaced by smooth walls, one lapis, one malachite, and one jasper. The floor beneath him remained the same. Warily he picked up the ankh and jumped back as a section of floor rose, waist high. Then all was still again.

The risen part looked like a stone trunk. Cheftu nudged what he presumed was the top—back and forward. It wouldn't budge. With an exasperated sigh he remembered the ankh and placed it in the hole. Nothing happened. He placed his ear on the stone, turning the ankh until he heard a series of clicks. Of course, three turns to the left, three more right, and three more left; Egyptians and Aztlantu had that much in common.

He pushed the top off easily and stared.

A small trough, a square, a wooden box, a plumb line, a level, and a trowel. He laid each of them on the table. At the bottom of the box were two linen bags and three jars. He took them out, opening as he went. A white powder, with small pebbles; he tasted the next—natron; a brown slime; a big bag of larger pebbles; and a jug of water. Cheftu paced. What could these have to do with each other?

What had Chloe said? The ability to pour stone, shape rock, and transform?

He had studied at the Temple of Amun-Ra before choosing medicine and joining the House of Life. He had learned how certain substances and liquids interacted with each other, forming new substances. Enamel was created by mixing *mafkat* powder with niter and holding it over a flame. He sped back to the table with its odd assortment.

Niter and water and lime—the white powder—made a caustic substance; add *mafkat* until it dissolved, then mud. When it thickened, he would pour in the stones. Cheftu stripped off the remains of his finery and began to measure and mix, pulling from recipes and rituals his mind never forgot.

He would succeed.

When the food appeared, Cheftu could not say. Yet it was there—roasted meat, sea scallops, and a salad of sliced citrus and onion. A flask of watered wine complemented the meal. He glanced over his shoulder; his experimental mixture was setting in the wooden box. Already it had taken on the appearance of limestone, its edges sharp and clean, the faces smooth and sparkling with bits of mica and ore. The art of *al-khemti*—even *called* Egyptian, after the land of Kemt.

Dion had said the priests, the *mnasons*, trained a lifetime learning to form *ari-kat* stone. They had constructed the many buildings on Aztlan Island using their series of secret gestures and their tightly knit clanship.

This *ari-kat* stone had built the Pyramids. Cheftu was certain of it. The limestone looked the same, and it would explain how such enormous, perfectly shaped rocks fit together flawlessly. They were *poured*. He smiled. Not only was Pharaoh Kufu's Imhotep brilliant, but he was wily, passing on the legend of thousands of workers quarrying immense stones for tens of Inundations.

Now Cheftu understood why no one had ever known anyone whose family had worked on the Pyramids. Most likely the priests had poured the stone into molds, then poured more when they dried. In a land built of mud brick, it really was no surprise. It would have taken a few thousand people as opposed to hundreds of thousands of people.

Cheftu ate, then slept. When he awoke in the jewel-toned room, he ran over to his brick. It was cool, so he pulled away the wooden blanks and looked at it. A rectangle of limestone that looked as if it were quarried from the finest veins in Aswan. It weighed like limestone also. Cheftu was laughing to himself when he heard a faint noise.

Turning around, he saw that his breakfast had appeared—fruit and bread. He turned back to the table; the entire table, including the *ari-kat* limestone, was gone.

Another table was in its place, with another box, another flat surface. Except this one had a throwing wheel. Eating his fruit as he unpacked the box, Cheftu frowned over the ingredients. A vial of natural acid, a block of alabaster, rags, oil, and a template drawn on linen, round and fat on one end, narrowing, then bulging again before the neck. Last, a dried bladder. He picked it up, turning it over and around. A dried bladder?

Cheftu paced, drawing on his lessons and ideas. He had no idea how many days it had taken him to make the *ari-kat* stone or how many days he was expected to be in the pyramid.

What was he to make from this? He toyed with the block of alabaster. The stone was pleasantly weighted, the height just right for a perfume vial. Acid. Alabaster. Another Egyptian skill, praise Ptah!

He opened the acid vial and poured a little on the stone. . . . The reward was a satisfying hiss as the acid began to eat at the stone. Hands trembling, he poured the acid into the bladder, squeezing the flow onto the stone, controlling how and where the stone was formed.

The ability to shape stone.

CHAPTER 12

CHEFTU HAD BEEN IN THE PYRAMID FOR TEN DAYS. Chloe only hoped they were feeding him. What could take ten days? Instead of worrying, she was letting Atenis kill her. Slowly, painfully, and thoroughly.

Today they were working on pace.

Chloe thought she knew how to run; she had done a lot of it in the air force, and she had spent a fair amount of time running in ancient Egypt. However, according to Atenis, Chloe didn't know the first thing about it.

First there had been the discussion of her running posture. She clenched her fists, a no-no; she also looked down. If I don't, I will trip and break something, Chloe argued, but Atenis chided her: looking down shortened her stride. Sibylla had long legs, she should be able to eat up the *henti*. It was a major advantage over Ileana, who was shorter.

Then there was the critique of her footwork. No slapping, no heels hitting the ground. Run only on the balls of her feet.

The calluses Chloe was developing were as thick as bubble wrap, complete with popping blisters. If she were running a long distance, she needed to run heel to toe, propelling forward with her toes.

Chloe followed the path's curve, wiping sweat off her brow with her elbow, keeping her hands loose. Running this way, on her toes, her shoulders immobile, did feel a lot better. She felt fleet, graceful, and the stretch of her leg muscles was . . . nice.

Most important, she was too busy to focus on Cheftu.

Chloe slowed to a stop before Atenis. The gray-eyed woman did not offer her encouragement, just put a hand on Chloe's elbow and turned her around.

Another field away, Chloe saw a woman running. Her shift was short, her hair bound up, but she was poetry in motion. Fast, graceful, and like all great artists, she made the skill look effortless.

"Who is it?"

"Kela-Ileana."

Chloe and Atenis watched the Queen of Heaven as she ran rhythmically. Chloe doubted she'd even broken a sweat. Not only did she look good in Aztlan's elaborate clothing, but her body hummed like a working Jaguar auto. Chloe watched her competition, feeling more and more deflated. The earth shifted beneath them, and Chloe touched Atenis' arm for support. A tremor. They were so often and so gentle that Chloe was not quite certain when they hit. Another? Or was she just nauseated from watching Ileana?

"You have a good chance," Atenis said. "You need to find your pace though first."

Chloe started to stretch, feeling her muscles bunch from stopping cold. "Teach me," she said. "I'll do it."

After all, if this race were part of the reason she was here, she should give it her best.

Sibylla, if she still lived, said nothing.

THE VESSEL WAS FLAWLESS, SMOOTH, AND EVEN, so fragile that Cheftu could see light through it. The art of shaping stone. Two meals lay uneaten on the floor, and he rose from his crouched position and grabbed a piece of stale bread. Determined not to turn his back when the table changed, he yawned, forcing his eyes open.

He had no concept of day or night, he felt neither heat nor cold. Even his beard had not grown. He stretched his legs, touching the floor with his hands. A soft whirring made him look up, but he had missed it. This new table was higher, with a new box and a beehive-shaped clay vessel on top.

Cheftu ate some fish, still warm, and an olive-and-wild-lettuce salad while he paced the chamber, easing the ache of his muscles and allowing the tension of the past decans? days? to pass through his body.

He rinsed his fingers, then rubbed and massaged his neck as he prepared to go into what he hoped was the final pyramid test. This must be the quest to transform.

Transform what? Into what? *Mon Dieu*, be with me.

After staring at the beehive for a decan or so, it came to him. The clay beehive was an oven! He'd seen a picture, a picture in his own time, of one. *Intéressant.* Also, there was a bowl, a lump of dark rock, three or four vials of liquids, a box of dried herbs, and a gold ingot.

Ovens and gold, ovens and gold. Cheftu gnawed his upper lip as he searched through his memories. The oven was an *athanor*, the container in which an alchemist heated his lead, creating gold. Transforming the everyday into the sacred.

Transforming. Surely Aztlantu couldn't change lead to gold even in this mythological land? He turned over the dark rocks in his hands. Not lead; lead had not yet been discovered. Transform . . . transform through heat. He opened the vials. Chemicals and herbs?

He'd read that alchemists in imperial France believed each object carried within itself the ability to develop, to metamorphose into that which was beautiful, powerful, and useful. Each man and woman had the same ability. The art of alchemy was not just knowing the properties and reactions of liquids and solids, but the art of refining the coarse into the perfected.

It was the ultimate search: to sift and modify until godhood was achieved. Alchemists claimed it was a spiritual quest, the refining, the most perfecting skill of all.

How? he thought, staring at the oven, the vials, and the rocks. These skills, if they were known in Egypt, had not been part of his education. Cheftu felt cold, sick, and panicked.

How much time had passed? Did they know he was stymied? Running his hands through his sweat-soaked hair, Cheftu fought for calm. *God, there is nothing I can do. I know nothing here. Please, help me.*

Trust me. . . .

The voice was solid and reassuring. Cheftu took deep, calming breaths, then returned to the table. Chemicals and heat interacted. Order was significant here. He sniffed each vial, forcing the scent to recall its name and properties, how it could be used, and for what.

His mind narrowed to a nib of intense concentration, Cheftu leaned on his instincts and tried to transform fear into faith. He began mixing and measuring.

The stench of the *athanor* was repellent after a while, and his eyes ran with tears as he fought for breath. There was no way out of the room, and he wondered if asphyxiation were the price of failure in this exam. The room shook slightly, another earthwave, Cheftu assumed, but when he opened his eyes again, he saw an obsidian sarcophagus.

Not only am I killing myself, I'm to bury my corpse also?

As it heated, the *athanor* was taking the air Cheftu needed into its red-hot body, spewing out poison. Cheftu stripped off his clothes and walked to the sarcophagus. It was cool to the touch, deep and curved to fit the shape of a man's body.

Dizziness assaulted him, and Cheftu knew he had only a few minutes of consciousness. Once, in the initiation of Amun, he had learned how to send his spirit away, slow his body down to the sleep of death. Could he do it again? Place himself in an attitude of stasis?

Tired muscles screaming, he pulled himself over the edge and into the depths of the sarcophagus. Lying down, he breathed deeply. *Please, God, please.* He could not see above the edges of the sarcophagus. Closing his eyes, Cheftu steadied his racing pulse, counting and resting, slowing his body. A whirring noise touched his ears, but he refused to splinter his attention. He felt his body gaining weight, growing heavy and slow.

It was similar to the sensation of moving through time, when his body had first slipped off him, like a heavy coat, and he had sailed naked both soul and body through . . . Cheftu's mind ceased to process, and he rested, above his body, above the room, above the pyramid, above Aztlan.

The Council wandered around the chamber, eating and drinking, glancing at the serfs, who would run to check the sky and report back.

The new Spiralmaster was running out of time.

Chloe's fingers were like ice around her rhyton, and she'd already bored Dion and Vena to death when they'd tried to engage her in conversation. *Come on, Cheftu! Think! Work! Do what it takes! The sands are running down!*

Selena had mentioned, obviously aware that Sibylla was very interested, that Phoebus and Niko were in the Rising Golden's apartments, preparing to celebrate when Zelos went to kill the failed Spiralmaster.

These people take competition way too seriously, Chloe thought.

Come on, Cheftu!

CHEFTU WOKE WITH A JOLT—his body cold as snow, the sarcophagus sealed. With a great gasp, he breathed. The stench of the *athanor* filled his nose and he coughed, staring up at the black lid across his lower body. He was immobile. He forced his fingers to move, pumping blood back into the digits. He ran a shaky hand over his face— once again his beard had not grown. Easing up, he leaned against one side of the sarcophagus. It was lighter in the room, lighter than it had been when he had fallen "asleep."

Muscles shaking, heart pounding, he crawled over the side of the sarcophagus. Cheftu leaned against it in shock. Before him on the table stood a lump of *shalcedon*. It was the size of the *athanor;* indeed it *was* the *athanor*. This was how the Aztlantu built the pyramid, he realized. They made faux jewels from ordinary stone through *al-khem* and heat. Their incredible wealth of precious stones was nothing more than a facade! Cheftu walked over the *shalcedon*, touching the still warm stone. He scratched it with his nails.

Grâce à Dieu!

The *shalcedon* was smooth, lumpy only from the ridges on the clay base. Cheftu tried to move it, but it wouldn't budge. Remembering the last thing Dion had told him, Cheftu ritually baptized the stone with a quick slice to his wrist. He hadn't died in the testing; still, some blood was demanded.

The floor fell away from beneath him and he went down in a wild slide, swallowing his screams. He shot out into a pool, beneath the fading blue sky. Water closed over his head and he came up sputtering and stared in surprise at the Council members in the room. They stared back, equally surprised. Chloe's face was white, her eyes as wide and green as the *shalcedon*.

Had he succeeded, then?

Zelos reached out his hands, hauled Cheftu from the pool. "Welcome to the Council and to Aztlan, Spiralmaster Cheftu!"

Cheftu's first official duty was to go to the deathbed of one of Zelos' *hequetai*. The man was young, only a few summers Cheftu's senior, yet he moved as though he were decades older. His babbling and hysterical laughter terrified his wife. Tears of fear streaming down her face, she refused to be in the same room with him. Already the serfs had placed him in the lustral bath.

Cheftu was there when he began his journey. Despite the power, position, and wealth the dying man possessed, none of his friends or family dared get close to him, fearing the illness. Afterward, in his library, Cheftu looked through the notes Imhotep had dictated. A scribe had been the former Spiralmaster's constant companion, taking down every word as though it were holy writ.

Unlike illness brought on by *ukhedu*, the body was not fighting this sickness. The lack of immune reaction—no fever, no sweating, no vomiting—was the most puzzling element. Later that night, as Chloe lay in his arms pillowed on his chest, he explained the fear that was growing around the illness about the lack of symptoms.

"It's completely fatal?" she asked.

"Aye. No one has recovered, or survived."

"Did the victims have anything in common?"

"All were part of Zelos' cabinet."

She was silent, her fingers beating out a rhythm on his stomach. "A germ, maybe?"

Cheftu listened as she explained the tiny animals that could inhabit one's body through improperly cooked food, a dormant illness, or even the air. "These germs make you cough and sneeze and run fevers, you say?"

"Aye. The common cold is everywhere. It's a real peach to land a cold account 'cause cold, fever, and sniffle relief is responsible for half the advertising in the U.S."

He eyed her warily, then spoke. "There is no fever. If this illness was something from outside the body, the body's defenses would react."

"So do an autopsy, see if the insides of the body tell you anything."

"A what?"

She sat up, her face animated in the lamp's light, her hair mussed and falling over her shoulders, tangling with his. Cheftu felt a surge in his groin as he watched her. "In murder mysteries they always do an autopsy when someone dies and no one knows why. Could this be poison?"

"I am fairly proficient at identifying poisons, but I will inquire. Perhaps they have one here that is unknown to me. Though I wager Imhotep would have recognized it long before."

"Just so," she said, staring at the designs painted on the wall behind him. "Look at that design. It starts out as a square, then turns into a diamond, then bends into that star shape, and then fills out into a circle. An example of Bronze Age morphing," she said, smiling.

He rolled over, pulling her beneath him, sliding inside the tightness of her body. He felt her stiffen and then accept him, her mouth and hands as hungry and seeking as his own. "You are morphing from medicine man to macho man," she whispered between kisses.

He gave himself over to sensation, the silk of her skin, her taste, her feel . . . and reminded himself to have her explain "morphing" later.

"I CAN DO NO MORE, MY FRIEND," Phoebus said.

Niko clenched his fists, and Phoebus watched the one-handed girl Neotne duck her head in sympathy. "If the Rising Golden is helpless, then I am resigned also," Niko said slowly.

"Cheftu passed the tests. He poured the stone, shaped the rock, he even transformed and survived."

"I could have passed them also, Phoebus."

"Niko . . ." Phoebus swallowed; this would be hard to say. "Spiralmaster had many summers to name you his inheritor. He chose not to, in all that time. He'd been sick for a while, and still he said nothing."

Niko's white skin flushed. "You say that Spiralmaster intended this all along?"

Phoebus shrugged; the facts spoke for themselves. Niko, his closest and dearest friend, turned his back on Phoebus. For the first time in his life, Phoebus was being dismissed. He saluted Neotne and left, walking down the long hallways to his own apartments.

"How did he receive your thoughts?" Dion asked, joining him as he crossed one of the large rooms.

"How would you receive them? Niko never mentioned his aspirations. I didn't know he wanted to be the Spiralmaster."

"I think he just assumed he would be. Not an aspiration as such, just an understanding."

"Apparently Spiralmaster did not have this understanding."

The two men walked in silence. "Speaking of the Spiralmaster, Cheftu approached me on two counts."

"What does the interloper want?"

Dion laid a hand on Phoebus' arm. "Zelos himself has welcomed him. He was tested by the most trying tasks. Spiralmaster instantly saw something in him that gave him trust in the man. Do you not think you could learn to—"

"He is a usurper," Phoebus ground out. "No better than Ileana."

"You are wrong, Phoebus." Dion's voice was implacable.

Phoebus sighed. "I want no more conflict today. Niko . . ."

"He holds you accountable?"

Phoebus shrugged, looking away. "What does Cheftu want?"

Dion refrained from commenting on Phoebus' deliberate rudeness. "He wants Nestor to work at his side. . . ."

"He is my inheritor! Until Kela-Ileana is full with child, at any rate."

"Aye, but how would training with Spiralmaster Cheftu interfere with his position? He would still devote most of his time to you."

Phoebus wished he were with Eumelos, playing in the garden, far from friends who thought he was all-powerful. "What is the other request?"

Dion indicated a tree in the garden, and they crossed the pavement and sat beneath it, the shade just touching their feet. "He wishes to open the body of the most recently deceased *hequetai.*"

"Profane the dead?"

"Phoebus, not as a profanity, but to determine why they are dying."

"He cannot tell from what we know? What kind of mage is he?"

Dion gazed at him. "Spiralmaster did not know why people were dying," he said dryly.

"Just so," Phoebus agreed reluctantly. He looked toward Mount Krion on Folegandros, the island of the Cult of the Bull. "I want you there, Dion. I want you to watch, see this man's magic and skill."

"No magic, Phoebus. A lot of skill, though."

Phoebus rose abruptly. "I must train."

Walking away, Phoebus felt as though the sky were falling in. He wanted Irmentis. All I must do is wait the twelve decans till the sun fades and she awakens, he thought. He gritted his teeth. Today he would outwit his trainer in practice. He needed to win in some arena.

"WHAT DO YOU MEAN, I AM NOT PREGNANT?" Ileana screeched.

Embla shrugged. "My mistress, I cannot root the seed in your body."

"Then what good are you!" The Queen of Heaven tapped her fingers, for once unconcerned about her frown lines. If these men didn't have powerful enough seed, her skin would be the least of her worries. *Ohk* Kela.

"Are you sure your lover is virile?"

"He has children, Embla. However, if he is not impregnating me, then I must find another."

"What are his children's ages?"

"Young. The newest not even a year."

"Take an additional lover," Embla said. "You do have another selected?"

"Aye," Ileana answered distractedly.

"Drink this manroot infusion twice daily and more when the moon is upon you."

"Aye," Ileana said, grasping the vial as though it were her crown.

"Sleep with this beneath your pillow," Embla said, giving her a packet of herbs. "Drink a lot of nanny goat's milk. A strong nanny with many offspring."

Ileana grimaced as she stood to leave. She snapped her fingers and three serfs came in, bearing baskets and trays of food. "My gifts, Embla," Ileana said.

The priestess fell on the baskets as Ileana closed the door.

Embla had one more chance to make the seed root; Ileana had to get pregnant.

CHLOE HAD JUST FOUND HER PACE, that rhythm that lifted her over hills and sent her sailing down them, that quickened when she was in shade and slowed down in the growing heat of the sun. As best she could figure, the competition would take place midsummer.

July. Running in July. On purpose.

She nodded at herself, then remembered to look up, her hands pumping from her face to her hips, her fingers open. An earth tremor made her stumble. She was facing east when Mount Apollo coughed for the first time in five hundred years.

The mountain's top, at one moment stark against the blue sky, was suddenly obscured by a gray cloud. Chloe felt a low rumble like a train, but this was Aztlan; there were no trains.

She froze while the cloud swirled artfully across the hills, bits of it misting away as the wind caught and diluted it. If she'd not seen it happen, she'd not have believed it. Now the mountain looked the same.

The puff of smoke? *Ash* had blown away.

Swallowing, she stretched a little and began to run back to where Atenis waited, where her time was now twice as long as usual.

As she ran, Chloe felt the mountain behind her.

That was a warning shot, it said.

She ran even faster.

THE END OF JUNE, the eve of the Season of the Lion, was hot and dry. Grain harvested from Caphtor was sent to Aztlan's clans. The seed would be stored during the rainless summer and planted in the fall.

Cheftu put his head down on the tall table. This room, lost in the bowels of the palace, was cool, but the mingled stink of flesh, blood, and the sewer made his stomach curdle. He had a perpetual headache, and Chloe had chided him for not eating enough. He was losing weight.

He grinned. Chloe. She had suggested autopsies. Only after he'd opened the first body, moons ago, had she remembered that he'd have to compare diseased insides with healthy ones. He and Phoebus had almost come to blows regarding his inquiries, Cheftu petitioning for approval on new methods in doctoring and Phoebus blocking his every move.

Thank the gods the Rising Golden was preoccupied training for the upcoming *Megaloshana'a* rituals. The table shook. Another earth-wave, Cheftu thought wearily. He stood, fighting for balance, and walked to the freshest corpse.

The first autopsy had made him sick for days, but Chloe was right, he'd built a tolerance. Nestor slammed into the laboratory, Vena trailing him. Cheftu slipped into the back room. The couple fought constantly. Nestor did not want her to challenge Ileana; she was training vigorously for the race.

Cheftu dared not think what would happen if Chloe won. The one time he'd broached the topic she had flatly refused to withdraw, claiming she'd made an agreement with Sibylla. He suspected she liked running, liked the discipline of training, despite her lengthy complaints about it.

He looked at the cadaver. *Mon Dieu*, what was killing these people? He'd seen so many hearts, livers, intestines, and lungs in the past few moons that even thoughts of foie gras were nauseating. His gaze rested on the man's face; it was frozen in a perpetual grimace. What more can I see? Cheftu asked himself, staring.

That *is what I can see!*

Stricken by what he proposed to do, Cheftu retrieved a utensil Imhotep had brought from Egypt. A brain hook used in embalming. Egyptian custom required removing the brain and entombing it with the body. Cheftu concentrated, summoning skills he'd learned long ago.

Navigating the hook up the nasal passage, he turned his wrist when he felt the tool was slightly past the forehead's heavy bone plate. The instrument slid and sliced into the soft tissue, then Cheftu reversed the process. Laboriously he retrieved the man's brain in tiny pieces.

When Nestor and Vena finished fighting and reconciling, Cheftu set Nestor to work on another corpse. During a plague, however subtle, there was no dearth of bodies.

They set the specimens side by side for inspection and comparison. Chloe had said he needed a microscope—not that she could explain what it was—yet before the invention even of plain glass, lenses were an impossibility. To compensate they looked very, very closely, the scribe in the corner taking down every word of their discussion.

When they had worked so long he could no longer focus, Cheftu sat back. "I cannot think of another location to look." Nestor shrugged weary agreement, and they climbed the spiral stairs into the land of the living.

Later, lying clearheaded and heavy limbed beside Chloe, Cheftu told her about his examination of the brain.

"You saw nothing? Well, chances are if something is infecting the brain, it is too small to see." She was quiet, and he kissed her forehead. It was a marvel to love her body and learn from her mind. What a blessed man he was.

A tremor rocked them, and Cheftu shielded Chloe until it stopped. Whitewashed dust had rained on them, and they got up, cleared the bed, and resettled, skin to skin. As he was almost asleep, Chloe sat bolt upright.

"Ninth grade!"

Startled, Cheftu cursed, but she was babbling in a mixture of English and Aztlantu. "Ninth grade. Anatomy. The brain is the center of the central nervous system, which controls motor skills, coordination, and . . ." He felt her tapping her foot against his shin. "Damn, I don't remember! But Cheftu, didn't you say the symptoms are loss of speech and swallowing? They can't walk, they stumble at first. Wouldn't that be the central nervous system?"

"Aye," he said slowly.

"Well, that's not the front part of the brain, it's the back. Did you, oh this is gross—did you get it all out?"

"You, *ma chérie*, are brilliant!" he said, kissing her head and springing from the couch. He snapped for serfs, sent a message to Nestor, and was racing to the laboratory in moments.

Nestor joined him, and Cheftu turned a bodiless head toward the man. "How do we get into the back of the brain?" he asked. Nestor blinked, rubbed his eyes, and showed Cheftu the fragile part of the skull.

It took force to crack it, but he proceeded through, getting to the back of the brain. Seeing the untidy job he'd done on extracting the frontal lobes made him wince, but the back part was untouched. Gingerly he and Nestor pulled it out, setting it on the table and ringing it with oil lamps.

After dividing the back portion into two sections, they began to look. They looked for decans. Cheftu stared long and hard, moving the light and the fleshy parts, seeking out aberrations in the tissue, cutting it into fractions. The texture was consistent until they reached the innermost part.

"Nestor."

Little black dots were sprinkled through the mass. Hands trembling, Cheftu lifted the flimsy sample so they could examine it better. Nestor, over his shoulder, raised the lamp, casting a shadow onto the table.

"Do you see what I see?" Nestor asked after a moment.

Cheftu looked at the black dots, trying to see what else might be there. He glanced toward Nestor and saw that the young man was looking not at the section but at the table.

A hundred pinpricks of light shone through the thin matter, not visible to their eyes, but discernible with shadow. There were holes in the brain. *Mon Dieu!*

CHLOE KNEW WITHOUT LOOKING she was neck and neck with Selena; she could feel the woman's breath on her arm. The finish line was just ahead over a small rise, and Chloe threw back her head, taking the hill as though she were racing up stairs, her heels not even touching the ground.

As Atenis had trained her, she surged over the hill and crashed through the line of nymphs awaiting them. Selena was two steps behind her, and they hugged, panting and sweating.

It was bloody hot, six days before the start of the midsummer festival, roughly June nineteenth, Chloe thought. The earth shook, and no one even stopped talking. Mount Krion had puffed several times, and Mount Apollo had even sent down ash on Daphne, but the Aztlantu had grown accustomed to the frequent interruptions. Ash was just one of the drawbacks of living on a land where the ground was fertile and magma chambers kept the water hot for bathing.

Tonight was a kickoff feast for the whole fourteen-day festival, and today was the last time Chloe would train before the race. Her body and mind needed rest in preparation, Atenis said. My body needs a few days to forgive me for what I've done to it, Chloe thought wryly. The differences were marked, though. Where she'd always been lean, now she was toned. Nothing jiggled except her breasts, a circumstance Cheftu gave thanks for every night. She smiled. It was good to be alive.

The ground twitched again, and she and Selena began walking back to the palace. Traveling through the residential wing toward the

Scholomance, she admired the wall paintings. Selena departed to Kela's temple, and Chloe went to Cheftu's apartments.

She learned from Cheftu's serf that he was in the laboratory. The lab was a dark, dank place with sickening smells. At least Cheftu kept it well lit. Sneaking exaggeratedly on her tiptoes toward the back room, she thought she might surprise him and—

Chloe tripped over something in her pathway, barely catching herself. Cheftu!

He was crumpled on the ground, and Chloe searched frantically for a pulse. Yes, still steady. She ran her hands over his body, searching for wounds, abrasions—he'd really gotten thin. He was still major hunk material, but thinner, a runner's body instead of a hiker's.

Chloe called for a serf as she turned Cheftu onto his back. Nestor came running in behind the serf. "Spiralmaster!" he cried. "Come quick—By Kela, what is the matter?" he asked, kneeling by Chloe. The two men carried Cheftu to his apartments and placed him on his couch.

"What is wrong with him?" she asked Nestor.

"I cannot say, Sib. No one can examine him. You know that no one can treat Spiralmaster."

"What?" Chloe asked in outrage.

"He is the master. If he falls ill, then—"

"Then he perishes from neglect? Get out," she said.

"My mistress," Nestor protested, raising his hands.

"Get out, I said. I will take care of him."

"My mistress, Kela-Ata Embla is ill," a serf said from the doorway. "She needs attention."

"Nestor will take care of Embla," she snapped.

Chloe was shaking with fury as she tried to figure out what to do. Cheftu had no fever, no sweating, just chills. He tossed and turned as though he were in the throes of a bad dream, and he was badly dehydrated.

With the serf's help, she undressed him and massaged peppermint oil into his skin, feeling helpless. Was his collapse merely exhaustion?

"I came as soon as I heard," Dion said, closing the double doors behind him.

"Thank Apis. What can you do?"

The chieftain visually inspected Cheftu and declared he was well, but in need of rest and food. Sibylla, however, was needed at the swearing-in of the new Kela-Ata, he said. Embla was dead: apparently her indulgence in food had been fatal. She'd been found with a half-eaten shrimp in her hand, her throat clawed as though she'd tried to dislodge something.

Too much information, Chloe thought, running through the palace corridors and halting abruptly. She snapped for a carrying chair. Don't forget you are trying to rest your body these last days before the race, she thought.

DION PULLED BACK THE SHEET and gazed at Cheftu's body. He'd known it would be like this, perfection in every lean line, the sensitivity, power, and control of the Spiralmaster tangible even in his flesh.

With a glance over his shoulder to make sure no one watched, Dion touched Cheftu's skin. He shaved and waxed like an Egyptian even in his pubic area, but bareness only highlighted Apis' gifts to him.

How Apis had gifted him.

Dion's breath caught as his fingers slid along the man's skin. His complexion was a shade lighter than Dion's, though still dark. He touched the man's flanks, and Cheftu jerked in his sleep. With a wary eye on Cheftu's face, Dion slowly moved his hands up Cheftu's body.

That was when he felt it. A lump, a hard protrusion beneath the oil-smooth skin of the Spiralmaster. Dion leaned closer, focused on the sore, very aware of how close his mouth was to—

Cheftu's knee caught him in the jaw, and Dion spun away, eyes watering.

"What in the name of Apis were you doing?" the Egyptian snarled. He covered himself and glared at Dion, fury sparking from his sand-colored eyes.

Dion wiped a streak of blood from the corner of his mouth. "You were ill. I was flouting Council decrees, endangering my own chieftainship to examine you. I was being a friend!" He ended on a tone of outrage. "This is your gratitude?" Glaring at Cheftu, he tested his teeth and jaw, all of which were still fixed in his head.

Cheftu looked away first, his face and chest darkening with blood. "My apology, of course you were. I . . ." He looked back. "Why am I here? It is yet daylight, and I am in bed? Where is Ch—Sibylla?"

"Training, I would think," Dion said. "She has a good chance of becoming the next mother-goddess. I believe she would be excellent, do you not? Phoebus is anticipating bedding her, I can tell you," he said with a laugh.

Cheftu laughed, but he didn't seem happy.

Interesting, Dion thought. "As for your being here, instead of in the laboratory. I think you fell, hit your head, and were sleeping it off." He refused to voice his fear, the possibility that Cheftu had this strange illness. After all, Spiralmaster Imhotep had gotten it from caring for the ill. Cheftu was doing no less.

Frowning slightly, Cheftu agreed that must have been the cause.

"Tell me," Dion said, touching Cheftu's leg, ignoring his flinch, "how long have you had that *bubo?*"

"What *bubo?*"

"May I?" Dion asked, tugging at the linen. Reluctantly Cheftu let him take it. Dion pointed at the sore on Cheftu's groin. "What is that, if not a *bubo?*" Dion fought for calm as he watched Cheftu touch his own body. His hands were darker skinned than his groin, and Dion concentrated on being composed. If he became aroused now, he would stand no chance with Cheftu.

The Spiralmaster focused on the sore. It was about the size of a child's fingernail and seemed to cause no pain as Cheftu poked it. Spiralmaster brushed his member and Dion saw a response. He had to leave, immediately.

With lies for excuses, the clan chieftain escaped the room.

THE *MEGALOSHANA'A* ARRIVED. Every nineteen summers the fields and hills of Aztlan were covered with the visiting clans. Azure, saffron, and crimson tents scattered across the green hillsides like overgrown flowers. The wind died and the sun shone hotly on the golden-topped Pyramid of Days.

In fourteen days, the Aztlantu world would change.

Events were scattered throughout the days, in accordance with the prophecies and charts of the Daedaledai and the cycles of the moon and sun. Tonight, a feast. Tomorrow, the first race for mother-goddess. Though only the Olimpi ever won, hundreds of young women raced in the hope that they might catch the eye of the Golden.

Once the mother-goddess claimed her position, then the Rising Golden was tested, first in the bull dance and then in the pyramid. Then he was *Hreesos,* his predecessor was *athanati,* and the people were blessed in the blood of the bull. More feasting and later, when the sun and moon, Apis and Kela, were joined in the sky, the new *Hreesos* would be conceived in a ritual for women and *Hreesos* only.

The feasting had no end or beginning, Coil Dancers were free, wine flowed like seawater, and the Aztlantu congratulated themselves on their good fortune to be born on these islands.

Beneath them, the earth churned; their fortune was changing.

CHLOE FELT THE EXQUISITE TENSION EBB AWAY and collapsed on Cheftu's chest.

"You," he said, trying to catch his breath, "have developed stamina."

"Almost kill you?" she said with a smile. "Desserts will do that, you know."

His eyes closed, and Chloe looked at him in astonishment. Cheftu went to sleep? Immediately? He must be exhausted from working so late every night. This festival time would be a good holiday, she thought. No students, no corpses, just a vacation.

Pulling away from his body, she noticed that he'd stopped being shaved Egyptian style. When in Aztlan, do as the Aztlantu do? Chloe grinned and got out of bed, covering Cheftu. She would go see Selena, who was more than freaking out at her new responsibilities. Then meet with Sibylla's clanspeople, who never wanted more than "just so" anyway.

She had no memories regarding Sibylla's clan chieftain duties. Sibylla herself had disappeared. Chloe had apparently absorbed her, though it wasn't flattering to see herself as a psychic vampire. She kissed her husband's forehead and bounced out of the double doors.

"Do not forget tonight," she whispered.

He muttered, and Chloe laughed.

The *Megaron* was filled with torchlight and the smell of flowers. The night was hot, and Chloe felt perspiration building up where she touched Cheftu. They looked as Aztlantu as the rest, and Chloe grinned at Cheftu's visible effort to keep his eyes above the necks of the many bare-breasted women moving around the room.

Chloe twisted the skin on his arm, and he glared at her. "Stop it!" she hissed. He frowned, then tried to look innocent. "I'm your wife," she said. "I'll always know what you are thinking." They walked toward their respective clan tables and, with a quick hand squeeze, separated.

The feast was elaborate and exquisite: lobster, shrimp, crab, squid, cucumbers, figs . . . all seasoned and placed in arrangements before her. Chloe glanced over her shoulder and saw Cheftu walking away, Dion beside him. She turned back to her conversation with Selena. Acrobats flew across the pavement, some playing the bull and some enacting the bull dancers. They juggled grapes, then clay *pithoi*, and finally two of *Hreesos'* newborn sons.

The Golden Bull rose, and the court grew silent in fear, admiration, and respect. "Citizens of Aztlan! My brothers, my sisters, my lovers." That got a laugh. "My fellow clanspeople! To Kela, the voluptuous earth goddess! Celebrate her life and love tonight!" Zelos' toast was slurred and full of good humor. Serfs appeared to refill the many rhytons.

The mood was expansive, sensual and carefree. Selena excused herself to pursue the stag Adonis, one of Dion's castoffs, and Chloe found herself alone, picking at congealing seafood and wondering why she wasn't satisfied. She still didn't know why she was here. This was nothing like Egypt, she had no guidance, no clear path. *Just enough freedom and rope to hang myself.* It was a discouraging thought.

She shook her head politely as *Hreesos'* gaze fell on her. Phoebus inclined his head and turned to kiss a dark-haired nymph at his side. She was a dead ringer for Irmentis, Chloe thought.

A gentle caress of her shoulder made her turn. "Are you well?" Chloe asked as Cheftu sat down. "You were gone so long I was afraid you'd slipped through a portal and were now in JFK's time."

"I was needed," he said, avoiding her gaze.

"The dancers will be here in a moment," she said. "The acrobats were good. Not quite Cirque du Soleil, but impressive."

"You speak in riddles," he muttered. "Has everyone seemed well?" he asked clearly.

"Well, do you see that tall lady over there, the one with the pierced—"

"Aye, I see her."

"Well, before the second course she and that gentleman over there were—"

Coil Dancers, without snakes, began to writhe before them. The women danced around the fireplace in the center of the room, twisting and turning, their pupils pinpoints in their eyes from *kreenos*. Chloe joined them, spinning and swirling, enjoying the freedom of the movement. Since purloining Sibylla's skills, dancing had become a lot of fun.

Her stomach began to cramp and she sat down, motioning for water. Maybe the wine was upsetting her system?

A while later, Cheftu sat down next to her. "Why are you not dancing, Chieftain?"

"Not in the mood," Chloe said. "I overate, I think."

His gaze was tender but quick. "Go rest, then, belov—er, Sibylla." He smiled over his cup. "As Spiralmaster, I command it."

"I think I will," Chloe said, rising. She *really* didn't feel good.

"Do you need to be tucked in?"

Chloe shook her head. "*Just* tucked in, though."

Immediately Cheftu's gaze sharpened. "What happened?"

"I ate too much," she said, then clapped her hand over her mouth and exited through a side door.

As he held her head, smoothing her hair while she threw up, Cheftu asked her about what she had eaten. Anything that she alone had eaten? Chloe couldn't remember; the thought of food made her sick to her stomach. Again.

"I think you were mildly poisoned," Cheftu said. "It wouldn't take much to weaken your body a little, throw your system into turmoil."

"Why?" Chloe croaked.

"Ileana."

The name was answer enough. As Chloe rested between bouts, her face cold with sweat, she became even more determined to beat the Queen of Heaven. Anyone who would poison just to win a competition was not fit to be a ruler.

She laid her head on the pavement, nice and cool. Cheftu stroked her head. "Shall I take you to bed?"

"Only if you promise to hold me," she said, sniffling. *God, I hate it when I'm weepy!*

"*Eee, ma chère*," he said, lifting her into his arms. "Do you think I am a beast? You are unwell—"

"I didn't mean it like that. I just didn't want you to leave me alone." Chloe snuggled closer to him, feeling safe, secure, and comforted. He kissed her bowed head and started up the stairs.

"I need a witness, Sibylla."

Chloe rubbed her eyes, then covered a yawn. "It is late, Selena. Can this not wait?"

"Revenge has its own schedule," said the new Kela-Ata.

Chloe sighed. "Let me get a cloak."

"We can do it here," Selena offered. Thinking of Cheftu sleeping in the next room, Chloe declined. Her relationship with the Spiralmaster was a secret she wanted to keep. She threw a cloak over her running shift and followed Selena down two floors to her apartments. Selena walked into the cleared room, and Chloe propped herself against the wall, wishing for a toothbrush.

Selena chanted to Kela, drawing elaborate patterns in sand on the floor. "You must defend my body while I am away," she said.

Chloe yawned again. "Defend?"

"Aye. While I spirit travel." She looked up at Chloe. "I mean no offense, but I do not want to wake up with a changed appearance. I don't want to be like you."

"My gratitude," Chloe said dryly.

THE PATTERNS DRAWN, Selena stepped into the center, bowing to each of the four elemental points—fire, water, wind, and earth—then sat down, naked and crossed-legged. From the satchel around her neck she withdrew poppy gum and placed it under her tongue, reciting the formula that would help her *psyche* leave her body temporarily. Feeling her body grow heavier, Selena loosened her grip on the flesh, fastening a silver noose tightly around her spirit self. Selena's *psyche* flew across the black skies, then sank into the palace building, passing through walls and ceilings like heavy air. She floated over her quarry and spoke, bringing him into the state between waking and sleeping.

"I HAVE A TALE FOR YOU, Phoebus."

The voice rose out of the darkness, out of Phoebus' thrashing, sweat-filled dreams.

"Once lived a woman so beauteous that even her brothers loved her. One became her husband, another her lover. Her husband was unfaithful—he found new women endlessly appealing. He could not have enough of them. This burned into his wife's heart. She vowed her children would never know this grief."

The voice, low and melodic, continued. "When her oldest daughter was yet a babe, merely three summers, the mother took her to an exiled priestess who lived in the mainland forest. There, for a price of precious stones, she had the girl's sex cut."

Phoebus jerked on his couch, cupping himself in sleepy protection.

"It was a tiny cut, but the mother knew it would forever rob the girl of her desire for men."

He tried to open his eyes, but he couldn't. His limbs felt weighted, and he was condemned to listen to a story whose end he did not want to hear.

"The youngest was not so fortunate. By the time the girl was five summers, the mother's fears had grown larger; her ability to reason had fled. The girl had caught her husband's eye, and rather than attributing his attention to paternal affection, the wife imagined he lusted after his child. The woman feared her daughter would rise up and take the mother's role. The priestess in the forest had long since died, yet she had to do something, strip the girl of her desires. The mother waited, planning carefully, for the child's clan brother, the heir, was the girl's constant companion. He could prevent this deed from being done.

"Then one week, her prayers were answered. The boy was gone.

"So the wife got out her own blades and she cut the girl. It didn't seem enough, however. She cut more, then more, then stitched where she could. The child bled badly and only intervention by a Kela-Tenata protected the girl from dying of poisoned blood.

"Then the mother killed the priestess to protect her actions."

Phoebus felt tears burning down his face, a welling of pain in his chest. Please don't let it be who he thought it was! Please, please, for the love of Kela—

"Irmentis was the girl; she is condemned to live her life beyond pleasure's touch. Slowly she kills herself in the arms of a green, insidious lover who fills her veins and twists her mind. Ileana did this; she murdered, she mutilated, she robbed you of your heartlove."

He was shaking with rage, with fear, with revulsion. Irmentis had never disrobed before him. Never had he seen her without her tunic. Could this be true? Could this be why she'd lain still in his arms a dozen times?

"Revenge, Phoebus. Revenge. You will be *Hreesos*, the time for your revenge is dawning."

He hissed as he felt something across his palm. His hand was wet, then his lips were wet, coated with blood. "Swear vengeance, Phoebus. Speak now."

The constraints on his movement and speech were gone. He muttered his vow of vengeance, then felt his sticky fingers wrapped around the haft of a blade. The vow kiss made him moan—such passion, such love, such lust! He could not kiss deeply enough.

Then he was kissing only air. Tears, semen, and blood mingled in his linens.

SELENA FELT HER SPIRIT RETURN to the cavern of her body. In the flickering light, she could see Sibylla's features masked in horror.

"How could you do that? Now that he knows the truth, he will never forgive her. You promised Ileana sanctuary; it was your duty. What is your purpose with revealing this story?" Sibylla protested.

"Phoebus will destroy Ileana now. It will be justice," Selena said.

"Do you seek to take her place?"

"Do not we all seek it? We all run the race."

"He loves Irmentis."

"Aye. She loves him, but she doesn't feel *eros* for him. Irmentis' greatest love is for the wilds. And her potion."

"Potion?"

"*Okh*, Sibylla! For an oracle you can be so blind! The drink Phoebus concocted for her. It eases the pain she lives with in the darkness."

Sibylla looked at the elaborate patterns of colored sand on the floor. Her eyes were growing paler as the poppy burned and her pupils contracted. "Ileana is the mother-goddess; you are sworn to protect her."

"Aye."

"But—doesn't this undermine your promise?"

"She should die," Selena snarled.

"I would have thought death too easy an answer," Sibylla said.

"She will die unbathed. Forever she will wander, a *skia*." Selena leaned over the poppy and inhaled deeply. "Death is but the beginning of her harvest in this life," were her last coherent words.

CHAPTER 13

UTTER DARKNESS CLOAKED THE NIGHT OF THE RACE. Kela was now the hag, newly deceased, waited to be reborn. In this blackness the race would be run, over the rough hills, through the winding passages, and finally across the bridge onto Aztlan Island.

It's dark, I'm barefoot, with decidedly aggressive women on my heels, Chloe thought. These people could really use an Olympics committee. Observation was forbidden; lamps and direction were not allowed, violators were punishable by banishment. It was not only a test of the body, skill, temperament, and endurance, the race was a search of the *psyche* through the shadows of night.

They would run from almost midnight until dawn. Fortunately it was summer, so night was only six hours.

Six hours; don't think of it like that, Chloe. You can do this. You know how. You can do this. She repeated the words continuously to herself as she stretched. The cooler night breeze ruffled the skirt of her shift and tossed tendrils of hair into her eyes and mouth.

A final strip of cloth around her forehead, a test of her "bra" bandage, and Chloe was ready. It had come down to a four-way battle: Selena, Vena, Sibylla, and Ileana. Just as long as one of the challengers, though preferably not Vena, won, it would be okay. Ileana would be deposed.

The Minos had his bull head on and sprinkled scented water on them. "By the serpent of Kela, may the vessel of the goddess be revealed." He extinguished the torch, and they started.

Though Chloe had to fight her desire to use her energy now and whip in front, she remembered Atenis' words. Pace, conserve, relax, look up. The night began to reveal itself in the silhouettes of ink black trees against blue-black sky. No stars, no moon . . . just silence and darkness and her own body.

She was so aware of her blood pumping, her muscles stretching and moving, her bound hair as it slapped her back, the slight jog of her breasts . . . Chloe allowed her mind to quiet, listening to her rhythm, resting and preparing for the mental side of the race.

Her shift was soaked; before her to the left she could almost make out the shape of Vena, her milky skin more visible in the darkness. Selena was ahead of them both, Ileana far ahead.

The aching had begun, and Chloe realized it was like sex in that aspect. Sometimes you had to strive, even suffer a little, until the pleasure began. They were going downhill, and Chloe kicked back with her stride, letting the pull of gravity do most of the work. She passed Vena in a burst of momentum and was in a copse of trees when the earthwave hit.

Chloe banged against an olive tree, slicing her shin as the ground continued to fibrillate. Swearing at the pain, the loss of her pacing, she waited until the earth stopped moving and limped back onto the path. Slowly she started again, her shin throbbing with every step.

Damn, damn, damn! She was still swearing when the next wave hit, throwing her to the ground, where she clung, sweating and nauseated, until it stopped. Hesitantly now, she got to her feet. Her shin was slick with blood, and she ripped a strip from her tunic and tied it over the gash.

She couldn't see or hear any other women. Chloe began to run again, starting slow, then picking up speed as her heartbeat easily leapt back to where it had been. More hills, more valleys: *Keep going, keep going.* She didn't think of the others, or how far she had run, or the distance to the finish line; there was only her body, the wind, and the earth.

Forward, keep going.

Blood was streaming freely down her shin. Finally she couldn't take it and slowed to a stop, looking for some way to stem the bleeding.

The quake hit violently, bouncing her around like a body surfer on a wave. *Thank God I wasn't running.* The two minutes of the quake were two of the longest minutes in her life. After coughing up the pomegranate juice she'd had hours ago, Chloe began to walk, then jog, then run—again.

She didn't care about the race anymore, she just wanted to get back! To Cheftu, to safe ground, to light! Following a sharp curve, she caught sight of the land bridge and, across it, Aztlan. No signs of anyone else.

At least I'll finish the race, she thought, encouraged by the sight. It was a straight shot from here to the island, mostly downhill to boot! *This will be the easiest part of the night!* She was flying down the hill when she passed Selena.

"Win, Sibylla!" the priestess cried after her. *"Yazzo!"*

Gaze fastened on the ground as she negotiated the uneven rise, Chloe almost ran over Ileana. With a yelp she sidestepped, wincing as her ankle turned a little. Ileana didn't waste a second, she put on a burst of speed as Chloe hobbled a few steps.

The vicious witch who'd kept her up half the night with dry heaves was not going to win.

Her shoulders as relaxed and motionless as she could make them, her hands pumping from her face to her derriere, Chloe kicked back all the way down the hill, propelled halfway across the bridge. She was catching up!

Ten steps behind Ileana when they crossed onto the island, Chloe knew she had minutes to overtake the older woman or she would lose. Extra energy, she told her body. More! Give me more!

Flick your feet, she remembered Atenis telling her.

The distance was closing, and Chloe hadn't felt her heels hit the earth in forty paces. She flicked one foot back, then the other.

In her mind's eye she saw the Road Runner's legs in a flurry of motion.

There! Just ahead. Ileana was wasting precious energy weaving, and Chloe ran taller, passing Ileana and crashing into the line of nymphs first.

Their hands pushed her, and Chloe dazedly realized it was a maze. Art, think artwork! She didn't ask how it came to be here or what the whole point was, she jogged through. It wasn't a Greek key, it wasn't a spiral. She turned another corner, and they cheered her.

Ileana crashed into her, jabbing her knee into Chloe's thigh, and Chloe staggered, catching her balance.

It was moments too late.

Ileana had won!

Dazed, on a dread high almost like a car accident or IRS audit, Chloe could only stare. Ileana's pupils were huge in the darkness as she magnanimously thanked Kela for selecting her again. She curtly reminded Chloe to be in her chambers at tomorrow's dawn to learn about her position as inheritor.

Above them, on the pyramid just tinted with light, Minos cupped his hands and cried out, "Kela-Ileana, consort of *Hreesos!*"

Chloe wanted to cry, she wanted to scream. Ileana had cheated. How could she win? She stood silent, gazing over the land bridge. She had never failed, not really. Almost anything was attainable if she worked hard enough. Atenis touched her elbow. "She has yet to get with child. There might still be hope."

She hugged Atenis. "My sorrow. I tried, dear Kela, I tried."

"She is a viper; she has always won." The chieftain's gray eyes were sympathetic. "You didn't race like she did. No one is more vicious than a cornered predator."

"What did they mean by 'inheritor to the consort of *Hreesos'?*" Chloe asked, striving for calm, coming to grips with losing. No wonder Sibylla had been so quiet. Chloe had been manipulated, and she had lost to a cheat.

Atenis stepped back, looking at her strangely. "She won the right to be mother-goddess. If, after thirty days of mating, Ileana is not pregnant, you will be Queen of Heaven."

If Sibylla still existed, Chloe would kill her. "Meaning exactly what?"

"The sacred marriage. You will bear *Hreesos'* children, be his wife. Sib, you are acting oddly. Are you well?"

Chloe couldn't quite take it in. She'd run this race, she'd almost killed herself, to oust Ileana. That she knew. She'd lost. She knew that, too. That she could still become Kela, the mother-goddess in every last way, was news. This is what I get for leaping before I look, Chloe thought.

For the first time she considered how nice it would be to live in her own body for a change.

Without Cheftu?

THE DAY OF THE BULL DANCE ARRIVED in a haze of beauty. Colored tents contrasted with the sea and sky, flaunting their clan emblems. The chieftains would conclude the meetings of the Council. Then, Phoebus alone would undergo the rituals of Becoming Golden.

He stood silent as attendants dressed him in the elaborate ceremonial robes of the Clan Olimpi. He would ascend the Pyramid of Days and emerge a changed man: no longer only the firstborn son of Bull Zelos, but the embodiment and incarnation of a god. A ruler in his own right, able to convene with the Council. But first the Bull Dance, the ritual, the sacrifice. Then one moon cycle with Ileana—his skin crept at the thought—and he would be the supreme ruler of the thalassocracy.

What a threshold in which to assume his throne. A plague was killing off the Aztlantu elders, two clans had been all but obliterated.

It was a good thing he was moving against Egypt and the eastern mainland. Aztlan would soon need their food, men, and resources.

He exhaled as his dresser laced a red leather corselet around his waist. The man deftly tucked the edge of the loincloth under the corselet and called for the ceremonial kilt. It wrapped low on Phoebus' hips, the elaborately patterned cloth swathing him and then falling into a waterfall of fabric that reached his sandals in the front. Phoebus held out his arms as bands of gold were strapped on his biceps and forearms. The heavy pendant of the clan of the Triton, Clan Olimpi, was laid around his neck. He clenched his teeth as he submitted to the formal twisting and binding of his waist-length hair. His eyes were lined with gray kohl, and golden earrings pierced his ears.

"Phoebus?" Her low voice sent a shudder throughout his body. He snapped the dresser away before turning. Instead of her tunic, she wore the attire of a highborn Aztlantu woman: a tiered skirt and fitted jacket, which covered her shoulders and arms, then tied tightly around her waist, leaving her white breasts with their painted nipples free.

He heard the low whine of her hounds in the corridor. Would that he could be her dog! "Irmentis," he said, coughing, "I welcome you, sister. My gratitude for coming."

"You know I hate court, but I could not miss your Becoming. How do you fare?" Though the question was courteous, her blue eyes seemed to see deep inside him, and he knew that she alone really cared.

"Nervous," Phoebus said, crossing his arms so he wouldn't reach for her. "It is odd to realize that in this twenty-four decans I will make earth-shaking decisions, choices that will craft me into another person."

"Your life will no longer be yours. You will belong to Aztlan."

I want to belong to you, he thought. "Aye. My days of mingling freely with the clansmen are finished." Phoebus flexed his jaw.

Irmentis walked to the window, looked out, then over to his dressing table. "I cannot stay for all of the ceremony," she said. "The sun, you understand."

"Aye. Nekros tendered his apology as well."

They stood in awkward silence, and Phoebus wanted to weep.

Until recently there had never been tension or discomfort between them. He crossed to a woven chest and pulled out an alabaster vial he'd filled for her. A wrapped parcel lay next to it, and he gave both to Irmentis.

She ripped the fabric away from the honeycomb, and he watched as her trembling hands poured some of the opaque green liquid over it. As if it were the finest of delicacies, she bit the comb—the honey and artemisia mingling in her mouth and veins. Phoebus watched in sweet agony as she licked her fingers, sucking the honey from her nails.

"I have some news," he said, unable to look away.

"Aye?"

"Ileana has won the race."

Irmentis froze for a moment, then continued to clean her hands. "It is no more than we expected."

"You could race her anytime you chose, Irmentis. Only you can beat her. We could be together." The words came in a rush. She stood perfectly motionless, not looking at him. The vial and honeycomb lay before her. She'd eaten almost half. Was Niko right that she was becoming dependent on it? He stepped forward. "Irmentis, my sister, we can wed. You can easily beat Kela-Ileana. All of our dreams can come true! The race isn't even in daylight." He saw her smile for just an eyeblink; still she would not look at him. Gently, as though approaching a fawn, he stepped to her. He pulled her chin up. "Irmentis, this is what we have always wanted, my sister, my love. We can be together! We can mix our blood—"

She jerked her chin from his grasp. "I came to tell you I am leaving, Phoebus."

"What?"

"There is an islet off Nios. *Pateeras* has gifted me with it, and I am going there. It is well wooded, and I will have my nymphs for companions. . . ."

Phoebus shook her in rage, ignoring the warning growls he heard from her hounds. "Leaving? I have offered you my crown and couch! You tell me you are leaving?"

"I cannot marry you, Phoebus. I have told you that as many times as there are stars in the heavens. Dreams are not real."

"You mean you *will* not marry me." Phoebus dropped his hands. He heard her snap her fingers, and the dogs sat, watching him but silent. She didn't move; neither did he.

Finally she raised her gaze, her eyes filled with unshed tears. "Nay, my brother, I cannot." Her words were slow, enunciated carefully.

"I am sick beyond bearing of hearing that, Irmentis!"

"I am sick beyond bearing of your selfishness!" she screamed. The dogs' low growls underscored her ire. "Never have you asked me, consulted with me, about the future you so easily create! You simply choose your path and expect me to chase behind you. I will not continue this, Phoebus! I cannot marry you! Should you wish to know why, should you ever *listen* to me, Ileana can tell you!"

Phoebus felt stricken. Her breasts moved with her agitated breathing. "Ileana?" he repeated.

Irmentis turned away, staring into the brightly sunlit day of which she could have no part. "Wed whom you must," she said in monotone. "Leave me to my peace."

Desperate, Phoebus pulled her to him, plundering her mouth with a hard kiss. He pressed her jaw until her mouth opened and thrust his tongue in, savagely searching for a response.

A dead octopus was more passionate.

He pulled away, immediately contrite. Irmentis' lips were bruised, the light color she'd painted them was now smeared across her face. Red marks showed on her white breasts where he had handled her. Her eyes were flat, and Phoebus felt a wave of shame. The dogs were on their feet, snarling, showing their teeth. Phoebus half wished they'd fall on him, end this misery. What had he done? "My sorrow," he whispered, straightening her jacket and rubbing ineffectually at the smudges on her face.

Someone knocked at the door. "My master! Time grows short!"

"Please do not leave me," Phoebus begged. "Not like this, Irmentis. Please."

"There is nothing more," she said. "We cannot go forward or back."

"Please. We can find some compromise, we can walk a joint path. Please, Irmentis. . . ."

She pulled her hands from his and smiled softly. "We cannot."

With a gentle hand she traced his lips, and Phoebus felt his breath catching. "Wed another, my love," she whispered.

Phoebus stared at her, lost in her gaze, her touch. "When do you leave?"

"Tomorrow."

Phoebus whirled away—he couldn't seem to control his anger now that it was out. "Tomorrow? This is all the farewell I get? When were you going to tell me? Or would you simply leave and let me wonder if some animal devoured you?"

"Phoebus, don't be a child. I will only be a day's sail away. It is no time. I was going to tell you, I just had not decided when. I had to stay a while, though, to know that you—"

"Will survive?" he asked bitterly. "What difference will it make to you?"

She dropped her gaze at his words, and Phoebus stepped into the path of sunlight, looking blindly toward the sea. After tonight he would no longer live two lives, one in the day as the Rising Golden and one in the night as Irmentis' fellow shade. Could he give up the night? The silvery moon? The cool quiet of wind through the trees, the heavy fragrance of night flowers? The golden glitter of a wolf's eyes, the shriek of the bats? The warmth of Irmentis' body beside his as they ran over hills and through valleys, their bows beneath their arms?

He had never spent more than a week away from her. She was his friend, his partner, his dream lover. To her he could confess his fears as prince. To her he could entrust the details of his experiments. To her he could rage over the precarious state of Aztlan's bloated chieftains and bickering clans and discuss his new plans to resurrect his empire. With her he could plot revenge against Ileana.

Could he survive?

He turned to her, her frail figure clad in clothing abhorrent to her yet worn for his sake. Where were her tunic and sandals? Where was the silver circlet that held back her long, curly hair? Would he train her like a hound? Was that what marriage would do to her? She was a wild thing—was it fair to tame her?

He read the answer in her eyes.

Let me be free.

She edged around a patch of sunlight on the floor and then stepped into the dark corridor. Phoebus watched as his heart, his dreams, his reason, walked away.

THE PYRAMID OF DAYS rose high, visible for *henti*, its multicolored sides inscribed with the history of the empire, its golden top throbbing with the power of the sun. The red, black, and white buildings of the palace contrasted against the dark soil and vibrant greenery. The nobles' regatta sailed beneath the graceful arches that spanned the lagoon between Aztlan and Kallistae, accepting the outpouring of flower petals and praise as their due.

The procession entered the tunnel.

The ceremonies were begun.

The Ring of the Bull was not actually a ring, but rather a rectangle that ran the length of the palace. Complete with balconies and overhangs, it seated more than three thousand people.

The men and women of the Decan Council were stripped to loincloths, save Nekros, who wore an all-concealing cloak that he would discard when they moved from the sunlight. Their long hair was bound up and crowned with feathers, their bodies prepared for burial from lustral baths. The table in the center of the room was empty, its surface inlaid with the decapod crab and the emblems of Aztlan's ten clans. There was neither head nor foot at the oblong table. Though *Hreesos* had ultimate power, in the Council chamber he was only another clan chieftain.

To the solemn march of drums, they walked in and took their places.

They followed the ritual of Becoming.

"I am the Clan of the Muse, Chieftain Atenis."

"I am the Clan of the Stone, Chieftain Nekros."

"I am the Clan of the Horn, Chieftain Sibylla."

As they spoke, all placed their ruling trident on the table, so that the tines met in the center. Each wore the golden seal of their clan, and male or female they wore the ritual dagger of Olimpi, given to them when they assumed the chieftainship, in the understanding that they would sacrifice even themselves to prevent internal war.

"I am the Clan of the Vine, Chieftain Dion."

"I am the Clan of the Wave, Chieftain Iason."

"I am the Clan of the Flame, Chieftain Talos."

Cheftu rose, ruler of the Scholomance. "I am the Clan of the Spiral, the Spiralmaster."

The two religious orders representatives spoke. "I am the Cult of the Bull, the Minos."

"I am the Cult of the Snake, the Kela-Ata."

Hreesos rose, laying down his triton with finality. He would not be present at this table again. "I am *Hreesos* Zelos, Clan Olimpi."

Together they spoke the creed that was the foundation of Olimpi Aztlan.

> For the benefit of all, the detriment of none,
> No people, no property, shall break our bond,
> We ten rule alone, yet reign as one.
> Formed by fire and flood,
> *Ellenismos* our blood,
> We live, rule, and die together
> Aztlan *athanati!*

While cheers filled the hall, serfs removed the table. Doors that had been closed were opened, forming a labyrinthine maze of rooms and corridors in which the chieftains would seek the face of Apis. The ten men and women removed their heavy gold pectorals and waited in silence.

Each chieftain was handed a noose and picked up his or her triton. Serfs came forward and removed the center prong, leaving them with staves. Chloe put the coil of brightly colored braided flax over her shoulder and looked up. Thousands of people watched from the balconies and lofts around the arena. They would remain there all day, throughout this ceremony and Phoebus' Becoming Golden.

The noise of the crowd was a low hum in her ears as she listened for the rumble of the Apis bull, somewhere in the palace. He was the bull they were to corner and tie.

Hreesos stumbled, catching himself against the wall. The other chieftains frowned and whispered among themselves. As they waited, Chloe knew palace serfs wove through the many hallways and rooms of the maze, clearing hallways and damping fires for the ease of the chase. Cheftu seemed lost in another world; she had not seen him since she was declared the inheritor of Kela-Ileana; she was not supposed to be with any other man. *If only I'd known that before.*

Hindsight really was twenty-twenty.

The serfs ran into the arena, handed *Hreesos* his stave, an indication the ritual was to begin.

The plaintive groan of the bull echoed throughout the palace, the sound building into a massive roar that silenced the chattering citizens. Chloe was petrified and electrified. They would stalk the bull through the labyrinth of rooms, and whoever noosed it would receive a boon from *Hreesos* and the Clan Olimpi.

"*Yazzo!*" he cried, and the chieftains ran into the winding darkness. The chanting of the crowd swept into the many chambers like a flood, rising to the painted roof and falling down again. Each chieftain set out in a different direction, and Chloe took the skinniest, darkest hallway. Surely it was too narrow for the bull?

Reminding herself that caution was the better part of valor, and surviving this was her goal, Chloe walked through the deserted hallways. Unless she had a rifle she wasn't going to deliberately seek out a creature with horns and an attitude. She'd *seen* bullfights!

She froze as a low rumble echoed through the hallways. Dear God, where could it be? Listening for anyone else—especially Cheftu—Chloe wondered through how many rooms she was required to wander.

She guessed there were at least a hundred rooms in this wing. Divided by ten crazed Council members and one hungry bull. If she tried just ten rooms, she would at least be doing her share. Did this incredibly long, dark hallway count? she wondered. Glancing to her right, she saw a glow of light. Would the bull head toward the light or away? Cautiously she poked her head into two rooms. Both were empty: no bull, no people.

She passed through the light well and into another hallway, more chambers. Chloe walked through at least six hallways before she heard the bull again. Louder? Closer? The walls vibrated.

The acoustics are probably distorted, she assured herself, peeking into another half dozen rooms. Aztlantu interior design was all or nothing, she decided. Either every square millimeter was covered with pattern and painting or the walls were plain white, or red, or the shrieking yellow Dion called "saffron."

Two more rooms before the next light well. Nothing in either. Nevertheless, the hair on the back of her neck began to rise, and she walked forward slowly. Then she heard a scream, a terrible, agony-filled, high-pitched scream.

Chloe ran, through the light well and down another hallway, heading in the direction of the sobbing screams and another light well. She stopped abruptly at the doorway. She could see nothing, her eyes were adjusting to the sudden brightness, but she could hear panting. Slowly she canvased the chamber with her gaze. Wall, doorway, wall, painting—the gaze dropped down, and Chloe felt her stomach heave.

Against the wall, beneath a painting of butterflies and lilies on the typical rock-strewn background, lay a body. The lower half was covered in blood, the body angled so Chloe saw only a lot of dark hair.

Blood spattered the floor and wall, an abstract swirl across the many cubits of geometric symmetry. The only sound was heavy breathing.

Feeling very much like the dense heroine who goes into the basement after the scary music begins playing, Chloe continued her survey of the room.

And stopped.

A pair of rolling brown eyes watched her from not five cubits away. What had happened here? With peripheral vision, she kept her eye on the body, hopefully unconscious and not dead. What had the bull done? The chieftain moaned, and the bull turned, licking its blood-stained mouth.

Chloe's mind went completely blank. Not one rational thought, but a host of instincts controlled her. She stood motionless, gazing into the mad eyes of the bull. She'd seen bullfights in Spain. Movement incited the bull, as did color, right? Good plan to wear a red loincloth. I should have just painted a damn target on my chest, she thought. Her heart pounded in her ears, and she stayed still. Where could she go?

The bull stepped forward, and Chloe gritted her teeth, staying still. Bile filled her mouth and she swallowed it down, her gaze fixed on the rolling eyes of the bull. Behind her, moving an inch at a time, she felt for the doorway. Was she close enough to back through it? Was there a huge door she could close on the bull's anger?

No. The doors had all been removed. Chloe swallowed, and the bull nudged closer. She could hear the whimpers of the victim, possibly bleeding to death, but if she moved and the bull got her, they would both die. Hideously. Out of sympathy her knees began to knock, and Chloe alternated locking each knee, trying to maintain control of her body.

She could smell the bull, a smell that reminded her of Cheftu's lab. Strange to smell it on a live bull, but what did she know? She'd never been around beef while it was still on the hoof! The bull finally glanced down, edging sideways, its head cocked as though it were hard of hearing.

A groan came from the chieftain on the floor, and the bull made a strange hissing noise, stepping even closer to Chloe. She took another step back, bringing herself even with the doorway. Was it narrow enough to prevent the bull from chasing her?

She had never realized how big a bull was. A deep freezer was positively petite in comparison. The bull shuffled forward, and Chloe knew if she stepped back farther, it would have her trapped. She would never make it completely across the room without being trampled. The bull made a small bleating sound and licked her arm.

Licked?

Chloe was frozen, watching the long tongue sweep against her bare arm a half dozen times. Then the bull turned slowly, lurching into another hallway.

Chloe sagged against the wall, giving in to her knees for a moment, then she ran to the victim. Blood spread in a radius around a woman.

Chloe brushed hair away from the victim's face. Selena—oh no, not Selena! She was bleeding from several different wounds, and Chloe wondered if Selena had been gored or bitten. Did bulls bite? For that matter, did they lick? Chloe knew nothing about livestock, but she would have sworn cattle were herbivores. This was the strangest-acting bull she'd ever heard of.

Blood was pumping from Selena like a hose on high. Could Chloe fashion a tourniquet? After ripping off a length of her already short loincloth, Chloe attempted to tie off the woman's leg. Knotting tightly above Selena's knee, Chloe tied the blood-soaked cloth elaborately, hoping it would help. Selena was unconscious, but she was still breathing.

Sounds from the other rooms filtered back to her. The bull. Shouting. Selena needed medical attention. Where was Cheftu? Chloe rose to her feet, uncertain where to go. Terrified, she followed the map she had in her head, moving through doorway after doorway, a brilliantly patterned maze where she was a rat in search of cheese. Finally she emerged in the arena.

She looked up, stunned at how late it was. The sun had long since passed its zenith, and many of the citizens were gone, presumably resting. She looked for a serf, a chieftain, anyone! A man's triumphant cry sent her racing into the opposite side of the labyrinth.

When her eyes adjusted she saw Chieftain Talos leading the bull. The noose was around its horns, and he was using his stave to prod it forward. In the arena a chorus of serfs announced that the competition was complete. Some of the chieftains ran through, ignoring her calls. Where was Cheftu? *Hreesos* entered, limping slightly, and Chloe ran to him, halting him with her hand on his chest.

His blue eyes narrowed on her. "Someone was hurt," she said.

Hreesos removed her hand, his grip firm around her wrist. "Who?"

She hesitated an eyeblink. "The Kela-Ata."

He snapped his fingers, summoning serfs. "How badly?"

"She . . . is bleeding horribly."

The Golden Bull crossed his arms over his chest. Blond hair matted his torso and arms, and his long hair was stuck to his neck and back with sweat. "This is why we all have lustral baths before the ceremony. She is ready to begin her journey."

"Nay! She is not dead, not yet."

Hreesos took her by the shoulders and moved her aside. "You know the laws, Sibylla. Any chieftain who cannot freely take his or her seat at the Council table—"

"Must defer to the inheritor. But she is not—"

"If she cannot walk, then she is dead as clan chieftain." *Hreesos* walked by her. "Into the arena, Chieftain, or you shall be declared likewise."

Chloe was tempted to flip him off and go after the broken body of the Kela-Ata. She grabbed a serf and told him to find Selena, bring a Kela-Tenata, and get her healed. Zelos glared at her, and Chloe followed him into the arena.

The high priest Minos, his bull-head mask pulled over his head and shoulders, giving him the appearance of a Minotaur, stood next to the real bull, still bloodstained and standing strangely off-balance. On the other side Talos stood at attention, his graying hair blowing in the afternoon breeze.

"Clan of the Flame!" *Hreesos* shouted. The citizens went wild. One by one the chieftains laid their staves down on the table. The Cult of the Snake was noticeably missing, but before anyone could ask, Minos and his priests were ushering them out.

It was the time for the Bull Dance.

Chloe ran back to Selena.

PHOEBUS STOOD, HIS SWEATY HANDS CLUTCHING THE RAILING. Ileana stood beside him, the proud tilt of her breast pressing into his bare arm. Arus was on the other side, watching their naked relatives as they ran from the room.

"You will be down there next Council," Arus said. His huge arms were crossed, and Phoebus wondered briefly how Arus felt: he was one of *Hreesos'* offspring, but he had never had a chance at Zelos' position, not being born of the mother-goddess. Would that be how Eumelos felt?

For decans sounds of screams, running feet, and hooves had drifted back to the assembled group. The citizens outside and around the island had feasted, waiting for news of the outcome. Phoebus could eat almost nothing, though he tore at the meat viciously, as befitted a man about to be blooded. Niko had refused meat, a distant expression in his eyes.

Talos now limped forward to accept the court's cheers and the Council's vow to provide his clan products for free the remainder of the year. Phoebus knew it was his turn. He had trained a lifetime for this. Adrenaline raced like fire through his veins, and he slipped down the stairs, where the priests stood waiting for him. He was stripped bare, his sex massaged to full strength, his hair freed, and the ritual boot put on his foot, laced up his calf. Wearing the traditional boot was a challenge, the one thing for which he'd not been allowed to prepare.

They handed him the short, vicious ceremonial blade and a double circle shield. Priests hustled the bull into the outside ring, while the nobility watched the Rising Golden walk in proud nudity from the interior of the Council chamber, through the obsidian tunnels, down, down into the actual bull ring.

Phoebus stood while he was showered with praise and flowers. The crowd was a sun-limned border of lumps and angles. The bull dancers, orphaned children, had entertained earlier in the ring, and smears of blood stood out on the sand floor, testament to the intensity of this diversion. Phoebus turned and gazed at the bull, trapped behind gates. He tensed his muscles, then jerked his chin toward the priests. He was ready.

If he survived unscathed, he would be tested further, the same testing the Spiralmaster Cheftu had endured. Once he passed those tests, he would become the Sacred One, learning his kingly duties during a year of abstinence: no meat, no wine, no sex. His energies would be focused. He would deny himself the pleasures of the flesh—save for mating with Ileana, if that could be called pleasure. Thus he would prove his worthiness as *Hreesos*, the Golden One, purified and selected for the work of serving Aztlan. It was the process by which man alchemized into more than mortal.

Today, however, he could kill, couple, and feast.

The bull charged at him and Phoebus dodged, using the reflection of his blade's handle to distract the creature at the last minute. Phoebus dropped his shield, clenching the short knife between his teeth. They circled, measuring each other, communicating from brown bovine eyes to pale human eyes the truth that only one would leave the arena alive. The sun came from an angle, the heat intensifying as it gathered in the black lava stone walls. Phoebus tried to keep the light behind him, blinding the bull, but the bull moved too fast and often Phoebus was the one blinded.

The bull charged again, backing Phoebus into the corner. As he'd practiced all his life, Phoebus grabbed its horns, flipping himself with the upward motion of the bull's head, touching on its back, then flipping off, landing on the ground. *He was a wave, crashing on the shore.* The boot hampered the grace of his movement a little, but no one realized it. The crowd went wild, and for a few seconds Phoebus relished the chant of his name. The bull charged, and Phoebus twisted over its back.

It charged again, and Phoebus feinted, then leapt, landing lightly on its other side. He was getting used to the boot now, the imbalance was beginning to feel normal, and his other leg was compensating for it. The court's excitement thundered in his veins as he rolled and dodged, tossing himself over the beast's powerful back.

Sweat blinded him, and Phoebus rubbed his forehead, having only an eyeblink of time to dodge the bull, forcing himself to roll beneath it during its charge.

The crowd went wild, and the air was filled with a rain of flower petals on the arena.

Phoebus was so hard, so full, he thought he would burst. The bull screamed at him: kill or be killed. The dance was complete; now it was death. He stopped moving, catching his breath, watching the creature's eyes. His trainer always said there would be a warning flicker in the bull's eyes the very breath before it came in for the kill.

Wiping sweaty hands on his thighs, Phoebus crouched. The beast came, full speed, its head lowered and eyes gleaming with blood lust.

Phoebus reached out for its horns, almost lying on its face, flipped and twisted his body over its head, and landed on its neck, his legs spread wide, riding on its shoulders.

He slit its throat with the knife, his body low over the creature, flat between its horns. He tightened his thighs, digging his bare and booted feet into the animal's large chest as it bellowed its death cry. Hair and sweat marred Phoebus' view, but he could feel the lifeblood of the creature, hot and thick, pour over his leg and foot.

Livid with pain, the bull bucked and fought to rid itself of Phoebus' weight. His hand gripped the sweaty fur on its neck, and Phoebus held on, his legs tight even as he lost his seat, even as the bull turned and twisted, its bellowing and roaring echoing back from the black walls a hundred times.

Finally the bull fell to its knees, jarring Phoebus as it nodded, sluggishly trying to get free. It stopped moving, collapsing heavily, and Phoebus leapt off a heartbeat before his leg was crushed.

Every muscle in Phoebus' body trembled, his breath was loud in his ears, and he felt the same rush that came just before climaxing. He wiped his hands in the dust, looking up at the crowd. They chanted his name like a prayer, and he closed his eyes, welcoming the homage of his people. He had been born for this adoration.

The priests came out, bearing large basins. Phoebus had severed the bull's jugular, and now the priests stood while he cut off the bull's head, spattering his body and face with crimson. The warm blood was poured into the copper and gold vessels, and Phoebus knelt before the priests.

The Minos came out, dressed again as a priest, and poured the blood of the beast on Phoebus. It coated him from the top of his golden head down his tanned body, mantling the stiffness of his erection. He closed his eyes as it dripped off his nose onto the ground. The warm copper smell both sickened and enticed him.

"Hail, Phoebus!" Minos cried.

"Hail, Phoebus! *Hreesos* Phoebus! Hail, Phoebus!" The crowd took up the chant deafeningly.

"Rising Golden Bull! Take the powers of Apis into yourself!" Minos shouted.

Phoebus drank the offered cup of blood.

The crowd screamed.

"Take the strength of Apis into yourself!"

Phoebus ate the offered bloody, raw meat.

The crowd roared.

"Take the fertility of Apis into yourself!"

The crowd applauded, and Phoebus accepted the still warm testicle. Hiding his revulsion, he slit the pocket and drank the creamy fluid. Swallowing quickly so he wouldn't gag, he was baptized again in blood.

The priest's words were lost on the crowd, frenzied at the sight of the golden prince, standing aroused in the blood of his victim. The primal urges in the polished ladies and nobles of Aztlan were rising.

Huge basins of blood would be placed throughout the arena for the populace. Each citizen would dip their cloth in the life of Apis and place his mark on their forehead, praying the blessing of blood would protect him or her throughout the coming year. Nobles would receive the bull's blood, and they would partake of its flesh.

The organs were saved for the priesthood, the brain for the Golden and his selected *hequetai* alone.

Thousands filed into lines to walk by the basins. They chanted Phoebus' name, and he felt the wind dry the blood on his body as he walked from the arena.

As he entered the darkness of the tunnel, his heart was still pounding, his erection throbbing, and his ears ringing with the sound of his name. *Hreesos* Phoebus. The blood had dried into a thin skin, and as he ducked under one of the black lava beams, he felt the drying coating crack.

He had succeeded. He'd leapt on time, his turns were tight enough. Not even a scratch! Giddiness was rising like a bubble within him, and he wanted a woman, badly. In the distance he saw a priest; would he know where the nearest Coil Dancer was?

If only it were Irmentis, her body bared to his gaze, her eyes glowing with invitation.

The priest took Phoebus' blood-caked wrist and led him to a blank wall.

Concealing his movements, the priest pressed part of the stone and a faint whirring noise echoed through the black tunnel. Phoebus

watched as an even darker square opened. They stepped in and began walking up. Then the floor angled downward. Phoebus could see nothing; he kept his hands on the shoulders of the priest before him, sensing the changes in the flooring. They'd walked for what seemed whole rotations of the sun, when the priest stopped. He'd still not said a word.

Another click and whir.

The scent of fresh blood filled his nostrils. Phoebus stepped into the space alone. The priest shut the door behind him, and Phoebus breathed deeply.

"Step forward, *Hreesos,*" Zelos, his *pateeras,* said.

It was suddenly light, and Phoebus blinked at the harshness. "You enter the sacred threshold of the priests," his father said, stepping forward. His blond hair caught the light, and Phoebus was struck with how young and handsome Zelos still was. He glanced around at the handful of men who flanked his father. They were all that remained of Zelos' *hequetai?*

"Come, *Hreesos,* sit," his father said, indicating a leather stool. Phoebus sat down hesitantly, and the low murmur of voices filled the room. The body of the bull he'd killed in the warm sunshine lay in a trench before him. The head sat before his seat.

"Take the organ and cut it up, serve a piece to each man you want in your cabinet," *Pateeras* instructed in an undertone. "Take the largest portion for yourself, but do not eat it until you have received the oracle of the Minos." Phoebus took the head and, with set jaw and watching audience, extracted the warm mass of brain.

He was having difficulty focusing, but still the brain pieces looked strange. It was filled with holes, unlike anything he'd ever seen in his experiments with the Spiralmaster. The Spiralmaster! Phoebus looked over the company carefully; the Egyptian did not defile this gathering with his presence. No one Phoebus' age was here, just a bunch of old men. *"Pateeras,"* he whispered, "is this what the brain looks like?"

Hreesos stared at it. "It looks the same as what I have eaten every summer for nineteen summers. Have no fear, Phoebus. Eat it. Take the strength of Apis into yourself."

Phoebus sliced it.

The Minos stepped forward. Intoning a lengthy prayer in the

founding language of Aztlan, he offered the horns back to Apis. Two other priests stood to the side as he gutted the bull, then flung its entrails against a huge gold plate at Phoebus' feet. The priests lit more lamps, and Phoebus saw the lengths of twisted intestine. The Minos' eyes were shut as he moved back and forth.

The incense that filled the room was making Phoebus feel lightheaded, and he desperately hung on to the details: the contrast of deep bloody red against the gold; the masked face of the Minos and how ridiculous the huge bull's head looked atop his shriveled body. They needed a high priest who looked the role, Phoebus thought. Young and virile, the epitome of Apis.

The man was speaking, his voice high-pitched and slurred. Zelos laid a hand on Phoebus' shoulder. "He is a frightened old man and speaks nonsense sometimes. We have nothing to fear."

Phoebus shook his head in agreement, but the thoughts tickled the back of his consciousness. They had everything to fear: earthquakes, eruptions, plague. The Minos suddenly screamed and fell convulsing to the floor.

Leaping to his feet, Phoebus stared as the other priests carried the old man from the room. The nobles were speaking, casting wary glances toward Phoebus. What had happened? The hair on Phoebus' neck had risen from that shriek. He turned to Zelos, whose face was ashen in the light. "What does this mean?"

"Select them now, Phoebus. Now!"

Phoebus looked over the company. They were sickly, shuddering and drooling, a few could barely walk. He needed young men!

"We enter a new era!" he cried out. "An era of expansion and prosperity as never before seen in any land!" He would go ahead and share his wishes to conquer, Phoebus thought. "No longer shall we barter for what we want; we will be rulers of it! Egypt cowers before us! The cities of Canaan can be our market basket! My wish is for every people related to the sea to be Aztlan's vassals!"

The thunderous applause he'd expected did not come. They stared in stunned silence. None of these men shared his vision for a new Aztlan.

A priest ran into the room, screaming. "Minos is dead! Minos is dead!"

"What have you done?" Zelos hissed. "The high priest is dead? Speak now, before they leave you!"

Phoebus was losing his kingdom before he'd even inherited it?

"Is there another bull?" Phoebus asked.

"Another?"

"Aye, more of the sacred Apis bulls?"

"Aye, of course! Choose, Phoebus."

Phoebus sat and picked up the first piece of hole-ridden meat. It was the symbol of power for his minister of finance. Phoebus ate it. Everyone straightened, and Phoebus fought to keep a smirk off his face. They were aware of his insult. Next, he took the piece for his minister of public properties. Phoebus ate it. His minister of barges, Phoebus ate; minister of canals, he ate. Were they getting his point?

He rose, drunk on power. "I am *Hreesos*. I am ruler of Aztlan. I will rule with your sons." Phoebus walked out, the direction he'd seen the priests go. Another silent priest met him and led him to a tunnel. Another tunnel. Phoebus felt hot but invincible. The priest opened another door, and Phoebus stepped through. The smell of manure touched his nostrils, and he glanced up and down the passageway. There, in the sunlight, was a nymph.

"You!" he called. She looked up, a figure in the distance. "Come to me," he commanded. He would prove he had gained the virility of Apis, despite the Minos' death. He would fill her with child; spite Ileana.

That was it, he realized in a flash of clarity. He would have his revenge; he would withhold from his stepmother! If she were not pregnant by the dark of the moon, she would be sent to the Labyrinth or killed. He smiled at the nymph again; she backed away, then fled.

No mind, he would sate himself with Coil Dancers until he met with Ileana.

It was the perfect revenge: Ileana would lose that which was most dear to her—her precious position.

The new *Hreesos'* drugged laughter echoed through the obsidian tunnels.

THE CITIZENS REVELED IN THE BLOOD. The stink of it, the thickness of it, their sanctification in it. Though Apis was their god, they were the rulers of the god, for they could destroy and devour him. The bull of spring was gulped by the lion of summer.

The day was fading, the crowd more boisterous as peddlers with spicy wine and honeyed treats moved by those still standing in line. Dancing had begun, and everyone bore the crimson stains of the celebration. This was *kefi:* abandonment, revelry, thrilling to life when death was so close. Wearing the bull's blood was a triumph, a blessing, and a recognition that death came to everyone.

Kefi rejoiced that death had not yet come.

Blood had dried on the layered skirts of the women; it had caked the carefully extended eyebrows of the men. It was smeared on the faces of children, and even the aged wore traces of it on their wrinkled brows.

Its stench was a perfume; it boiled in their veins as they laughed and cavorted, a people bigger than their gods, their land, the earth itself.

A voice, a single voice, high on the wind, cut through the blood-crazed shouts of the populace. A white-cloaked figure stood on a ledge of the Pyramid of Days. The Calling Place, where by some magic, every word uttered from that height was audible for *henti.* The crowd became silent, all of Aztlan became silent, watching the woman as she walked the narrow ledge. She spoke clearly, authoritatively, her voice rolling away from the pyramid like waves on a beach.

The Lion creeps up on you
The storm clouds gather
Darkness, fire, blood, and water come
Mercy beckons; flee while you may
Seek the truth, the stable ground, the power you worship will destroy

Flee for your lives
The Lion growls
Flee for your lives
The Bull rumbles
Aztlan will be a cavern of bones, if you pay no heed!
Your children will be dust; your legacy will be ashes.
Death comes, guised as a dance.
Flee!

From the crowd a drunken voice called out, "Olimpi power will destroy you!" The enchantment was broken, though everyone heard the woman's next words.

"This is cursed land! We have all wisdom and treat it as dust! Learn from the past; our land was shaken to pieces. We must now flee before we are submerged in our arrogant pride. Do we seek to die? Do we wish our weakest vassal to be remembered as the greatest culture? Flee, citizens, flee!"

Was that the Sibylla? Prophesying *against* Aztlan?

Hreesos' private guard could be seen scaling up one side of the pyramid, the fading sun glinting off the gold in their clothing.

CHLOE LOOKED DOWN FROM THE IMPRESSIVE HEIGHT of the temple as it perched above the ring. The citizens were tiny creatures, and she thought, You are born in blood today. The smooth rock of the Pyramid of Days felt odd to her bare feet, and she felt dried tears on her face.

Selena was dead; they had danced while Selena was dying. These people had no heart, no sense to listen, neither to her nor to the ground that shook beneath their feet. They were suicidal.

She felt the presence and turned. A cubit away stood a crop-haired guard. "Come with us, don't disturb the festival," he said.

Chloe nodded her head; she would not go with him.

He took a step forward.

She took a step back.

Into air.

CHEFTU WATCHED AS THE WHITE-CLOAKED FIGURE fell backward off the Pyramid of Days. The crowd screamed and rushed forward in a mass; the two guards stood on the edge, looking down. Nestor grabbed his forearm. "That was Sibylla."

The news hit Cheftu like a kick in the gut, and he hissed in pain. The two men moved forward quickly as the arena balconies emptied. Cheftu caught fragments of conversation.

"Where is she?"

"I saw her fall!"

"Kela—"

"A sign—"

"Not dead?"

Nestor's grip had not lessened as they pushed through the crowd of gawkers. Cheftu stiffened when they saw the white cloth on the ground. Then he frowned; there was no one and nothing inside it. Immediately he looked up, searching the side of the pyramid for any clue.

"It is a great miracle!"

"A priestess of Kela, certainly!"

"She is above the clan!"

"She's gorgeous—"

What had Chloe been thinking? What had possessed her? She was bewildering, his wife; he never knew what she would do next. A beautiful, magnificent, amazing creature. He squinted into the shadows around the pyramid. Also a cunning woman . . . and very, very agile.

CHAPTER 14

CHLOE SAT IN THE SHADOWS, WHIMPERING. Her heart still pounded in her throat, and if her hands stopped trembling before the year I A.D., it would be a miracle. The crowd swarmed like ants over her white cloak, and she could hear the bewildered comments of the guards above her, wondering about the penalty for murdering a Golden, Kela-Ileana's inheritor.

Leaning her head against the stone, Chloe replayed the last few seconds. Stepping backward into nothing, she had fallen. Because of the shape of the pyramid—smooth casing stones with narrow staircases that scaled its sides—she had fallen over the smooth part but managed to roll onto a step. Her cloak, which had come loose, had continued to fall. It must have been quite a sight, the white against the rainbow background, distracting enough that the thousands never saw her body, a tiny figure against the mass of stone. Chloe had immediately rolled into the shadow of the step. A little cubbyhole beneath a larger set of steps was the perfect hiding place for a terrified, sweating, mostly naked impostor oracle.

Or was she?

The group was dispersing along with the sunlight, and she could hear the guards coming down the steps above her. What should she do?

I ruined the Bull Dance ceremony, the kefi *of the day. Phoebus would not be happy.*

I had no choice, Chloe thought. In those few moments I was compelled. She realized with a shiver that she would have given her life to speak those words. Where had they come from? They sounded vaguely like a song she'd once heard . . . a prophecy of disaster gone unheeded. The mountains were coughing ash. Did the Aztlantu think they were *athanati*, that they wouldn't perish, that Aztlan couldn't fall?

Please, God, don't let it happen to them. Even though they let Selena die, they aren't any worse than any other people.

Every civilization was good and bad; no culture was pure.

She shivered as the guards walked past her, still arguing.

Chloe huddled under the stair and wondered what to do. A chilly breeze began blowing at dusk. Could she return to the palace? Just how irritated would *Hreesos* be? Curling into herself, she napped, waking to a black summer night.

Seated in her perch between heaven and earth, she thought the world seemed like a pointillist masterpiece in silver and gold. Fires burned golden below her: homes, taverns, palaces, and gardens. Silver fires burned above her, constellations yet unnamed.

Talk about a paradigm shift.

"Sibylla!" the night air seemed to whisper, and Chloe smiled, feeling the comfort of the darkness.

"Sibylla!"

She raised her head: the night air was sounding rather irritated.

"Sibylla! Where in the name of Kela are you?"

She recognized the 1-900-FONE SEX voice as Dion's. How did he know? "Here!" she whispered.

The sound of sandals on steps, and then she saw a flicker of light, quickly extinguished. "Come out and do not speak!"

Covering her very bare, very cold breasts, Chloe unbent herself from her hideaway. Wincing with stiffness, she crept down the stone steps. They were worn in the middle, and she was grateful she was barefoot. She didn't remember climbing them. All she remembered was holding Selena's hand as the life faded from her eyes, Atenis' muffled sobs in the background. Chloe pressed her lips together. Poor Selena.

Dion stood in the darkness, his smile and the whites of his eyes the only things visible. She walked down to him, and he pulled a frontless jacket over her shoulders. Chloe tugged it on as he handed her a tiered skirt. She shimmied into it, trying to tuck in the top. "It is no matter, come along," he said.

Like *skia* they slid from shadow to shadow until she felt the rock-strewn concrete pavement beneath her feet. Dion put his arm around her waist and pulled her against the wall. Voices first, then people passed. Chloe's heart was pounding again, and she wondered why he was being so secretive.

Slowly they made their way from the temple complex, past the snake goddess's temple and into the palace area. Hundreds milled about, dancing, drinking, and making out. Dion pulled her beside an oleander bush, and they fell to the ground. Chloe groaned as her back hit the less than padded turf. What was going on? He loomed over her, his bare chest against her naked breasts. He was undoubtedly one of the sexiest men she'd ever seen, but there was absolutely no chemistry.

"Phoebus would like to push you from the pyramid again," he said quietly. Chloe tried to sit up, to face him, but he moved his lips close to her ear, speaking softly. "Why would you say such things? Why did you do that?"

"I—"

"Do not speak. Everyone thinks you are quite dead. Maybe that is for the best now. You can return to life later. Phoebus is furious. So is *Hreesos*. Kela-Ileana claimed you offended the goddess."

Chloe blanched. Zelos angry would not be a pretty sight; trust Ileana to manipulate facts to suit her. Where was Cheftu? "Atenis is willing to smuggle you away," he said.

She nodded her head.

"Why do you say nay? Are you mad?"

Damn reverse gestures, she thought. I really am frazzled. Frantically she shook her head. "Wise choice," Dion said. His mouth hovered over her collarbone, and though their proximity was devoid of sexual tension, Chloe was beyond uncomfortable.

She rolled over, pinning him to the ground. His hands automatically grabbed her waist, and she resisted the urge to bat them away. "I said aye. Where do I go and how long should I stay away?"

His eyes were night dark, his mouth against her cheek. "Tonight Atenis will take you to Prostatevo."

Phoebus' new city, she thought. Sweet Atenis! "May I masquerade as an artist?"

"Aye, if you want."

Thank God, no more lame-ducking it as the chieftain of the Clan of the Horn.

"If anyone asks you, claim your husband was lost in the eruption. Grief has kept you from the festival. You will wear a tattoo, and no one will look twice."

"Just so."

"Stay for a day or two, let Phoebus' anger cool."

What would she miss? Didn't she have responsibilities? Chloe was opening her mouth to ask when someone recognized Dion. She quickly lay on the chieftain's chest, hoping it would prevent the man from inquiring further.

"By the gods, man, can you not restrain yourself for one night? Cheftu is very upset, worried," Nestor said.

Chloe froze. If Cheftu heard about this, she didn't want to think what he would do.

"Greetings, Spiralmaster."

Was it her imagination, or had Dion practically purred that?

"Greetings, Chieftain," Cheftu said.

Chloe could have screamed with frustration. This looked bad, really bad. She and Dion were lying with legs tangled like frisky teenagers. Leave! she thought. Cheftu, walk on by! Please don't think the worst. Would Cheftu recognize her? Horrified that he would, Chloe debated how to extricate herself. Literally.

Dion propped himself up on his elbow. "What did you think of our bloodstained ritual today? I don't see the blessing of Apis on your forehead. Join me."

Chloe dug her nails into his side. That was the *last* thing they needed.

"*Okh*, I think you have more than a lapful," Cheftu said, his voice sounding strained. Had he recognized her? Oh dear, oh no.

"Dion?" another voice called from the darkness.

Dion bolted upright. "Ileana," he hissed. "Nestor! You must distract her. Pretend you want to seduce her!"

"She's my stepmother. Let the Egyptian pretend to seduce her!"

"Seduce?" Cheftu said.

"Seduce?" Chloe echoed.

"Delay her with flirtation, anything," Dion commanded. "I must get"—he paused—"this nymph away."

Dion gripped her arm, pulling her up, her back toward the two chieftains. Cheftu grabbed her shoulder, turned her around for a brief moment, and she looked into his eyes. Forgive me, she pleaded. Understand what is happening! Dion whipped her around and they were off through the gardens, Chloe stumbling as she blinked back tears.

Dion's pace was impressive. In drag he could have beat Ileana flat and married Phoebus, Chloe thought. However, the fertility angle would be challenging. . . .

In the dark they ran down whitewashed steps still warm from the day's sun. The one time a couple approached them Dion pulled her into his arms and kissed her. It was like kissing a mirror when she was teaching herself—she thought—how to kiss. Dion pulled away and they raced down more steps, zigzagging in the half-moon night.

The smell of the sea enveloped her, and Chloe grimaced when she saw the boat. The small boat. The tiny, rinky-dink boat. It bobbed in the water, and Dion whispered that he would keep her clan seal until she returned, and he would send her messages daily. Then Chloe was sailing away, the rower a silent old woman with impressive biceps who shushed Chloe until they were a considerable distance from Aztlan Island.

The wind was brisk and the voyage incredible. Chloe felt as if they were rowing across the river Styx, it was so dark, so silent, within the lagoon. Walls of stone towered on each side of them, and her feelings of claustrophobia were only slightly assuaged by her tremendous nausea.

The rocking motion grew worse as they pulled into the more open channel south of Aztlan Island. Chloe patted seawater on her forehead and throat, trying desperately to think of anything but her roiling stomach.

Normally she did not have motion sickness. She'd traveled on planes, trains and automobiles. She'd been in cargo jets, on camel backs, and in hydrofoils. Little boats, however, were her nemesis. When Mom and Father had first taken her and Camille to their getaway on Santorini, they'd thought it would be so much fun to sail there.

Instead of the normal tourist transport, Father had chosen to hire a small boat. Within fifteen minutes Chloe, even at fourteen, would have given anything—her dog, her beloved grandmother, heck, she would have given her virginity—just to get off that boat. The nausea had continued for three days after landing, and she'd hated Santorini because of the association.

The rower stopped, fished beneath the boat with her hand, then brought up a clay pot. She opened it and passed it to Chloe. Desperate for anything to soothe her stomach, Chloe drank. Sweet wine, tart and clean. It tasted like pomegranates. The woman clicked her tongue, and Chloe passed it back. After taking a swig herself—so much for not boating and drinking, Chloe thought—the woman sealed it and dropped it beneath the water again.

They sat in the silent night, drifting slowly, but the motion was gentler now and Chloe felt much, much better.

"It is another decan or so, my mistress," the old woman said. "Lie down and rest, the bobbing won't upset you so."

Feeling suddenly sleepy, Chloe leaned against the side and laid her head back, staring into the stars.

Cosmic geography tests haunted her dreams.

His THOUGHTS WERE SOUR, and Cheftu could feel his body tensing in anger as he, Nestor, and Dion, having gotten rid of a very intoxicated and provocative Queen of Heaven, walked through the gardens to Dion's apartments.

The Aztlantu could teach Egypt much about revelry, Cheftu noted grimly. A trail of women and men gathered behind Dion as they walked through the lamplit chambers, the stench of food, sex, and sweat permeating the very plaster.

Chloe and Dion. Cheftu gritted his teeth. Dion had laughingly told him that she was a nymph with a jealous father, and very shy, which was why she had hidden her face. Why would Chloe pretend to be Dion's lover in the garden? Why had she gone with Dion and not waited for him at the pyramid? Did she think he was so simple that he believed, as the people did, she had vanished? He would have taken care of her; she had no need to turn to another man. The scent of honeysuckle was heavy in the air as Cheftu listened to Dion spin his lies about Chloe. Cheftu had forced himself to smile, realizing that honeysuckle would always smell like betrayal to him.

The door to Dion's apartments swung open. Exquisite women of every description wandered around, sipping wine, kissing, and flirting with an assortment of men.

Cheftu good-naturedly accepted a rhyton of wine but refused the petals he saw everyone chewing. Feeling at once upright, hypocritical, and priggish, he declined offers for walks in the garden, kisses, and . . . other things. No one held allure for him. Just Chloe, he thought. In whatever body she happened to be inhabiting.

"Do you not enjoy women?" Dion asked, sitting next to him. Although he appeared to be a man of honor and was a reasoned, literate, cheerful companion, Dion put Cheftu on edge.

"Not tonight," Cheftu said.

Dion leaned closer. "Do you wish for something more. Something different?" The man's eyes glittered, and Cheftu felt even less comfortable.

"Actually, I think I see a fair-haired nymph across the way," he said, rising.

"*Eee*, Laurel."

Cheftu moved toward her slowly, Dion behind him.

"My mistress," Dion said to her. She was talking to another woman, and both fell silent. Cheftu noticed her teeth were stained, the consequence of the flower she was chewing. She stared at Dion with adoration. "The Spiralmaster has chosen you tonight." Dion caressed her rose-tinted cheek. "Make him happy for me, Laurel, will you?"

She shook her head, and Dion tipped her chin, her huge brown eyes rapt on his face. "To please him is to please me, Laurel. You do want to please me, do you not?"

Her green gaze moved to Cheftu, and he knew she would neither please nor be pleased tonight. She wasn't Chloe.

She held out her small hand with the petals in it.

"*Kreenos*," Dion said. "It is a gentle expansion of your senses, my friend. Take, it will not harm you." Cheftu arched a brow, and Dion said, "Well, this one time it will not harm you." He leaned closer and whispered into Cheftu's ear, "A warning, Egyptian, she uses her teeth. Be wary, unless you like a little agony with ecstasy?"

Cheftu felt incredibly uneasy. He muttered noncommittally, and Dion walked away. Laurel took his hand and pulled him with her. He'd feed her the petals, maybe she would forget. If only he could.

Chloe and Dion.

PHOEBUS ROSE FROM HIS COUCH; the priests stood around him. The Coil Dancers would leave him to a cold couch for an entire year. This period of self-denial was supposed to give him discipline, teach him self-sacrifice, attributes needed in *Hreesos.* How his father, Zelos, had survived this was a mystery.

He kissed each of the women, lingering on the pale, dark-haired one. But she was not Irmentis. At least he had spent himself with them. Ileana would not swell with his seed. The women left and the priests assumed their positions, his guardians for a year. Phoebus' head ached as the sound of chanting, waking the bulls, drifted in through the window.

The light scent of burning herbs floated over from Kela's temple. He watched the sun rise, thinking of Irmentis, alone as she descended into the darkness to sleep. Her words "Marry another" echoed in his mind. Try as he might, Phoebus could not detect any manipulation. Did she really want him to forget her?

He snapped for a bath.

A decan later, sitting before his reflecting pool, he heard the giggle of a boy and turned in delight. Eumelos moved stiffly in his embroidered tunic, and Phoebus grinned when he saw the child's shaved head and painfully tight braid. "I thank you for honoring me, princeling," Phoebus said, crouching down to be face-to-face with his fair son. The *maeemu* on his shoulder chattered, then hopped down, scampering across the floor to the table where food was set.

"I love you, *Pateeras*," Eumelos said. "Mother tied my braid too tight." His dark blue eyes moved around the room, seeking a woman to help him. He turned back to his father. "Can you untie it?"

Phoebus loosened the formal braid Kassandra had woven. The mother of three of his children, she was her most demanding with Eumelos. "Better?" Phoebus asked.

"Aye, *Pateeras*." Eumelos ran and jumped on the bed, singing a new composition commemorating Phoebus' victory over the bull. "Mother said I would never stand in the blood of Apis," he said, playing with the edge of Phoebus' cloak. The *maeemu* took to the game, pulling at the gilded feathers. The serf pounced on the tiny gray creature and scooped him up with an irritated sigh.

"That is true," Phoebus said, biting his lip, wishing to silence Kassandra. Couldn't she see how her words hurt? *Okh*, Eumelos, he thought. Would you look forward to this day if you knew you would stand in my place? "You have other duties. Your birthdate was too early, my son. Consider it a blessing from Apis." He brushed his hand over the boy's lean back. Eumelos was already tall, but thin. As I was, Phoebus thought.

"Then why did you name an island after me?"

"All princes are immortalized in some fashion. Zelos renamed Mount Apollo for me when I was born—"

"How come I did not get a mountain?" Eumelos asked suspiciously.

"Because there were no more, brat," Phoebus said. "You have a whole island instead." My other children have only brooks and beaches named after them, he thought. Take what little I can give you.

Eumelos shrugged, satisfied. "Can I ride with you today?"

"Nay. You must accompany your mother, son."

Eumelos groaned. "All she talks about are clothes and other men and women. It is so boring! Do I have to?"

"It is our custom. You must obey our customs; they are the backbone of Aztlan."

Eumelos shook his head, unhappy but obedient. Phoebus hugged him, then gave him back to the serf. *Do you know what our customs are, son? Would you be able to face this day unflinching?* With a grimace of distaste the dresser put the *maeemu* on Eumelos' shoulder.

"Am I ready?" Phoebus asked.

The dresser looked at him coolly. "You wear the golden feathers, the golden corselet, the long kilt in purple and gold." The man twisted his forelock. "You have your pendant, your rings, your seals." He tapped his face, his bejeweled hands graceful as he gestured. "Once we strap on that feather blanket, you should be ready."

"Then do it."

The dresser gathered the ceremonial cape. It was indeed feathery. Peacock feathers formed a ruff around Phoebus' neck and ran down the front at right angles, bordering the whole cloak with Theros blue, the iridescent purple-blue of the sea. The rest of the cloak was made of white feathers that had been dipped in gold. It stank, it was heavy and awkward, but it was the custom. The dresser's two assistants helped Phoebus straighten it, then opened the door.

Phoebus turned, ignoring the sniff of the dresser, and gestured to the four Mariners who held the carrying chair. From this day forward,

Phoebus would ride. The Golden Bull did not walk or run in the eyes of the citizens.

"To the Pyramid of Days, Rising Bull," the serf said, helping him into the golden chair and arranging the fall of the gold-feathered cloak.

The noise of chanting reached his ears before they even had descended to the main floor of the palace. The throne room was filled with representatives from the many colonies and vassals of Aztlan. The peoples they had conquered through commerce. How many more would be conquered? he wondered.

He was carried past two enormous red columns and down the passageway to the Ring of the Bull. Today it was filled with the court of Aztlan, their brightly colored skirts and glittering jewelry brilliant in the full of the day. Phoebus directed his attention forward, past the milling thousands that blocked the flagged walkway from the palace up to the heights. Already he felt the draw of the temple, the draw he'd felt even as a boy.

If only Irmentis were here. . . . He shut his mind against the thought and stared at the temple. The Egyptian had passed the pyramid tests; he would also.

CHEFTU AWOKE, staring at the geometry of the ceiling. Drool trickled from the corner of his mouth, and he had less than an eyeblink to make it to the commode before nausea overtook him.

Sweating and shivering, he huddled on the painted floor.

He was sick.

For months he had been shivering. Strange episodes of euphoria engulfed him at times. At other times he became disoriented and got lost in the palace.

Now this.

Stretching his leg out, Cheftu stared at the sore on his groin. It was swelling. Two moons ago it had looked like a bruise, red tinted and tender to the touch. Now, now it was swollen, and it hurt when he moved his left leg.

He put his head on his arms, frightened. His thoughts seemed unmanageable, and he didn't know how to regain control of his mind. The bite on his shoulder was healed, but he could think of nothing else that could have hurt him. Had the bull passed something on to him? Five things were carried through the body: blood, mucus, urine, semen, and air. He'd not had contact with any of those, only saliva. *Mon Dieu*, what to do?

Wiping a streak of spittle from his mouth made him grimace. Chloe hadn't questioned his decision to allow his body hair to grow. It was disgusting, but it had hidden the sore from her sight, and he'd managed to distract her away from touching. He looked at his groin; he didn't want her to know. Was he contagious? Would he infect her? Could he keep this information from her? *Should you?* he heard her voice say in his mind.

Groaning, Cheftu rose to his feet, steadying himself against the painted wall. The low rush of water came from the framework of clay pipes throughout the palace and carried refuse, and the contents of his stomach, to sea.

He walked to his couch and sat down with an exhausted sigh. He had planned to go to Chloe today since Atenis had finally confided Chloe's whereabouts to him. A kilt would cover him, but since when had he stayed covered around Chloe? Yet even the thought of her lean, flexible body gave him no pleasure. The room suddenly swirled around him. . . .

Before Cheftu met with Nestor he needed to bathe and change. His beard was steaming beneath a linen towel in preparation for shaving when he heard someone else enter the room. A quick snap dismissed the serfs, and Cheftu felt other hands lift the towel. His eyes were still covered as the new person lathered his chin. The long fingers were rough, the hands of a laborer, not a body serf.

All thoughts of relaxation left Cheftu's mind as he was shaved. He didn't dare speak for fear the man would cut him. But the stranger's touch was curiously gentle and caressing, and Cheftu's muscles tightened in unconscious defense.

"How are you feeling today, Cheftu? Ready for the feast tonight?" Dion said as he pulled the towel off Cheftu's face with a flourish and a smile.

The fears, unbidden and unacknowledged, that had risen in Cheftu's mind melted away. This, after all, was Dion! The chieftain for whom women went mad. He was even said to bed them in multiples. Cheftu smiled back. "I'd heard this festival is more of a sensual rite than a religious feast." He accepted Dion's hand to get out of the chair, and Dion snapped for serfs, who brought clothes.

"Aye," Dion said. "Have you been disappointed thus far?" He seemed unconcerned that Cheftu was naked before him, and Cheftu pulled his mind to other things, trying not to feel disturbed as the serf wrapped an Aztlan kilt around his hips. After all, Dion had been the first to see the *bubo*, a recollection that still made Cheftu cringe.

Cheftu focused on the kilt, another of the outlandish patterns that would please even a Parisien couturier. It came up high in the back, and its heavy front was finished with a reptile border and a huge tassel that tickled his knees. It was a mélange of colors and patterns that made his head spin.

Together they entered the laboratory, and Dion promised to bring both Nestor and Cheftu lunch. Already Nestor was working on copying formulae; he wore last night's clothing, and Cheftu knew from Nestor's glare that he had also spent the night alone.

Suddenly it was too much; why was Cheftu here while Chloe was there? "I leave for Prostatevo," Cheftu announced.

Nestor smiled. "Be back by moonset, and safe until my eyes hold you again."

Cheftu opened the doors, halting at Nestor's next comment. "Greet Sibylla for me also."

Spiralmaster left without comment.

DAYS, CHLOE THOUGHT. She had been here for days, alone. She couldn't completely hide her smile, however. She was working with paint! Glorious paint! Finally she was back in a world she knew. It was a wonderful, marvelous feeling, so much better than faking it as the chieftain of cows.

It would have been nice to hear from Cheftu, Spiralmaster hotshot himself. Chloe shrugged and tried to be charitable, but honestly, he could have sent a message bird, at least! She was certain he'd seen her, recognized her. Surely he didn't think she was dead?

Chloe rubbed away the line and frowned in concentration. She picked up her paintbrush and looked around. According to Atenis, this was going to be a children's room. Yet nothing felt light and fun enough. Imitating Atenis' style, she'd painted part of one boy, still with youthlocks and those wonderful liquid Aztlantu eyes. Doing what?

Chloe stared at the wall. What did little boys do? Fishing? Not here. Basketball? Not hardly. Nintendo? Chloe laughed at herself. She was getting loopy.

Two boys, maybe? Doing what? Chloe began to sketch in another body, then teasingly drew his arm extended toward the nose of the other. Take that, she thought. It seemed familiar, as though her hands knew exactly what to do, and how.

Eyes narrowed, she picked up her brush and began to paint. "You can be Cheftu," she told one sketched boy. He had almond-shaped eyes and winged brows. Not quite Cheftu, but close enough for the funny papers. With rapid strokes she gave her "boy" a boxing glove. Now her boy was nailing Cheftu's boy's nose, right on target. "That is for not following me," she said to the painting.

"I dared not draw the attention."

Chloe whirled around, lost her footing, and fell against the wall.

Cheftu stood in the doorway, leaning on the frame as though he'd been there for hours.

He was so gorgeous, Chloe thought. He'd made an art of adapting. His kilt was more subdued than those of most Aztlantu, and his clan pendant lay in the center of his chest. The funny disk he always wore around his waist moved a little with his breathing. Black hair fell over his shoulders, the elaborate braiding in of the extensions woven with gold thread. His skin seemed a bit paler than usual, but it should, because he spent all his days inside. Kohl ringed his eyes, making them look even lighter, and his expression was unreadable. They just stared at one another.

"I do not get the benefit of a glove," he said with a smile. "That seems rather unfair."

"Who said life is fair?"

"Touché." It was particularly incongruous to hear the French coming out of his ancient-styled body. Chloe turned back to the painting, inking in her boy's eyes. "This is hardly the welcome I had hoped for," Cheftu said from beside her.

Chloe jumped, painting one eyeball slightly askew. "Then maybe you should have showed up yesterday," she said archly.

He laced his fingers in her hair and pulled her head back, gently, but with no question of who was in control. "I could not. So now we have time to recoup, *oui, ma chère?*"

Looking into his eyes, she tried to see his thoughts, his feelings. He was holding something back, she sensed. "Let go of me."

He released her and she knelt down, mixing turquoise paint in a clay bowl.

"I have found the holes in the brain, the sole symptom of this plague," Cheftu said, his tone clipped. "Thank you for inquiring."

Chloe stirred the *mafkat* powder and water with a dowel, her lips pressed together. "Congratulations." She rose, her paintbrush laden with turquoise paint.

"I have had strange . . . feelings recently. I am out of sorts," Cheftu said. "The Aztlantu are an odd people. They care little for human life, would sacrifice anything for sensation."

"You don't make sense," Chloe said, testing the texture of the paint on the back of her hand.

"*Merde*, Chloe! I miss you! I need your decency, your humor!" He turned her around, turquoise paint spattering them both, brilliant against his crimson-and-saffron kilt. It also flecked her painting.

"Dammit, Cheftu! I've worked for hours on this painting, and if you think you can just wander in whenever you feel like it, then ruin my painting and expect me to fall into your—"

He gripped her around the jaw and kissed her hard. Chloe pushed him away, spattering paint on them both. "You're ruining my work," she hissed. Cheftu glared, pulled both of her wrists behind her, and snatched the paintbrush.

"You have become so Aztlantu," he said. "Dancing half-naked in the court, the inheritor to Kela-Ileana." She struggled and he moved his grasp up her arms, holding her still and arching her back. "Do you want to bed Phoebus?"

Chloe hissed in response and refused to admit his grasp hurt. She forgot it hurt when he began painting her nipples with the paintbrush. The tiny hairs of the brush tickled, and she felt herself growing tighter, hotter. "Do you wish Dion were holding you, Phoebus painting your body?" He was angry, his eyes betrayed his hurt.

"It wasn't what you think."

He began to paint a design on her breast, moving it up toward her esophagus and down close to where her jacket was loosely fastened. Chloe couldn't tell what he was painting from her angle; all she could see was the swell of her breasts, a pale gold against the brilliant turquoise. Hieroglyphs. He'd painted her with hieroglyphs.

Chloe struggled again and Cheftu yanked her closer, his hard grip unyielding. He held the paintbrush in his teeth and slid his hand beneath the waistband of her dress. Pressing his mouth to hers, the tangy flavor of the paint between them, he drew Chloe's tongue into the jail the paintbrush made of his mouth. "I am very angry, Chloe," he said against her lips.

A ripping sound filled the room, and Chloe screeched in outrage, struggling against him. He pulled her to him, making her kicking ineffectual. Chloe was dizzy, flooded with mixed emotions, and . . . well . . . hungry for him.

Cheftu walked her backward, against the wall, and Chloe twisted, trying to get away, though not as wholeheartedly as before. He might be angry, but she knew he was also turned on. He ripped a ruffle off her skirt with one hand, and Chloe felt her knees weaken. With quick movements he tied her wrists behind her and laughed while she strained. Now she was hopping mad.

Until he dropped to his haunches, the paintbrush forgotten as he dipped both hands in the paint and massaged it into her skin. It was thick, gloppy, and so cool it made her shiver. Cheftu treated it like lotion, rubbing the pigment deep; she looked as though she were swirled in ocean waves from the waist down.

Chloe was trembling, barely able to stand. Cheftu's touch was magic, and it was unspeakably erotic to see herself transformed with color and pattern. She had *become* art. Leaning her head against the wall, she concentrated on sensation. The cool paint gained her body's heat. The places where it was heavily applied felt solid and thick, versus the parts barely washed with color, a coating so light it felt like cobwebs on her skin. Cheftu picked up her foot, rubbing in the paint, stroking his fingers between her toes, slowly, the sucking and slurping of the paint reminiscent of . . .

"What flavor?" he asked hoarsely. Chloe slowly slid down the wall, her knees over his shoulders, sitting on his thighs. She blinked and inhaled as he painted her face with the most eloquent of touches. The paint had thickened and felt luxuriously smooth. "What flavor, my faithless madame?"

Baskin-Robbins, she thought, they haven't invented this flavor yet! She groaned as he touched her intimately, the visions behind her closed eyes waves of blue and lapis and turquoise rising higher and higher, straining to crest. Cheftu whispered words against her lips, suggestions and sensations, stoking the fire, making her as hot as the blue center of a flame, until she was consumed.

THE BLACK, CAVERNOUS CHAMBER WAS ECHOINGLY EMPTY. Torches affixed to the walls cast an almost daylike brightness, the different heights dispelling shadow. The Council stood on the first balcony, where the nobles of Aztlan had stood merely days ago.

The final test had come.

Phoebus stood, forcing the trembling throughout his body to stop. He'd bested the Apis bull, proved his worth in the pyramid, survived the Labyrinth; now the final test. He must choose to do what benefited the many but hurt the few. The fertility of the fields must be assured.

The king must die.

I will stand here in nineteen summers, he thought. I will look in the face of my son and know I must kill or be killed. He dared not think beyond that, beyond the ritual. He was Olimpi, he would be victorious.

It was silent.

He raised his gaze and looked around him, not daring to move his head. Niko leaned against the far wall, his arms crossed. Next to Niko stood Phoebus' triton, the prongs polished and sharpened, ready to pierce skin. Phoebus looked away. His body smelled rank, fear in his sweat. His bowels were loose, and he felt nauseated. Thank Apis that Eumelos would not one day do this. Better an unloved son to destroy him.

The crash of wood against stone reverberated throughout the chamber as the double doors opened. Phoebus' palms were wet, and he unlocked his knees. Zelos walked through the door, Spiralmaster trailing behind, Dion holding the Golden Bull's triton.

Zelos didn't look as though he were past his prime, Phoebus thought with a rush of pride. He was still the tallest man in Aztlan, and his fine blond hair floated over his shoulders, though streaks of white were visible. His body was tight, trim, golden skinned, and the dozens of offspring from a wealth of nymphs attested to his virility.

The blue eyes that both Phoebus and Eumelos had inherited were pale and sad. The new Minos motioned both contenders forward. Phoebus stepped to his father, trying to delay the sunrise, trying not to drag his feet and humiliate his clan.

Only once had the tradition not been fulfilled. Golden Bull Kronos had defeated his son and ruled for thirty-eight summers. By the end of his reign he was weak, puny, and the fields were wasted. Zelos had won the battle easily and partaken of the sacrifice, though very little power had been left in Kronos.

Pateeras' hands gripped his forearms, and Zelos smiled. "You are worthy, my golden son," he said. His voice was thick, and his expression was resigned. "Still, the clan and the empire demand our best in this battle. You have proved your mind to be sound, your reflexes to be fast and sure, your intellect to be superb, and now you must prove your will and your obedience are without question."

Phoebus shook his head in agreement.

"Afterward, you must prove your self-control. No man can lead where he has not walked. Aztlan is experiencing pangs—birth pangs, I hope—of a new, glorious generation—" Zelos' voice broke. "I regret I will not see your rule."

Phoebus' grip grew tighter.

"Fight me now, Phoebus. Show me that my pride is not misplaced. I will not have it whispered that *Hreesos* Zelos was an easy victory."

"I hear you have bested almost all the Mariners," Phoebus said with a smile. "I shake in my sandals."

Zelos laughed, a lonely, desperate sound. "Do your duty by Ileana," he said.

Rage, carefully banked, filled Phoebus. "I shall, *Pateeras.* I shall do well by Ileana."

His father looked at him, searching his gaze. He then looked at their linked arms, hands clenching tightly to each other, just below the elbow. Golden Bull Zelos straightened to his full height, saluted his son and heir, and waited for Phoebus to do the same.

It was too fast! Phoebus thought. Nay, this could not be it! But he had turned on his heel and Niko was handing him his triton, his gaze turned inward. A sense of isolation pounded in on him, and Phoebus feared he couldn't go through with it. He'd lost Irmentis, he'd lost his youth—and now his father?

He turned again and walked back to the floor. Zelos, the triton held loosely in both hands, stood easily on the balls of his feet. His dignity was awesome, even here, fighting the last of his life's battles.

A serpent was thrown onto the sand, signifying the start of the final battle. Spring versus winter, youth versus age, will against will.

Phoebus turned in a small circle, watching Zelos' triton, uncannily aware of the swishing sound of their bare feet in the sand. A low hiss gained his attention, and he leapt back an eyeblink before the horned viper struck out at him.

His hands were wet, his grip on the triton tight. Zelos was closer, and Phoebus dodged his first strike, parried his second, and ducked the third. What would happen if no one won? It was an impossible thought that died at birth. Only one man would leave this arena. His father would not be shamed.

Zelos attacked again, and Phoebus rolled beneath the tines, grabbing his triton before Zelos turned. If he didn't kill Zelos, he would never be allowed to punish Ileana. The thought of Ileana broken and begging—pleading, her lovely face distorted, her aging body revealed—filled Phoebus with a rush of pleasure.

He jabbed at Zelos, not an attack, just a show of engagement. His father smiled, and Phoebus knew he would kill him and feast, as generations of golden-haired and blue-eyed men had done before him.

He would make Ileana suffer.

Another serpent was thrown onto the sand. Two to avoid, while attacking Zelos. Phoebus struck out, the contact with Zelos' triton sending shock waves up his arm, jarring his bones into his teeth. He opened his mouth, releasing the pressure on his jaw, and moved sideways.

They clashed again, high, then lower; closer, farther away. The sound was almost rhythmic, and Phoebus virtually danced in the arena, running and dodging and striking. Zelos was skilled, but not fast, and Phoebus realized that at thirty-eight summers his father was old and weary. Phoebus moved in closer.

First blood was Zelos' calf, an accident as Phoebus rolled away. A line of red beaded up, and Zelos charged him. The end of Phoebus' triton caught Zelos in the stomach, then the chin, giving Phoebus time to retreat.

Another serpent.

Quickly Phoebus wiped his hands on his legs, not daring to dust them with sand. Zelos' triton cracked across his left arm, and the instant numbness made him drop the lower half of the triton. He was unable to defend and felt Zelos' tines scrape his abdomen.

Three lines of blood. He raised his gaze to his father. Second blood. One more round. The look of horror on Zelos' face was quickly masked, but Phoebus knew that was the last time his father would really try.

Two more serpents.

The speed of the final dance had increased, and Phoebus attacked, lashing out, focusing his hatred for Ileana on the father he'd always adored. Zelos defended well, but he didn't strike back. The snakes were restless, moving, confused by the action, and striking at anything—each other, the shadows.

Phoebus crashed against Zelos, their tritons crossed, held perpendicular by their intertwined bodies. The Golden Bull's face was streaked with sweat and dirt, and his jaw was gritted with the strain of battle. Phoebus loosened his grip, feeling the slide of the triton against his palm.

Staring into his *pateeras'* eyes, he murmured, "For the clan and the empire," and stabbed Zelos with an uppercut, feeling the triton pierce through skin, the tine slip between his ribs and enter Zelos' heart.

His father sagged, groaning in pain. The clang of falling metal sounded in the distance, and Phoebus held his father, feeling the warm, heavy flow of his draining life. Zelos cried out, and Phoebus saw a serpent slip away. Zelos had been struck.

Life and color faded from the Golden Bull, and Phoebus saw the sweat that covered his face. Zelos opened his eyes, gasping for breath. "Wor-thy," he whispered. Phoebus felt a split in his chest. Zelos was gone.

"Hail, Golden Bull Phoebus Apollo!" he heard.

Hands touched him, propelled him, and Phoebus walked unseeing. The chanting was soft, stern, and he couldn't see anyone's face. Through the hallway and into the final chamber, the final honor. The final horror.

The warmth and scent of Zelos covered him, and Phoebus looked into the corpse's expressionless face.

A blade was pressed into his hand. "I honor the *athanati* Bull," he said. Closing his eyes, he felt his fingers move, hacking away at the listless blond hair, finding the still-warm skin beneath. He pressed the blade hard against the skull, his hands slippery, from sweat or blood he didn't know.

The crossing lines. He took a deep breath and pulled, rending the skin from the skull, a sharp sound like coarse linen being torn from end to end. Breathing deeply through his mouth, he drove the fine edge of the blade in above the right ear. The crack made his stomach roil, and quickly he cut—a jagged edge, to be sure, but all the way through.

Better to absorb the power of a fallen god than to bury the husk of a withered man, he thought. Better that my father dwell in my heart, soul, and veins than in the cold, dark earth. Zelos would Become one with Phoebus. He would flow in Phoebus' blood; he would fertilize Phoebus' seed; he would inspire Phoebus' thoughts. Zelos would become *athanati* . . . in Phoebus' body and later in Phoebus' son. It was the way of Aztlan. It was honor and tradition.

Phoebus tugged on the skullcapping, then grabbed the bone tighter and tensed, pulling away. Another shrieking, tearing sound. Phoebus paused, looking down; this was an honor. Better to consume the power of Zelos while his blood was still warm, before his *psyche* journeyed to the Isles of the Blessed.

A skin the thickness and tightness of a sheep's bladder covered the brain. Ignoring the hot rush of blood against his clammy cold hands, Phoebus cut into the pyramid sac between the two sections of the brain.

He cut into the pinkish, coiled mass and pierced a section with the blade, carving a bite-size portion and holding it up for the Council and the priests to see. It was filled with holes, fine holes, like pumice—like the brain of the bull.

"I take the power of Zelos into myself." He put it in his mouth and chewed.

Phoebus Became the Golden Bull.

CHLOE WOKE UP CONFUSED. It smelled like a chemistry lab, but she had taken all her chemistry last year, right? She had a horrific crick in her neck and slowly opened her eyes.

The recall was so fast, it was almost painful. Worst yet, Cheftu was gone. The sun had come out just in time to set in the west, and light washed the room in shades of gold—where it wasn't already turquoise. Her fresco was spattered, probably ruined. Then she looked down.

Her body was unrecognizable. Not like when she woke up in Egypt, which was jarring enough. *Now* she was alien. She was blue! From just above her pubic bone she was inscribed in graceful, sweeping hieroglyphs; below she was painted with swirls, arabesques, and waves. Painted blue. Very blue.

A Matisse mermaid.

With a groan, Chloe got up. Every muscle hurt, and she blinked back tears that she blamed on her aching body, not her bruised heart. Cheftu had been a different kind of lover, and unless she'd fallen asleep beforehand, this was the second time she'd brought him no satisfaction. Was something wrong with her? Surely he would have told her?

So why? The thought was disturbing, and she stepped over the skirt and went into the back chamber, where she'd made a pallet. No one. Swallowing back tears, she crossed the room and ran up the three steps into the street entrance. It was silent, a breeze blowing, fading golden light, and completely deserted.

Biting her lips, Chloe walked down the steps. The boxing boys stood frozen, polka-dotted, and Chloe picked up the paintbrush. The spots on her boy's arm and ankle could be disguised as beads. Amazingly enough, Cheftu's boy had been struck only on a few strands of hair. Chloe finished the boxing glove in black, then changed the direction of the waist sash to cover even more blue and grimaced at the whole thing. It was hardly worth lasting the ages.

The urn of water was icy cold, and Chloe hesitated to wash herself. What had Cheftu written? With the brush in one hand, she read the upside-down glyphs slowly, writing them on the ground. The floor would be covered in shells or stones eventually.

When she'd gotten them all, she read the passage. "My heart aches for that which it cannot have and loves what it cannot love."

What did he mean? Why had he left? Things had been going just fine, hadn't they? Surely he didn't really think she was having an affair with Dion? If something were wrong, wouldn't he have told her? Had he tried to? Relationships were based on open and honest communication.

What did Cheftu's heart ache for? What did he love that he couldn't love? Why hadn't he stayed? She was weeping as she traced the markings on her skin, the hieroglyphs and swirls and arabesques.

Did he still love her?

She would leave at dawn, ask him face-to-face.

CHEFTU WAS IN THE LABORATORY, thinking of what he had seen during the night. Holy saints and Mother of God! These people were *cannibales!* He was relieved beyond telling that Chloe had not been there, had not participated in this most gruesome feast.

Certain that he was alone, Cheftu pulled out the squishy, deteriorating piece of brain he'd sneaked out. Hands shaking, he held it, then raised the lamp, casting the light down through it.

Holes.

Covering the piece, he sent for a scribe. The rituals would be recorded on tablets and scrolls in the library, would they not? He could simply ask, but he was afraid his distaste would show. Cheftu no longer trusted the Aztlantu to behave as other people. No wonder the earth was seeking to rid herself of them!

The scribe returned with the writings, and Dion. They spoke for a few moments, then Cheftu couldn't help himself. "How long has that last ritual been enacted?"

"Zelos becoming *athanati* in Phoebus' body?"

Cheftu swallowed the bile in his mouth. "Aye."

Dion leaned back, stretching out his legs, bracing his hands on his hips. "Since the reign of the Clan Olimpi, I would guess."

Cheftu crossed his arms. "Who usually participates?"

"Only the Council and the new Golden partake of the departed

Hreesos, though the entire priesthood and his cabinet eat the organs of the Apis bulls."

The key was here. Cheftu didn't exactly understand, but the key was here. When he finally persuaded Dion to leave, he sent for Nestor.

Decans later, the two men looked over the papyri and damp clay sheets they had covered. Apparently whatever it was, the killer was in the body of the bull or the man. When it was eaten, it moved to another body and ate holes in its brain also.

The warning signs came too late. Only when one saw the brain's holes did one know for certain what the killer was.

"Are you saying that everyone who ate the bull today is at risk?" Nestor asked, aghast.

Cheftu ran a finger down the columns they had assembled. In every case, the victim had partaken of the bull or of Zelos' forebears. It was a bloody legacy, a costly one. The illness waited a long time to develop. Nineteen years was the last time anyone had . . . dined, Cheftu thought with revulsion.

"The bull ritual takes place every midsummer festival, though. Each summer *Hreesos* proves that he is strong and wise and takes Apis and shares him with all."

The priesthood! "How do we tell them they are doomed?" Cheftu said.

Nestor was silent, the weight of the reality sinking in on him. "By the gods," he whispered. "Aztlan has committed suicide!"

BY BLOOD PHOEBUS HAD REVEALED HIMSELF as *Hreesos,* the power, the spirit, the incarnation of the Apis bull. In the pyramid he had proved his scholarship, intellect, and reason. Here, now, in a tradition

even older than the Clan Olimpi, he would be the springtime renewing life with the earth.

He looked up one last time; soon the moon would be one with the
sun. In a moment of timeless night the most intimate of cosmic
dances would take place between Kela and Apis, the moon and the
sun. Priests all over the empire would fast tonight, their eyes on the
sky, waiting for the first omens for the next nineteen summers. Phoebus fisted his hands and forced himself calm, then stepped down into
the womb of the earth.

The scent of burning herbs filled the air with a heavy smoke, coating his nostrils and blinding his eyes.

The women—Kela-Tenata, Shell Seekers, clanswomen, and serfs,
for all were welcome—filled the cave. In their hands they held clay
votives of birds, butterflies, snakes, priestesses, and poppy pods. Their
mingled voices rose and fell, disorganized but loose and natural, rife
with mystery.

> Mother Kela
> source of all creation
> In whose great breast flows life and death
> with the wind and rain.

Was this how Dion felt? Phoebus wondered. One man among hundreds of women, whipped to a frenzy? However, there was a difference. Any and every woman was available for Dion's touch; Phoebus'
purpose lay in one woman.

Defeating one woman.

He felt *Pateeras* in his belly, thoughts, and blood. His stomach knotted at the thought of what he must do. He was certain he was
drained; Ileana would not win, she could not, not again. In thirty days
justice would begin.

This cavern on Kallistae was one of the largest in Aztlan. It consisted of four grottoes, with narrow connecting passageways. Between
the flickering lights and shifting bodies Phoebus saw the stalagmites.
A phallus of stone rose upward, penetrating the depth and darkness
of this cave. The women touched and kissed the stone monoliths, and

Phoebus wished he could trade any nymph, mistress, or matron for the mother-goddess horror who awaited him.

He found himself thinking of serving Sibylla for twenty-eight days. Thank Kela he'd been told she wasn't dead, just in hiding. He felt no anger toward her; he wished it were she awaiting him in this grotto.

> Bring life again!
> In the passion of conception we renew you
> Mistress of animals, the butterfly, the snake
> She serves as your body.

Slowly Phoebus was pushed through the narrow entrance tunnel. Sweat soaked his neck and back, and the air grew closer, the slight touches he'd felt grew bolder. Illumination was tiny pricks of light in a cloth of gray, choking darkness. He'd never wanted so desperately to flee. He'd never felt so very alone—removed from men, isolated from the protection of his name and bearing. Here he was a petitioner, a stud to serve one purpose. His vanity pushed him forward through the mass of loud, swaying women.

His *pateeras* had done this with Rhea. It was the Olimpi way. Spring returned, fertilized the fecund earth. Did he have the right to change tradition? To break the cycle? I will take pleasure in renewing with Sibylla, he thought. Ileana is the poison of the cone shell, but I will serve the clan admirably with anyone else.

Phoebus' head felt very heavy, his neck no stronger than the stem of a flower. He felt the new Kela-Ata's hand on his shoulder, guiding him to a narrow set of stairs. The women's voices had darkened, become more sensual, and he could almost feel the pulse of mother earth increase beneath his feet.

> As the spring is brought forth in a gush of color
> May life begin anew with the rush of seed.

Phoebus stumbled, and the priestess caught him around the waist. "It is the poppy," she said. Tendrils of burning opium rose from the crown of pods on her brow. They climbed—slow or fast, Phoebus could no longer tell—until they reached a stone balcony. Women surrounded him, ecstatically aware and singing, grouped to watch him.

The poppy faded when he saw her before him. His flesh recoiled; he could not do this. Not even revenge was worth joining his body to the murderess of his mother! He accepted gum from the priestess and chewed it. The overlaying tang of cinnamon could not disguise its bitterness.

> We grasp the root of creation!
> And flow with the font of life!

She sat on a stone throne. Elaborate wedding paint gleamed across her breasts and torso. A diadem of poppies and pomegranates decorated her brow, a forelock of her corn-colored hair fell over it, touching the perfect blush skin of her face. The rest of her hair, unbound, flowed around her, a river of gold and silver. She wore only a multi-tiered skirt which fell to the ground from her small waist.

He stared at her. His stepmother, Ileana, made not one move of recognition.

The Kela-Ata stepped forward, her hands raised, her husky voice throbbing in the dense, drug-filled cavern. Snakes coiled around her arms and throat. He watched as two women—he thought Vena and Atenis—stepped forward and moved Ileana's legs, pulling her to the edge of the stone chair, draping her knees on opposite stalagmites.

Lastly they moved her skirt, baring her completely to him. In ritualistic movements they rubbed her with oils and perfumes. The high priestess asked Kela for healthy vegetation, prosperity, victory, and fertility.

Ileana raised her gaze to his; her eyes were pools of blue, her pupils barely dots. Still, enough of her lingered for the look to scorch. *Are you not man enough? Zelos would weep for shame at your weakness. You are not a worthy Golden.* She was the personification of the nurturing mother-goddess, yet only derision danced in her poisonous gaze.

Phoebus felt his reason harden and stepped forward. He didn't know where he'd lost his clothing, but it didn't matter. All he sought was to wipe the simper from Ileana's perfect face. Fortunately his sex ignored his emotions, and his fury and loathing was fading on a wash of peace and drug-induced contentment.

The chanting rose in volume and tension, and the Kela-Ata mouthed, "Now!" Unwilling to touch Ileana more than necessary, he braced his arms on either side of her head. Her eyes widened at his brutal entry. His lips felt thick, and his mind was fogged. Where was his hatred of her, his desire to punish? "I know what you did," he whispered. She absorbed his motions. "You will pay, *skeela*-goddess." Even in his own ears, his words had no heat.

"Surely enduring you is punishment enough," Ileana muttered, her eyes closed.

Her words were insulting, and Phoebus wanted to retaliate, but nothing came to his lips or mind. Through a haze that grew as the gum in his mouth diminished, he felt his hand on her hips. Lost in a blur of desensitization, he could barely feel the tiny pieces of gravel embedded in her cold skin. Phoebus pressed them deeper, a shallow gratification.

Ileana's hissing insults faded to little groans and grunts, and Phoebus disliked his body's response to her. Self-control, he had to use it. "I hate you," he whispered, his words slurred. She was approaching the apex, her hands touching him unknowingly, fluttering over his chest and face. "I wish I were a blade," he muttered. "I would carve you as you carved Irmentis." He couldn't continue to stand, he realized. His legs were collapsing, and he just, he just—

She cried her mother-goddess pleasure, and Phoebus ground his teeth, resisting the seduction of her body. Would she know? He slumped against her on the stone chair, shaking and dizzy.

The Kela-Ata tried to pull him away, but Phoebus resisted; he needed more time or she would know he'd withheld. "Come along!" the priestess said, and Phoebus tried to cover himself. Ileana was being served a poppy-mandrake drink to help his seed find a fertile root. Her legs were tied over each other and elevated. He was free—she didn't know! Phoebus closed his eyes. He only had to do this twenty-nine more times.

The sacred marriage was over.

Phoebus and Niko were in a meeting with Nekros when the new high priest demanded entry. His greeting was perfunctory, and Niko sharply reminded him of Phoebus' title. After sharing the prescribed wine, Minos claimed Phoebus needed to climb the mountain summit and sacrifice to Apis.

"Climb the cone? Are you quite mad?" Niko yelled.

"It is tradition."

"I have never heard of such," Phoebus said. He watched Niko as his friend's gaze turned inward. If it had been written down, Niko would recall it. "When was the last time this was done?"

"Just before Clan Olimpi took power," Minos said. "It was their rationalization for no earthwave activity. It is an accepted alternative now, however."

"Why does *Hreesos* need an alternative? What are you talking about?" Niko asked.

"The priests refuse to follow a Golden who killed Minos in sacred ritual. If Apis takes the offering, then Phoebus will be vindicated. The skies themselves commanded it," Minos said.

"I didn't kill the Minos," Phoebus protested.

"He died prophesying concerning you. That is what the priests see and why they demand this duty," Minos said.

"He speaks the truth," Nekros agreed reluctantly. "If you do not do this, the priests will believe that Apis is against your rule."

"We no longer live in superstitious, ancient times!" Phoebus protested. Walk to the edge of a volcano, even a resting one?

"What mountain is he supposed to climb?" Nekros asked, his words slurred.

"Mount Krion."

It was silent in the room for a few moments. "Mount Krion has long been asleep," Nekros said to Phoebus. "It would be the safest choice."

"It has been a fearful year," Nekros continued. "Citizens are wary, skittish. This would do much to restore their faith."

"Provided Krion doesn't blow the new ruler to the Isles of the Blessed," Niko said dryly.

Nekros held Minos' gaze. "There are priests who specialize in watching the Nostrils. They will be able to foretell the best time to visit. Of course, Phoebus will not go alone. A contingent of guards, perhaps even several boatloads of people to watch." Nekros' tone of voice had become ruminative. "Minos, get us the right day. Niko, arrange a barge party to set sail at a moment's notice." He looked at his nephew. "Prepare your heart, Phoebus. This is unfortunate, but it must be done."

CHLOE HAD FORGOTTEN THE MIDSUMMER FESTIVAL was just concluding. The roads were packed, the streets were blind alleys, and no matter how she tried, getting through to Aztlan Island seemed impossible.

The news spread through the group like wildfire. Minos had demanded *Hreesos* offer sacrifices to Mount Krion, begging the Bull to forgive him for the death of the former high priest. Clansmen were invited to follow; they were loading their vessels now.

Chloe pushed through the crowd and began to run down the zigzag steps to the harbor.

She hoped Phoebus was through being angry; she was definitely through with playing dead.

IN TYPICAL AZTLANTU FASHION, even this grim journey became a festival, Cheftu thought. A day of *kefi*. A flotilla of vessels: small fishing boats, Mariners ships, pleasure barges, all assembled for the short sail to Folegandros. People clustered on the edges of the high cliffs, and he knew elaborate picnics were being hosted in the multicolored houses that scaled the sharp edges of the lagoon.

The boat he was on, with Dion, Nestor, and a bevy of bare-breasted beauties, was outfitted with garlands of flowers, delicately scented lamps, and rugs on the deck for comfort.

The ship ahead of them held *Hreesos* Phoebus, Niko, Nekros in an all-encompassing cloak, the new Kela-Ata, and the Minos. Trailing in their wake was the entire contingency of *Hreesos* guards in smaller boats. On this hot summer day, in the Season of the Lion, the hills were dried brown. The ships, brightly painted above the waterline, looked like ducklings following their mother across the azure sea.

Different sails proclaimed different clans. According to Dion, Phoebus had expressed interest in speaking to Sibylla, so Cheftu knew Chloe could return. Was she here even now, sailing beneath her clan's emblem? Would they have a chance to talk? Just as soon as he returned from this fool mission he would seek her out, Cheftu thought, still-ing the trembling of his hands.

One of the nymphs began to sing, the melody soothing against the lull of waves and the creak of wood against sail and wind. Dion handed him a rhyton, and Cheftu drank, staring into the cloudless sky, his kohled eyes squinted against the sun.

"Are you happy?" Dion asked.

"Happy?"

"Aye."

He had wine, women, and song. He was in a beautiful place, with anything he wanted at his beck and call. However, he was also faced with a ghastly plague, an angry wife, and a bevy of spewing volcanos.

Cheftu felt like Nero, fiddling as Rome burned. He still did not know why he was here. There seemed no way to stop the plague, not without changing the many brain-eating rituals they had. If they chose to eat the lung instead, would the same thing develop? Were they all destined to die? If so, why?

In Cheftu's opinion, the Aztlantu cannibalism was a vile tradition. But *le bon Dieu* was far more gracious and forgiving. This plague was no punishment; perhaps it was an inborn consequence? Why was he here? Because Chloe was here? Why was she here?

Nothing made sense; his brain was as cloudy as ash.

"So, Egyptian, what *would* make you happy?" The underlying humor in Dion's words made Cheftu grin despite himself. "Knowing the secrets of the universe? Reading the minds of the gods? Living forever?"

"The secrets would be too much to know," Cheftu said. "The minds of the gods would terrify me. Living forever sounds exhausting." Though his words were glib, he knew if Chloe had asked, her eyes burning into his with indefatigable curiosity, he would have bared himself to her, shared his heartfelt responses.

One of the women began to rub his feet and calves. Her touch was nothing like Chloe's, and he refused her gently.

Dion watched with knowing, dark eyes.

Unnerved, Cheftu rose and walked to the prow. Folegandros shared a narrow channel with Nios, the Cult of the Snake. Mount Krion was on the southeast edge of the island, the green-sloped cone visible to the ship.

"So it is safe?" Cheftu asked, indicating the summit.

Nestor sighed. "Aye, well, that is what the priests say. They have studied the Nostrils for generations, so they should know."

Hreesos' ship docked first, and Cheftu looked up to see that the switchback path to the summit was studded with people. From here he could hear the low chant of "Phoebus, *Hreesos,* Phoebus, *Hreesos!*" The ship with the sacrifices docked next: goats, sheep, rams, and an Apis bull.

Phoebus stepped into a traveling chair, and the youthlocked child with him stepped into the next one with Niko. A contingency of guards followed at a quick pace, then the Council members Phoebus had requested. "Can we go?" Cheftu asked.

Dion shrugged, and Cheftu and Nestor took a small boat to shore to join the cluster of hangers-on following *Hreesos* to the top.

Mount Krion was one of the highest peaks in the empire. It rose 2,400 cubits, a dark pyramid against the blue sky. Feeling reckless and vibrantly alive, Cheftu declined a chair and settled into a fast pace. According to the ritual, Phoebus alone would stand on the edge of the cone. The rest of the followers would wait on the flanks.

The sun was high by the time Cheftu and Nestor were halfway up. Many of the women and quite a few courtiers had dropped out, choosing to wait in the shade with a rhyton of wine instead of continuing the hike. A few hours later, Nestor also chose to wait. Cheftu walked on alone. The carrying chairs were far ahead of him, and he saw no one behind him. The wind was stronger, a cold breeze that chilled the sweat on his back and forehead. Cheftu attributed his faint tremors to the weather and walked on.

The sun was on its westerly path when Cheftu heard steps behind him. Pausing on the narrow path, he looked back. A woman walked alone, with a leggy, long stride that sent blood rushing to his head and groin. As an Egyptian or Aztlantu, she was the mate of his very soul. Though her black hair was now to her waist and her costume shamelessly revealing, it was Chloe. In any guise, she was his. Would she forgive him?

Would he forgive her?

As she turned the bend, two levels beneath him, Cheftu knew the answer to the question. Just seeing her made the day brighter, the scents sharper, his blood pound heavier. She was his impetus to make each moment count for more. Resting against a boulder gray with ash, Cheftu watched her approach. She wiped her forearm across her head without breaking stride. Her tunic was short, and he saw the muscles in her thighs tighten and release. Her breasts were covered, but sweat darkened the cleft between them, and Cheftu's palms itched with a need to touch her.

CHLOE FELT HIS PRESENCE BEFORE SHE SIGHTED HIM. The question was, was it her imagination manifesting him? Or Cheftu actually in the flesh? She raised her head and saw him. Aztlantu, with hair extensions and elaborate kilt, yes, but his eyes were molten gold and filled with love.

She walked into his opened arms, feeling the heat of his satin-smooth skin, the pounding of his heart, the scent of him engulf her. The anger melted away, replaced with joy. *This* was how it should be!

This sense of homecoming, mingled with security and danger. "I love you," Cheftu whispered, and Chloe's blood raced through her veins. "Just let me hold you."

The scent of crushed thyme, rosemary, basil, hyssop, lavender, and sage surrounded them as they sat overlooking the water, the distant glitter of Aztlan. It was so perfect that she didn't want to say anything, to destroy the moment. "The mountain awaits," Cheftu finally said, and they walked on, hand in hand.

PHOEBUS GOT TO HIS FEET, taking the reins of the many sacrificial animals being offered to Apis Earthshaker. The cone rose ahead of him. Niko and Eumelos waited by the traveling chair. The *Hreesos* guard fanned out around him, and the Minos sprinkled Apis' blood on his shoulders. With a deep breath, Phoebus began the short climb. The animals were nervous, tugging away, and Phoebus grimly pulled them along. There was no smoke, no clouds of ash. They were safe.

He was one with Apis; he would not be rejected.

Waiting just behind him, the guard watched. This is what it means to be a god, Phoebus thought. To walk to the edge of the Nostril of the Bull and not fear destruction. Crawling over a low ridge of rocks, Phoebus pulled the animals, now protesting loudly, with him.

He froze.

Krion was no longer resting. When had this happened?

The crater gaped like a black mouth. Hair rose on his arms, and he shivered in the cold wind, despite his cloak. Puffs of gas rose from the hole, and Phoebus could see the smoldering core, a wicked glint of red, like blood in the body of the earth. Yellow crystals had formed around the rim of the hole, and black blood oozed out the top. The ground was hot beneath his feet

Feelings of godhood blew away like smoke. He was merely a man, at the mercy of this fury in the earth.

He looked back at the Minos, who motioned him to continue.

Phoebus needed to deliver the animals to the fiery cone itself. Picking his way carefully over warm earth and around boulders, Phoebus stepped down. The air was still and hot. It stank, and Phoebus walked faster. Fear flooded him, and he ran the last distance. Shoving and pulling, he got the animals around the depressed area. Their plaintive cries rent the air, and Phoebus paused long enough to wedge the end of the rope beneath a boulder.

Fleeing with no dignity and even less concern, Phoebus leapt up the side. Rocks fell in small showers around him, and he felt heat rise from pockets that opened suddenly in the earth. He had just crawled over the shallow lip when a noise rocked him, threw him flat.

Phoebus scrambled to his feet and ran, dodging debris as a roaring rumble completely filled the air. A blow to his leg knocked him to the ground. He rose and ran on, hobbling. When something else struck his other leg, his scream made no sound against the continuing roar. It was becoming hard to see. Phoebus crawled, panting, through the thick air. His hair caught on fire and he rolled, putting it out with his back. On pure instinct he huddled behind a boulder and watched fire fly through the sky.

Then it was over.

Through a fog of pain he tried to see around him. No lava, just rocks and gas. Apis had taken the sacrifice and rejected it. Phoebus trembled; what would sate this angry god? He wondered if Apis wanted *him* as a worthy sacrifice. He didn't want to die! He couldn't die!

Pulling himself along the hot, rocky earth, the Golden Bull of Aztlan fought to stay conscious. Blood streaked his wounded legs, his burned back, and he pulled on. "Help!" he cried faintly. "Help me!" This was probably the first time he'd ever begged, he realized. He couldn't tell how far he'd come. Everything was gray, the ash still smoking, burning his skin. "Help me," he whispered. Something flew at him, piercing him, and Phoebus screamed with the pain as he sank into thoughtless oblivion.

"*Hreesos?* Phoebus?"

Phoebus opened his eyes. "Ni-ko," he gasped out. "Help me."

CHAPTER 15

CHEFTU BARELY HAD ENOUGH TIME to throw himself over Chloe, shield her from the small landslide of rocks and dirt that rained from the upper path. When it was silent again he lay still, panting, reassured by her breathing.

He felt the cuts and bruises on his back and legs and rolled away gingerly. Chloe leapt up, brushing pebbles from her skin. "Was that an eruption?" she asked, searching the peak for signs of lava.

"Nay, just a cloud of gas." He winced. "It loosened the rocks."

"If it loosened the rocks here . . ." Chloe trailed off.

"*Hreesos*," Cheftu whispered, and they took off, hiking quickly up the path, crossing over rock slides and stepping carefully around the edges. Nothing was sturdy here. The screams were faint but audible. Chloe and Cheftu pulled up onto the plain and halted.

What had been green grass before was now scorched earth. The skeletal remains of the traveling chair were visible in the distance, with carbonized figures beside it. . . . "The carriers," Chloe whispered.

They ran to the west of the scorched flank, where the flower-dotted grass still waved, untouched.

"Your gas cloud is capricious," Chloe shouted.

"Is not nature always?"

They walked through the field; the cries were growing softer. "Here, Cheftu!" Chloe shouted, kneeling. Niko was holding his dying friend in his arms, sobbing. What wasn't burned was bleeding, and Chloe didn't have to be a medic to realize *Hreesos* would not last the night. A little boy stood to the side, trying not to cry as he looked down on the blond-haired man.

Cheftu's hands were gentle as he cataloged the ruler's wounds. "Broken leg, bleeding ear, possibly deaf; back burns and"—he paused when he saw the broken tree limb, spearing Phoebus as effectively as a blade—"belly wound." His gaze met Chloe's, and he winced. *Hreesos* was losing blood rapidly.

Of the thirty men who had accompanied *Hreesos,* only four survived. Another Minos was dead. They met Nestor on the way down, then gathered the others. A few citizens had been wounded in landslides; even more of them were drunk. Those in the regatta had watched in shock as the mountain had plumed gray smoke. Very few had waited the unlikely return of *Hreesos* and instead had sailed quickly for Aztlan.

The gods were against them.

Phoebus awoke once, screaming for Irmentis. Dion shared his opium gum to ease the Golden's pain. Birds were sent to all the clans and to Irmentis' small island. Niko held his cousin's hand as the timekeeper quadrupled the pace for the rowers. Night was falling, and the long shadows of the canyon walls clutched the Aztlantu, pulling them into the growing darkness.

PHOEBUS WOKE BY ROLLING ON HIS SIDE. He was hot, cold, lonely, and hurting. The new moon glowed outside, reminding him he lived still. He knew his breathing was growing shallow, too shallow. This is not like the pyramid, he said to himself. I won't wake up in three days, unharmed.

Irmentis! his soul cried. *Please, let me see you just once more, just once!* He felt his body gaining weight, heavier and heavier, as his *psyche* rose to leave. He sealed his lips, squeezed shut his eyes. He must stay alive, just to see Irmentis. He could not die without looking on her face once more.

Mustering all his concentration, he pulled his spirit back, focusing on the pain, connecting mind and body with shackles of blood and agony.

NIKO REFUSED TO LOOK AT THE BLOODSTAINED BODY of the Golden Bull. His heartbeat was dreadfully slow, the cloths wrapped around him were saturated in blood. The jolting of landing and carrying had loosened the tree limb that had served as an admirable plug to the wound. The ship had cast everyone off except a skeleton crew and the Egyptian physician. A strong wind had easily swept them back to the island.

Just in time for Phoebus to die on Aztlan.

Irmentis' shrieks filled the air. She was forcibly restrained by two burly Mariners. Her dogs were leashed, held by a scared nymph. Irmentis' face was blotched with tears. "Save him!" she cried. "Take me! But save him!"

If Niko knew a way to take her life in place of the Golden's, he would have done it in an eyeblink. The upstart Spiralmaster observed all, and when their gazes met, Niko knew the Egyptian had resigned himself to Phoebus' death.

Niko's eyes narrowed, and he gestured for the Mariners to take Irmentis and her hounds away. He would meet with her in her *Megaron* momentarily. First he would see *Hreesos* stabilized.

He gestured to the Egyptian.

Irmentis' fists were clenched as she turned to the Spiralmaster. "He is dying! Surely with your foreign ways you can do something?" Her hounds were seated behind her, their pleading eyes fixed on the Egyptian.

The Egyptian sighed. "His loss of blood is too great. His wounds are too severe. He might not even be able to walk."

"What about the elixir?"

"The elixir?"

Niko smothered a smile. Two things the Egyptian didn't know. But Niko did, and Irmentis was right, they could give Phoebus the elixir.

"Who will be *Hreesos* if you let Phoebus die?" Irmentis' voice was wheedling, hints of Ileana's temper in her intonation. "Nestor isn't man enough to lead Aztlan, the chieftains will fight against him. It could mean civil war, Spiralmaster. You are sworn to protect the empire. Phoebus *is* the empire!"

Niko considered her words as the Egyptian thought. As if the comment needed thought! The glory that had taken centuries to develop and mature was falling like ash on their heads. Nestor was a nice boy, but not the stuff of rulers. The chieftains would pull against him.

"If he needs blood, give him mine," she said.

Cheftu paled.

Irmentis stared at him. "I know it is thought that I am ill, but aside from . . . a few things, I am healthy as a young calf. I am pure blooded, Spiralmaster. Both Ileana and Zelos are my sires. It would be pure blood of the Clan Olimpi."

"You speak nonsense, nymph," Spiralmaster said without conviction. "There is no way."

"There is," Niko said in a rush, stepping closer. "I know of experiments. I know you can take blood from one creature and put it in another." Irmentis knelt before Cheftu, her lithe body etched with muscle and sinew, tinted with the blue of her veins. She took his Egyptian hands into her own, scarred from sun exposure.

Spiralmaster looked from one of them to the other. "What if he should take on your aversion to the sun? This is an empire in the sun, how could he rule? Will your clansmen trust a Golden king who can't abide the light of day?"

"Nekros rules his clan easily in the dark," Niko said. "Irmentis lives there peaceably."

She clenched his hands, staring with wide, black-lashed eyes up into his face. "Better a ruler in the dark than no ruler at all, Spiralmaster. But you must act! Phoebus begins his journey as we speak."

The man sighed. "I do not know this procedure of taking blood and replacing it." He looked at Niko, beseeching.

Niko turned to Irmentis. "We will use your blood, see if we can restore *Hreesos*."

She rose. "And the elixir?"

"Nay! Nothing unknown!" the Spiralmaster said. Niko sent her a silencing glare.

Irmentis turned on her heel, calling her hounds and snapping for serfs. She gave them low-voiced commands and turned back to Niko. "The sun is setting on Phoebus. Hurry!"

When we give him the elixir, Niko thought, he will have forever.

Cheftu watched as Niko checked the Golden's temperature. Phoebus' harsh breathing filled the room, and Cheftu could see black blood rising in the belly wound. Cheftu's every instinct said that *Hreesos* of Aztlan would die.

Death might be preferable to living in that wreck of a body, Cheftu thought, looking at the man's burns, the damage to his left leg.

The door burst open and he looked up. Irmentis' face was unnaturally flushed, and her gaze skittered around the room. At least she'd left her hounds elsewhere. Her left hand pressed a cork down on the vial tucked in her sash. What was this?

She strode to Phoebus' side, her gaze caressing his face, his body. "Niko has a remedy."

"A remedy?" Cheftu snorted. "Phoebus has been near gutted, mistress! Only direct intervention of the gods will save him. Even they cannot restore him to fullness."

"The gods," she repeated softly, her eyes on her brother. "Zelos has Become a god. He is *athanati*. Are you watching him, *Pateeras?* Will you allow your Golden son to die before his *Megaloshana'a?*" She spoke in a monotone, and Cheftu began to fear she would fall into a fit.

"Spiralmaster Cheftu?"

Nestor stood in the doorway, a line of serfs behind him holding all manner of objects.

"This is a sickroom," Cheftu said in exasperation. "My patient needs prayers and peace, not a thoroughfare of people in his chambers!"

"This is the method of transferring blood," Niko said, stepping into the room and directing the serfs. "It will take only moments, Egyptian, to set up. If we are disturbing you, please step into the corridor."

Cheftu looked at Nestor, who was setting the objects down in the room: coils of fine wiring, bandages, needles, and vials of wax. Swallowing his fury, Cheftu bowed curtly and stepped into the corridor. A group carrying a low bed passed him, then a few Kela-Tenata. He ran down the stairs, spotted Dion, and grabbed his arm. "Do you know of this?"

"The transfusion. Aye."

"Has it been done before?"

Dion sighed, clapping his hand over Cheftu's. Cheftu withdrew his in confusion. "Aye. Done before."

"Did the patient live?"

Dion looked away. "Aye. It did."

"I cannot be part of this," Cheftu said stiffly. "I neither know nor have heard of such a practice."

"So learn," Dion said equably.

"It is unconscionable to experiment on . . . on . . . a human being!"

"Better a man than a corpse," Dion said.

"At least we should use someone else's blood!" Cheftu implored. "Irmentis is ill."

"Aye, that is known." Dion's gaze became intent. "Do you know the nature of her illness?" he asked.

"There is a rare blood weakness. She seems to have all the characteristics. I cannot know until I test her urine."

Dion blanched. "Her blood is weak? How would it affect *Hreesos?*"

In the miraculous event that he survives, Cheftu thought. "He would gain Irmentis' abnormalities."

"Blood lust," Dion murmured.

"Your pardon?"

"Nothing," Dion said, giving him a quick glance. "Nothing of importance."

They walked in heavy silence back to *Hreesos'* quarters.

The Kela-Tenata watched the sun while saying the prayers of healing and protection, begging Kela to touch *Hreesos* with a healing hand. Clustered around his bedside were Aztlan's Kela-Tenata, each prepared to pierce the Golden's flesh with gold tubing as they pierced his sister's. The branch in his belly would then be extracted, and they would learn if the Golden Bull would live or die.

The priestess sang out sharply; the time had come. Cheftu looked into Irmentis' eyes, dark and unfocused, probably from the pain of hundreds of tiny tubes forced beneath her skin. A priestess tied her arm to force the blood from her body into *Hreesos.* Niko watched, his amethyst eyes narrowed to slits. Nestor and Dion stood motionless, and Cheftu wondered if they wished for Phoebus' death or life. Was not Nestor the inheritor of the throne?

Hot wax sealed the tubes to flesh, and the Kela-Tenata moved around, adjusting and monitoring the transfusion process. The final tube was attached, and all stepped back. The two royals slept on, connected by golden veins of blood. Niko would extract the stick once *Hreesos* had received two *heqat* of blood. The Kela-Tenata walked around the room, lighting pots of healing herbs and chanting her series of prayers.

Cheftu watched the system work, fearful of its failure. What if Phoebus died? What if this killed him? Could he live with himself?

Would the Aztlantu let him live? Despite the fact he'd had no hand in it, he was the foreigner—immediately suspect. Would *Hreesos* live?

Dozens of Kela-Tenata held and eased the golden tubing, raising it on Irmentis' side and lowering it into Phoebus. Still, Phoebus' breathing was shallow and ragged, his eyes fixed behind his closed eyelids. The scent of fresh blood hung in the air, and beyond this room Cheftu could hear the corridor filling with worried courtiers and citizens.

The transfusion would take several hours, several tries with Irmentis' blood. The tubing was tiny, and blood ran through very slowly. In between she would drink cow's blood to renew her. Each drop she gave would enhance *Hreesos'* chances of survival, encouraging his heart to keep pounding.

Cheftu noticed that Nestor and Dion had left him all alone with the patient and Niko.

He could almost hear Chloe saying, "Can you spell s-c-a-p-e-g-o-a-t?"

IRMENTIS' VISION WAS A GLADE, *like one of the many on her beautiful island, yet different. The trees breathed, the water sang, everything around her was filled with life. She was the same yet different—her skin glowed, her unbound hair danced on a soft breeze. The luminescence of stars glimmered within her.*

"Irmentis, my sister." The voice was weak, borne to her on the air. Phoebus, whole and healed, stood before her, his strong body gilded in the silver light. His hair hung over his broad shoulders, his eyes were lit from within like silver disks. "You are giving me that of which you have so little, your blood."

Irmentis shook her head in agreement, unable to move her gaze from her brother's body. A delicious heat stole through her, the light within her began to throb. What was this? As if he could read her mind Phoebus answered, "You are feeling the want of a whole woman, Irmentis. What you would feel had not Ileana . . ."

She cried out when he touched her, then heard his thoughts, felt the pounding of de-

sire in his body, and knew that despite the women he'd bedded and the children he'd formed, there was no one and nothing else he wanted more than her.

It frightened her.

She did not want this; she loved him, but not in this fashion. He was to be loved from afar: this was too close. "You reject me here, too, Irmentis?" he said. She opened her mouth to tell him it wasn't him, not his fault.

Then she was awake, her body weak and shaking. Tears poured down her cheeks, mingled fear and sorrow as she looked at her brother. The golden veins were being carefully removed from his body, while they prepared to pull the wood from his belly. Niko was directing the extraction and she turned to him, wincing from the many pierce marks.

"He lives, Niko." His gaze, purple and tortured, met hers, and Irmentis realized that Niko too loved Phoebus, loved him more than as a clansman. "Give him the elixir, Niko. He has nothing to lose. Do not let the Olimpi, your dearest friend, die."

He walked out, as though he didn't hear her.

NIKO RAN THROUGH THE HALLWAY, down the twisting stairway, and knocked on the door in series of pressures. It swung open.

He stood in Spiralmaster's laboratory. The vials and jars and flasks were as well-known to him as his name. Where would Spiralmaster have hidden the elixir? Knowing the cagey old man, he would have placed several vials in different places, with some form of coding so they were discernible only to one who knew Spiralmaster's thinking.

"Looking for this?" Ileana said, stepping from the shadows. Her beauty was invisible to him. All Niko saw was the vial.

"Give it me, Ileana."

She hid it in her palm. "Why, Niko? You seek to prolong the life of a man who hates me, who has not gotten me pregnant. I will lose my power, respect, and adoration of Aztlan, if I do not swell with child."

"Your concerns matter nothing to me, Ileana. Give me the vial."

"Are you certain it works, Niko? Are you certain it won't further poison his already crippled body?" She laughed, and Niko's blood simmered like lava.

"What do you want, Ileana? To be *athanati?* I can make that a reality. I can give you eternal youth and beauty."

"It means nothing unless you can also make me pregnant," she spat.

"I can do that." For Phoebus he could do anything. Even touch this spider of a woman.

She smiled, her gaze caressing him from head to toe. "You are comely, but you do not care for women, do you, Niko?"

He actually didn't know, but he wasn't going to admit it.

"When shall we arrange an assignation?"

"My offer is this: I will fill you with child, here and now; you will give me the elixir the moment my seed is spilt."

She was breathing faster, her breasts swelling before his eyes; by the gods it was repulsive! "I will give you some of the elixir, Niko. Enough for the service you will render me. If you want more, you will know the cost."

"All I need is enough for Phoebus, but I need it now!"

"Swear it, and your Phoebus may live."

"I swear by the Spiral and the Shell."

He watched as she poured a little of the elixir into a smaller flask. "Swear by blood."

Cursing, shaking, and afraid he would vomit on her, Niko slashed his palm with a broken blade, swore again, and rubbed blood on his lips. Ileana's hot mouth was aggressive in her desire. She kissed him until he was dizzy, licking the blood from his lips. "Does it excite you to know that Phoebus kisses like I do?"

It did. Tremendously.

She turned her back to him, releasing her skirts. "Now, Niko."

Caught between revulsion and pounding lust, Niko moved to her as he'd seen a dozen friends do over the summers. Her hands were sure in guiding him, and nineteen years of abstinence made the experience very short.

Ileana's glance was disparaging, but she climbed onto the table, crossed her legs, and lifted them. With one hand she began to touch herself. With the other she handed Niko the small flask, keeping the vial at her side.

"Where were you?" Irmentis hissed. "The Spiralmaster and Kela-Ata have concluded Phoebus is dying!"

Would this work? How could he know? The stones. "Go speak to them, cry, wail, distract them after a few moments. Go!" he instructed her.

"Niko—"

"Do it!"

Niko stepped into Phoebus' bathing alcove and pulled a stone from each of his pouches. Setting down the flask, he bent close to them, as though to an elderly relative. "Will Phoebus live with the elixir?"

He tossed the stones and watched as they turned. Aye!

Niko grabbed the flask and ran into the Golden's apartments.

The stones continued to turn. "I-n-d-a-r-k-n-e-s-s-a-n-d-l-u-s-t."

Niko stepped in, watching those who were allowing Phoebus to die. The Kela-Tenata, the Egyptian, were focused on Irmentis' hysterics. They had their backs to him. Phoebus lay silent, but Niko heard his labored breathing and knew *Hreesos* was still, barely, alive. He was not yet gone, but they had bathed him and arranged his arms in a position of death.

Irmentis fell to the floor with a cry, twitching violently. The Kela-Tenata grouped around her, and Niko sprang toward the couch. Niko saw that Phoebus' skin was drained white. His hair and body were drenched in blood. How to administer the elixir?

Niko wrenched back the blood-soaked bandage, swirled the liquid, and then poured it into his belly wound. Phoebus convulsed with a shout, and the Kela-Tenata turned as a body. Irmentis threw herself on Phoebus, her lips pressed to his ripped abdomen.

Her screams filled Niko's ears. He watched in horror and barely conscious jealousy as she licked at Phoebus' wound, her salty tears falling into the gash, blood coating her lips and cheeks. She was immersed in the taste and scent of Phoebus' life. The magi pulled her away.

Niko had to restrain his own screams of fear. Phoebus was still, so uncommonly still. The elixir had killed him? The stones had promised it wouldn't. They had said Phoebus would live. While all eyes were on Irmentis, Niko raised the flask to his lips, but the liquid was gone. Niko staggered back into the alcove, pocketed his stones, and crept out the serf's passageway. He heard shouting and yelping from afar as they led Irmentis away, down corridors.

The Kela-Tenata believed Irmentis had killed Phoebus. Ultimately Irmentis would wander in the punishment of the Labyrinth.

Niko knew the truth: He had misused his gifts and murdered his friend. His just punishment was to live without Phoebus.

PART IV

CHAPTER 16

AZTLAN

P HOEBUS WOKE WITH A SUDDENNESS that was shaking.

He felt well-being flow through his body; his sense of smell, hearing, and sight had never seemed so strong. He realized that something heavy was across his face, but he didn't have the energy to move yet. He smelled fear and death and something, an aroma so tantalizing that his mouth filled with liquid. Not saliva. It was a virulent bile that burned his tongue and throat, ate at his teeth.

Slowly he opened his eyes. His lashes rubbed against metal, and he carefully removed the mask from over his face. A death mask? He looked around, wondering where he was. He knew it was cold, but he didn't feel it. There was no decoration on the walls; indeed it seemed more of a cave than a room. Why was he in a cave? His brain flitted in his head, seeking a solution for this madness.

Shakily he sat up, clutching with both hands the leather-strip stretcher he lay on. The floor was dirt, cold, and powdery—like a cave. He rose to his feet, strength and power flowing through the strange quietness of his body.

Spying a jug, he walked to it, lifting it with ease as he poured it into a shallow bowl. Sloshing water over his face, he wondered what to do. Was this some unknown trial for the throne?

He glanced down, then braced himself against the wall. Dizziness and disorientation engulfed him. Phoebus closed his eyes as he fought what had to be sheer exhaustion. Opening them, he gazed into the depths of the water. Water that always, his entire life, without fail, returned his blue-eyed, golden-haired appearance.

Nothing.

It reflected back the ceiling well enough. He moved a jar right beside the water. The edge of the jar was visible. He dropped a comb in the water, and it caught the reflection before it rippled away. But *he* was not there.

Swallowing, wincing at the bile he tasted, Phoebus turned away.

Eumelos lay asleep on the chalk floor, curled tightly into himself. Phoebus stepped to his son, blindsided by the hunger that suddenly arced through him. A smell filled his nostrils, and he felt a seductive beating inside his head. He sank back on his heels. "Eumelos? Son?" He shook the boy's bony shoulder and flinched when Eumelos screamed.

Then his son was in his embrace, crying like the child he was, and Phoebus' arms were around him, feeling his bones beneath his hands, the pounding of his small heart as he sobbed. "You're alive! They said you were dead! I didn't believe them, but they said it, they did, they did!"

"Son," Phoebus said, keeping his voice steady. "Who said I was dead?"

Eumelos' blue eyes were glistening with tears. "The new Spiralmaster and Dion. They brought you down from the mountain, you were all bloody and dirty."

Faint images of fire and pain floated in his head. "But I lived?"

"They traded your blood with *Theea* Irmentis' and something went wrong. There was a lot of shouting—" Eumelos was getting too excited, his breath was raspy, and Phoebus held his son tight, soothing him. Why would Dion and Cheftu tell such falsehoods? Why would they terrify his son?

"Where was Nestor?"

"He cried a lot and they made him go away. They wanted to make me go, too, but I wouldn't, not even when Nekros came. He made a mask and left it on you." The boy's sobs were getting softer, and Phoebus changed position, his legs were sore.

"As you can see, Eumelos, I am well." Then he looked down at his legs. Strong legs that were supporting him. Hadn't they been hurt? Yet both ankles worked; Phoebus inhaled deeply, then moved his hand from Eumelos' back to his own belly. Only a faint scar remained where a stake of wood had impaled him.

"How . . . how many sunrises has it been?" he asked Eumelos, setting the boy on his bent knee.

"I do not know." Eumelos wiped his nose, smearing it across his face. Phoebus smiled at the gesture. By the gods, he loved this child! "Maybe five?"

Phoebus felt his arms begin to tremble, and he grabbed Eumelos close, this time to comfort himself. He remembered it in patches. More images, Irmentis—her ultimate rejection. His whole lifetime he had hoped she would turn to him, but in that shaded glen of her mind her *psyche* had forsaken him. Phoebus moved past his fury, the love that was mutating into hate, to his next memory. Blood and a fire that had roared through Phoebus' veins when Niko poured something on him.

The elixir?

The boy coughed, and Phoebus touched his forehead. He was hot, though to Phoebus everything felt hot. "I need you to do something for me, Eumelos. I think someone wants my throne, do you understand?"

"They want to be Golden?"

"Just so." Phoebus' heart ached when he thought that Eumelos would never inherit the throne. It would be worth the self-sacrifice just to see this bright child rule Aztlan. Far preferable to any whelp Ileana would birth. He shuddered. "Go to the pyramid and ask for the Minos. Do not leave until you bring him back here." He looked around. "Where am I?"

"In the caves beneath Kela's temple."

"Tell only the Minos that I am well, Eumelos. No one else. Swear to me?"

"He died, *Pateeras.*"

He died and I live, Phoebus thought. "Just so, tell whoever is wearing the Minos mask." Surely the inheritor had stepped into his position in five days? "Swear."

They linked their smallest fingers and swore; blood was too much for a boy this young. But it was never too early to learn the concept of honor and keeping one's word. Phoebus kissed his son's head, assuring him he was fine, and lay back down on the stretcher, touching the shallow scars that covered wounds that should still be seeping.

What was in the elixir?

HUNDREDS OF LUNCHING CITIZENS were scattered about the hillsides of Aztlan and Kallistae. Sunlight glinted off the Pyramid of Days, and the deep blue of Theros Sea was capped with white waves. Chloe relaxed in the sunshine on her balcony, feeling its heat steal over her bared body. She'd been in meetings all morning, and between the lingo she didn't understand about cattle and the gnawing lust she felt from just seeing Cheftu across the room, it had been both stressful and frustrating.

Hreesos' demise was a carefully guarded secret, and her husband was sequestered until further notice. The populace knew nothing officially, though she was certain rumors were flying thick and fast. The eruption of Mount Krion had been visible from Aztlan, and the consequences were hard to hide.

The death of the Minos was on everyone's lips.

In the beauty of the sun, it was hard to imagine widespread destruction. A breeze across her skin offered relief from the heat, and Chloe imagined how wonderful it would be were Cheftu beside her. She smiled while dozing.

Suddenly all over the island, birds flew up screaming as they fought for airspace. Then she heard it, a dull rumble that seemed to reverberate deep in her breastbone like a bass guitar. She ran to the balcony's edge, looking out toward the land bridge and the adjoining island.

"The Bull roars!" she heard someone shout. She saw citizens running for the sea, leaping in from hundreds of cubits above the water, racing down the zigzag path, pushing into boats so full they capsized almost immediately.

She crouched and fought a wave of nausea as the balcony trembled beneath her. The air was thick with cries, and Chloe hunkered down, her hands flat against the colored stone. The rumbling grew louder, deafening, and she raised her head.

Across the churning waters, on the island of Kallistae, the cliff's edge seemed to shudder, and one section, dense with people, fell crashing into the sea. A human avalanche.

Then it was still.

"Citizens!" A voice rose on the wind.

Chloe turned, shielding her eyes, looking toward the pyramid. A white-cloaked figure stood at the Calling Place, his arms wide. "Fear not," he cried. "The Bull has rumbled his last!"

Around her she heard the caustic comments: "What assurance is that?" "Shut up, you old fool," "Tell that to the dead." Chloe watched as the robed figure made a sign, a blessing or a curse, she didn't know, and turned slowly in a circle, showing himself to all. *Hreesos!*

"I am *Hreesos!*" he whispered . . . a soft declaration that grew and swelled like a tidal wave.

"He's dead!" some brave soul shouted.

The white-robed figure pointed. "I have become *athanati*, and yet I will rule. I have faced Apis and I won. Join me, citizens! Eat of the flesh of Apis and rejoice in his strength. In my strength."

From the bottom of the pyramid priests led out dozens of bulls. Some were black Apis bulls, some were just cattle. An altar was set up, and as Chloe watched, a bull was sacrificed. She looked toward the sea, where nothing seemed changed—as if those lives hadn't even rippled the surface of the water. Did no one realize it would take more than a bull snack to save them?

Hreesos continued to speak, telling of his triumph over Apis Earth-shaker.

How was this possible? How was it that he swept down the stairs and handed out bloody bits of bull to the cautious few who grouped before the pyramid? Five days he'd been dead! At least, that was what rumor said.

Was this like a soap opera—don't believe the dead are actually dead unless you pinch them in an open casket? Chloe shook her head, watching as *pithoi* of wine, then baskets of bread, were brought out. What was *Hreesos* doing?

"My mistress?"

She turned to the unknown serf. *"Eee?"*

"The Kela-Ileana requests you present yourself in her *Megaron* as you are bid. The serfs will bring your belongings."

"You are from Kela-Ileana?"

"Aye."

"People are dying in the lagoon, shouldn't she be helping?"

"The Queen of Heaven requests you," he said, his tone firmer.

"Where is your heart? Hundreds of people are down there," Chloe said, tying on sandals.

"You are the inheritor; the fiancée of *Hreesos* requests you."

"Until a few moments ago, there was no *Hreesos* and nothing to inherit!"

The serf smiled tightly. "Come with me, mistress."

"Nay," Chloe said from the doorway. "These people need help."

"My mistress kindly requests your presence."

"There are things more important than her request," she said, stepping over the threshold.

"Nay. There are not," he said sternly, following her.

Chloe turned around, tapping her foot. "She may be Queen of Heaven, but she can wait. *They* can't."

He grabbed her around her waist, and Chloe struggled, getting away, turning to tell him off.

All she saw was his fist.

CHEFTU LAY ON HIS BED, SHIVERING. He didn't feel cold exactly, just . . . unsteady. Turning on the couch, he brought up his leg, easing the sore that grew larger and larger each day. Another had started on his side, usually hidden by his corselet.

"Spiralmaster!" Nestor called. "Cheftu, where are you?"

Struggling upward from the morass that he seemed to be wallowing in, Cheftu tried to cry out, to call the young man, but he heard the doors close and Nestor's footsteps against stone as he ran upward.

What was happening to him?

You've got the disease, his reason said. *You have seen this happen a dozen times. Can you still walk?*

Determined to prove himself, Cheftu forced his body upright and took a step away from the couch. Then another. His legs didn't seem to be working together, and sweat soaked his kilt from the effort. Steadying himself against a table, he tried to think, tried to reason.

Later, he would try later.

He fell onto his couch.

CHLOE CAME TO IN AN UPSIDE-DOWN WORLD. Her head throbbed in counterpoint to her head bobbing.

She *was* upside-down.

I'm going to be very sick, she thought. She twisted as her carrier walked down a set of steps. Chloe tried to pull away; his shoulder was gouging her stomach.

"Cease moving!"

Oh great, the Tyson wannabe.

"Sick," Chloe gurgled.

He bounced her into his arms, his touch as impersonal as a masseur. Not a moment too soon, either, Chloe thought. Her head was splitting, her jaw ached, and her normal sense of outrage was muffled by her desire for Excedrin. Had she ever been hit like that before? She certainly couldn't recall it.

Double doors opened before them, and Chloe was set on her feet in a room of great beauty.

Dolphins swam gracefully on the walls, their humped backs forming a dado around the room. Beneath that ran a bench of gray stone, its back waved to follow the dolphin design. Four-pointed stars covered the ceiling, and lilies bloomed between the open doors. Chloe jumped at a piercing scream, then saw a peacock stroll in, his tail open and proudly erect. She heard a snap of fingers, and her carrier pulled her into the next room.

"Greetings, Sibylla. My gratitude for accepting the invitation that you take your rightful place here."

"Correct me, Ileana, but am I not a clan chieftain? So wouldn't my rightful place be the island of Hydroussa? Or perhaps my own apartments?" Chloe didn't even bother to keep the sarcasm from her tone.

"Your position as inheritor to the Queen of Heaven takes precedence," Ileana said.

"Are you still not with child?" It must be weeks into her month-long mate-fest with Phoebus. Of course, he had been allegedly killed toward the beginning of it. Would Ileana get a complimentary month? When would this be over?

Ileana's gaze was as warm as an ice cube. Her fingers flexed on her still-flat stomach. "Sadly, Phoebus has weak seed."

"Or you are infertile," Chloe quipped.

Ileana's turquoise eyes narrowed like a bushy-tailed cat's. Apparently it had never dawned on the Queen of Heaven that something might be wrong with her. Chloe took a step back.

"Since the goddess has not yet blessed me, I must remove Phoebus' options."

Chloe began to feel a tad nervous.

Ileana smiled at her like the Grinch on Christmas Eve. "You are sailing away—"

"Nay, I am not." Not yet, anyway.

"Nay, of course not," Ileana said, further confusing Chloe. *Do I stay or do I go now?* The question was answered as Chloe's arms were jerked behind her and tightly bound. She opened her mouth to scream, but that just made it easier to stuff a wool scarf in. "Your ship has sailed, the clan horns were visible for *henti* around. You will be lost at sea, though because you are not expected, no one will know until it is too late to seek you out."

No! I can't do that to Cheftu! But she couldn't speak—she was eating a sheep, whole.

"Enjoy the Labyrinth, Sibylla."

She was taken, sometimes carried, sometimes dragged, through narrow hallways and convoluted staircases until it was very, very dark.

Blinking at the sudden brightness of two torches, she read the name above the doorway, then read it again. In Aztlan it was a name too profane and too powerful to be spoken aloud.

Hades.

Eee! the things Edith Hamilton didn't include!

The serf blindfolded her, and Chloe twisted back and forth; it was inevitable that the serf would win, but some instinct rebelled at the thought of blindness. He slapped her, and in the ensuing dizziness that reawakened her headache, her sight was hidden behind a linen scarf.

Her last vision was of fire.

The serf pushed and she stumbled. Unable to catch herself, she fell forward into open space. Air rushed by her, and her muffled shriek was the only sound in her ears.

"I TRIED TO WAKE YOU, MASTER, but I couldn't find you," Nestor explained.

Cheftu clenched his fists, gritting his teeth. Mon Dieu, *as soon as they find the cause of the illness, the entire populace is fed it!* It was too late. He'd forsaken his reason for being in this time, and because he could not rise from his couch, a whole culture was doomed.

Surely he was not solely responsible for their demise? But ultimately those who were infected would die. All this vast knowledge, wisdom, and experience would be lost. *Mon Dieu*, what could he do? "Is Commander Y'carus in port?"

Nestor didn't know, so Cheftu sent a serf to learn. He gestured for the younger man to sit down and wondered how to say what he needed to. "Your Spiralmaster selected me for this role because I know the future." Nestor blinked, at once fearful and suspicious. "In that future, Aztlan falls." Cheftu looked away, brushing his long hair over his shoulder. "The legacy lives on, and we must see to it that some people live on. Who would not have eaten the bull?"

"Anyone not on the island."

"Nay. Here. Who on Aztlan would have been overlooked?"

Nestor sat back. "The serfs, the infirm, the poor."

"I haven't seen any poor."

"They do not live side by side with the citizens. Ofttimes they were cast out of their clan for personal offenses and must beg or leave Aztlan altogether in order to live."

Cheftu stood up, holding on to the back of the stone chair. "We must find them, get them out of here."

"I will call some Mariners."

"Nay! I fear we must do this in secret. No one must know what we are about, and no one who ate the bull must be on that ship."

Nestor paled. "Do I have it?"

"I know not. However, I do."

CHLOE GULPED FOR A NONSHEEP—FLAVORED BREATH. She needed air. Nasty! What was that smell? She choked on her hard-won breath and vowed to use only her mouth for breathing. Sulfur!

She really *was* in hell.

Her fingers twisted and turned at the knot holding her wrists together. Swearing at the rope's burning, she slid it higher up on her hands. She couldn't see to know if anything sharp, like a razor blade or a pair of scissors, were conveniently stuck in the wall, so she'd have to get her now bleeding wrists to her mouth and gnaw through, like a giant rat.

As if on cue, Chloe heard scampering and flinched. Maybe her blindness was a blessing incognito.

Holding her arms as straight as she could, she lay back on them and strained to inch her backside through the loop of her arms without dislocating a shoulder. It hurt, she felt sweat on her forehead, but then her arms were beneath her legs—and fourteen layers of ruffles. She wasn't wearing the best exercise gear. Pulling her knees to her ears, she got her hands clear of her feet and chewed on the knots.

It was actually easier to untie them, despite the straining that had tightened them. The serf was no Boy Scout, and the rope was tough. Blindfold next. Another few seconds and she was free! Sight, at last.

Chloe blinked a few times, rubbed her eyes, and looked around.

There were many shades and terms for black: Mars black, black as night, black-cat black, midnight darkness, dark as a dungeon, Stygian darkness. Black as Hades.

Oh God, oh God.

She felt panic rising in her throat like a tunnel being sealed shut. *Don't freak! Oh God. You can get through this. Take it one step at a time.*

One. You can't see a bloody thing. That's okay—still, you have four senses and intuition. She felt the ground. Hard-packed dirt.

The stink of sulfur. It was hot as an August night in Texas with no breeze, and it sounded eerie. Sad, whispering calls and plaintive moans did nothing to encourage her.

Hopeless cries. Dante's warning flashed through her mind: "Abandon hope, all ye who enter here."

She shook her head and continued her pep talk. *What do I already know?* Sibylla's brain remained silent, so Chloe pieced together what she could.

The Labyrinth, Hades, was a maze by definition. There were no light sources. She'd fallen down, way down. Or at least it had felt that way. But not far enough to break anything.

She was expected to die.

Bad thought, Chloe.

She put her head on her knees. *Think! The maze you beat before was art—a design motif. Maybe this is the same? How can I know when it's too dark to see?*

She'd pretend she was Helen Keller.

On her feet again, she took a step and slipped, falling down a vertical shaft, her flailing hands finally catching a ledge. She scrambled up the sheer chalky sides with bare toes and fingers. Chloe huddled, her breath loud and her heart pounding.

Part of her just wanted to fall off a ledge and be done with it. She was terrified, trapped in a place designed to kill—or send you round the bend.

Then she thought of Cheftu. They'd been through so much, yet here they were. Together, no less. She still hadn't drawn his hands or told him about her family. Or had his children. No, leaving Cheftu was not an option.

Her stomach growled and Chloe realized that her ability to think clearly would be pretty limited. She could survive without food. Not happily, not in a good mood, but she would live. Water—water was trickier, especially since she was sweating like a mule. *What I wouldn't give for a squeeze sport bottle!*

On her hands and knees she crawled forward, away from the ledge. Standing carefully, she reached up and touched ceiling. She'd walk as far as she could, see if she could understand the plan better. There had to be a method. One didn't just construct something without a method, a blueprint; it had to make sense to somebody! She just had to guess the right somebody. Swallowing dryly, Chloe walked forward.

THE GODS APPEARED TO LISTEN TO PHOEBUS. In the days that followed his ascension of the pyramid, utter calm descended on Aztlan. Not a tremor shook the earth, not a wave flickered high on the sea. The wounds that gaped in the soil of the empire became green with growth, and the fire that had warmed the citizens' feet in warning, cooled.

The anger of Apis seemed dissipated; no stench of sulfur, no pockets of steam. The sky was blue, swallows fluttered on the breeze, butterflies lighted on buildings, a blessing of the goddess Kela. The dead had been peaceably interred in the caverns of Paros. A few clansmen returned to Delos, now two slivers of island, and began to design a newer, better city for the Clan of the Muse.

From around the empire, citizens came to clean out the burned fields of Naxos. Mariners and engineers from Siros updated the irrigation system with better aqueducts. Women from Tinos brought seedlings and laid them in the ash-coated earth with love, honoring the dead and praying to Kela for fertility.

Priests journeyed from Folegandros, set about pouring new *ari-kat* stone for buildings, watchtowers, and walls. Mount Krion slept, not even a puff of smoke emitted from the pointed cone. Priests monitored Mount Stronghyle and Mount Gaia, but Apis rested. Phoebus had assuaged the gods. He was one of their number now.

Hreesos was seen everywhere. Always white cloaked, his blue eyes and a flash of gold were the only things visible beneath his hood. Niko, his mage, was ever at his elbow, as was Eumelos, his firstborn, who trembled when his father left his sight. From the tip of Hydroussa to the pylons of the Breakwater, the Golden Bull inspected, encouraged, and supported his people.

As proof of his kingship, his worthiness to rule and omen of the bounty he would bring to Aztlan, the Queen of Heaven was rumored to be with child. Every night they coupled, and every day she was carried from the palace to the sprawling temple of the snake goddess for the Kela-Tenata to observe her. Though her waist was still tiny, citizens speculated that her breasts grew heavier and noticed she no longer wore her cincher.

Had Aztlan ever had such a powerful, magnificent ruler? He was *athanati* already; he'd battled the bull god and won. He was everything a ruler should be—fertile, wise, handsome, strong, and mysterious.

His people would do anything for him; Phoebus was a god.

NIKO SLAMMED THE DOOR, and Neotne looked up. He dismissed her with a snap and walked to his chest where the stones lay hidden. Phoebus was being difficult, refusing to believe the peace would end.

The stones had spoken, though Niko hesitated to share their prophecy. The stones were Niko's secret.

More danger approached. Niko had been trained to see the signs of impending eruption. The priests had quietly informed him of the newly poisoned water, the activity of the snakes.

With shaky hands Niko pulled out the black and white stones, tossing and throwing, asking mundane questions as he worked up the courage to ask the difficult ones. He checked what he knew of the language against the chart he'd made. The letters were confusing, and a single misread mark could change the meaning of the word or sentence.

Phoebus had not mentioned Irmentis, not even asked after her. He had to know she'd been thrown in the Labyrinth. He cared only for Eumelos.

A child.

He let Niko handle all the questions citizens asked, he just moved through the day, smiling, waving. The clansmen were dazzled, but Niko alone knew the Golden Bull had lost his energy, his will. Phoebus never spoke to his childhood friend, he just smiled. It was as though Phoebus had died; being with Eumelos was the one thing that kept him from lying down and embracing the Isles of the Blessed.

It was clear he no longer cared for Niko. The realization cut him to the quick: first Spiralmaster betraying him, now Phoebus' passive forsaking him. If only Niko could win back his love, his friendship, his old, easy companionship, he would never ask the gods for another thing. He questioned the stones. "Will the Scholomance survive?"

"T-h-e-e-s-s-s-e-n-c-e-w-i-l-l."

"When will the mountain erupt?"

"T-h-e-S-e-a-s-o-n-o-f-t-h-e-L-i-o-n."

"Which day?"

Niko felt someone watching him and turned quickly. No one stood behind; it must be his fear, his imagination. He wrapped the stones in cloth and snapped for a carrying chair. He needed to speak to the Council.

Aztlan was dying.

THE GIRL WAITED UNTIL SHE SAW HER PROVIDER'S CHAIR take him away. She crept into his chambers, looking around for his hiding place. Those stones were talking to him; she could see the answers in his pale, burning eyes and flushed face.

Neotne wanted some answers.

Her teeth permanently gritted against the ache of her missing hand, Neotne used it as a brace while her right hand sifted through her benefactor's possessions. Two squares of silk from Kos were set on opposite sides of his chest. She pulled out one and recognized the black stone she'd seen over Niko's shoulder. She unrolled the second and laid it beside.

The stones moved!

Stifling a shriek, Neotne watched as the stones flipped and turned. Faint markings in some mysterious text colored their sides, and she felt tears prick her eyelids. It was a language she didn't know.

The stones were twisting and tumbling as though caught in a violent wind. How would she get them back inside? Despair had almost drowned her until she saw the crude clay tablet. Beside each of the markings from the stone was an Aztlantu translation.

Trembling with fear and anticipation, Neotne picked up the struggling stones in her one hand and tossed them, as she had seen Niko do. In a voice that was low and rough from weeks of silence—why should she speak if the gods would not heed her—Neotne asked her question.

"Does Y'carus live?"

The stones flipped three times, and she quickly compared the markings, then again. Elation flowed through her so quickly she felt dizzy. Aye! Y'carus lived! The next question on her lips was how to find him, yet her eye was drawn to her hand.

From her hand, to her arm, then her marred breasts. She could see through only one eye; grasp with only one fist. Y'carus lived, and he had loved her. The woman she had been was dead, though. A new creature stood in her place. A being that most found repulsive; she couldn't bear to see that pitying, fearful look in Y'carus' eyes.

She wouldn't find him. She would leave Aztlan, go far away. Perhaps in summers to come she would find the courage to take up life again. "What is there for me?" she whispered, blinking away tears. She must be strong; she was alone now. Niko had treated her well, saving her from a painful, certain death, but he didn't need her. He tolerated her, but he had no warmth, no love, in his *psyche*.

The stones slipped from her fingers onto the table. The answer took much longer, as she thrice verified each letter. "B-e-r-e-a-d-y-t-o-s-a-i-l-f-a-r."

"Who are you?"

"T-h-e-v-o-i-c-e-o-f-I-A-M."

The stones seemed to burn in her palms as Neotne slipped them into their silken pouches, separating them enough so that they were still, then putting them inside the box. She had to ready herself to sail. She had to be brave.

CHAPTER 17

THE CALM BEFORE THE STORM started to give way. Small quakes, deep beneath the earth's surface, began. They shifted rock and jostled lava that surged from the earth's core, racing like molten blood freed from a tourniquet. As the shifts moved higher, the level of the lava rose. On the ocean floor silent plumes of rock, gas, and steam burst forth, incinerating fish and roasting flora.

The quakes continued, a ripple effect in soil as they moved higher, above sea level, into the remaining channels of the Aegean ocean rift. As indigo-sailed ships rowed above, the sandy bottom of the sea cracked, a break that ran north and south, east and west, causing a dozen, then a hundred other fissures.

Slumbering inside the towering cones, the liquid rock surged and fell, compressing, tightening. The hundreds of earthquakes felt and not felt each day thereafter shifted and irritated the boiling, writhing mass.

THE ADEPTS WANDERED like *skia* through the back alleys of the city. Y'carus was indeed in port. Cheftu felt a burning inside that warned him time was slipping through his fingers like seawater. Today he felt well, and he thanked God for that, for there was much to do.

The adepts were seeking those who would survive. Ostensibly those they asked were being taken to the pyramid to receive the bull. Cheftu took only those who protested, who had chosen not to eat it because they found the idea distasteful.

Chances were they would find the idea of breakfasting on each other even more so.

Cheftu was amazed at the squalor that lived behind the palaces and villas of the wealthy. Open ditches were filled with refuse that plumbing did not carry away, rotting food was covered with flies as the starving forsaken children and adults of Aztlan ate.

These people were not allowed on the streets, nor were they allowed in the fields or on the walkways until well after dusk. No religious ritual was allowed them; they were utterly and completely ostracized. Nestor gathered a few, and they promised to meet him at the doors of the pyramid after nightfall.

Cheftu left Nestor to take care of things and went in search of more people. Keep looking, his intuition said. Search, you will find.

He was in a wealthy section of town, lush greenery draped over the brilliantly painted housing. He went from servants' quarters to servants' quarters, asking who had partaken of the bull.

His band was pitifully small when he knocked on the door of the largest house. A young woman opened it, her face badly burned, her arm cradled against her breast.

"You have come . . . to . . . sail away?" she whispered.

Cheftu was so stunned at her guess that he shook his head silently.

She reached behind her and pulled a woven bag awkwardly onto her back. "Take me."

By the rising of the moon, the motley crew had assembled. Cheftu and Nestor walked them down the zigzag steps to the docks. Water slapped against the hulls, and laughter seeped out from the doors and windows of brightly lit taverns. These were the few who hadn't eaten the bull, who weren't infested with the illness that ate holes in the brain.

Y'carus' gaze was bright as he watched the remnants of Aztlan march aboard his ship. He and his crew had not eaten the bull; still, some wanted to stay with their wives and children. Those who remained on board knew the purpose of this voyage, and each man's expression was bleak. Cheftu handed Y'carus a huge trunk of scrolls and tablets from the library: the plans for diving bells, indoor plumbing, maps of the seas, an Aztlantu dictionary, the cherished formula for alchemy. These secrets would be shared with the world.

"Aztlan will soon be but a memory. You carry your empire on your ship."

Y'carus looked over the broken and rejected people. "We start with poor stock."

"Do not see them as clansmen; free everyone from their class and clan and then begin to see anew."

The commander looked at him. "My eyes will not hold you again, my friend."

"Not in this lifetime." He and Y'carus embraced as the last of the passengers, the prepared young serf woman, stepped aboard.

Cheftu walked down the gangplank. He looked back for a moment and saw the serf and the commander step closer and closer, then finally fall into each other's arms.

Cheftu smiled; apparently the commander wanted to set about improving the stock immediately.

Under the waning moon, the huge Aztlantu ship pulled away, the sound of the timekeeper's drum faint, a throb in Cheftu's temple and throat.

So the Mariner and the Dyer sailed for the open sea, journeying beyond the channels of Aztlan, through the wine-dark Aegean and into the Great Green. On the shores of the Mediterranean they founded small cities beneath graceful cedars.

The three hundred grew, the boats multiplied, and the tribe became famous for their skills: sailing and dyeing. Though they stayed by the sea, they kept to the plains, avoiding the fury and madness of the earth within its mountains.

So the Phoenicians, who worshiped an angry god who demanded blood and fire, circumnavigated the globe. They brought cedars to King Solomon, took Egyptian faience to the Caspian, and left coins in the Azores, consulting the same maps Alexander the Great would use. Maps found in the ancient texts of the library in Alexandria, written in an alphabet the world has used ever since, taken from a land called Atlantis. . . .

Cheftu couldn't believe his ears. "You are certain?"

"The serf said her mistress has sailed for Hydroussa. This is for you."

Cheftu opened the tiny slip of papyrus and frowned. Chloe wrote to him in tile typing? This was new and odd. "Dearest Cheftu, Clan business calls me away. I cannot wait to return to your arms and languish there. Sibylla."

He dismissed the serf and stared at the note. Chloe used the word "languish"? More significantly, she had signed it Sibylla. He looked at the typing carefully. Was he being paranoid? She wouldn't flee Aztlan without him; that wouldn't be her way, unless she were forced.

But who could force a clan chieftain? There must be another explanation. If she were gone, she would send him a message. Perhaps she had been watched or knew someone would read the note. If he had not heard from her in a few days, then he would react. However, he could do nothing now.

He left for his next medical call. The last of Zelos' *hequetai* was dying.

As Cheftu walked across the footbridge set in *ari-kat* stone that spanned the shallow lagoon of Aztlan Island, far, far beneath the surface time ran out.

The hairline cracks and crevices had widened to the span of a man's hand. The basket holding the bay began to unravel. The earth shuddered, splintered, and heaved, and the strands unwound faster.

Beneath the lagoon hairline fissures filled with water and grew. The pressure and weight of salt and fluid rushed into the cracks until the section broke completely, the first of many that would crumble away.

Cheftu was halfway up the steep walk to the dying man's villa when the terrified cries wafted up to him. He ran back to the cliff's edge. He watched, speechless, as the lagoon began to drain.

Huge waves created by suction swirled at the far end of the bay, then crashed against the dock. The few brave sailors fled up the zigzag path in a frenzy.

Ships were smashed against the rocks as the water level dropped. Cheftu was deaf to cries and screams. The bay was falling! In moments Aztlan's flotilla had become driftwood.

"The Sibylla warned us!" was the first clear call he heard. What did this mean? How could they flee, if there were no ships?

The waves had gained strength and rose high against the rocky walls of Aztlan.

"Flee for the mountains!"

"Run for your lives!"

Theros Sea, the beautiful, bountiful sea of summer, had become Therio Sea—the Beast.

He hoped Y'carus was safe. It would be aw—Chloe! *Mon Dieu,* she was at sea!

TIME HAD NO MEANING. The darkness was unrelenting. Bouts of terror gripped Chloe like fits, and she fought herself for calm. She now knew the maze was constructed in three dimensions. Not only were the passages vertical, the side ledges led into horizontal mazes of their own. How deep was a question she didn't want to have to find out.

Her clothes were drenched, and she'd ripped at the seams of her skirt fruitlessly, settling for taking it off and wearing just the apron. It covered front and back, arcing from her hips to her knees and back up. Great for movement and a thousand times cooler.

She'd twisted her hair up and around as she'd seen Cammy do a thousand times, but there was nothing to secure it. Her head pounding again, she slid down one wall, her tears mixing with sweat on her cheeks.

The last maze had been a square with a swastika, the first one a five-point star with a Greek key pattern beneath it. Patterns, patterns, these people had a thing for mutating patterns.

How long had it been? Eternity was one night, Chloe thought. One sulfur-scented night. Patterns swirled beneath her closed eyelids, morphing from one into another. Greek key, swirl, swastika, star, rose, key, swirl.

Incredibly, Cheftu was sucking on her fingers . . . ouch! with his teeth! Chloe jerked her hand away, contacting flesh with a scream. Darkness, sulfur, Cheftu wasn't in hell with her. Chloe kicked out instinctively, and her ankle was caught.

"If I had known you were alive, Sibylla, I would not have tried," a woman's voice said. Chloe struggled to place it, low, husky, almost masculine. She heard a whine that had nothing to do with humans. Hot breath, long, sloppy tongues . . .

"Ir—Irmentis?"

"Who threw you down here?"

"Ileana."

The woman laughed, bitterly. "It would be a justice if all the *skia* she has created haunted her at once." The dogs were panting. They threw Irmentis' dogs in here, too?

"Why are you here?"

"The Kela-Tenata thought I killed my brother."

"Who? Phoebus?"

"Aye. My brother?"

"He lives. He's fine." What a very weird conversation to be having in utter darkness with hound breath in your face!

"Then he has left me here as punishment for not returning his *pothos.*"

Not sure she wanted to hear more about irresistible longings, Chloe got to her feet, her hands outstretched against hot, furry bodies.

"Would you like some water?" the huntress asked. Greedily Chloe slurped it down.

"How are you living down here?" Chloe asked.

She felt Irmentis' shrug. "I have always lived in the dark. Here is really no different than my grove. I have my hounds," she said with warmth.

Chloe heard voices around them and then heard Irmentis' sniffing, then the dogs' sniffing. "Someone is dying," she said. "Come quickly."

Are we the graveyard detail? Chloe didn't ask, she just followed, wondering how she could help. "By the way, where did you get fresh water?"

"The lowest level. There is a well."

Chloe was thinking a well on the lowest level of a dungeon was ridiculous as she tried to follow Irmentis and her four-legged entourage through the darkness. The huntress stepped confidently, and Chloe followed, stumbling on the changing turf, trying to visualize the pathway. Lots of left turns; familiar. What was the pattern?

They stopped.

"Do you have a blade?" Irmentis asked in the constant darkness. Chloe began to feel a little nervous. Something stank, a sickly sweet smell. The dogs were going nuts! "They took mine before they threw me," the woman explained.

"Nay, I do not."

"Very well, you take the other side. He'll be tough, but fairly fresh. We'd best go before the hounds."

Before Chloe's mind could interpret it, she heard a sound she would never forget, the sound of human teeth sinking into human flesh. Irmentis sighed as she chewed noisily, and Chloe ran. Down the darkness until she felt the floor beneath her drop away and she was sliding into midnight.

TWO DAYS AGO CHEFTU HAD RECEIVED A MESSAGE that Chloe's ship had landed at Hydroussa. The note was not from Chloe, but rather a serf saying she arrived. Now, today, another message that she was lost at sea.

Not for a moment did he believe that. She was alive; moreover she was nearby. At night he could almost sense her calling out to him.

Aztlan was in chaos. Cheftu had gotten back to the main island the day the harbor sank, but not before the city of Daphne had effectively emptied itself on the slopes of Mount Apollo. Like chicks under a hen's wing, the citizens fled for the hills, fearing the water's rage.

At some point in that night the bowl of the bay had crumbled utterly. Not a ship was left. Kallistae was now a much larger island in the middle of a very deep sea. Even if it were still there, the port would be useless, impossible to anchor in. How such a thing had happened, Cheftu could not explain, just marvel.

The moon was out tonight, shining on the distant waters. The palace was full to overflowing, for those who had not fled to the mountain had run here. Cheftu had been taking care of a young Mariner who'd gotten trampled in the panic, among many others. Where was Chloe?

"Do you gloat in the moonlight?"

Cheftu sighed and turned around. Niko. Couldn't the man be satisfied with ruling Aztlan through his patron? "Why would I gloat? Aztlan is destroying itself, yet the Council refuses to meet."

"I think you are more concerned about the whereabouts of a certain clan chieftain."

Cheftu licked his lips. "Why would I be concerned?"

"Possibly because Ileana had her thrown into the Labyrinth?"

Cheftu laughed, genuinely amused. "Why would I care? Tell your tales to someone who will believe you."

"You laugh at me? I've seen the way you look at her. Don't dare laugh at me, for I am the one who knows! You may have deceived Spiralmaster, but I have the stones! I have the elixir! I visited the island!"

Rubbing his face, Cheftu shrugged. "Do not tell me falsehoods about Sibylla, and I will not laugh."

"The stones say she will die."

"What stones?"

"The talking stones."

Cheftu stilled. Stones had been mentioned in the chamber where he'd undergone the various testings. Mystical stones that enabled the Aztlantu to ask questions of the former god of this place. "Take some wine with me?"

"You think I am such a fool as to drink your poison?"

"Nay. I would think you know I'm not such a fool as to murder you in my own apartments," Cheftu said acerbically, stepping away from the window and pouring a cup of wine. "Tell me about this island."

"You cannot find it," Niko said, strutting around the room, touching various objects, running his fingers over the furnishings. He thought this would be his chamber, his possessions, Cheftu realized. This is painful to him.

"I cannot imagine that I would."

"I was taken there, taken to the altar with the archway and the colored stone pavements."

Coughing, Cheftu asked, "Archway?"

"Aye. As fine as anything built by the Scholomance. Red stone that reached into the heavens, protecting the place where the speaking stones lay. Their god gave me a vision, inviting me to join him."

Cheftu somewhat doubted the veracity of the invitation, but he wanted Niko to continue talking. A red stone archway, could that be the way out of here? Out of this time? Was this the counterpart of the gateway in Egypt that had ultimately delivered him to this myth-shrouded island? Cheftu hoped it was a sign to leave Aztlan.

Someone knocked on his door and Niko opened it. "My master!" a serf said. "Eumelos has fallen ill! *Hreesos* commands your attendance." With a smug smile, Niko bade Cheftu a cool, confident farewell and followed the serf out. Cheftu closed the doors behind them and leaned against the wood.

There was a doorway; all he had to do was find his wife.

NIKO'S HANDS TREMBLED AS HE TOUCHED EUMELOS. The boy was not hot, he was not vomiting, but he was sick. Phoebus' expression was taut, his eyes pleading. He knew. Eumelos had the illness, the plague, that had struck the *hequetai* and was decimating the populace.

"Where has he been these past days?" Niko asked.

"He stayed with the priests for a few days, then rejoined me. He was well, until he fell last night." Phoebus swallowed audibly, and Niko pulled back the linen sheeting. Ataxia was setting in, already Eumelos' wiry body was twisting, his shoulder and arm held awkwardly.

It had struck so quickly!

"Do something, Niko," Phoebus pleaded. "You are the best, the brightest. Please, help my son." Niko had never heard Phoebus sound so weak, so needy. Part of him wanted Phoebus to fight for him like that, the other part wanted to heal Eumelos and receive Phoebus' adulation. Yet nothing could be done. They had seen that. Once death set in—

The elixir!

Niko covered the boy, trying to stop his shivering. "He will live, Phoebus," he said. Though he hated to touch Ileana, the elixir had saved Phoebus from certain death. Would it do the same for Eumelos? If Niko saved Eumelos, then surely Phoebus would love him, Niko, again.

"You swear to me?"

Niko looked into the weeping face of his dear friend. He touched Phoebus' pale skin, still darker than his own. "By the Spiral and the Shell, I swear it. I will return. Do not leave his side."

Running from the room, Niko stopped a serf and gave him a message, then ran down the steps to the laboratory. He would look for the elixir, see if he could uncover Spiralmaster's hiding place. If that failed, he would mate with Ileana and take it from her.

Eumelos must live so Phoebus would be Niko's again.

She arrived faster than he expected. Niko spun around.

"Do you seek this?" She held out the vial, and Niko's hands clenched.

"I need more. Your grandson is dying."

"Children often die. There are always more," she said. "He's no blood relation to me, at any rate. Are you willing to agree to the terms?"

"I said as much in my message."

"You are fortunate I came on such a rude, flimsy request," she said coldly.

Niko ground his teeth. "My apologies, mistress." Slowly she smiled. Niko forced one foot before the other, walking to her. "What must I do to have the whole supply, Ileana?"

She laughed. "You think I will give you all? You are an idealistic fool, are you not?"

He placed his hands on her breasts, squeezing until she panted. "I need the rest of it, Ileana. Give it me."

Her face was growing flushed, her eyes losing some of their glitter. "I will tell you what to do, and if you please me, I will give you all of it. If not, I will give you a generous portion. Training does take time." He hated her smile, her hands that worked the bindings of her skirt.

This was for Phoebus. He could do anything for Phoebus, suffer any indignity, endure any trial. "What do you want me to do?" His voice sounded strange in his ears, and he felt his body stiffening as more and more of her white skin was revealed. He hated her for making him feel this way, hot and unfocused.

"Worship me, Niko."

PHOEBUS KNELT BY EUMELOS' COUCH. His fingers trembled as he brushed the boy's hair from his face. Where was Niko? What of his promise? His vow? "It will be well, son," he said. "You will be fine. Niko has sworn it. Niko has never broken his word to me, you will be well."

Eumelos' blue eyes were stark with fear, and his breath was rasping and rough. How many decans had passed? What illness could strike so suddenly? Surely it wasn't the plague. The boy was not in Zelos' cabinet, so how could he have gotten it? "When this is over we will go on the air sail," he said. "Remember Dion's air sail?" He waited for Eumelos' jerking head shake. "We will sail over the island and you can see all of Aztlan and Kallistae, the pyramid so small it looks like your plaything! Won't that be fun, Eumelos? Won't you enjoy that?" Again the boy jerked, the tremors seizing his body until Phoebus half laid on him just to still the motion. He pulled back, trying not to weep. His son was getting sicker. The fits were coming on faster, more frequently. Where was Niko? "You must get well, though, Eumelos. You must be healthy before we do that. Can you get well?"

Tears raced down the boy's tanned cheeks as he opened his mouth, trying to speak. The clicking of his throat and tongue terrified Phoebus, who lifted him up, setting him on his leg, trying to ease his breathing. Eumelos was limp, his body sagged and jerked, his mouth worked, but no sound issued forth.

"Niko is bringing a physic, son," Phoebus said. He was sure Niko would return with the elixir that had saved him. "Niko will be here soon, just wait for him. Just wait." He held the boy's frail body to his chest, rocking him back and forth. "Remember the potion Niko gave me? He is going to give it to you. You will be better, Eumelos. Never again will you get sick. You will be *athanati*." He smiled through his tears. Even if he had to shatter the foundations of Aztlan itself, Eumelos would rule next.

For his son, he could give his life.

Eumelos began to make gagging sounds, his clawed hands scratched at Phoebus, his eyes darted, terrified. When his face turned blue Phoebus shouted for help, for the Spiralmaster, trying to hold Eumelos' head up, to get air into him. The boy was thrashing and wheezing, fighting for breath, his body jerking, his eyes on Phoebus. *You promised,* they seemed to say. *You promised and you are foresworn.*

Serfs helped Phoebus hold Eumelos still, but he hadn't gotten a breath in moments, his eyes were glazing. "Nay! Nay!" Phoebus shouted, opening Eumelos' mouth, arching his throat. No sound, no air.

His son went limp, his fluttering heart stilled, his eyes saw a different horizon.

His journey was begun.

CHEFTU MET NESTOR IN THE HALLWAY, and together they ran for the Golden's chambers. The sound of weeping met them before they turned the corner, and Cheftu saw the doors open, the hallway filled with nymphs in blue.

The color of mourning.

Entering the room, he learned that Phoebus was already gone no one knew where. *Hreesos'* face had been ravaged beyond recognition, a dreadful sight to behold. Nestor crossed to the couch, and he and Cheftu exchanged glances. The child was dead.

"*Kalo taxidi,*" Nestor said, closing the boy's staring eyes. "Has he been bathed?"

"Nay, my master. *Hreesos* refused," the priest said. "He said that Eumelos would not die."

Cheftu looked at the still, twisted body. Another one; the sun was not yet at its zenith, and already five more had died. He felt an ache that permeated beyond body into spirit. There was no way to win, there was no way to save them. He was living with corpses; he was a corpse, just waiting for the time to lie down.

"Call Nekros," he told a serf.

"Chieftain Nekros began his journey this dawn," the serf replied. Again, Cheftu's gaze met Nestor's. They both looked away and began to arrange the body.

NIKO COULD NOT RECALL when the hardship had become pleasure, he couldn't think. But sometime, lost within Ileana's scent and taste, some buried part of him came forward. He was cruel, pounding into her; she begged for more. His reason had fled, the world had been reduced to the parameters of his sex. Sweat dripped from his forehead onto her breasts, her knees were locked tightly, he could feel the muscles of her calves on his neck.

The shout shook him; it didn't sound like Ileana, and he was silent in his task. Pain ripped through his back and he arched deeply as Ileana climaxed, her screams of pleasure mingling with his cries of pain. White fire burned through his body as he was wrenched around, sent spiraling into a table, then crashed against a wall.

Glass vials and noxious fluids crunched beneath him as Niko rose, swaying, his mind perceiving what his heart could not. Phoebus, his features wreathed with hatred, his hand gripped tightly around the same knife he had sworn on just weeks before.

Blood dripped from the knife, the same blood that even now was sliding over Niko's sweaty body.

"Betrayer!" Phoebus hissed.

Suddenly Niko realized Phoebus didn't understand. "Nay," he wheezed. "It was for the eli—" Phoebus' hands were around his throat, squeezing, his words flying like spittle on Niko's face.

"He died, just like this. Coughing, gasping, wheezing. I promised he would be *athanati*, and he died." Niko fought his dearest friend's stony fingers, his sinewy wrists. Niko's vision began to purple. "I trusted you with my son's life and you betrayed me. With a whore!" The grasp was tighter; Niko couldn't breathe, he couldn't see, he thought he heard popping—his own bones? "You killed my son, you apostate! You killed him!"

THE LAST WORDS WERE LOST on Niko, as was Phoebus' final blow. Niko was insensible, the stones of prophecy in his pocket, the elixir in his pouch.

"He was doing it for you," Ileana said. *Hreesos* turned on her, and she scrambled backward. She'd never seen Phoebus like this. She was a fool to have reminded him she was here.

"You *skeela*," he cried, then ran toward her. Ileana swung off the table, ducking behind it as Phoebus crashed into it. Weapon, she needed a weapon. He threw the table aside and she scurried on hands and knees to another, picking up a broken vial. He charged after her, treading on glass in his bare feet. She backed up, drawing him closer. His hands reached for her, and she swiped at him with the jagged edges of the glass.

Phoebus stumbled back, tripped over Niko's motionless leg, and fell, catching himself on his elbows. Ileana leapt at him, plunging the glass through his stomach with all her strength. His hands flexed in agony as he rose upward, a twisted imitation of a lover's surrender.

Turning on his side, he crawled after her. Ileana ran, fell, and ran again. His hand grabbed her ankle, and she tried to kick free. Blood covered everything, so slippery she couldn't get a grip. Groping for another weapon, she landed on the ground.

Phoebus had stopped moving. She tried to slide away, only to have him drag her over his body. Throwing her runner's muscles behind it, she waited until her knee was even with his chin, then rammed upward.

His howl surrounded her, and his grasp weakened enough for her to get away. Ileana ran to the door and closed it, breathing, listening for any sounds. The crash of more glass—he'd turned over another table—the thud of wood on wood . . . then silence.

She looked at herself. Naked, coated in blood and seed. Glancing at the door, she saw that her handprints were everywhere. On the other side were the bodies of *Hreesos* and Niko. *Okh* Kela, what had she done? She'd killed the Golden One? I had no choice, she told herself. He would have killed me.

The Council would not care; they wouldn't listen to her side. Her life would be forfeit: death or the Labyrinth. Hades, where Irmentis, Sibylla, and countless others awaited her. They would tear at her, kill her. Ileana swallowed, trying to calm herself.

If there were no bodies, no one would know what had become of *Hreesos* and Niko. Get rid of the bodies. She had to get rid of the bodies. Cautiously she opened the door, peering into the torchlit room. It was worse than she had thought.

Total silence, blood everywhere, broken glass and overturned tables littering the room. Could she ever clean up this mess? Maybe just leave, let whoever found them assume that Phoebus had attacked Niko and killed him? It was the truth; no one would know she'd ever been here. Her gaze went to the bloodstained door, where delicate crimson handprints made a stark pattern on the wood.

She stepped over *Hreesos'* body. A pool had formed beneath him, and she saw another piece of glass had pierced his throat. Not allowing for thought, Ileana ripped at his kilt, sopped it in blood, and painted over her handmarks on the floor, the table, and the door.

Hesitantly she walked back to Niko.

His body was not there.

Ileana took a breath to scream, but a metallic-tasting hand silenced her. "You killed Phoebus, whore."

She went numb, limp; then fear seized her and she fought. Niko hung on tightly, swearing as she kicked and struggled. When she finally tired, she opened her eyes. "I was defending you!"

"You were protecting yourself," he said in his hate-filled voice. "You will die for killing him."

"He wanted to kill you!" she said, his arm around her waist as he walked her backward.

"It was his right. He didn't understand. Every thrust of my body was a betrayal. I deserved to die." Niko turned to look at Phoebus, his grasp suddenly looser. Ileana reached out and grabbed a curved shard of glass. She brought it back, in between her waist and arm, and plunged it into his belly.

He dropped to his knees, his hands flying to his wound. Ileana pulled free and grabbed a spare torch in a metal cone leaned against the wall. Coming from his side, out of the reach of his grasping arms, Ileana swung it at his head.

He collapsed like a drunk, finally still.

She could see nothing except shades of red. There was too much blood now, she had to get rid of him. He'd not even bothered to undress fully, just entered her as though she were a Coil Dancer! At the time it had been arousing, but now it infuriated her.

A slight sewage stink wafted through this lower level of the palace, and Ileana's stomach clenched. Niko was not dead; his blood was still warm. He had been a powerful mage, a perfect lover. She didn't need to kill him, just get rid of him. She walked down the hallway. The stench grew worse; some older latrines were here.

Running back to her victim, Ileana approached carefully, wary of Niko attacking again. She tried to pull him, but he was too heavy, too slippery to get a good grasp. She crossed to the back of Spiralmaster's lab, looking around frantically. There! Beneath a pile of dried skins was a wooden cart. After tugging it free, Ileana pulled it to the doorway, where Niko was yet motionless.

Grasping his body under his arms, she pulled upward, backing onto the low cart. Half of his body dragged, but she could still maneuver the cart forward. A streak of blood pointed like an arrow to the latrine, and she realized with a grimace she would probably have to clean it.

Choking at the stench, she pulled off the wooden seating and a breeze rushed up, stirring her hair and making her gag with the smell. The opening was wide enough for him, but high off the ground. How would she lift him so far? Carefully she untied the sash, then

Ileana picked up his legs and dangled them in the hole that fell straight into the channel beneath the island.

She pulled and yanked his heavy body upward onto the latrine seat. He wasn't going! Once she had tied his sash tight around his chest and under his arms, Ileana climbed on the stone support, straddling the hole. Standing on the ledge, she had to duck because of the torch burning above. His legs were down the aperture, his torso falling backward—all she need do was move him forward and nature's force would tug him down.

Pulling on the sash, she leaned his body forward, still not enough. Ileana crouched, grasping him around the waist, scooting him.

Niko's hands tangled in her hair as he laughed, a rasping, wicked cackle. "You go with me, Ileana. I will finally prove my devotion to Phoebus."

In the eyeblink she had, Ileana kicked his back, hitting the shallow knife wound Phoebus had made. Niko's scream deafened her, and she stepped back, leaping from the stone to the ground. He teetered a moment, then slid downward with a grunt.

Shaking, Ileana looked inside the latrine hole. Fingers clenched the side, elegant, blood-caked fingers. Then a hand appeared and she heard him groaning to pull himself up. The same hand that had held her breasts, cupped her sex, now sought to kill her.

She grabbed the torch from above and brought it down on his hands. His scream echoed in the shaft, but he didn't let go. His purple eyes were black with hatred as he pulled himself higher, his white blond hair swirling over his shoulders. "You *skeela*," he hissed.

Ileana stretched out the torch, touching the locks of his moonlight-colored hair, igniting the young body that had served her. "My passion has set you afire," she whispered as the flame took hold. Niko swatted as his eyebrows caught fire, losing his grip.

His agonized scream stayed in the air long after his burning body fell.

The scent of his burned flesh stayed in the air even longer.

PLASTER WAS RAINING DOWN ON CHLOE'S HEAD, chalk rising from her running feet. Hacking and coughing, she ran down a corridor that seemed alive. Aztlan must be having another earthquake! She wasn't looking and tripped, her shriek bouncing around her as she slid down a well, Ping-Ponging from wall to wall, and landing in a heap on the ground. The still ground.

Thank God.

Rising, checking that all parts moved, Chloe looked up. For the first time she could see. This must be the very bottom, she thought. Hopefully she was far away from Irmentis. Chloe couldn't even voice what she thought of the huntress. The ground shook again, but it was a faint tremor, and Chloe ignored it. She must be on the outside rim of the Labyrinth. The only way she'd ever followed mazes was from the center out. From the outside in, she always got confused.

She could see up the chalk-white passageways that opened suddenly and spat the unfortunates down here. She looked around, wondering what she could set afire if she found tinder. Cammy always said that Twinkies made great torches. Chloe had told that one to the guys in her outfit, and once they'd stopped laughing and set a few afire, they'd taken her words a bit more seriously.

Her stomach growled, and Chloe realized if she had Twinkies, it would be a hard choice between lighting them and eating them.

Since Aztlan was running short on Twinkies, how could she get light? How would she know which way she'd come?

A memory of hunting in East Texas hit Chloe powerfully. Her grandmother Mimi's second husband (she'd lost the first one when she was very young) was a strapping oilman named Jack. He'd adored Mimi, spoiled her children like his own. Aside from Mimi, his other passion was hunting. Chloe, as she had gotten older, had never understood how such a gentle man could be so bloodthirsty. Jack had hunted and fished all over the world: safaris in Africa, expeditions to

Canada and Australia, even China. One day he'd taken his little granddaughter out on his ranch to share the finer points of how man outwitted beast.

He'd probably get on really well with Irmentis.

Chloe had liked getting to see the animals. Up close, not like a zoo. But pencil on paper had made too much noise for a deer's sensitive ear, so she'd had to sit motionless and quiet. It had been torture for a seven-year-old, until she'd realized that if she paid a lot of attention, she could draw them from memory later.

So after Jack had taught her how to find animals at their watering holes, he'd showed her how to track. Scat told the tale.

It was a disgusting option, Chloe thought. But it would answer both questions: one, she would know where she'd gone, and two, if she could light it, it would burn.

My Mimi is rolling in her grave, Chloe thought, blushing despite it all.

Irmentis would also be able to find her, but then again, she'd had no difficulty finding Chloe before, so leaving a more visible trail would hardly matter. *Was she starting to chew on my fingers when . . .* Chloe shuddered and walked to the first spot she needed to mark.

For the first time in her life, Chloe wished she were male. She could use the aim. If she could point, this would be easy. No wonder females never marked territory!

Walking from one end of the tunnel to the other, she marked and marked. *I feel like a tom in heat!* Immediately it was useful, since she backtracked on herself twice. It was amazing how the acrid scent was instantly identifiable, especially in this darkness. *Okh, what levels have I sunk to?*

Survival of the fittest was a grim, gross thing.

The next question was, how to get up to the other layers of the maze?

The earthquake threw her across the room, showering chalk and rock on her body, silencing her questions.

AZTLAN'S LAND BRIDGE ALWAYS PROVOKED QUESTIONS: How was it created? How could it stay? The answers were buried within the earth's history. The two islands had been one, and as the lagoon shaped, it eroded the connecting land to such a degree that a suspension-style bridge was formed.

Today, far beneath the earth, the Aegean microplate subducted at an angle to the African plate. For a few moments the whole Aegean plate twisted on a bias, tearing the earth and sending panicky fissures throughout the landmass from which these islands rose.

On Aztlan and Kallistae, the stable legs of the land bridge shifted, and a massive crack appeared on a diagonal from northwest to southeast. The two man-made footbridges fell first, casting the few hardy souls who were crossing them into the gorge between the islands.

Some citizens were crossing the land bridge to the island of Aztlan, hoping to wait in the pyramid, certain that Apis would protect them from his wrath.

A mother, her son's tiny hand in hers, had broken into a run when she felt the quake hit the land bridge. Hundreds of years of erosion had taken their toll, and the bridge began crumbling. People collided—those who saw the crack widen and the others radiating out from it, and those who saw the pyramid and imagined safety there.

Screams, shouts, and cries were lost under the mighty roar of Apis, and the earth moved as though trying to throw them all off. The mother hung tightly to the hand of her son as the ground gave way a step ahead of her. With a grace and determination she'd never known she possessed, she jumped forward.

The bridge shattered, huge pieces of rock and earth falling to the crashing waters below, people like ants struggling to stay on the horizontal, even when it joined the iridescent waters of the sea.

Those on the mountain watched in horror, considering themselves safe, as the bridge that had linked the two islands fell into the now bottomless depths of Therio Sea. A sense of isolation settled on them as they watched their countrymen die at the hand of Apis Earthshaker.

The mother had been fortunate; one hand grasped roots, her legs dangled over the edge. Her child was wheezing with fear, swung between heaven and earth, safe only in his mother's slippery grasp. With a strength and ferocity that only maternity gives, she heaved her right arm up, screaming at her child to grab hold with one hand and climb over her. He was a dumpling of a three-year-old, fussy most times, with pudgy cheeks and plaintive brown eyes. His feet found purchase, and she encouraged him to walk up, high, keep walking, and she would catch up. "Don't stop walking!"

Dirt dried her tears, muffled her screams, as she felt herself slide and felt his little hand let go of hers. He called for her, and she stifled her cry as another length of root was pulled from the ground. With both hands now she tried to pull herself up, but she was too weak, too heavy.

"Go on, Akilez," she ordered her son. "Walk on! *Manoula* loves you." Pain ripped through her arms and she tried to kick upward, to pull herself higher, but her corselet was too tight and her skirts too cumbersome.

Her son was crying as she slid another length of root. The waves were closer now, a vicious mouth to chew and swallow her. Not my baby! she thought. He was her birthchild, not yet gone to the Clan of the Wave that would one day claim him. Pulling her face from the earth, she began to sing, shouting up to him, encouraging him to sing too as he walked toward the big gold building.

The pain eased as she heard his voice grow stronger. "Go on now," she cried. The tremble began, she felt it in the plant she held, in the portion of Aztlan that would be her *tholos*. "Run go sing for the priests!" she screamed. "Run!"

His voice was submerged in the final dance of death, beneath the roar of the waves, the crush of rock, and her own screams as she fell into the sea.

CHAPTER 18

Someone was banging on Chloe's head. When she finally came to, she had only a moment to shield herself and roll out of the way of the falling rock. Up, she had to get up. On instinct, she crawled forward and entered the chute that led upward, to what she hoped was the entrance. Bracing her arms and legs so that she fit like a chimney sweep, Chloe began to inch her way up.

The aftershocks sent her sliding down several times, but she didn't think, didn't reason, just kept heading up. About halfway, from what she could tell, she found a landing. The earthquake had stopped and she marked her spot, then crawled down the passageway. Left turns repeated, she was in a Greek key. The passageways were getting shorter and shorter! She should be at the center any mi—

The shaft swallowed her astonished cry, and the words beat around her as she fell through the air. "Oh shit," Chloe said before the breath was knocked out of her.

Landing was painful, bruising all her cuts and cutting all her bruises. I should get hazard pay for this, she thought, forcing herself up on badly rubbed hands and knees. Two things were instantly noticeable.

One, fresh, albeit stinky, air.

Two, the sound of waves.

Dizzy with adrenaline, Chloe ran toward the sound of the water, the passageway twisting and turning, not like a maze, but like a mountain pass. As she rounded a corner, air blew at her, blinding her with her hair and freezing the cold sweat on her body. The brightness made her recoil, even though it was only half-light. Chloe swallowed a sob when she realized she was free of the Labyrinth.

She was in a dark cave, the ceiling obscured by shadow, the sound of water splashing over wood more exquisite than any symphony. Live water! Wood! Probably boats! And there, in the distance, was a sliver of sky. When her eyes adjusted to the faint light she saw the boats were nearly submerged. There were no ships, just small rowboats. Chloe realized she was beneath Aztlan island.

She stepped to the least damaged of the vessels and searched for a bottle, giggling with relief when she found a jug of wine. She smashed the top off, took a swig, dumped it, and began to bail.

CHEFTU RUBBED HIS EYES and surveyed his makeshift hospital. Bodies, some dead, some wounded, lay with not a hand span between them, throughout the feasting hall. These had escaped to Aztlan at very great cost. The land bridge was gone, the corpses washed away by the water, the cracks on both islands widening with every decan.

In another room lay those who were dying and dead from the plague. The same illness that had taken decades to manifest itself was now killing people in a matter of days.

Time was running out, yet Cheftu needed to help these people and *mon Dieu*, find Chloe! He heard someone enter the room and turned, squinting through the darkness. They were using only torches, for oil lamps were too dangerous during an earthquake due to fire.

"The Council is calling a meeting, Cheftu," Dion said.

"I have not the time, Dion."

"Phoebus is still missing, as is Niko. Ileana has called the meeting."

Cheftu looked up from sponging a fever victim's forehead. "She is not on the Council, how can she do this?"

Dion sighed. "Since Phoebus is missing, she is acting in his stead. Nestor needs to be sworn in as Rising Golden."

Cheftu stood up. "When will you realize there is no need for another Rising Golden? The only thing rising is the water level! This is a ruined land, Dion. The Council needs to help the others flee! Ritual will not save us now!"

"It is all we can offer. The pyramid is sealed, messages to Minos return unanswered."

"We have no access to food?"

"Some, not much. The stores in the palace will last a while."

Cheftu sighed, moving to the next patient, a man with a broken arm and foot. The little boy he'd found on the bridge had finally stopped singing, and Cheftu touched them both. No fever, thank God. "Do I dare ask how long 'a while' is?"

Dion brushed against his back. "You do not, my master. Tell me, how can I help?"

Grateful beyond words, Cheftu set the dark chieftain to work and walked back into the room with the dead and the dying.

THIS IS WHAT THEY MEAN BY LEARNING PATIENCE, Chloe thought. It had taken a thousand years of bailing, then digging around for a plank, a board, something to use as an oar, then plopping herself into the driver's seat and rowing for the mouth of the cave. Then she realized she was on the wrong side of the island and had rowed back into the cave, hoping to find another way out. Finally, she was approaching the steps to Aztlan.

Or was she?

New earth was brightly colored against the older, and Chloe felt her heart pounding in her throat. The earthquakes, oh my God. She rounded the bend and saw the destruction of the land bridge, now just two nubs jutting out from opposite sides. Tears streamed down her face unnoticed. She saw that the zigzag pathway was also gone. How would she climb back up?

Her hands were bleeding with blisters on top of cuts, and she fought not to barf as the water bobbed her around. She turned back to the cave. Only by chance did she see the small cut in the rock and steer toward it.

Miraculously, she found a small landing with stairs leading up. She had no idea where they led, but she would be closer to the palace, and that was where she needed to be. *Cheftu, we gotta get out of this place. We tried to help, we tried to warn, now we just need to lead the way out of here.*

"YOU ARE EXHAUSTED," DION SAID. They'd been working side by side for decans, and Cheftu knew he was swaying on his feet. "My apartments are just a hallway away. You can get some rest. Then and only then will you be able to help these people, Cheftu." Dion's arm was guiding, and Cheftu stumbled. The heavens knew he was tired, worried, and his mind felt hazy. Just a little sleep, a little food; that was what he needed. Dion had been telling him this for decans, and as a physician he knew it was true. He would be of more use when he was refreshed.

Leaving Atenis in charge, he followed Dion into the dark hallway, down it, and into the chieftain's spacious apartments. Like a child, he ate and drank, following Dion's bidding. The chieftain talked constantly, his words lost to Cheftu. His voice sounded as if it came from a great distance.

Cheftu lay back on the couch. It was labor to lift his aching leg. His eyes were closing, even as he hovered around sleep.

"You do not know for how long I have wanted you here."

Some part of Cheftu's mind registered that Dion was next to him. Cheftu wanted to move away, but it was such an effort.

"A man of intelligence, of wit and style. *Eee*, Cheftu, let us away from this island. We can start anew! Come with me!"

"No . . . boats."

"The air sail, Cheftu. We can get to Prostatevo, then take one of the ships from the new harbor there." He touched the streaks of gray at Cheftu's temples. "We can leave this land. We can be together. I see how you avoid women; we are made for each other! We can take the elixir and remain eternally young. Eternally healthy." Cheftu was motionless, feeling Dion's fingers touch the lines beside his eyes and the brackets carved around his mouth. His touch was intimate.

Dion's voice grew more intense. "Imagine never aging, Cheftu. Imagine a dozen—nay, a thousand lifetimes to learn and study, to explore, to know!" Cheftu opened his eyes. Dion lay beside him, his face close, his dark eyes wide. The emotion in them was eerily familiar. "Imagine a thousand lifetimes to love."

He covered Cheftu's mouth with his own.

CHLOE OPENED THE DOOR and stepped into the huge apartment. Apparently she had discovered someone's secret passageway. Her eyes adjusted slowly. As though it were a stage, a covered couch was centered in the room, lit by torches so that the two figures on it were clear.

Two heads of dark, flowing hair.

Two bodies, plastered together. A hand hung off the bed, the ring on it twinkling like a laughing demon's eye. Thoth, god of healing. The fingers wearing it were long, strong, and sensual, two scarred forever.

The bottom fell out of Chloe's world.

My heart aches for that which it cannot have and loves what it cannot love.

Cheftu's words echoed in her brain, and Chloe crumbled against the wall, her hand over her mouth.

Cheftu and Dion?

Cheftu was gay?

Chloe couldn't look away. She saw the shadow of the cleft of Dion's buttocks and wondered if Cheftu were also naked. Dion's hair shielded her view of Cheftu's face, and she was unspeakably glad. To see passion in his golden eyes for someone else—for a man!—was not something she could endure.

Stumbling backward, she ran to the spiral of the staircase. This explained why he hadn't been searching for her. Chloe fled down the steps, her hand over her mouth, seeking a way out, darkness—solitude. She fell to her knees, sobbing, blindly groping the wall.

Cheftu was gay? Think about it, she chided herself, striving for calm. It wasn't possible. She'd been around gay men most of her career. Surely she would have known, have recognized? *But you saw that kiss with your own eyes; they were in bed together. It's not like Cheftu was tied down and being forced.*

She curled into a ball, the vision of two beautiful men embracing inscribed on her brain. Down was becoming up, black turning to white. It couldn't be true. It couldn't!

Had Cheftu grown bored with her? Why didn't he say he was confused? Chloe thought. Why didn't he tell me what he felt? Had the opportunity to try something different, possibly more erotic, been undeniable?

He had been angry with her, he'd been unmoved by her, unwilling to touch her, he'd been silent, withdrawn. Oh God!

A dizziness enveloped her, the minimalist chords of a forgotten violin concerto filled her ears. She saw her life with Cheftu. Slowly she rethought every word, every gesture. *He'd never truly wanted her.* He had hated her in the beginning. He thought initially in Egypt that she was a whore, and when she had been with him, she'd acted like one on several occasions. Teasing him.

The violins rose.

He'd felt responsibility for her because she'd also been a time traveler. They had a great deal in common; neither of them actually belonged in ancient Egypt.

The slightly mutating repetition of violins swelled in her head.

He'd married her only to save her life.

The cellos joined.

He was an honorable man. He'd vowed to love her and protect her, and he had. But he hadn't *wanted* to!

The deep, resonating mourning of strings in her head drove her hands into her hair. She must be crazy! This was *Cheftu!* She thought of the ring he'd given her, the ring with topazes the color of his eyes, a woven band of gold and silver. "I love and I hope," he had cried in French as she was lifted from Hatshepsut's time.

But there was love between a man and woman that was not sexual. Or personal. You could love and not *be* in love: what else was friendship?

He'd lied to her. He'd lied in their bed, and he'd lied in her body!

Chloe rose on unsteady legs. She had to get out of here. She couldn't bear to be so close to him. But could she be wrong? Was Cheftu still in there with Dion? Had he walked out in a rage? Had they? Her imagination failed her. It had been at least an hour.

She crept back up the staircase; the sounds were unmistakable.

The violins screamed in pain.

"SPIRALMASTER! WAKE UP, WAKE UP!"

Cheftu rolled over, instantly awake, on guard. "Who is it?" he called.

Stunned silence. "Nestor, why?"

Throwing on a kilt as he limped to the door, Cheftu rubbed his face. Surely last night was but a fevered dream. He touched his mouth and swallowed. The knuckles of his hand were split; no dream. *Okh!* He threw open the door.

"The mountain has been coughing smoke all morning," Nestor said.

"Why did you not wake me earlier?"

Nestor shrugged helplessly. "What can you do?"

The two men ran up the stairs to the main chamber of the second floor, then down the long portico. Cheftu pulled up short when he saw Dion. His jaw was purpling, his gaze reproachful. With a stiff bow in Dion's direction, Cheftu looked out at the mountain. Where was Chloe? She hadn't contacted him.

He noted that Niko and Phoebus were still missing. Perhaps Niko was comforting Phoebus on the loss of his son? He shivered at the new interpretations "comfort" brought. Images from the past twelve decans filtered through his mind.

Mount Apollo's sides were dusty with ash. The two man-made and the one gods'-made bridges were gone. The ships were dashed into kindling, and the waters were too rough, too deep, to swim.

An Etesian wind began to blow from the northwest. Faint tremors shook the earth, so commonplace they were ignored. The group watched as various puffs of black were released into the air. Cheftu felt panicky. Where was Chloe? He'd checked on his patients—twelve more fatalities—and rejoined the group on the portico. Many more had arrived: serfs, citizens, parents and children, priests and priestesses, all the human remnants of Aztlan.

They saw the mountain move before they heard it roar. The top did not blow off; instead the side slid away. He watched a huge section of mountain glide down the left-hand side of the slope, shattering into pieces of rock and earth as it moved. The boom that had taken seconds to rise into the atmosphere dropped back to earth, felling them all.

Cheftu lifted his head as a cloud of red and black rose, growing exponentially larger even as he watched. It blew westward, revealing ripples of fiery blood trickling from the inside of the mountain, molten rivers rushing across the island. Cheftu wiped his mouth, his blood was already a strange concrete having mixed with the hot ash.

Before anyone could speak, the clansmen of Daphne were dead. The mountain they had trusted to protect them had destroyed them. Their god had cannibalized his people. Waves rushed up the sides of the island, rocking the harbor as the earth heaved and tore, a painful, gory birthing. A cloud of stinging, biting ash rained down, dusting the whole of the island. Multicolored lightning flashed in the growing blackness, and Cheftu felt his hair crackle with the power of the air.

Green life became red death as the mountain vomited. Deep within, the emptying chambers collapsed in on themselves. Magma pulled from the adjoining Mount Stronghyle had weakened both islands' infrastructure. The empire's showplaces began to sink.

Around the Aegean, clansmen watched, their eyes drawn toward the gray column of smoke that reached to the heavens. From the shores of far-off Hydroussa they sent birds, questioning the fate of the clans. In Delos they wept, for they knew too well what would survive.

Nothing.

On Folegandros and Nios the religious orders prayed and cried, realizing that the anger of the earth could not be assuaged. When Mount Gaia began to smoke the priestesses did not wait. They piled into boats, sailing north, a band of strong, self-sufficient women. They would land on some northeastern shore, where their skill with nets would become a skill with spears and their earth goddess would transform from a nurturer into a conqueror.

In far-off Egypt, Imhotep wept as Ipiankhu stared toward the far horizon. They had sought only to protect Egypt; they'd never desired the annihilation of their cousins. Had the room that was now so far under construction been for naught? Ipiankhu looked at him, as though he discerned his thoughts. "We are to be faithful and trust."

Imhotep nodded and muttered through his rotting teeth, "May we live forever."

In Knossos, Daedelus watched, tears streaming down his face. The palaces were ravaged, razed from oil fires. Daedelus instructed the people to secure their boats and run inland to the mountains. They were blessed to have no Nostrils of the Bull.

Would the Clan Olimpi escape Aztlan? he wondered.

In the rush from the villages and towns to the mountains, a young Caphtori girl named Psychro got separated from her mother. She found herself in a wide cave littered with empty votives. Through her tears she heard a sweet voice that comforted, consoled, and convinced her to open herself.

When Psychro awoke, she carried with her the wisdom and experience of a clan chieftain. Though she was but a child, a wandering spirit had stepped into her body. She stayed in the cave for the rest of her days. Her ability to read omens and foretell the future became known far and wide. The legend of Psychro's Cave grew. On the eve of her death, the spirit moved into a younger woman, who in her turn became Psychro.

In the end, nothing save the crescent-shaped land would remain. The island in the bay would sink, then rise as magma flowed again into its subterranean passages. It would grow tall and verdant, seducing the descendants of those who had fled. Like sheep to the slaughter they would return to its heights, settle their country, and in less than four centuries flee one last time.

Only their legend and artwork would survive. Their destruction would play a role in world history. Days of blackness, a cloud of fire, and rivers of blood delivered by the eruption would serve to convince a leader on a far-off shore to "let my people go."

From the ashes of the first great civilization would be born an everlasting race.

It had been a bright day for humankind, then night fell. A long, pervasive night, which lived on in history and myth forever. A lesson to those who sought to be gods.

CHAPTER 19

CHLOE WOKE UP, CRUMPLED IN A HEAP. Walking carefully, as though sudden movement might shatter her, she picked her way down to the hidden cove. Dion's cove, obviously. Earthquakes rained bits of stairway on her, but it didn't matter. None of it.

Was she being presumptuous?

She had to know; she had to hear it from his lips. Cheftu had assumed the worst when he'd seen her with Dion. Perhaps she had done the same? Nothing sounded like sex except sex, Chloe thought, choked on tears. She stepped onto the rocky landing. Her boat was bobbing wildly, and she dragged it farther on the shore. Looking outside, she saw it was night. Still?

The air was filled with strange noises and the smell of fire. She'd taken two steps when she saw movement at the water's edge. Within moments she was dragging a man out, flipping him over and pounding on his back. Her hands came away pink with blood, but he coughed, vomited, and inhaled deeply. With feeble gestures he tried to move farther up the rocks. Chloe grabbed his hand to help him and barely kept from shrieking as she saw the creature she'd rescued.

In the torchlight it was hard to discern his features, but she knew of only one albino on the island. "Niko?"

He shook his head, and she pounded his back more, wincing when she saw the burns that covered his upper body. He needed medical attention. He needed Cheftu. Chloe pressed her lips together—could she stand to see her husband?

Did she really plan to *not* see him?

More of the odd noises . . . bringing to her mind the national anthem "and bombs bursting in air." Who would have firecrackers or arms in Aztlan? Suddenly she understood and grabbed Niko's arm, dragging him into the boat. He was burned, but he could still move. She gave another oar to him. "It will take both of us," she said, and they began rowing out of the tiny cove, into the waters of Theros sea.

They were both coughing in moments, and Chloe ripped Niko's sash in half, despite his protests, tying a half over each of their faces. It was still dark; the only light was the reflected lava as it dripped over the edge of the cliff. Aztlan itself looked unharmed. The waters were strangely quiet, placid, the shorelines seemed wide, speckled with darker spots that Chloe supposed were beached aquatic life.

As they rowed, she recalled her disaster training. She'd heard volcanoes discussed, but not with any real conviction. There were only a few active cones in the Pacific Northwest, about as far away from Texas as one could get. Still, she remembered a couple of things: often those closest didn't hear them erupt; poisonous gas was a silent killer; water was usually contaminated; there were no rules. Most chilling was that eruptions could set off a series of disasters.

Often the sea pulled back, then came rushing in with tidal waves called tsunami.

Mount Apollo had erupted, judging from the lava slithering toward shore. "Turn around!" she shouted, rowing madly. Niko didn't hear her, so Chloe kicked him, screamed again on the rising wind, and rowed for all she was worth. The waters were still because the tsunami was gaining strength.

The large cavern, would they be safe there? Her arms were numb, and she felt no pain, only the sensation of having realized too late. Then, as they heard the roar of the returning waters, she saw the entrance, maybe ten feet away. "Jump!" she cried to Niko, then took a flying leap over him and dove deep, fighting her way forward. She felt a shape in the water beside her and broke the surface. Inside!

Just then a sweep of current dragged at her feet and she felt a hand around her wrist, pulling her to the dock. What was left of the dock. Shaking, trembling, they crawled out of the water, clinging to the splintered wood as they saw the white-capped waves rising and crashing outside. This was where she had come out of the Labyrinth.

"My gratitude," Chloe said once she caught her breath.

Niko waved a burned hand before it fell beside him. Chloe crawled over; he was unconscious. After dragging him up as high as the shore went, she left him. Holding a torch she'd taken from its sconce, she walked the length of the harbor, looking for a way up. The only opening she could find was one leading to the Labyrinth. Raising her light, she saw that a ladder was carved into the side of the chute.

Eee, shit. Gripping the torch between her teeth, Chloe grabbed the lowest rung and began to climb. Sweating, swearing, and drooling from the torch, she finally climbed out onto the landing. The pungent stink of her own refuse welcomed her, and Chloe realized her life sucked when she looked forward to smelling her scat. Dear God, this was disgusting.

However, when lit, it did burn! Triumphant, regardless of the grossness scale, Chloe tried to backtrack. This level was a Greek key, the chute was in the center. She found herself on the outside again, another noticeable pile for marking, which she lit. Then, because she had the torch, she could see the ladder and let herself down the outside chute. Once on ground level she walked until she hit the other side, another chute. Holding her torch high, she thought she saw it turn. Another Greek key?

Wincing at the blisters on her palms, she climbed up. On her right she passed two landings. One whiff of the first and she knew she'd been there, done that. The second was laid out the same way. After peering down the center chute again, she found her way out and back up the outside chute. The torch was getting low, burning dangerously close to her hair and face, so Chloe put the end in her mouth, climbing faster.

This chute rose high, zillions of steps, but she'd left the other layers behind. The ladder ended, and she saw a ledge above her. Sweaty hands shaking, she moved one, then the other, to the ledge. With a groaning heave and much scrambling for footing, she pulled herself over as the torch fell down into the darkness.

Resting her head against the stone, Chloe fought for breath, to stop shaking, to calm down. Once she felt a little less like screaming and crying, she raised her head. To her right was a doorway. Cold with sweat, she stepped through it and turned back.

She'd escaped Hades.

She was in the palace!

Chloe took off at a run, taking the first set of steps in twos and threes. Niko needed help, she needed answers, and they all needed to get the hell out!

EVERYTHING WAS BURNING, Cheftu could feel nothing except the heat, smell nothing over the acrid stink of the fuel. Human bodies. Just as Mount Apollo had incinerated thousands hiding on its hillsides, so Cheftu had personally overseen the burning of the corpses. So many, all stricken down by the plague.

Bathing them, as Aztlantu custom declared, was a massive production lacking elegance. Serfs held the bodies, drooling and jerking but still alive, by shoulders and ankles, dunked them in the lustral bath, and laid them down in almost endless lines. Then, when they died, they were taken out and set on the earth as macabre kindling.

I will soon be among them, he thought with some effort. His mind grew increasingly confused. The only reason he could imagine he'd lived this long was that he'd not eaten the bull . . . or the man. Absently he fingered the pink scar on his shoulder. The bull must have bitten him, some of the illness coming through with its saliva.

He stared across the sea. Patches of flame danced next to rivers of fire. It was beautiful in a hellish way. Cheftu looked away as he arranged yet another body in the position of death. Who would do this for him? Nestor? Dion? Chloe?

Scampering down the falling, sliding hillsides of Aztlan, the truly desperate were trying to flee, to swim if they could. Frantically they made for Prostatevo, now a place for refuge, far from the fire-foaming mountain and the cruel sea. Cheftu turned back to another patient, checked for breath, did not even pause when he didn't feel it, then crossed her arms, too.

Dion came running in. "Niko! He's been found! Come quickly!"

Cheftu didn't even turn. "By whom? Where?"

"Sibylla," Dion said.

Cheftu turned and stumbled back, glimpsing his wife in the door-way. She never ceased to steal his breath; he never stopped wanting to give it to her. She was battered, filthy, yet she felt so good against him, in his arms. He held her until he was trembling.

Dion left to retrieve Niko. Cheftu felt him go, then tilted Chloe's face to his, seizing her mouth, groaning against her lips as he felt his blood move, his heart sing, once more.

Her response was as desperate, as fevered, and Cheftu felt tears slide down his cheeks. She was here! She was his! He broke away from her mouth and held her tight, pressing his cheek against her head. Her hand gripped him, and Cheftu stiffened.

"I guess this means you are bi?" she asked in English.

"Bi?"

"Not gay?"

"To see you *chérie,* to touch you, fills me with great joy and gaiety."

She chuckled, confused. "I can see we are hitting one of those time-comprehension boundaries," she said, searching his face.

Cheftu kissed her again, reveling in the relaxation of her body against his. For moments he forgot he was also ill, that the mountain was on fire and the island sinking. For a short moment he forgot his hopelessness, for when Chloe was with him, he had nothing but hope. Hope they would be together always; hope that they would grow old in each other's arms; hope that he would see their flesh mingled in a child. Children.

He felt another quake.

"*Eee,* Cheftu, the earth moved," she said in his ear, her tongue trac-ing the outer whorls. His hands were on her breasts, his hips moving against her. He needed her, now, here. Before he could voice his need, they were knocked flat.

Silence.

"A sonic boom?" Chloe asked in the darkness. Her voice was tremulous. Cheftu took her hand, and they ran out the door, up the stairs to the portico.

Where once had been the mountaintop, now there was only black smoke. Chloe was transfixed. "It's stunning," she whispered. "Red and black: look at the patterns and swirls."

As Chloe and Cheftu watched, the pyroclastic cloud rolled down the mountainside like a ball, bouncing and turning, reducing everything it touched to cinder yet leaving some areas unmarred, except for a hot breeze. Temperatures of 750 degrees reduced all other living things into rolling puffs of atmosphere, vaporized even before the citizens heard the eruption. All the dwellers of Kallistae saw were crackles of heat. All they felt was pressurized air. Vineyards and flowers were laid flat, ash even before they touched the ground, bowing in obeisance to the fury of the earth. Buildings of red, black, and white stones were crushed by the hoof of Apis.

As Chloe and Cheftu watched, two hundred million cubic feet of rock spewed from the mountain. The gargantuan cloud of red and black rose, growing exponentially larger with every breath. It rushed like water down the slope. The cloud grew like a wide-topped pine, branches of scorching death reaching out to encompass the entire horizon.

To encompass them.

Cheftu pulled Chloe, running down the stairs, shoving and pushing through screaming, panicked people, never losing his grip on her hand. They reached the underground level, and Cheftu kicked open a door. A storage room.

For once, being in the storerooms was where he wanted to be.

A thunderous clap, a noise so pervasive that he felt his blood vessels expand, knocked Cheftu flat. When he could see again, he noticed blood dripping from Chloe's chin.

Cheftu ripped off his kilt, tearing it in two. He urinated on both pieces and wrapped a wet piece around Chloe's face. She tried to back away, but Cheftu forced her face in it, barely finishing tying the other piece over his mouth before they were knocked down again.

Screams were cut short, and there was no sound except the roar of destruction. He lay across her, his breath shallow through the fabric. His body shielded hers, one arm protecting their heads, the other covering his groin. His bare backside was pelted with falling stone. A jar exploded, and he screamed as boiling olive oil rained down on his head and back.

PART V

CHAPTER 20

I T WAS SILENT, but Chloe knew she wasn't dead. She hurt too much. The cloth over her face was dry. She pulled it off and threw it away, watching in horror as it burst into flame midair. She tried to swallow but couldn't. Panicked, she touched her face, only to find that her hands were blistered, scorched.

Cheftu!

He lay facedown beside her, his body half shielding hers. His back was a mass of swelling blisters, and one side of his head was now bald. Chloe touched him. He didn't move.

Crawling to her knees, which seemed unhurt, as did the rest of her front, she tried to turn him over. Dead weight. *No! No!* she screamed, though the words didn't come out. She fumbled at his neck for a pulse—nothing.

Be calm, she told herself. Check again! His hands were beneath him, and she couldn't pull them free. She grabbed around him, feeling for the other side of his throat. Something moved beneath his skin, and Chloe held her breath. It moved again. He was alive!

He wouldn't be for long. She rose slowly, taking stock of her own body. Nothing broken, burns on her back, but her face and lungs had been protected. She looked down at Cheftu—he'd protected her. Her neck was scorched and she felt her exposed, burned scalp. What remained of her luxurious hair snapped like broomstraws.

The room was lighter, and Chloe realized the two floors above them were missing. Sheared off. Where had they gone? She walked to the doorway and almost stepped into a puddle of still simmering olive oil. She hobbled into the corridor.

The cloud had sliced off the two stories of the wing they were in and had deposited the remains twelve feet away.

Warm snow was falling, covering the crushed buildings. Everything was gray. Without thought Chloe pulled off her apron, her only remaining clothing, and covered her face to breathe.

Squinting through the falling ash, she began to make her way through the remains of the Scholomance. Nothing stirred. All she could see was wreckage. A low moan caught her attention, and she watched helpless as a man stumbled over ruins, trails of fire following him like an unholy wake. He fell down, and Chloe smelled his burning flesh.

Chloe walked to the steps and found herself in a haphazard balcony. Bodies were laid in straight lines—a signpost for the direction the cloud had come. One body was moving, and Chloe stepped closer. Before her eyes his chest expanded, as though being pumped with air. His middle erupted, and Chloe saw the snaking form of his entrails before she ran away, gagging.

Bile burned in her throat, irrigating her scorched esophagus. Dear God, was she the only one alive?

The building was flat from here to the sea. The Scholomance was a mausoleum, the botanical gardens were cooked spinach. Chloe turned back in despair, then squealed.

Standing solid, pristine clean and bright beneath the fall of ash, was the residential wing of the palace! It was postcard perfect and cut away from the Scholomance as though someone had taken a cross section. She took off at a run, stumbling occasionally but remaining upright. Her apron fell from her face, and she was blinded by ash but fueled by hope. She felt the velvet of grass beneath her feet and dropped.

Voices cried around her. Her mind swam before she recognized one. "Where is Cheftu?"

She opened her eyes. Dion, looking perfectly normal save the gray in his hair, knelt beside her, Atenis stood behind him. Chloe swallowed with difficulty. Atenis gave her a sip of water, and Chloe almost wept. It tasted good and it burned. "Hurt," she managed to say. "Badly."

Dion picked her up and carried her inside. "Where is he, Sibylla?"

Having her burns touched was almost enough to make her scream, and Chloe pushed away from him, out of his arms, supporting herself against the wall. "Come with me," she whispered, coughing.

"Nay, I will go alone," Dion said.

"You need a guide," she rasped.

"It is chaos out there," Atenis argued. "She can show you where he is."

"Get her a traveling chair."

"She cannot sit, Dion," Atenis said, gingerly taking Chloe's hand. The dark chieftain walked around her, and Chloe heard his hiss when he saw her back. "By the gods—lead," Dion commanded Chloe, touching her cheek gently.

Back through the falling ash, which now covered everything like two thousand years of dust, they walked. Somehow Chloe led them to the room where Cheftu lay. Dion pushed past her, running to kneel beside Cheftu. He issued a series of curt commands, and Cheftu was lifted and laid on the stretcher, still facedown. Dion walked beside the stretcher, and Chloe wondered if he knew he was crying. They reached the undamaged section, and Chloe saw people had begun to gather.

People. They barely looked human. Faces and bodies burned, pummeled with falling debris, coughing up blood. Those who could move fetched and carried water, oil, and the few herbs that were available.

Of Kallistae's 55,000 inhabitants, a few hundred remained. Vaporized, Chloe thought. Heat so extreme that the meat and bone of human and animal instantly became gas, air, mist. Vapor. Lava had flowed north, covering the towns of Hyacinth and Daphne, and flowed south over Echo.

Indeed, the strangest thing was how the pyroclastic cloud had bounced from the shore of Kallistae to the shore of Aztlan. They'd thought they were safe being on a separate island; the lava hadn't touched them. They'd not counted on the cloud's demonic ability to bounce from shore to shore. She glanced over the mass of destruction.

Now the volcano rested, but for how long? Hours or aeons? They needed to flee. They could run to Caphtor, though no swallows had returned with news of how the Caphtori had fared or the fate of the other islands.

Chloe doused cloth strips with wine and poppy and dribbled it into the mouths of the victims. For those who had no lips she set it on their teeth, letting them suck the liquid drop by drop.

Mechanically she moved, her body screaming with pain, but activity kept her from thinking about Cheftu, about what had happened. She tried to barter with God. She'd always sucked at negotiating, but the outcome had never been more precious. Let him live, please. Just to breathe and laugh and smile?

If I were in a movie, Chloe thought, I would vow to God that if Cheftu were allowed to live, I would let Dion have him. I would sacrifice his love and my happiness to save his life.

This was not a movie and God knew her better, Chloe realized.

No amount of lying to the Almighty was going to be convincing. Cheftu was hers. Please let him get better and she would be a faithful, understanding, wonderful wife.

And if Dion stepped in her way, she'd stomp him.

"FIND HIM," DION SNAPPED.

Nestor sighed. "We combed the cavern Sibylla said he was in. What more can be done? He is one man, Dion. There are thousands who need aid."

Dion looked at the back of the man lying so still before him. Imhotep was gone—as was the intellectual wealth of Aztlan. The snake goddess's temple, enclosing the Kela-Tenata, had been shattered during the last earthquake, pieces of column and fresco crashing into the sea as the island seemed to slant more each decan. Dion possessed simple healing skills, but Cheftu needed more, far more. "There must be someone, some way."

Nestor laid a hand on Dion's shoulder. "It is not destined, brother. The man is beginning his journey. Leave be, Dion. Bathe him if you will, but others need you more."

Dion ground his teeth. Others might need him more, but he needed Cheftu. He would not let him die, even if he had to face death in his place. He shrugged off Nestor's grasp. "Return with Niko or die in the fires!"

Night had fallen, though how they were supposed to know the difference between night and day, Dion couldn't say. He sluiced water over Cheftu's back, trying to cool the angry red welts. A fine coating of glass splinters had showered him, so Cheftu looked as though he'd been pierced by a thousand pins. Instructing two serfs to hold lamps so that the tiny particles, almost amber in color, caught the light, Dion had plucked them out.

The opening door made him turn. Nestor, stained with sweat and gray with ash, entered. "We found Niko, Dion. But I doubt you will be able to use him."

Dion barely had time to turn before he vomited. Nestor handed him a cloth for his mouth. "It strikes without warning," he said.

In the name of Apis, what had happened? Dion looked again. Niko, distinguishable only by his violet eyes, seemed to be wearing a cloak. Nay, no cloak; his skin was so badly burned it left him a pulpy, massive wound. His hands were twisted into claws. Next to him, Cheftu seemed an ideal of health.

Dion caught Niko's gaze. "What happened?" Dion asked.

Niko tried to blink, but his eyelids were burned.

Nestor whispered in Dion's ear, "His throat is scorched. It's hard to speak."

Dion bit back his howl of frustration. If Niko could not help, why had Nestor brought him here? To watch him die?

"You wanted him. No one should die alone, Dion. No one," Nestor said softly. He began to wash Niko's face and shoulders, preparing him for the Isles of the Blessed.

Shaking his head, Dion looked over at Cheftu. He wouldn't die alone. Sibylla had collapsed, and they'd taken her outside to lie with the other corpses. It was some small satisfaction that he'd have Cheftu to himself, if only for a while.

"Aeeeh . . . Aeeeaaah . . ."

"He's trying to speak," Nestor said.

"Bring him drinking water!" Dion shouted.

"And a reed!"

"A reed?" Dion asked, then watched as Nestor deciphered the agitated sounds from the thing that was Niko. Slowly Nestor began to hover his hands over the length of Niko's body, moving down. He stopped at Niko's groin, where amazingly he seemed mostly undamaged.

The serf returned, and Nestor took the water and reed, sucking water through the reed, then slipping the other end into the cavern that Niko had left for a mouth. Slowly Nestor released the drops of moisture into Niko's throat, drop by drop. Dion's eyes filled with tears as he watched.

"Try the pouch."

Nestor again searched, following Niko's raspy commands. Nestor slipped his hand in and brought out a flat black stone, the length of his palm and oblong.

"Uuurrrrmm."

"What?"

"Uurrmm."

"Try the other one, Dion."

His hands suddenly shaking, Dion felt in the pocket of Niko's kilt. His fingers closed around a stone, and he brought it out. Like the other, it was oblong and sized to fit in his palm. But it was foamy white, pearlescent. He held it up.

"Thhhhhmn," Niko panted. His violet eyes were wide, excited. "Urrmm thhhmm urmm thmmnn," he repeated, then choked. They turned him to the side, trying to clear his throat. His breathing was even more labored. Dion listened as Niko fought for breath, the painful gagging sounding magnified. His eyes ran with tears of staring, but they didn't plead or beg for life. Frantically Nestor bathed his legs and chest, blessing him, wishing him *Kalo taxidi.*

A long hiss signified his death. Nestor slipped his hand inside Niko's pouch again and brought out a vial. "The elixir." Gently Nestor laid a linen over the mage's face, gesturing for the corpse to be taken outside.

The rhyton-shaped vial of blue glass was the purpose of it all. The true method for living eternally. Dion snatched it from Nestor and ran to Cheftu, pulling out the cork. He poured the liquid on the man's wounds.

"Nay, Dion!" Nestor caught his hand. "Think, brother. Do you have the right to change his life?"

"If I do nothing, he will die!"

"If you give him this elixir, he may live, blind and crippled! Do you have the authority to decide his destiny? Aztlan lies in ruins because we believed we were gods. We thought we could order men's lives. Spiralmaster was wrong, we are not gods. Do not make this man *athanati,* Dion. Prepare him for eternity and leave be."

Dion felt the sobs gathering in his throat. His chest convulsed painfully, and his hands fell to his sides. "I love him," Dion croaked. Nestor pulled him close, standing between Dion and Cheftu.

Tears and mucus smeared on the Golden's chest as Dion sobbed, racking, painful gasps that made Nestor hold him closer. Behind Nestor's back, Dion's hand held the unstoppered vial. Carefully he moved his finger from the top and poured it into Cheftu's slack-jawed mouth.

Easing the vial to Cheftu's side, Dion clenched Nestor closer, looking over his shoulder. Cheftu's lips glistened with moisture, and Dion felt a fierce surge of delight.

He had the authority because he loved Cheftu. Now there would be time enough to wait for his love to be returned. Dion would take it, too.

We *are* gods, he thought. Nestor just didn't know it yet.

CHAPTER 21

CHLOE WOKE UP IN THE FALLING ASH. It was clogging her nostrils and her mouth. She coughed, then struggled up and ran for the still standing wing of the palace. She would not be left outside like trash! She had to see Cheftu.

He'd been so still, so silent. Her burns hurt, but nothing like the agony she imagined he was suffering. Was Dion taking care of him? The thought brought her up short, but Chloe straightened her shoulders and walked on. If he had tired of her, Cheftu would have to tell her good-bye. His kisses had not been the kisses of a woman-weary man. She was a novice in some ways, but she also had excellent instincts and knew Cheftu's body and desires better than her own.

If he were gay—she'd better say homosexual or they would have another talk about joy and happiness—he would have to come right out of the closet and confront her face-to-face. Otherwise he was hers! Bug off, Dion, she thought, marching now down the hallways. Mimi had once told her crazy Aunt Rina, not to be confused with her twin, crazy Aunt Lina, that any woman who could not hold her man was not worth the starch in her petticoats.

Chloe had stripped off her petticoats, but she still had Kingsley blood.

Cheftu, if he lived, wasn't going anywhere.

Please God, let him live.

DEATH WAS EVERYWHERE. People with a spectrum of wounds covered every available surface. Cheftu blinked, opening his eyes—one eye. The oil had blinded him, he realized. But he was alive. He inhaled—the air was filled with the smell of fire and roasting flesh. He was lying on his stomach, facing a wall. His hands were numb beneath him, and he turned his head, pushing himself upright.

Recognition and recall flooded his mind: the eruption, protecting Chloe, screaming as hot oil rained onto his back, his head, his hand.

Blackened, misshapen things were lying on the floor beside him.

Burn victims.

I am a burn victim, he thought, looking at his hand. Blistered and broken, two useless fingers, and the other hand? Cheftu sat on the edge of the couch, looking at his hands. He was horribly burned, huge blisters rising up on his skin. Would he be able to practice doctoring again? Did he dare touch Chloe with these talons?

Would she want to see him? Half-blind, nearly maimed? With trembling fingers he touched his eyebrow and felt the puckers of skin that covered the side of his head.

He stood slowly, stepping away from the couch. He ached, and blisters pulled and tightened as he moved. Aye, he'd been hurt, but he could walk. How was Chloe?

A scream made him turn, and he saw a serf faint dead away. Nestor, stained and rumpled, his blond hair dark with ash, stepped toward Cheftu. "By the holy bull of Apis," he breathed. "You live?" Atenis stood behind Nestor, her gray eyes wide.

"Should I not?"

"I'm here to bathe you. You were but a mass of wounds, with little hope."

"I still am, my friend," Cheftu said. His throat hurt dreadfully, but his mind felt clearer than it had in many moons.

Nestor walked around Cheftu in silence. He picked up a vial from the couch; just a few drops remained in the bottom. "He did it anyway," Nestor whispered.

"Did what? Who? Why are you so shocked?" Atenis asked.

"Do you recognize the vial, Cheftu?" Nestor asked.

Cheftu looked at the glass vial. Of course he didn't recognize it. Abruptly he turned to Nestor. "Wait! The—?"

"Say it, Cheftu."

"He gave me the elixir?"

Nestor turned the vial, watching the drops fall and merge. "It would appear so."

"The immortality elixir?" *Mon Dieu!* It was unknown, not tested! Cheftu tried to check his fear. "This cannot be. Where is Sibylla?"

Atenis laid a hand on his shoulder, "My sorrow with you, Egyptian."

Cheftu blinked. Atenis was sorry? Realization dawned on him, but Chloe could not be dead. "Where is she?"

"She has begun her journey." Nestor nodded his head in regret. "She seemed well enough, but she collapsed and Dion had her laid outside with the others."

"It was too late for a lustral bath," Atenis whispered.

Black rage shielded what remained of Cheftu's vision.

"You live!" Dion cried, running into the room, embracing Cheftu.

Livid, Cheftu swung at Dion's jaw, then his gut. His fists connected with satisfying thuds, the reverberations traveling up Cheftu's arm. He was amazed at how good it felt to hurt the man. "You gave me the elixir?" he hissed.

"I wanted you to live. Beside me," Dion whispered, panting. Atenis helped him up, and Cheftu smiled grimly when the chieftain winced.

"You took my choices from me, Dion!"

"I could not let you die."

Cheftu continued to glare at Dion, his hands clenched into fists. "Where—is—my—wife?" he asked, enunciating every word.

Dion rubbed his jaw, frowning. "I didn't know you had a wife, Cheftu. You don't wear a tattoo."

Blisters on his hand stretched as Cheftu tensed. "Where is Sibylla?"

"Sibylla was your wife? She was not your equal."

"By the gods! Are you insane, man?" Nestor shouted at Dion, stepping between them.

"Show respect, Dion," Atenis said, pulling on Dion's arm.

"She began her journey, Cheftu. I laid her in the ash myself."

Cheftu didn't step forward and break the man's neck. Chloe was alive, and every minute spent killing Dion was a moment not spent finding Chloe. "My wife is a warrior. An artisan. She loves with a grace and power that leaves me weak." He stepped back from Nestor, picked up a kilt discarded on the floor, and belted it, then threw the stone disk he'd worn around his waist for months onto the floor. It shattered on contact. "You, Dion, are the one who is unworthy even to speak her name."

"I have given you life!" Dion cried.

"What was that?" Nestor asked as Atenis knelt over the pieces of stone.

Cheftu turned at the doorway. "I am sure my wife will thank you for my life, for I will spend it with her." He looked at Nestor. "Get your cloak and come with me. Now."

"He is my clansman and brother, Cheftu."

Atenis was gathering up the shards of stone, stained with Cheftu's blood. "What was this, Spiralmaster?"

Cheftu looked from one face to the other. "The recipe for the elixir. Spiralmaster gave it to me. There will be no more grasping at godhood."

It was utterly silent.

Cheftu stumbled through the palace to the gardens. It was impossible to discern whether it was night or day. Everything was gray. Looking southeast, he saw naught but destruction; looking back to the section of the palace he had just left, it hardly seemed the world had rocked and regurgitated.

"They were laid there," Nestor said, pointing to ash-covered lumps. He didn't meet Cheftu's glance, but the fact that Nestor had accompanied him needed no words. Cheftu knelt and felt beneath the warm coating of ash, trying to touch any limb that seemed familiar.

The bodies were closely lined up, but there were a few gaps. Nestor dug on the other side. "Cheftu," he said into the stillness, "come see this."

Footsteps led away, hidden by dustings of ash. Big feet.

Grâce à Dieu!

JUST AS CHLOE HAD BEEN READY to break into a chorus of "Stand By Your Man," she heard a voice in the darkness. Though the accent, even the language, was different, the tone was the same. A voice that pleaded, terrified because the owner's world had crashed, collapsed, fallen around her ears. The same cry that had gotten her into a mess of trouble in ancient Egypt.

A voice asking her for help.

More specifically, asking Sibylla for help.

Before Chloe had the option of literally playing dead, a chorus joined it.

"Mistress Sibylla! Praise Kela!"

"I knew you were right, mistress, I told my husband I did, but he never did listen to me—"

"Help us, lady! Please!"

There were dozens of them, asking for help. She, after all, had predicted this collapse. Fire and water—oh, aye, those had been her words. They wanted to leave; there was no way out.

Well, there was one way.

Chloe blinked in the night like darkness. She knew the passage now, was that the point? The Labyrinth was easy—she should have figured it out before. Daedelus had constructed it, and the man knew one symbol. The Greek key. She'd seen it on his clothes in Knossos; it was the only piece of jewelry he wore. She obviously hadn't been thinking clearly. One Greek key depthwise, three widthwise. That was the Labyrinth. Would the boat below hold this motley crew?

Their voices grew louder, yammering at her, pleading with her. "I will take you!" she said. "But it is not an easy journey. We travel through Hades itself."

Silence.

One brave soul spoke. "With you we will get through. Left here we will die."

"Are the Golden fleeing, mistress?"

I really don't know, Chloe thought. *But Cheftu is not leaving with Dion, that I can promise you.* "If we are going, we need to go," she said.

As if they were first-graders on a class trip, Chloe paired them up, swiping torches as they walked through the deserted palace. Instructing them to be quick and quiet, she led them down the steps. *Please let the boat be there. Please let everyone fit!* She hardly wanted to exercise values clarification by deciding who stayed and who fled.

The first complaints came when they actually saw the lintel marked Hades. Chloe wiped her brow and led on. The starting point was the scariest, to her, anyway. Her arms braced on the ledge, her feet flailing for the shallow steps of the ladder, she stopped sweating only when she felt her toes touch, then grab.

After crawling a ways down, she coaxed the first few through the tunnel, then scampered farther below, listening to them talk to each other. Great, building teamwork! They passed the first level, then reached the second. Chloe stuck her head in the horizontal passageway, sniffed; wrong one. Down again. The trek was very recognizable now.

She wasn't going to tell them about the chute. She'd just step and they'd follow.

There was another smell, though, beyond the scat, the torches, and the general sulfuric decay. A briny smell. They were approaching the chute and Chloe turned, telling them all to follow her, she knew what she was doing. Like good little recruits, they shook their heads. Chloe stepped into the chute, bringing her knees to her chest to try to control her slide.

Halfway down, water closed over her head, extinguishing her torch and stealing her breath. Uh-oh.

ATENIS FOUND CHEFTU AND NESTOR as they attempted to follow the large footprints through the ash. They'd quickly lost the trail and were searching in circles. Atenis said that Dion needed to see them both, that it was dire. Cheftu tried to refuse, but she said they needed a physician. Her gray gaze pleaded, and Cheftu reluctantly agreed.

They trailed her through Spiralmaster's chambers and into the laboratory. Even before they reached the door, the stink forewarned the putrefaction within. Atenis opened the door and stepped back, allowing them to enter.

Cheftu looked at the room, his nose covered. It was foul; brown stains covered everything. Phoebus' remains lay in the center of the room, crawling with minuscule white insects. Cheftu averted his gaze, looking toward Dion.

As Nestor caught sight of the dead Golden, the last vestige of boyishness vanished from his features. His eyes hardened as he took in the murder of his clan brother . . . and the feminine prints that were not completely obscured.

Ileana had killed *Hreesos.* Had she also burned Niko? How had he wound up in the sea? The two men had disappeared at the same time.

"Detain the mother-goddess," Dion commanded the few remaining Mariners. "Bring her to me now, here."

"Retrieve Irmentis from the Labyrinth," Atenis said. "Leave her in the *Megaron.*"

Swallowing his distaste for rot, Cheftu knelt over the body of the king. Shards of glass were scattered around him in a radius, and the neck of a jug stuck out of his belly. A long sliver of glass protruded from his throat. Apparently even the immortality elixir couldn't prevent death when the recipient had such grievous wounds. Cheftu had rarely seen so much blood.

What kind of woman could do this to her stepson? Her spouse?

"Niko lay here, I'd guess," Dion said from across the room.

"Why do you say that?"

With a finger Dion touched a tuft of white blond hair affixed to the floor. Cheftu felt sick, dizzy, when he heard Ileana in the corridor. Nestor's glance was sharp, and Cheftu and Dion stood straighter. Atenis stepped backward, into the shadows.

Ileana entered in on the arm of the Mariner. He was already charmed: despite the destruction of the palace, the Queen of Heaven was perfectly coiffed. Cheftu thought of his wife, filthy with sweat, blood, or volcanic ash; still her spirit, the beauty of her heart, shone through.

He spat at Ileana's feet.

The room grew silent as she lifted peacock green eyes to him. "Foreigner, retract your insult or face the Labyrinth."

"You are a foolish woman to make threats in the same room where your victim lies," Nestor said. He moved away from Phoebus, and she saw the rotting corpse for the first time. Unlike most, she didn't turn green, get sick, or faint. She stared with distaste and looked away. "Do you deny that you murdered him?"

"He was *athanati*, by his own declaration. How could I, or anyone, kill a god?"

"Perhaps with a broken jug neck, Ileana?" Cheftu asked. "The elixir granted Phoebus immortality while he still had blood. When he was wounded before, Irmentis gave of hers. When you attacked him, he drained of blood."

"Stay out of this, foreigner."

Dion stepped forward. For the first time Ileana looked fearful, just a little tightening around her eyes and mouth. "Could you not get pregnant, Ileana?"

"I already am, you fool," she said haughtily. "The throne is mine, it always has been. It always will be."

"Not by Phoebus, though, *eee?* You raped Niko—stole his *psyche* and his seed."

She laughed. "Unlike you, Dion, I needn't *persuade* men to my bed."

He slapped her, and Cheftu felt his cheeks redden. She deserved justice, but could he stand and watch her receive it?

With a motion that was seductive and repulsive, she licked blood from the corner of her mouth. "Do you feel like a real man now, Dion, instead of a misshapen woman?"

Nestor caught Dion's hand before he struck her again. With a stern look he stepped to Ileana. "Break a jug for me, Dion," he said. "You also, Spiralmaster."

"How sweet, you think to avenge Phoebus. Do you not realize that if he were not dead, you would still be nothing but an errand boy?"

Nestor's blue eyes were icy. "Many vows have been made to destroy you, Ileana. It was Phoebus' fondest wish. In his own way, he is bringing it about. As my first official duty, I will avenge the death of Phoebus Apollo, lately *Hreesos*. Release her," he instructed the Mariners. "Leave this floor and do not return to it. Ever. You are released from clan and commission."

"Why, my master?"

"Aztlan is falling. Flee for your lives," Dion said.

The men saluted, and the five people listened to their footsteps racing up the stairwell. Ileana looked from one man to the next. Cheftu could feel her probing his mind, searching for a weakness. "Shall we make up now?" she said to Nestor, running a finger down his chest. Apparently she thought he was the weakest link. "I can serve you, while your Spiralmaster serves me and Dion can finally learn the ... *whorls* in the Spiralmaster's shell," she said with a laugh that was pure harlotry.

Nestor stopped her finger by breaking it.

Ileana screamed, cradling the wounded digit to her bare, heaving breast. "How dare you?"

Atenis stepped from the shadows. For once she stood tall, proud, an unknown elegance in her profile and demeanor. "You murdered Nestor's mother, Phoebus' mother, Dion's mother, your own mother, and two generations of the Kela-Ata, *eee*, Ileana? You threw Irmentis and Sibylla in the Labyrinth. Then you killed my clan brother, your husband, Phoebus."

"You can prove nothing!" Ileana hissed.

"Why did you harm Niko?" Dion interjected.

"You didn't even bathe him, did you?" Atenis asked.

"Atenis, my dear child," Ileana said, cradling her hand while sweat pebbled her upper lip.

"That is the most ironic part, is it not?" Atenis said with a sad smile. "I am not your dear child, nor is Irmentis. You have no maternal heart, Ileana."

"No heart at all," Dion muttered.

"I did not rear you to speak like this to me!" Ileana hissed.

"You did not rear me at all, Ileana. You avoided all your children, giving yourself and your affections to your lovers instead, yet hating Zelos for seeking the same surcease."

Cheftu watched the older woman's face pale. His glance shifted to Atenis, and he blanched when he saw the tool in her hand. *Mon Dieu!* She stepped closer to Ileana. "Do you recognize this, Ileana?"

The woman was still reserved, but her eyes were dark with fear. "Nay, I have not seen it before."

"Then you claim you don't know how it cuts? What it cuts?"

Cheftu and Nestor exchanged glances. To what was Atenis referring? Dion watched fixedly. Somewhere above them a hound howled. Ileana began to shake visibly.

"You know the greatest of your crimes, Ileana. Murder is not it. Stealing love, dreams, hopes, ambitions, these are all your product, but not what you will die for," Atenis said.

Everyone was silent, watching the Queen of Heaven. "What then?" she asked, a hint of hauteur still in her tone.

"Every person you killed you destroyed for eternity. You murdered them unbathed, you sent their *psyches* into oblivion. For that heinous crime, you will die."

"Slowly," Dion interjected. "Languorously." He cocked his head. "I hear Irmentis."

Ileana dropped all pretenses. "Not Irmentis, Atenis. For whatever love you have borne me—"

"I hate you," Atenis said quietly. "What you took from me I might never have used. Marriage and childbearing are not my interests; even were I whole they would not be. But you broke Irmentis' heart and turned her into a wild thing. You wounded Phoebus beyond bearing, a *pothos* love that ate away at him, his perceptions, his dreams. Then you murdered him with no hope of an afterlife."

Cheftu watched as Atenis stepped away from the wall. A marble lustral bath filled with water sat in the midst of the bloodshed. Nestor and Dion advanced on Ileana.

"Dion, don't let her—"

Ileana's words were cut off as she was submerged in the bath. Cheftu stood immobile until they brought her up, panting and drenched.

"I told you your death would be savored."

Cheftu listened to the silence following Dion's words. Ileana's makeup was running, her hair stuck to her scalp. She was trembling, her broken finger apparently forgotten. They helped her stand and then moved away.

"Shall we go, Ileana? Your death awaits you," Atenis said.

The Queen of Heaven took a reluctant step forward, then bolted, running out the door and down the corridor. Neither Atenis nor Dion moved, they just listened to her flight. "She is getting away!" Nestor cried.

Atenis turned around, her gaze bleak. "Justice will be served. Irmentis and her dogs are free." A rumble stirred above them, showering down a faint coating of plaster. "Ileana will pay."

"I cannot watch this," Cheftu said, starting toward the door. Dion and Nestor caught his arms. In the silence, Cheftu looked up. Irmentis stood in the doorway, bloodstained and grimy, her nails thick, her hair knotted; she seemed the embodiment of hell. Atenis embraced her sister. Cheftu saw the blade, the wicked hooked blade, pass from hand to hand. Irmentis flinched and asked softly, "This is it?"

"Aye, my little one," Atenis said. "The very same. I saved it for you. This is your battle to win."

Dogs barked in some distant part of the palace, and a low human scream floated above it. Cheftu twisted against his captors' grips. What were they going to do? Irmentis tucked the blade in the waist of her tunic and left.

"What justice is this?" Cheftu asked quietly. "How can murder be the least of her crimes? Why did you give her a chance at eternity?"

"Ileana broke hearts, foreigner," Dion said. "She took them, whole and beating, out of a trusted person's chest. The individual was condemned to go through the rest of life with a gaping, fatal wound that would never be healed." He turned the full fury of his dark gaze on Cheftu. "Tell me, Spiralmaster, is it better to wound and poison an entire existence or to just eliminate it?"

Cheftu bowed his head. What right had he to judge?

"Ileana will taste a little of the physical pain she put Irmentis through," Dion said. "It will only be the physical, but I think it will be all Ileana can experience. After death she will face judgment at the hands of the gods for her deeds. Our loved ones are *skia*, but Ileana will pay for eternity."

"Justice is served," Atenis said.

CHLOE BROKE THROUGH TO THE SURFACE, gasping for air, floundering in the rough water. It took her a moment to get her sense of direction, and then she realized what was wrong. The water was almost to the top of the cavern! The island was sinking! Or was the water rising?

My God, she'd brought these people down to die! With a deep breath she dove down, feeling around for the people. One by one she lifted them to the surface, then plunged again. When she found them all she popped up. "Everyone," she wheezed, "have their partners?"

"Where are the boats?" someone asked.

Bloody good question. "They are tied beneath us. The water is rising. You do not have the time to wait for them. Swim out of here."

Sputtering and arguments she cut short by banging her hand on the ceiling of the cavern. The water had risen while they were talking! "Grab some debris and float out of here. There is no other way. You have no time. Swim out of the channel, head for the outside of Kallistae. There is a harbor in Prostatevo. Go!"

She didn't wait to see if they listened; she'd seen a few snag the boards that were floating around. Cheftu was still on the sinking is-

land. She wasn't sure who was rescuing whom, or for what, or where, but she knew God did not demand they commit suicide. With a deep breath she sank below water level, feeling around for the chute. Touching the sides, she let the water push her up until she was in the air again. The water level was rising.

On feet that needed no guidance going around through the maze, she ran, then climbed up the ladder, hauled herself over the ledge, and ran for the next set of stairs.

And I thought training camp was a bitch.

THOSE REMAINING FACED EACH OTHER.

Dion. Nestor. Atenis. Cheftu. Vena and the little boy she had rescued.

There were two ways off the island. The air sail, still untested with the weight of two, and a diving mask. One.

Not a serf, a Mariner, or a Scholomancer could be found. Bodies lay in heaps, the stench of burnt and rotting flesh mingling into a tang Cheftu feared he would never purge from his nostrils. A bowl of chilled water was passing from hand to hand as the Olimpi prepared for the possibility of death. Quickly and quietly they bathed and blessed each other with *Kalo taxidi.*

The waters of Therio Sea were rising. Chloe was . . . he hoped to God she was safe, far away, and he thanked *le bon Dieu* for the chance to kiss her that last time. He dared not hope for more; it was time for him to be honorable.

"Cheftu and I should have the air sail," Dion said, wiping water from his eyes. "We are men of science, of courage. We can lead those who regroup in Prostatevo."

"You just want your lover with you," Vena cried.

"I am not his lover," Cheftu said through gritted teeth. "The women and child should go."

"Cast lots," Atenis said, offering Cheftu the bowl of water. He dabbed a cross, his protection, on his forehead and set the bowl down. He didn't need to check his belongings. He wore a kilt and belt, nothing more. Atenis had gathered the bloodstained disk pieces and placed them in a bag slung over her shoulders.

Nestor was watching Vena cuddle the little boy named Akilez, his wet head pressed against her breasts. Cheftu supposed they should anoint Nestor as the Golden Bull, but as there was no longer an Aztlan empire, there seemed no reason.

"Use these stones," Dion said, tossing them from his pouch.

Two oblongs fell into the dim light, one black and one white. Hebrew was scratched all over them, lined with gold on the inside of the letters. It was not possible, yet it made such sense, it was so logical! *Toss them,* he heard whispered in his mind. Cheftu licked his suddenly dry lips. "What language is that?" He knew, but he had to be certain.

"Ancient Aztlantu. Before the Olimpi."

Cheftu seized the stones, then tossed them, his words coming out in a rush of French. "Is Chloe well?"

The letters for the Hebrew "yes" flickered in the light as the stones turned in the air.

"What is this?" Nestor asked.

"Give them back!" Dion cried.

"Will we be together?" Cheftu asked, throwing them again.

"Y-o-u-r-d-e-c-i-s-i-o-n."

Cheftu steadied the rush of blood in his veins. His decision, his choice. He could be with Chloe if he decided. She was safe, the most important thing.

"Nestor, Vena, and the child should take the air sail. She is lighter, and they can, um, repopulate if needed," Cheftu said. "Atenis, you are familiar with the diving gear, you go alone. Dion can swim."

"What about you?" Dion asked.

"We cannot leave you," Atenis said.

"He will not be alone," a voice said from behind them.

Cheftu wanted to laugh with joy as Chloe walked in. Vena covered her nose, Dion snorted, and Atenis and Nestor smiled. Cheftu pulled her into his arms and kissed her, tasting the brine, the sweat, the blood. "The island is sinking," she said. "We need to go."

They turned around, Nestor and Vena were already strapping on the wings of the air sail. "Until my eyes hold you again," Nestor shouted. "In Prostatevo!" They ran off the edge of the portico and fell. Dion, Atenis, Chloe, and Cheftu ran to the ledge and looked down. Nestor and Vena were floating low, but floating. The white rectangle began to move southward. Barring another eruption, they had a good chance.

Atenis kissed Chloe's cheeks. "My eyes will not hold you again; I go to the mainland. Be well, oracle."

"I'm not—"

"You are not Sibylla, but you are an oracle, more than you know," she said. Holding her pouch of broken *ari-kat* stones, she walked out of the room.

Chloe turned to Dion. "Don't let us keep you."

Dion met Cheftu's gaze over her head. Cheftu braced himself, memories of that night flickering through his mind. The shock he felt when Dion kissed him. Then his horror as the dark chieftain confessed a love for Cheftu that Dion claimed surpassed the love a man and woman could know. A love of gripping passion, a unity of spirits, a camaraderie of minds. Cheftu's disgust had submerged into a grudging sympathy. Dion had shared impulses and desires that turned Cheftu's stomach, but he understood the man's need to reveal them.

Cheftu had fled Dion's apartment for his own, washing his skin until it was raw. He'd still felt unclean. A mouth is just a mouth, Dion claimed, yet Cheftu balked. Perhaps it was, if physical pleasure were the only end. Sailors used each other from necessity on the sea, yet most would prefer a woman. Dion claimed no woman could love as completely as a man.

Dion had given him the elixir out of love and a desire to be with him.

He was alive. Was it the elixir or just natural healing? Cheftu didn't know. "I have not changed my mind," he said.

Dion's hand clapped Cheftu on the shoulder, and he stood rock still. The man's voice was low, soft; Chloe was straining to hear what he said. Cheftu felt pity, revulsion, and great sorrow. "I am yours, Cheftu. I would give my life for you. I have given life *to* you. You learn late that women are for breeding alone. True love, passion, and companionship are found only between warriors and scholars and men who are equal. I will restore you when you realize womankind's perfidy. I will wait, for I too have taken the elixir. We are destined."

"Back off, cowboy," Chloe growled. "He's mine."

Cheftu stared at the stones. This was it! This was why they were there! These stones were a direct communication with God, for David, for Solomon. These stones couldn't be allowed to sink here, to be lost in the hands of this dying race.

"Let me take the stones, Dion," Cheftu said.

"Why? You are choosing to be with her."

"Why do you need them, Cheftu?" Chloe asked.

"I need them, Dion," Cheftu said, ignoring Chloe. "They mean the world to me."

Dion's eyes darkened, and he began to smile, "The world, *eee?*"

Cheftu's hands hovered over the stones, still lying on the low table.

"If you take these stones, I will never see you again," Dion said.

"You won't anyway," Chloe said.

A low rumble shook the room, throwing them all to their knees. Cheftu's hand skimmed the table and grabbed the stones.

Dion sat up, saw the stones were gone, and launched himself at Cheftu. He caught the Egyptian around the waist and bore him backward. "Get off him!" Chloe shouted as Cheftu and Dion rolled on the floor, Cheftu taking the blows from Dion, shielding his face with his arm, the stones jerking in his grasp.

"Give me the stones," Dion said. "If I can't have you, I want them."

Cheftu struck out, catching Dion across his jaw and cheek with his closed fist. The chieftain was stunned for a moment, and Cheftu rolled away. "Why do you want them?" Cheftu asked as the two men stared at each other, breathing hard.

With a chill Cheftu realized Dion was aroused. "Return them to me, Cheftu."

Another tremor. Chloe helped Cheftu up and they began to back away. "Cheftu!" Dion shouted. He crouched low, preparing to attack. Cheftu slipped the stones into his sash, feeling the inscribed sides against his skin.

A scream of tearing rock deafened them momentarily. Dion ran toward them, and Chloe leapt in front of Cheftu, kicking high into Dion's groin. He collapsed to his knees with a groan. Cheftu looked at him, his friend, the man he'd respected. "The stones were my reason for being here," he said. You want them only because you think they will bring me to you, offering myself into the bargain, he thought.

"We are not finished, Egyptian," Dion wheezed out, still doubled over. The floor shook as Cheftu took the stones from his sash, holding them securely in his palms. He couldn't lose them; the cost had been too great.

"Come on!" Chloe said, pulling him through rooms and down hallways. She dragged him out, into passageways, deeper and deeper into the palace. She halted at an inset altar and turned the ax. "We need all the luck we can get," she said, and pulled him along, down another hallway. They stopped to look out a window, and Cheftu saw the opposite cliffs were now higher. "You can swim, *eee?*" she asked.

"Aye, of course."

They stepped up to a gate. He saw with a shock that it was labeled Hades. "Three rules. Don't let go of me, don't breathe, and swim fast!" Chloe kissed his mouth hard, wrapped his arms around her waist, and pulled.

They fell through air, then down into water, and Cheftu had to fight to stay with her. He held a stone in each clenched fist, following his siren of a wife. She swam without hesitation, turning and twisting until Cheftu's head began to pound. Around and around they swam, then down, and farther down. His arms wrapped around her waist, his vision was spotted, and they swam yet farther. He was going to die, he needed to breathe!

Water battered them when they broke the surface. Cheftu hauled air into his lungs and looked around, trying to gauge where they were. "Outside Aztlan Island," Chloe said, still catching her breath. "I don't know where to go now."

Cheftu motioned and they started swimming across the channel, where deep water moved fast. He felt every muscle in his body, the jumping stones in his hands dragging at him. Cheftu and Chloe clambered up on the opposite shore. It was coated in ash, little blobs of lava still simmering red and black on the rocks. It was a brief stop; they had to get farther away.

The archway. That island. Cheftu pulled her close, feeling the firm curves of her body, the tremble of her legs and arms from the exertion of the swim. He could feel burns on her back as she curled closer.

"*Eee,* I want you, too," she whispered against his skin, kissing his chest, sending blood rushing wildly through his veins.

"Did I say it aloud?"

She smiled up at him, green eyes through seaweed curls of black hair. "Not in so many words." Her hand closed around him, and Cheftu hissed, then laughed.

"We need a boat," he said. *Do not think about the warmth of her body, the softness of her skin.* She murmured agreement as she kissed his hands. Then she froze, sat up, and stared at him.

"Your face!"

His hand went to his damaged eye; nay, it must be the other. He touched both eyebrows. Nay, it was the first? Only a scar left?

Chloe drew back, watching him with wide eyes. "You are healing. Major fast." Her cadence was very slow. "Even your hair has grown back." He touched the side of his head that had been a patch of blistered skin. Hadn't it?

Cheftu pushed Chloe off his side and lifted his kilt.

"What the——?" she shouted in English.

Moving his member aside, he ran his fingers through the wet hair. There was no *bubo!* He tried the other side. None there! He looked again.

"What in *hell* are you doing?" Chloe asked.

"Looking," he muttered. Nothing sensitive or swollen, no marks at all!

"Aye. I see that. What do you hope to find?"

He looked up. She was sitting back on her haunches, arms crossed over her chest, her expression somewhere between outrage and laughter.

Cheftu jerked down his wet kilt. "Nothing."

The shore shook. For once Cheftu was grateful for an earthquake. "Look for any wood you can find. Rope, too," he shouted, motioning her one way down the beach while he headed the other.

Ash began to fall; they must have been too close to hear the eruption. Another one. Aztlan Island was literally sinking as they watched. Cheftu turned back to the shore. Wood, *mon Dieu,* where was wood?

There was no wood, Chloe was convinced. Pretty soon there would be no water, either. Huge rafts of pumice were starting to gather, floating together, clogging up the sea. Exhausted, starving out of her mind, Chloe sat down.

The sapphire waters had turned gray. It looked like some bizarre traffic jam, with these big pieces lining up throughout the lagoon. If we could just walk from slab to slab, she thought, we could get to Prostatevo.

"Cheftu!" she screamed.

He came down the beach, running, limping . . . and looking even healthier. "What? What?"

"Tom Sawyer. Rafts. Hop on."

He looked from her, to the sea, back to her, and then Chloe saw the concept, not the reference, snap into place for him. She wouldn't tell him how long it had taken her to figure it out. The eruption has melted away my brain cells, she thought.

Grabbing hands, they began crossing the congested waterway.

Chapter 22

I T WAS HARD WORK MANEUVERING A PUMICE RAFT with no oars in a rambunctious sea. Chloe's knees were bleeding, and her palms were a strata of painful sores. All in all she felt as if she were on fire in a gray world.

Ash continued to fall as they paddled and pushed their makeshift vessel. The hazy twilight robbed them of their sense of direction. The wind kept them both permanently chilled. Prostatevo seemed farther away than Chloe remembered.

She was fighting tears when Cheftu called a halt. They were free of the other pieces of pumice, he said. Perhaps they would float for a while, carried by tides. She nodded, then shook her head, then rasped out, "Just so."

His hands on her shoulders made them both hiss—his blistered palms and her burned shoulders—and she lay down with her head on his leg, staring up. Not that there was anything to see. Chloe shivered, too tired to know or care anymore.

"Do you know what the Aztlan empire was?" he asked. His voice was almost back to normal, strangely enough.

"Santorini."

He was silent a moment. "I do not know that place."

"In the Aegean. My mother studied it. Though she thinks the Minoans lived here, but the Minoans never had pyramids. I don't know who these people were." She chuckled, half dozing. "However, my mother studies the painting I did."

Cheftu braced himself on his elbows. "The boys? Are you certain?"

Chloe giggled. "It's a really big deal because it's the first recording of anyone using boxing gloves in ancient times."

He was quiet. "I do not recall anyone using gloves for boxing."

"Nope. My point."

"*Okh,*" he said, laughing.

Chloe looked at her palms. She really should wash them, but salt water was going to hurt. "So if you didn't know it was Santorini, where was—is—was . . ." She rubbed her face. "Where were we?"

"Did you read Plato?"

"Plato?"

"Aye, the Greek philosopher?"

Chloe licked her lips. She hated to admit ignorance. "Not exactly. I've never been a fan of ancient times. Quite ironic, that."

"I thought women in your time attended university?"

"We do. We just have a lot of other things to study besides old Greek guys."

"*Eee,* for example?"

"Old . . ." Chloe paused for a moment. "European guys."

Cheftu chuckled. "Plato tells a legend, a story of a submerged island."

Adrenaline shot through Chloe's body. A submerged island . . . She had always imagined that underwater island kingdom looked like the palace in "The Little Mermaid." Could it be? "I thought it was in the Atlantic?"

He sat up. "An Egyptian named Solon told Plato the story. Beyond the Pillars of Hercules, Solon said. To the Greeks, this meant beyond Gibraltar, the mountains they called the pillars of Hercules—"

"But to the Egyptians?"

"It meant beyond the islands that began the Greek world. The

Egyptians called Crete and the islands beyond her 'Keftiu.' The root of that word is 'pillar.' We've seen the red pillars in their architecture. In Hebrew the word is 'Caphtor.'"

"Aye, also the Aztlantu."

"Aye," Cheftu said, looking startled for a moment. "For the Egyptians, Crete was a far western isle, one of the four pillars holding up the sky."

"So how do we get Atlantis from that?" Chloe asked.

"The Greeks thought Atlas held up the sky, so a daughter of Atlas—"

"Would be Atlantis?"

"Just so."

"So the Egyptians were telling a story about a kingdom by a sky pillar? And the Greeks believed that same pillar was in the Atlantic, so the kingdom was somewhere in the Atlantic." Perspective really was everything, she thought. "Yet Atlantis called itself Aztlan which sounds so Mexican to me. Their clothing and architecture was Minoan. Well, mostly Minoan." If you ignored the pyramids, she thought. "So what else about them was familiar?"

"I could tick them off on my fingers. Plato extols for pages the red, black, and yellow stones used, the hot and cold springs, the rings of land and water. Also, he describes the social structure. Each king ruling his island, then meeting in a Council; each island providing a certain product to the people at large. The citizens are divided into districts. The craftsmen, the warriors."

"The Clan of the Muse, the Clan of the Wave."

"Aye. Also, they have the wealth for leisure, competitions."

"They chased a bull, with nooses and staves, through the palace," Chloe said remembering hearing that from her mother. "History morphs into mythology. Wow."

His fingers played in her hair. "Which 'old European guy' taught you about Atlantis?"

"Wait a minute, mythology." Chloe sat in silence for a moment. "Did you study classical Greek?"

"The language?"

"The culture."

Cheftu shrugged. "It was not of particular interest, but I did read the classics."

She turned to him, shaking with excitement. "History morphs into mythology. Zelos was Zeus."

"Mount Olympus?" Cheftu blurted in French.

"Phoebus Apollo. Phoebus was Apollo. His sister Irmentis, the huntress. She could be Artemis."

"You claim we have been on Mount Olympus?" Cheftu asked, appalled. "Let me see your head, you are wounded."

Chloe pushed away his reaching hands. "Listen to me. I'm not saying these people were gods. I'm saying they were the inspiration for the gods. They were borrowed and shaped, sometimes even keeping the name."

"Dion was?"

"Dionysus," they said in unison.

After a moment Chloe whispered, "Athena taught me how to run. This is unbelievable, but don't you think it fits?"

"The original Mount Olympus was Atlantis, peopled with the Greek gods?"

"It sounds outrageous like that, but essentially, yep."

They sat in silence, and Cheftu reached out to her, caressing the side of her face.

Chloe turned her head and kissed his hand—then pushed it away. She scurried to the farthest corner of the raft. Cheftu fought for balance, before sliding off into the water. He came up sputtering and glared at her.

"What possessed you to do that!"

"Your hand is . . . healed," Chloe stammered. She felt her heart thudding, her own scabbed palms braced on the pumice. She held on as Cheftu hauled himself, dripping and shivering, onto the raft. She blinked in the twilight, looking at him. "What are you?"

"Cease being ridiculous, Chloe! I am Cheftu, your husband, *non?*"

"Your face. It's healed. Completely."

He touched his brow, closed one eye, then the other, touched his scalp.

"What happened, Cheftu?"

Slowly he turned his hands over. The skin was flawless. She saw the cuts were healed, the nicks and forming blisters were gone. He licked his lips slowly. "I was dying, Chloe. I had the plague."

"The shuddering-and-staggering-and-drooling plague?"

"Aye. The same. I had *buboes.*"

"*Buboes?*"

"Raised sores, in my groin. They were blackening."

"My God." That was why he'd ripped off his clothes and searched through his pubic hair—he was looking for the sores. "Do you still have them?"

She met his gaze, both eyes perfectly whole. "Nay." He looked away. "That is why I stopped, umm, being with you. Coupling. I was afraid you would become infected."

"That explains your reluctance in the paint."

Cheftu smiled. "Aye. If I'd not feared it would kill you, I would have made love with you. *Mon Dieu,* you have no idea how tried I was in those moments!" He touched his brow again in wonder. "If I have my way, you will always wear turquoise."

She wasn't sure what to say. Atlantis and Greek god prototypes were one thing, but this? She'd seen his eye heal, in two days. How could it be? Water ran over the edge of the raft, throwing her closer to the center. Closer to Cheftu, which was still a little eerie. "Why didn't you tell me?"

His gaze was direct. "I don't know. For fear you would do this, move away from me. Stop loving me. Leave me."

She reached out hesitantly, laying her hand on his knee.

"Please do not leave me, Chloe. I've endured your death once, I cannot abide it again. Promise me." His hand covered hers, holding her tight to him.

"When I thought you were wounded, that you maybe loved Dion—"

"Loved Dion?"

"Aye, well, I did see you kiss him."

"Did you see me blacken his eye also, *ma chérie?*" he asked testily.

"I ran away, and when I came back, I heard, well, unmistakable sounds."

"It was not me."

Her mind flashed the picture into her head again, and she saw details that had registered in the area of her heart, her intuitive under-standing of Cheftu, but had been missed completely by her tired, freaked-out consciousness. He'd not been responding, he'd maybe even been asleep. Did she really think Cheftu would be unfaithful?

Yes, he had slept with Sibylla, but it had been her body in Sibylla's skin, her face, her eyes. He'd known her instinctively, even if not ra-tionally. "I know it wasn't you, Cheftu. I know." She smiled.

He still wore a pained expression.

Inching closer, she touched his face, where only the tiniest ridge of scar tissue could be felt. It gave her the creeps. His gaze searched hers, moving back and forth on her face. *When you thought he was wounded, you wanted him.* It didn't matter, she reasoned with herself. *Now that he's whole, you don't?*

Hello?

"This is weird, Cheftu."

He kept looking, pleading.

"Something else puzzles me," she began.

"That is?"

"Why do I change bodies? Twice now you've been the same person, the same body. What happened to RaEm's body?"

"It was destroyed. Trampled." Cheftu's gaze flickered away. "If you'd been in it, you truly would have died."

Chloe felt her skin crawl a little. If the body she'd had was gone, where was the real RaEm? Still wearing Chloe's red hair and fair skin in nineteen ninety . . . six, now?

"Also, if you had not been Sibylla, how would I have found you again?"

"You wouldn't have deigned to look for me in a washerwoman?" Chloe said dryly.

"I carried your corpse, Chloe. I was not looking." His gaze was in-tense, unnerving Chloe more.

"How did you get well, Cheftu? What is the elixir?"

"What is the elixir? Herbs and fluids and essence of crab."

"Excuse me?" Chloe said.

"The formula. Spiralmaster gave it to me."

"Your photographic memory did the rest," she concluded.

"I never forget anything I read."

"Exactly. So how did it work?"

Cheftu looked away. The ash was falling lightly, not so cloying and thick that they needed masks. Chloe waited, watching Cheftu's healthy body. Still she was scared, almost repulsed, but she fought to get over it. *He's healthy, so be grateful.*

"In *al-khem*," Cheftu said, "oftentimes a reaction is arrived at only by adding two compounds in a certain order. Taking all of the ingredients and mixing them together would not work. But letting them interact with each other before combining, that is something entirely different."

"Just so," Chloe said.

Cheftu licked his lips, his long fingers picking at the edge of the raft. "The Aztlantu Golden, the people you call Greek gods, were cannibals."

"What?"

"It was a religious ceremony. Rather than bury the wisdom and accumulated knowledge of a leader, they would ingest it."

"Literally?"

"Aye."

"They ate his brain?" Chloe fought back a wave of nausea. Other cultures did things other ways, she reminded herself. "You know, the Aztecs ate the hearts of their enemies, hoping to consume their bravery. I wonder if the Aztlantu and Aztec civilizations are somehow related." The pyramids were certainly similar, she realized, and that would explain why the Aztlan empire initially sounded like a Mexican resort.

"So," Cheftu said, "the illness came from the cannibalism. I don't know how, but the bulls were infected also. They had the same holes in their brains."

"Everyone was dying? Slow or fast, they were all dying? Even you?"

"Aye. Then some of us, notably Phoebus and I, received the elixir."

"Phoebus is dead."

"Aye, it must need blood in which to work."

"You healed," she whispered. She brushed some ash off the raft.

"The elixir itself was not the thing. The interaction of elixir and the illness, that is what revived Phoebus. Somehow the sickness and the elixir mixed in the blood, an *al-khem* reaction that resulted in . . ."

"So . . ." She swallowed, feeling awkward. He was Cheftu, but he was also someone, something, new. "Are you . . . immortal?"

Cheftu laughed. "Phoebus died, and he had both. Longevity, I believe, is the most to hope for. It cannot work without a lot of blood. It does heal, however."

"Did you eat anyone?" she asked cautiously.

Cheftu just stared at her until Chloe was embarrassed. She fought not to scoot farther away. This was Cheftu! Her husband! Her lover! But he seemed so eerily alive, especially in these surrealistic surroundings. She'd seen him covered in blood. Now he was whole? "What now?" she asked hoarsely.

Cheftu reached out to her, laying her hand palm side up. "I have the stones."

"What stones? What are you talking about? Did you share *anything* with me here? Did you confide even one thought?" Chloe asked, crossing her arms over her chest.

"*Chérie,* don't be hurt—"

"You didn't trust me, Cheftu. You kept everything from me!"

"I did not know until the end about the cannibalism."

"When did you know you were fatally ill? Were you going to tell me or just let me wake up next to a cold body?"

Cheftu had the grace to flinch. "I didn't want you to—"

"To have a choice? To decide for myself?"

"Chloe—"

"I'm not some sheltered nineteenth-century noblewoman, Cheftu! I'm your helpmate, your partner, I thought I was your best friend—"

"*Chérie,* Chloe, forgive me." His hand was still held out, palm up, to her. "You did not answer my question. Will you stay with me?"

She looked away, aching without and within. He'd lied by omission, he'd not trusted her enough to confide in her. What did they have if he couldn't tell her the negatives? The raft ceased moving, the air turned static and silent. The hair on the back of Chloe's neck rose on end. Cheftu was frowning in the half-light.

The night around them turned instantly black. A sudden bone-rattling roar pounded into her skull. Chloe screamed as the air pressure suddenly changed. The concussive blast flattened her like a rag doll.

Chapter 23

THE FINAL ERUPTION PELTED FIRE AND LAVA on them. Chloe and Cheftu lay on the raft, paddling madly as rocks flew by. They hadn't known they were so close to the volcano.

Within minutes they were alternating the tasks of paddling and kicking hot ash off the raft. The stuff was cloying, irritating against their skin, clogging their ears and eyes and noses and mouths. Cheftu relinquished his kilt to tear into masks, wearing only his sash with the stones. He dropped into the water and propelled them deeper into the sea, swimming and kicking as Chloe directed them through the hazy, burning day. Or night. Who knew.

Chloe couldn't feel her arms and she wasn't sure if her eyes were open, because the scenery never changed. She was moving like a robot—in and pull, in and pull—feeling the water and current tugging against her, hoping that she inched them forward a little bit more in the gray sea. Occasionally she changed raft sides, always moving onward. They weren't heading to Prostatevo—Akrotiri—she guessed. Where were they going? It was too much effort to ask. Her stomach cramped with hunger, and her palms stung from salt and air.

She worked in a timeless haze of grayness. Cheftu's face was a paler shade as he moved around her to paddle on the other side. He kissed her forehead, smoothing back the tendrils of hair that still surrounded her face. The crown of her head was bald, blistered, her eyelashes and eyebrows singed from the heat. He touched her lips and her nose.

Pockets of hot air rushed by them. "Is the mountain still erupting?" Chloe asked.

"It is. We must find a way out of here, out of this time." He turned away, paddling again. "If only I knew where Niko's island was," he muttered.

"Niko's island?" Chloe said into the wind.

"The island of the stones," was the last thing she heard before pain and exhaustion pulled her into darkness.

CHEFTU GLANCED OVER and saw that she had passed out. She was bleeding from a dozen different wounds, though she had worked with superhuman effort to get them away. His warrior, he thought, smiling. Not only was his own body unscathed, he was seemingly impervious to fatigue. The elixir had worked.

Dion said he had taken the elixir also, but he'd not had the plague, had he? Did the elixir confer immortality? Or merely longevity? Not that it mattered right now. They needed to find the island. Cheftu checked to make sure the stones were secure in his sash. It was such irony! The Urim and Thummim of the Hebrew people had been used by Greeks, whose ways they would shun. Why did he have them now? Where should he take them? Where were they to go?

Had he and Chloe been in this time period for a year?

Worries engulfed him. He drew Chloe close, cradling her to his chest. She whimpered as the rough pumice tore at her skin, but she didn't awaken. Eee, *my beloved, what will become of us?* Brushing his lips over her brow, he held her, facing into the gray unknown.

MY SHEETS NEED A HIGHER THREAD COUNT, Chloe thought. These feel like sandpaper.

Then water drenched her and she reared up, only to be soaked again. Tossing brittle hair over her shoulder, Chloe tried to get her bearings. Cheftu was paddling furiously in the whipping water.

Cautiously she crouched on the raft, gripping the rough stone edges, resisting the waves. Where were they? Shadows seemed to lurk inside the gray, a darker, more solid gray.

Another wave almost washed Chloe overboard. Cheftu grabbed her wrist, and she squealed as her stomach and breasts were yanked over the pumice.

She joined him battling through the rough water. If only I knew how to surf, she thought as another wave hit her.

Ash continued to fall, suffocating. *Who needs bad guys when you've got Mother Nature?* Cheftu touched her hand, then pointed to the side. One of the darker shades of gray. Land? They paddled harder, trying to ride the waves. The breakers were getting more powerful, higher, slamming the tiny raft down onto the roiling surface of the water. As she was considering the relative benefits of swimming, the raft flipped.

She came up clawing for air. The current tore at her, pulling her, then tugging her away. She spotted an island and swam toward it, fighting the current.

Then it dawned on her . . . current . . . waves . . . shoreline . . . duh! She didn't have to swim, the current could take her.

Chloe tried to float, but the waves were too violent. She let herself be buffeted along until she crashed against a rocky floor. The jagged pebbles that lined the beach were not much more comfortable than pumice. For a moment she reveled in being on solid land, until another wave knocked her back toward the sea. Concentrating, she gained her footing and picked her way up the strange beach, forested down to the water's edge. Standing on shaking legs, she looked around. Vegetation, encroaching water, Cheftu approaching, stumbling on the stony beach.

She staggered up the shore to the center of the small island.

"Mon Dieu!" Cheftu shouted. "Of all the islands that surrounded Aztlan, we found the right one!" He ran to her, grasped her hands. "Chloe my love, be happy for this!"

Chloe looked above her. A red sandstone archway stretched over a fifteen-cubit span, rising high above them with no central support. Beneath the archway lay a mosaic made from rocks and shells. Her skin broke out in goose bumps the size of Volkswagens.

They had found the doorway. "What did being in this time mean?" she whispered.

Cheftu's glance slid across the mosaic ground, past the well, to the sea. "The sea is so close." He swallowed audibly. "The island is sinking. See the trees?" They stood in cubits of water. Waves lapped at the far edge of the mosaic pattern, mere cubits from where they stood. The tip of a hill was just vanishing beneath the waves. "How long do we have before we're immersed?" she asked.

He looked up at the sky, trying to see through the ash and haze that covered the sun like a veil, leaving them shrouded in half-light. Chloe forgot everything when she looked down at the stone-covered ground. A mosaic.

It was not Minoan work—that was a no-brainer. The design was less stylized. It appeared to be a chart of sorts. Chloe looked more closely. Two fish, together. A ram, a bull, human twins. She searched through her memories of art history. They were familiar, but these weren't depictions she'd seen in class. She'd seen this in person, not on a slide.

She halted, then counted the symbols. Twelve. "Holy shit," she hissed. It had been a while since she'd seen a daily paper, but it looked like a zodiac.

"What is it, beloved?" Cheftu asked.

"I've seen this mosaic before." Her scratchy voice rose in excitement. "In *Israel*. This one must be thousands of years older than the Israeli version. Why would a piece of Hebrew artwork be on this island?" she asked.

The Voice, the one she'd heard only a few times, whispered to her heart. *Trust.* The hazy light cast the lintel's shadow over Cheftu.

The alcove in Egypt, the cave on Caphtor, and now this sinking island. Chloe wondered if around midnight the moon's shadow would move to the goat—Capricorn—the sign for both of their December 23 birthdays. She shivered. If they were here, and Aztlan was gone, was God going to rescue them? Was it a year later? Would the door open tonight?

Would they step through the gateway in time?

Chloe and Cheftu sat side by side, watching the lintel in fear it would disappear if they turned away. If they could glimpse the sky, Chloe was certain they would see celestial bodies drawing into alignment.

Grapes and oregano had been their dinner. Not quite gourmet, but better than sand, the only other option. Cheftu had dragged her to the well, and they'd both washed and drunk until Chloe thought "marking" would be no challenge at all.

The bottom-line question was why.

Sitting here was worse than waiting in an airport. Chloe clenched Cheftu's hand. They had seen and done so much, but why? She turned to him. "What was the point?"

"Of Atlantis?"

"Of us here," she said. "Why bring modern people to this ancient world?"

He shrugged.

"Was it to help with the illness?"

"I cannot see that, since everyone died."

"What about the elixir?" she asked.

"Only three of us have taken it. Since I destroyed the disk that bore the formula, there is no way to pass it on. The illness and the cure are gone forever."

What if we were supposed to keep the disk? she thought to herself. "We didn't save anyone."

"We saved a few, Chloe. We did all we could do. We are not asked more."

She picked at the ground in silence. "What about the stones? What are they? Could they have been the point?"

Above them gray haze was melting beneath starlight and a half-moon. Cheftu sighed, then answered slowly, "The stones are Hebrew oracular stones. The Hebrew high priest used them to communicate with God."

"Easier than mere prayer," Chloe observed. "Why here, though?"

"These people predated the Israelites, but they worshiped the One God."

"Until they started in with the bulls," she said.

"Aye. Every nation has fallen away, though, Chloe. Even the Israelites themselves did. God forgave and forgave—" His words stopped as the shadow from the lintel became clearer.

It seemed to be growing brighter around them, a rosy glow. Was the lintel itself glowing? They crawled farther inland, onto the mosaic, beneath the archway. Chloe grabbed Cheftu's hand. "It must be the twenty-third of December."

"Aye."

The moon-cast shadow was moving, crossing the stones one at a time, shifting to the goat sign. They watched it, mesmerized. Finally Cheftu stood up, tugging her with him. Chloe fought the urge to giggle. Her husband wore only a belt around his waist, the two stones tucked on either side of his body. With his unbound hair waving over his shoulders and back, he looked as though he'd been lifted from the cover of a lurid novel. She, on the other hand, looked like a witch who'd been yanked from a burning pyre. Cheftu smiled as though he could read her thoughts.

He kissed her gently. She felt him lace his fingers with hers and opened her eyes. Water splashed up onto their calves. Time was almost gone.

Her husband pulled her closer, backing up until they were standing on the mosaic goat, its horns tinted with gold. They held each other, and she felt his heart pounding in his throat.

The water beat against the island. They were either going down or going somewhere else. The bases of the archway were long submerged, and the glow from the lintel reflected on the wave-soaked rocks. The water surrounded them now, and she didn't know if she felt his trembling or hers.

Cheftu stepped away, holding her at arm's length. He reached down, grabbed a broken shell from beneath the water, and scraped it across his palm. Blood beaded up black on his skin. He rubbed his lips with it and then hers.

The Aztlantu vow. The blood vow.

He spoke slowly, his English broken and thick. Chloe felt her eyes fill with tears. His gaze was intense, seeing through her, past a wreck of flesh and bone to her immutable soul. "We are entrusted with the life and welfare of each other. My blood is yours, yours is mine. I seek to love and cherish you all my days, in whatever world we live."

He kissed her, and Chloe tasted the hot silk that was his tongue, the copper liquid that was his life. "I love you," she whispered. "I'll be with you anywhere."

He clasped her tightly, whispering into her ear, "Dear God, how I feared you'd never say those words." His hands were trembling as he touched her wounded body. "Hold on to me. Don't let go."

She caressed his cheek, looking into his eyes. "I won't leave you. I vow it."

He closed his eyes, tears streaking the ash on his face. The one request he'd made: that she stay with him. She'd taken so long to answer. "We'll be together," Cheftu said, opening his eyes to stare into hers. "I promise. I will travel anywhere to find you, any time."

Oh God, they might not travel together. He realized it, too. Chloe whispered, "I promise, too."

The water was now to their waists. The island would be submerged in a matter of hours. They held each other's hands tightly, memorizing each other's images.

It happened suddenly. The familiar wind whipped around her and Chloe felt herself pushed, her battered fingers melting away from Cheftu's unscarred hand. Instead of water, she felt only space, and then a psychic roar as she was transformed from flesh to pure energy, lost in the cacophony of mixed senses.

Lost from Cheftu.

Help me keep my vow, she prayed.

EPILOGUE

CHEFTU WOKE WITH WAVES WASHING over his legs. The water was brisk and he sat up, shaking his head to clear it. Braced on his elbows, he looked around. The patch of ground he sat on was not big enough to be called an island, and there wasn't a jot of land anywhere else in sight.

"Chloe?" he called.

The water stirred. Grimacing and groaning, a woman pulled herself onto the islet. "I am thrice damned and beloved of Set," she cursed.

Cheftu's blood iced over. The woman in Sibylla's body looked up. Her brown eyes fixed on him, then narrowed. Her smile broad, her voice seductively sweet, "*Haii*, Cheftu, we meet again," she said.

Mon Dieu! RaEmhetepet! Cheftu recoiled, covering himself. If she were here, where was Chloe? He noticed the water was clear, the sky was bright, the ash had vanished. He had traveled. The islet on which they sat was tiny, but not underwater. The lintel was gone. Where had RaEm come from? "How—" He choked on his words. "How did you get here?"

Horrified, RaEm surveyed her new body, the body that had survived the eruption of Aztlan. "I had made love with Phaemon—"

"Phaemon? Phaemon was with you?"

"Aye, the soldier who was my lover." She licked her cracked lips and shifted her gaze. "The night I was transferred from our Egypt to that hell of the future, I had determined to rid myself of Phaemon. I was full with his child, and the fool thought I would leave Egypt to play wife and mother." She laughed, and Cheftu forced himself not to wince. How could he have mistaken Chloe for RaEm, even for a heartbeat? "While he was intimately occupied, I struck him."

"You were coupling with him and you slapped him?"

"Nay. I took a blade to his back."

"By the gods, RaEm!"

She shrugged. "We fought somewhat, then rolled beneath the archway to HatHor." Her gaze met his. "Then we began the descent into hell. We fought again when we awoke in the chamber, the same room, many years beyond what we had ever fathomed. I fled, hid in the catacombs beneath the Temple in Karnak. Phaemon recovered." Again she shrugged. "Eventually we made our peace."

"How did you get here?"

"I was walking in the desert close to our campsite. I stepped into a hollow beside the monolith and found myself sucked in by a mighty wind, awakening here."

The wind blew coldly across them, and Cheftu was reminded that it was winter, that they were stranded in the middle of an unsailable sea. No ships would chance crossing the Aegean or Mediterranean before spring. *Mon Dieu!* He touched the stones tucked in at his waist for reassurance. At least they were safe. Surely it was not his destiny that he die here?

"While I was Chloe I had the appearance of a *kheft*," RaEm said. She picked up a fragile piece of hair still attached to her burned scalp. "At least here I am black haired, as a woman should be."

Cheftu rose to his feet, suddenly trembling and sick to his stomach. RaEm had stepped into Sibylla's body, where Chloe had been. Sibylla's spirit had been left in the cave when Chloe had first "arrived." If Chloe weren't here, and RaEm was . . . then was Chloe in her own time? In her own body?

Foam and mist coated him, and he shivered, turning his back on RaEm, looking across the water. The empire that had once stretched from horizon to horizon was gone, the islands all sunk beneath the sea's waves. "Where are we, Cheftu?" RaEm said. "Why am I here? What happened to this body that my *ka* now inhabits?"

He quoted Plato: "'*There occurred violent earthquakes and floods, and in a single day and night of misfortune the island of Atlantis disappeared into the depths of the sea.*'"

He ignored RaEm's complaints, smiling in spite of himself at her language. She spoke in a bizarre mixture of ancient Egyptian and Chloe's American.

"So where are you, my love?" he whispered to the waves. "What body holds you? What time is now your home? When will I see you?" The words were carried by the wind over the sea. "Remember your vow, Chloe. Together. We will be together, again."

AUTHOR'S AFTERWORD

ENUMERATING THE DETAILS used in *Shadows on the Aegean* would fill another book. Essentially, the Aztlantu are a cross between Plato's Atlantis and what is known of the missing Minoans.

Plato describes Atlantis as a mountainous water-and-earth-ringed island. Volcanologists have concluded that the island of Santorini, pre-1500 B.C.E., was indeed ringed with water and land. What is today a crescent-shaped bay was then a shallow lagoon. Excavations at Akrotiri (Prostatevo) show us multilevel dwellings made from the black-, red-, and saffron-colored stone found on the island. Plato speaks of hot and cold running water, a geologic possibility in a volcanic environment. Excavations show pipes and sewer systems within Minoan enclaves.

From whence did these Minoans come? As suggested by my imagination, they are descendants of one of Noah's grandsons. I was startled to unearth a theory that agreed with my fictional premise. A Byzantine cartographer, Cosmos Indicopleustes, suggested that Noah was Atlantis's founding father. The ancient known world has been divided by the tribes who descended from these biblical characters. Javan (Iavan), son of Japheth, son of Noah, historically populated the eastern Mediterranean islands of Crete and Greece. Cosmos thought that Plato's account of Atlantis was originally Mosaic tradition. He suggested that Atlantis was the land of the ten generations of Noah and was in the east. Followers of this theory from the 1570s misread Atlantis into the Pentateuch as a part of biblical history.

The Urim and Thummim are virtually unresearchable, except through legend and the Book of Mormon. In a story preceding Moses, this was no help. However, I wanted to place Aztlan in a historical context, so I turned to Egypt. Recent Egyptological studies reveal that Joseph may have lived in the same time period that I placed Atlantis. These same studies show that a long period of famine did indeed take place during the reign of Senwosret III, and that it was caused by exceptionally high inundations. In a country as gingerly ecologically balanced as Egypt, a few inches' difference in the flood level can spell disaster.

The reign of Senwosret/Joseph coincided with a time in Crete/Santorini when palaces were destroyed—a time when the volcano was starting its preeruption show and we have very few facts. A perfect placement for Atlantis and nearly nine hundred years before classical Greece.

The Phaistos disk is on exhibit in the Heraklion Crete Museum. As of this writing it is undecipherable. However, it bears striking similarities to an astrological chart of Crete from late summer to early spring.

Prion diseases—including kuru, mad cow disease, Creutzfeldt-Jacob disease, and other spongiform encephalopathies—are frightening and true. All the symptoms portrayed in *Shadows* are accurate, based on medical journals and books. In the fall of 1997, Stanley Prusiner, who gave the prion its name, received the Nobel Prize.

The Clan Olimpi was the pantheon of Mount Olympus, loosely disguised. Classical mythology has dark, bloody roots, and many of the characters, names, and traits reflect that shadowy genesis.

Preclassical religion on many shores was goddess based. The earliest goddess in Crete was a pentad deity named Hera. She created and destroyed and ultimately was awarded the life of her consort, who was also her son. Owing to the obvious classical association, the mothergoddess needed a new name in this book. I chose Kela, a derivative of *kalos*, which is Greek for beautiful or charm. Phoebus was Apollo's first name. Dion is short for Dionysus. Arus is Ares. Nestor is a Greek name meaning "traveler," appropriate for Hermes. Selena is the ancient personification of the crescent moon. Atenis was Athena, who in preclassical times was a local patron goddess of craftsmen.

Irmentis was Artemis, a goddess whose roots are blood-soaked in preclassical mythology. The plant *Artemisia absinthium* (wormwood) is named after her, and I gave her character an absinthe addiction. It brings on madness and visions and quells sexual desire, characteristics for which chaste Artemis was known. Because of its bitterness it is consumed with something sweet. At the turn of the twentieth century, it was poured over sugar. Irmentis drank it with honeycomb.

Artemis was originally a vampiric figure. I gave fact to the myth by infecting her with porphyria, the disease from which the legends of vampires and werewolves grew. Greek folklore is filled with vampire tales: those who drink blood, can't abide the sun, whose gums draw back from their teeth, and who actually sweat blood. All of these are traits of acute porphyria.

Santorini was declared in the mid-1800s to be the most vampire-ridden place in the entire world. This was possibly a result of the embalming effects of the soil. The custom then (and today) on Santorini is to bury the deceased in the dirt, then dig up the body a short interval later for formal interment. In premodern times, if the body was not sufficiently decomposed, they claimed it had become a vampire.

According to fable the Scholomance was a school of life where all the secrets of nature, magic, and power were taught by the devil in person. Only ten students were admitted at a time. Nine were released to their homes, the tenth detained as payment. Masonic legend attributed Dionysus with first teaching these skills, in addition to architecture and masonry.

Aztlan is the name of the mythological birthplace of the Aztec civilization. More than any other culture, Aztecs are associated with Atlantis. Because of this association and the theory of Aztecs being the descendants of the Atlanteans, I incorporated assorted Aztec features into my Aztlan. The Pyramid of Days with 365 steps was borrowed, as was the feather-edged ceremonial cloak, the calendar, and the obsidian blade vow ritual. The reasoning behind Aztlan's cannibalism is similar to the Aztecs', and it fits modern understanding of the psychology of cannibalism. Essentially, the deceased have power that should be consumed. This consumption is a great honor and a religious rite.

The purpose and method of Minoan bull dancing has been explored by dozens of authors. The nice part of fiction is that one can suppose and theorize. Astrologically, the world had just left the Age of Taurus. During that time period, bulls were worshiped the world over.

If Atlantis and Egypt had enjoyed the close relationship that I portray, they might well have shared a common faith, namely worshiping Apis. The Serapeum in Egypt was built for the mummies of Apis bulls. Cretan legend and mythology is filled with tales of bulls, from the Labyrinth to Zeus' capture of Europa. Plato asserts the elders of Atlantis chased the sacred bull through the palace with staves and nooses.

The ritual of baptism in bull's blood, as described, is still practiced on the Aegean isle of Lesbos. To this day, churches in the Aegean have bullhorn-shaped belfries.

Normandi Ellis's beautiful interpretation of the Book of the Dead, *Awakening Osiris*, was especially useful and inspirational for the Egyptian scenes.

Six books guided me on this journey: *Unearthing Atlantis* by Charles Pellegrino; Edith Hamilton's *Mythology*; *The Pyramids, an Enigma Solved* by Davidovits and Margie Morris; *Pharaohs and Kings a Biblical Quest* by David Rohl; Fodor's *Greece*; and the most provocative glimpse into the Minoan mind I've ever found, *The Thread of Ariadne* by Charles Herberger.

Did Atlantis exist as a superior culture? I propose that archaeology and history testify that it did. Their superiority was only in their understanding of science, commerce, and society, as opposed to mainland Greeks, who were still living in huts. Did they circumnavigate the globe, discover chemistry, have an understanding of engineering, medicine, even aerodynamics and timekeeping? Allegedly, the library in Alexandria had scrolls attesting to all these things. Whether the Egyptians, the Chinese, or a culture like the Aztlantu discovered them first, we will possibly never know. The importance is to realize that ancient people did more, went farther, and were much more sophisticated than we believe.

Did they destroy themselves? Ultimately every culture has cannibalized itself. Egyptian, Greek, Roman, Byzantine . . . or perhaps the Atlanteans simply made awful real estate choices, seduced by the fertile volcanic soil. Like any people, they lived their lives, birthed, wedded, and died, unaware they were mythology in the making.

So, we sail into the Mediterranean.

Suzanne Frank
October 19, 1997
Dallas, Texas

ACKNOWLEDGMENTS

DOZENS AND DOZENS OF PEOPLE graciously shared their thoughts, expertise, and wisdom during the creation of this book. My thanks to those who have read for me, in part or in full: Melanie, Barbara, Eric, Erick, Dan, Dana, David, Dwayne, Diane, Hanne, Joe, Rob, Rene, River, my mother, and my class. Your perspective and ideas have been invaluable. Thank you for your time and patience.

I cannot possibly name all my on-line acquaintances who asked, "Have you thought of this, Suz?" or introduced a concept or an angle for further exploration. Thanks most especially to Matt, for the zebrafish, which led to the crab; Jason, for the information on the Urim and Thummim; Gary, for the gorgeous map; Dan, for the unpaid job of publicist/cheerleader/linguist extraordinaire; John, for how to run well; Eric, for prophets and pirates; River, for hunting and fighting; and Ira, for many long talks, hysterical laughter, and literary perspective.

Deep thanks to Diane Frank, my research scientist, who excels at explaining complex ideas in bite-size pieces; who gamely tracked down resources and articles on prions; who spent days with me in the University of Washington library as I read journal after journal. Diane, you are a goddess! Thanks also go to Dr. Farrell R. Robinson for unveiling the human brain to me. Literally. He showed me how to cut open a skull, how to extract a brain, what it feels like, what it smells like, what it looks like, and what it sounds like. (No, I didn't taste it.)

Always, thanks to my parents. They explored Mt. St. Helens in Washington because I needed to see another volcano; they collected all references to preclassical Greece and phoned me when I needed to watch the Discovery Channel; they listened to my ranting and raving about diseases, mythology, alchemy, ad nauseam. They asked questions that made me think harder. Most significant, they never doubted I could do it.

Heartfelt thanks to Susan Sandler and Jessica Papin, my editors at

Warner. Special heaping thanks to Susan, who said, "Antioxidants are old hat. Get another disease." Thus she inspired my search for prions. She also keeps me writing in actual English, and she always gets it. Enormous thanks to Jessica, who kept the *psyches* of my characters consistent, who always asks for explanations for the "historically impaired" and jumps into my worlds with both feet. These women saw my vision, they encouraged its depth, and most important, they trimmed away the fat and challenged me to work harder, stretch farther. Thanks to Jackie for her time and insightful V-reader comments. Thanks to Theresa Pantazopoulos for the *Reflections* publicity and the great support of the Warner reps.

A special thanks to Evan Fogelman. Without him there wouldn't be a trilogy.

Thanks to Beth and the staff at Hotel Kavalari in Santorini. It's truly the most amazing place to stay, with stunning views of the caldera and close to the heart of the town. Beth gave her time and knowledge of the island and its *shadowy* sides. Thanks to Kathy Stamm, who actually *got* us to Greece, despite the winds, the strikes, and the Athens airport.

Blessings on you all!

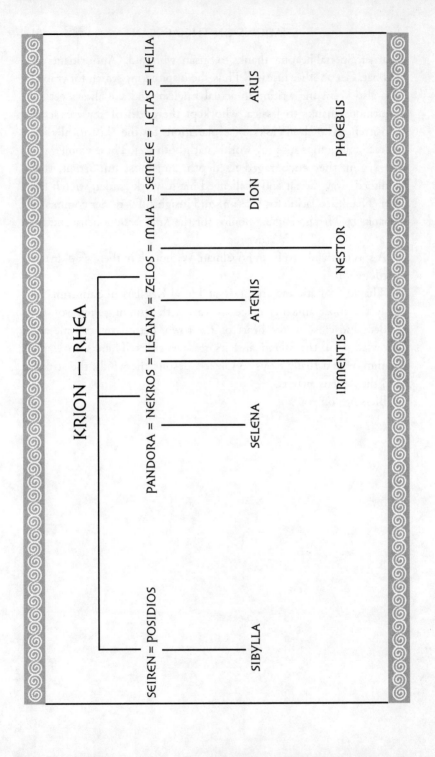

KRION — RHEA

SEIREN = POSIDIOS   PANDORA = NEKROS   ILEANA = ZELOS   MAIA = SEMELE = LETAS = HELIA

SIBYLLA   SELENA   IRMENTIS   ATENIS   NESTOR   DION   PHOEBUS   ARUS